# I SHOULDN'T BE TELLING YOU THIS

Also by Mary Breasted

Oh! Sex Education! (*nonfiction*)

# I SHOULDN'T BE TELLING YOU THIS

## MARY BREASTED

**HARPER & ROW, PUBLISHERS,** New York
*Cambridge, Philadelphia, San Francisco, London*
*Mexico City, São Paulo, Sydney*
1817

FIRST EDITION

*Designer: Sidney Feinberg*

Library of Congress Cataloging in Publication Data

Breasted, Mary, date
  I shouldn't be telling you this.
  I. Title.
PS3552.R3575I2 1983      813'.54        82-48141
ISBN 0-06-015092-0

83 84 85 86 87 10 9 8 7 6 5 4 3 2 1

*For Ted Smyth and Dan Wolf*

# I

Why did I accept Ron's invitation to lunch? I know I was nervous about it. The morning I headed out to meet him, I noticed peripheral things in a sharp way. Maybe I had not got over the shock of New York, even after four years. It hits you like an insanity, like too much love, when you come in from a small town. Or if you live there through a winter and come out one sunny morning to find a million people in Washington Square Park trying to be alone with nature. Which is the kind of morning it was. And I remember the park as a bright mass of noise smelling warm and earthy, and this conversation:

"It ain't no fren' a mine, man! Don' go layin' that trip on me!"

"You done the introductions, Freezer! Mothuhfuckuh come aroun' here again, he gonna catch some lead! Shoot! He ain' no Blood. He a 'Rican, you dumbass!"

"You jess pissed you stole a empty wallet, Sampson. Fuuuock!"

"Niggah, shut yo' face!"

The speakers had their backs to me. They were leaning against a bench on which a bum was sleeping soundly, and for a moment I thought he was the one they had robbed. I wondered whether I should wake him. And then I realized he wasn't a Puerto Rican. He looked, actually, a little like the mayor. He was snoring face up, with one arm dangling in the dirt near an empty pint bottle. His other arm was bent over his chest, the hand of it resting like the gentlest of consolations over his heart and a newspaper picture of Jackie Onassis, looking pop-eyed from flashbulbs. He had covered himself with newspapers from his armpits down to his ankles. Of course, he couldn't own a wallet, I thought. Then I saw the *Evening Star* headline flash up from his belly in the breeze:

THOUSANDS WAIT IN LINE TO SEE
FACE OF JESUS ON TORTILLA

The page fluttered down again, and I wasn't sure whether I'd read it correctly, so I moved in to take a peek.

"What *choo* want?" said Sampson or Freezer, spinning around.

I jerked my hand away and hurried off.

That is the last thing I remember before I met Ron, because, as I said, I was nervous and New York was overwhelming that day. I was poor at the time and not rigidly scheduled, so the promise of a free lunch in a French restaurant should have seemed like a good deal. But I planned to write up my host afterwards from the feminist perspective, and it bothered me: it didn't seem too feminist to let him pay for the lunch. Not that I had much choice. I had recently lost my job with the East 118th Street Block Association and very nearly gone to jail, a miscarriage of justice almost, which I shall presently explain, and I had been attempting to earn a living as a writer for *The Evil Eye*. That is, I had penned some recollections of the East 118th Street fiasco, which had emerged into print in the *Eye* including details and observations not my own, added by an astute and hard-swearing woman editor who said I had been screwed and would I like to cover a feminist teach-in the following week?

I had, as a matter of fact, been screwed enough times to have formed a habit of seeking further opportunities, but I felt it best not to discuss my private life with the hard-swearing woman editor, as she would be apt to put a few accurate details into her own column and screw me out of free drinks at the Poor Mouth, my favorite Village bar.

The Village at that time was my home. It worked a strange spell on a young woman not unattractive to construction workers and Puerto Rican garment district slaves, for it was, in 1976, the homosexual capital of the universe, San Francisco notwithstanding, and the Village fags looked at a woman as if she were a sheet of shimmering Saran Wrap, invisible and immaterial except when you poked.

Why I had chosen the Village to settle in when my first city job was in East Harlem, a good three-quarter hour's subway ride away, I do not precisely know, except that it was a sixties place, and I had not had enough of the sixties, an era I had spent fettered in the Regional High School of Four Corners, Massachusetts, trying to study hard enough to get out of there. I studied too hard, I guess, because I got into Radcliffe, where I had to study too hard to stay in, and even though I was class of '72 and got to partake of the thrilling occupation of Widener Library and to practice fellatio impromptu between the Conrad and Cooper stacks, I felt that the sixties had passed me by before I'd got started. You might say I had missed my generation. And there were times when I believed I had missed it by several decades. I might have been an ambulance driver in the Spanish Civil War or an organizer for the Wobblies out in Kansas or one of those pioneer women de Tocqueville wrote about who went from fine Eastern homes to "leaky cabins in the depths of the forest," where "fever, solitude, and boredom had not broken the resilience of their courage."

Not me. I grew up in the deadest of dead little towns that had not even a movie theater to keep us going on Saturday nights and where the most exciting two people were the town drunk, who used to flag down trucks in his underwear, and the town policeman, who used to arrest him. The town policeman was stone deaf and doubled as a taxi driver, which often perplexed visitors who came in on the train from New York.

Other people thought my father was the most exciting character in town, but to me he was just my father, whose opinions I had heard too often. He didn't have to work for a living because his ancestors had been bankers and left him a small fortune, which he frittered away on organic farming projects and campaigns to get Four Corners to secede from the state of Massachusetts. He was not easy to live with. He went to town meetings just to embarrass us. He'd raise his hand and try to filibuster on the Vietnam War when the selectmen were getting down to the real business at hand, maybe the sewage ordinance or the local property tax rate, and the good citizens of Four Corners would shout him down for a while, but he'd be up on his feet again in another half hour with a point of order about the Constitution, and then the sergeant at arms would kick him out. One year when I was in high school my father locked himself inside the town hall the night before town meeting and said he wasn't coming out until the war was over.

My older brother, Noah, who is some kind of a scientist now, had to take rations to him in the dead of night, even though Dad was pretending to be on a hunger strike. Noah got arrested, and it warped him permanently. He went off to commune with inanimate objects. I came to New York.

Anyway, I'm going to have to tell you my name sooner or later.

3

Sarah Makepeace. Dad's is Adam Makepeace, so you can see how he got so obsessed with stopping the war. His family weren't all crazy. They were descended from the original Noah and Adam Makepeaces who came to the Massachusetts Colony from England back in the seventeenth century. Their history is a bit vague because they believed that the written word was a form of vanity, but the two brothers are said to have broken off from the original Puritans to form their own religion, which they called Earthly Delights. Eventually the two brothers also had a schism. Noah went off to civilize the Indians and was never heard from again. Adam produced a huge family, which spread out all over the state and founded banks. My father's father was a Boston bigwig. He disowned his son, but that didn't stick. Dad had claimed conscientious objector status during World War II, and Grandfather thought this was a disgrace. But toward the end of his life, the old man got sentimental. He left Dad a nice set of stocks and the house in Four Corners.

New York in 1976 was about as different from Four Corners as the heart of Calcutta was from a Hindu saint's little cave. The kings of the world came through town looking for action. Their wives went to Bloomingdale's. One day Princess Margaret went in there and jammed up the place with Secret Service men all tuning up their earpieces among the perfume bottles. Rollerima the transvestite went skating down Third Avenue in long billowing skirts. There were mobsters infiltrating big business and sexy young cops infiltrating the mob. You couldn't tell who was who anymore. The rich dressed down and the poor dressed up. Parts of the city looked macabre, as though a giant beast had gone through eating out windows and crunching out chunks of brick wall, feeding on the taste of too many people in too small a space. It was fashionable to say that New York was dying. It was also fashionable to say that New York was the greatest city in the world.

I loved the place, even though a lot of hype had gone into getting people to say that. Every minute—no, every millisecond—you could see something interesting on the street, and what you didn't see you could hear. I was always hearing little snatches of conversation that conjured up unseen dramas. One day I heard a woman telling her companion, "But, Jenny, it wasn't the *shrink* Robert was paying for!" I think that was in front of the Jefferson Market, around the corner from the Poor Mouth. Another day, in Times Square, where porno titles beckoned their lewd baby-talk invitations—*Peach Fuzz, Liquid Lips*—I honest to god heard one man saying vehemently to another, "Forty fucking shots of penicillin!"

4

It was toward Times Square I was headed on the morning I passed the sleeping bum. For Ron Millstein worked near there, a mere stone's throw from the spot where the man uttered, "Forty fucking shots of penicillin!" Ron Millstein was the city editor of *The Newspaper*, the city's not largest but highest-brow metropolitan daily, where sexism was supposed to be rampant.

All I knew about *The Newspaper* then had come to me from outside its huge English manor gates, which had been imported by Old Man Kleinfreude just after the turn of the century, when unstable market conditions had driven certain aristocrats to sell their family treasures to rich Americans. The gates were ugly and useless. They were too heavy to be closed and too large for the building entrance. (No one had ever seen them closed in my lifetime, except once when the Columbia campus was raided by cops and someone purporting to be a member of SDS had called in a threat to the night city editor, saying he had a bazooka and would commence firing at the building in half an hour.) The gates would have gotten in the way, cost ponderous seconds in those rare emergencies of four in the morning when grumpy reporters would be summoned to come in for the special edition and write, with fingers faster than thought, "Early this morning the Empire State Building fell over after it was apparently hit by a meteorite."

At parties I would hear people quote from *The Newspaper* as if it were the Encyclopaedia Britannica or Freud or Karl Marx, so much did they respect its authority and rely upon its facts to make those who would belittle their opinions shut up and listen. They quoted from its editorials and they quoted from its columnists and they cribbed shamelessly from its movie reviews. They cited its public opinion polls to give numerical weight to their pronouncements that things were bad today and would be worse tomorrow. People took *The Newspaper*'s word for the word of God on their chances for getting heart attacks, cancer, gallstones, a centrist President, Asian flu Part One or Part Two, LSD flashbacks, tinnitus, or schizophrenic delusions. My own friend and former roommate Ellie Bliss, the Legal Aid lawyer, used *The Newspaper* on me soon after she married her shrink, Roger Einstein, and decided that everyone else in the world should be married. She sat me down in the Complaint Room of the Criminal Courts Building, and she made me read the statistics on a single woman's chances for going insane—four times those for a married woman my age—and she made sure I saw how they increased every year. It was on the tip of my tongue to tell her what *The Newspaper* had said about the suicide rate among psychia-

5

trists, but I didn't, and Roger is still alive. There are limits to the amount of statistical determinism people can take, and not everybody liked *The Newspaper*.

My father hated it. He had read it, thoroughly and vocally, for as long as I could remember. Never once had the paper printed one of his letters to the editor. Secretly he loved it, I think, and was unrequited.

My friends in the Village regarded *The Newspaper* as the voice of the Establishment, and mostly they listened to it to find out what not to do or think or buy, because *The Newspaper* told them what uptown was doing and thinking and buying, and so it was a kind of constant in their lives, a star by which their wandering barks could take bearings and be off from in the opposite direction. One of the staff writers on *The Evil Eye* told me he had spent the late sixties in a commune in Oakland stoned on mescaline and going blotto as his girlfriend discovered her lesbian potential, and the only thing that had kept him out of the loony bin was the closetful of old *New Yorker* magazines he would retreat to in times of intense group confusion. "They gave me the feeling that there was still a there there, if you get me," he said, and *The Newspaper*, for all its unhipness, could provide similar reassurance. It was like Grand Central Station—old, ponderous, gray, and resonant with the sounds of eras past, but a place where you knew where you were when you were in it.

In recent years, though, creeping subversion had spread from the outside world into the *Newspaper* building itself, carried there by a few young reporters and fewer older ones with youthful grievances. There had been snippets of gossip printed in the *Evening Star* and *The Evil Eye* about small battles and feuds brewing in the huge caldronous building. The most recent of these disputes and the most serious was between a group of women reporters and *The Newspaper*'s management. They called themselves the Feminist Faction, a name which bespoke their slight ambition for obtaining a majority in their kingdom, and they were threatening to file suit if the bosses did not give them editorial veto over all stories making mention of the female sex. Or so I had been led to believe by Jenny Locke, their spokeswoman, whom I was acquainted with telephonically and feared meeting lest she ask me face to face, as she had over the telephone, whether I believed in vaginal orgasms. She had a lot of axes to grind, to put it plainly, and she had first let my woman editor hear her sharpen them against the receiver, leading to my assignment to go forth to expose the male chauvinism of Ron

**6**

Millstein, Jenny's immediate boss, as well as that of Gilbert P. Foley, her ultimate boss, *The Newspaper*'s editor.

Prior to my luncheon with Ron, I had done a little background research. According to clippings from *The Newspaper*, these men were two geniuses who had both worked their way up from licking the floor to positions of awesome responsibility, so awesome that Ron suffered from a rare form of psychosomatic gout, while (fondly nicknamed) Gil suffered from a common form of insomnia. Gil was neither tall nor short but somewhere in between and had gone to Groton and Yale. Ron was described as "rotund" and "affable" and his schools were not included in the clippings. Gil and Ron were reported to be a "perfect team," the inward brooder and the extrovert respectively, the Anglo Irishman and the Estonian Jew, who made every decision together and trusted each other absolutely, ever since the first night they began simultaneously to work as clerks for the Sports Desk and confessed to each other their failures to make any of their high school teams.

But according to Lars Shield, the editor of *The Evil Eye*, Ron and Gil had discovered their true affinity the morning they each crossed a picket line of striking truck drivers to offer their services to management, an occasion when all the other *Newspaper* unions were calling for a sympathy strike. Lars said they were both immediately promoted to junior reporting jobs, "and they never forgot how to say 'Yassuh' from that time forward." Lars couldn't stand the way *The Newspaper* always referred to *The Evil Eye* as a "Greenwich Village weekly." "Shit!" he'd say. "We've got as many readers in Okinawa as they do." I think we had two.

Ron sounded pretty naive over the phone.

"I've seen your by-line," he said. "That's a very distinguished American name. Just the kind of name we like to see in *The Newspaper*. Wasn't there a writer?"

"You're thinking of Thackeray," I said. "No relation."

"Yes, I have *definitely* seen your by-line! Why don't we have lunch, Sarah? I don't like to do interviews over the telephone. Do you know Le Petit Enfant?"

"No," I told him. "*The Evil Eye* doesn't spring for haute cuisine."

"Oh, don't be silly! You'll be my guest!" he said. "Let me try to buy your understanding—ho ho, little joke! You don't mind a little joke, do you?"

"Well, if you are trying to bribe me, I could use a trip to Paris. You need a special feature on Paris in the springtime?"

7

"Uh, I'd have to ask Swope. That's his bailiwick, you know. But we might—"

"Little joke, Mr. Millstein," I said.

"You didn't think I thought you were serious! Ho ho ho, Paris in the springtime! I bet you don't even speak French," he said, starting to sound a little smarter.

"No," I said, "but I could learn it on the plane."

"I like your sense of humor, Sarah. We'll get along. I will *definitely* buy you lunch at Le Petit Enfant. Friday. Can you make it this Friday?"

"I might bite the hand that feeds me," I said feebly.

"Oh, ho ho! So we'll see each other Friday."

"All right, Mr. Millstein, but I warned you."

"Please call me Ron, Sarah."

"All right, Ron," I said, looking down at a Jenny Locke quote on my foolscap pad: "Ron's idea of women's liberation is letting his secretary take a piss when she wants to. You know who he took to the Guild dinner last year? Flicka Poinsby. She's a news clerk. The original sex object. She got drunk and sat on his lap in front of the five hundred most powerful people in New York. He thought that was cute. Flicka's so dumb she couldn't write her way out of a paper bag. Ron made her a reporter, but she flunked, so now she's Exhibit A: Cunts and brains don't mix."

## II

He did not look like a man who would take a girl named Flicka Poinsby onto his lap. He was too fat to take anybody onto his lap. "Rotund" did not do him justice. Ron Millstein was enormous.

He came waddling into Le Petit Enfant in that embarrassed, pitiable way a fat man has of waddling into a room, and he sort of ballooned between the tables to get to where the maître d' had pointed me out. Heads turned to look at him. Chairs had to be shoved back to make room for him to sit down. He was sweating, and he looked flushed and short of breath. Clearly he was going to die soon and awfully. The thought crossed my mind that he might die while being interviewed by me.

"Sarah Makepeace," he said before I could open my mouth, "no one told me you were such a beautiful girl, uh, woman—god, you can't tell who's going to be insulted—what are you having? Like a drink? I need one. The blinking city's going to hell today. Mayor Simon says he's closing down the Central Park Zoo, and the courts are on strike and the Lexington Avenue IRT is being marauded by a gang on skateboards. I tell you, I can't keep up with it all. They're filming on my street, and my wife is going crazy. What'll you have? I'm on bullshots, strictly bullshots. Try the brains here. You won't regret it. You know, when I first came to work for *The Newspaper*, I couldn't afford to buy a meal in an Automat. Ate all my meals in the soup kitchen they had for bums and people on the dole. Gil did too. We were so poor—why, we were so poor we used to walk to work forty blocks every morning and walk home every night, and it was rough then, too, not around here, but downtown on the East Side where I was living then. I lived in a flophouse with burlesque queens. There was one who did a trick with a cigarette. The things I learned from them! I bet you've never seen a burlesque show. Hello, Jacques! I'll have a bullshot as usual, and the lady will have— what's your pleasure?"

"Uh, I'll have wine, white wine," I said. That was, as I recall, the only thing I said during lunch.

Ron talked so fast you wanted to catch your breath for him. And when he talked, his whole face participated—the big lips, the wide nervous eyebrows, the broad, blunt nose, and all the chins. He made of talking a kind of totality, and it was a totality of self-love. He did not seem to believe that anything he said could be uninteresting. He was without fear.

"Sarah—you don't mind if I call you Sarah? That's a Jewish name, you know, Old Testament. I had a cousin named Sarah who ran away with a crummy guy named Hank Noble. He was a Gentile, so her family sat shiva when she left with him. You know what that is, don't you? A funeral? She ran away with him in high school because she was always a rebel and whatever her parents wanted her to do, she wouldn't do it. Her Hank Noble left her high and dry. He joined the Marines and disappeared. Her family eventually took her back because they weren't really married, and so the Gentile business didn't count. Women. In my family, they were the stubborn ones. They ran things and bossed everybody. I like strong women— I mean, I don't want to make you think I'm against strong women. But a really strong woman, you know, has ways of doing things which don't rub up against a man's pride, but of course I don't have

**9**

to tell you. My wife, Sondra, can let me know what she wants just by the way she says my name. When she says 'Ro-on,' I know she wants money, and when she says 'Ronald,' I know she wants me to cut back on my diet. When she says 'Ron!' very sharp like that, I know she's going to tell me that I forgot we were going to the theater and didn't dress for it. I always get that over the phone. I like women. Women, women, women. We didn't have any women on the paper when I came to work there. We had male clerks and male secretaries. There was one woman columnist in Washington, but nobody had ever met her, and she was supposed to be about eighty years old and very austere. Geraldine Paine. A very famous columnist in her time. She covered Washington society back in the days when there was a Washington society. Of course, now society is anybody's guess. Mrs. Simon said that to us the other day. We had dinner at Gracie Mansion, and she was talking about a fund-raiser for that new dance troupe, The Bodies, where the whole troupe appeared naked—not for a performance, which would have been appropriate. No, they came in naked and mingled with the party guests, just stood around with drinks in their hands, talking and laughing as though there was nothing whatsoever unusual in their appearance. Mrs. Simon said it was awful. She didn't know what to do, so she pretended it wasn't happening. I'm telling you this off the record, Sarah. I shouldn't be telling you this, but I didn't think the mayor looked well. He's feeling the strain. I'm sure of that. He didn't touch the cheesecake. Said he was off cheesecake. How can you be off cheesecake? They have excellent crepes here. I've got to keep one eye on the clock because we're getting early summaries on Lex and Park and Courts. You know what a summary is? I like to get a jump on the other desks. Gil may be my friend—of course he's my friend! Everybody knows how close we are—but he plays it down the middle on the front page, and so I have to fight. Boy, do I have to fight! I sweat blood for my stories. Yesterday I had six. Six on the front page. Metro usually gets two or three. Did you see Jenny's piece? Of course, she won't thank me. Jenny is—oh, she's capable. When she's functioning she can be—why, I've told her she's got the makings of a great reporter, a *great* reporter. But ever since she had that abortion last year, between us, she's been in therapy, and therapy is not good for newspaper reporters. Don't look back. Not in this business. You can't ever look back. It's fatal. I learned that a long time ago. If you want to be a psychoanalyst, you lose your news sense, you see. You aren't in therapy, are you, Sarah? A lot of my women, you'd be surprised how many women in the newsroom are

**10**

seeing shrinks. But what do I know? Sondra tells me I'm an oral compulsive. A lot of women aren't ready for the pressures; between you and me, Sarah, they haven't been prepared. You'd be amazed how many come to me in tears. I feel like a wet blanket sometimes. Ho ho, wet blanket! That's a good one! Off the record, as I told you. Hello, Jacques. Bring her just a taste of those brains and an omelet. I'd say she's an omelet person. White-wine drinkers always are. Good. Sarah, do you know how many women I've hired? I've hired five women in the last year. We get a hundred applications a week on the Metro Desk alone, and at least ten percent of those candidates are topnotch, the real stuff, white males, every last one of them. We can't touch them. Jenny doesn't realize what she's doing. If I hire five reporters a year I'm lucky. Are we supposed to make up for a situation that has prevailed for thousands of years? They all promised me they were not going to have children and now two of them are pregnant. What am I supposed to do? Set up a nursery? You want kids and the whole domestic package, you don't come to work for a newspaper. Do you see Gloria Steinem having children? She's one I really admire. We had her in for lunch, you know, we have these editorial lunches, and she was so cool and polite. She could kill you with a feather. I shouldn't say this, but damn it, she hasn't let it destroy her femininity. She charmed the publisher, charmed the pants off him. Charmed the pants off him, ho ho ho! *That's* a good one! I'll have to remember. But she really did. Rattling off statistics like a little cooing dove. Who was it said, 'Lies, damned lies, and statistics'? Bill was convinced—because between you and me, I don't think he had given much thought to the Women's Movement—in the space of an hour with her, he was convinced we should make women our number one priority. Jenny could sure as hell take a page from her book! She's the reason I've been hiring only women for the last year. Well, I had to hire a couple of sportswriters and take Arthur Gunther for Foreign because he'll be going to Moscow. We are a newspaper! We're not a charitable institution or government agency, where they have to make a show of a thing. You have no idea the headaches those women have given me. They complain about everything. They take twice as much sick leave as men do. They get hysterical on deadline. And now some of the male reporters are putting in for paternity leave. We don't give leaves, period. If we did, the whole staff would ask for a year off to write a novel and get nothing done and come back with writer's block, just like Figland, Steve Figland, who I never should have let go to the MacDowell Colony—he can't *write*

**11**

anymore. I don't know what they do up there in the woods. Steve said it made him crazy not hearing the telephones. He's still crazy, and now he blames it on the noise in the newsroom. I sent him out to do a weather story last week. Should have been a snap. Weather stories are easy as pie. Steve smoked up a carton of cigarettes and got three paragraphs done. Absolute garbage. He was doing a lead about the existential ache of the polar bear, for god's sake! I had to put him on rewrite. Do you think you'd be comfortable working for us, Sarah? How's your French? Seriously. Why's *The Evil Eye* so goddamn sloppy? Saying I gave Mayor Simon a veto on the subway series. Nobody has a veto with us. We can't get our own reporters to make changes we ask for. Damn it, they are the most independent, pampered bunch of journalists in the whole country! What time is it? What did Jenny tell you about me? Did she tell you I'm a male chauvinist? Sure I'm a male chauvinist! Everybody's a male chauvinist! You can't change the world overnight, and they don't all want it, you know. My own daughter-in-law *loves* to cook. You can't keep her out of the kitchen. How many Virginia Woolfs are there anyway? Talent doesn't grow on trees. We had to look far and wide to get our women, and what thanks do we get for it? I hired Jenny, did you know that? Gil didn't think we should take her. She was *my* choice. I got her out of Chicago. She was killing herself with that syndicated column. Jenny's not really a columnist. To be a columnist, you have to have—I don't know, what is it? A kind of stature. You can tell her I said that, too. Because she knows. Listen, if it weren't for me, Jenny Locke would still be earning fifteen thousand a year writing for little old ladies in Dubuque. Let's have coffee. I've got to run."

He must have signaled to Jacques, because the coffee appeared without his having to interrupt, and he signed the check while still talking and kept up the verbiage while waddling out of the restaurant with me. He had been able to stand up without assistance after all. When we got out on the sidewalk, he strode forth mightily, as if his weight gave him not less but more energy than ordinary men. He went on hitting at Jenny and then bouncing off into unrelated fragments of name dropping, observing, opining, mentioning plays he'd seen, a glimpse of Woody Allen, a lunch with the President's press secretary, a reception for the French consul general, his foot problems, Gil's insomnia, somebody's ulcer, the "nice, articulate" new FBI bureau chief, the "hopeless" search for a good black columnist, and the muggings of *Newspaper* truckdrivers, which had been getting worse since the latest Times Square clean-up drive.

When he got to the big gates, he stopped, looked me in the eye, and put out his big fleshy hand to me, smiling enormously.

"I don't know how long it's been since I've had such a good conversation, Sarah Makepeace. I like you. When are you going to come to work for us?"

"When?" I said from my daze of listening.

"You don't have to tell me today." He smiled on. "I look forward to reading your piece. Don't forget what was off the record, sweetheart."

And he went in through the gates. If Ron Millstein was a genius, what was Shakespeare?

---

# *III*

---

I needed a job, but I didn't believe for a minute that Ron was sincerely offering me one. I had ideas about how things were done in those days, and I knew *The Newspaper*, the fucking stalwart of the republic of journalism, did not hire nobodies like me. *The Newspaper* hired China experts and distinguished young economists, top political correspondents from other newspapers, Pulitzer Prize winners and Harvard *Crimson* editors, elegant punsters from *Time* magazine, people with brilliant but muted brains. Since my brain was neither brilliant nor muted, I did not qualify. I was smart enough to know that. How had Ron made it? The man was not muted, not in control. One could see he had energy and a sort of grotesque charm, and he was thoroughly New York, juggling all those balls in the air at the same time. But he had laid himself open to me to such a degree, with Gloria Steinem "like a little cooing dove," "women aren't ready for pressure," "you'd be amazed how many come to me in tears," and all the "topnotch" candidates being white males. Telling me that a truly strong woman knew how to get her way without rubbing "up against a man's pride"! Didn't he listen to himself? Did he think I wouldn't *write* the story after he "offered" me a job? Shit, the crudest public relations man in the city wouldn't try a trick like that. Ron Millstein was dumb, dumb, *dumb!*

I knew Lars would be overjoyed to hear all the things Ron had said to me, so I made furious notes on the subway and went straight to *The Evil Eye*.

Lars was reading a piece about Bianca Jagger's visits to the White House.

"Hey, Lars," I said. "Ron Millstein offered me a job."

"So take it," he said, without looking up.

"Come on, Lars! I'm serious. He wanted to do a little suppression of the news. A little bribery. Isn't that terrific? I got some great stuff for you, Lars. Ron Millstein just delivered himself of some choice inanities on the subject of women."

"Good, good," he said. "Go write the goddamn thing!"

"Why don't you hire me, Lars? I could interview all your favorite hates. I seem to have the kind of face they can talk to. You know, Gee Whiz from Massachusetts."

"Don't bother me, Sarah. Can't you see I'm busy?"

"I need the bread, Lars."

He did not respond, and when I raised the subject with Doris Munster, the feminist editor, she told me I had to "earn the credentials."

"What credentials?" I asked her.

"If you don't know what I'm talking about, I can't explain it to you. There are people around here, Sarah, who've been writing for us for years, and we haven't hired them."

"Maybe they don't need the money."

"Why don't you join a rap group, Sarah? You need to get your head straight on quite a few issues."

"Like?"

"Like you don't just jump right into the *Movement* where a lot of other folks have put in time and expect to be made a star, Sarah. You're only twenty-six. I mean, you're coming along. You're doing good stuff. But you don't understand yet. You haven't had enough experience. Have you lived with a man? Have you read *Rape?*"

"Who said anything about being a star? I just want to be able to pay my cleaning bill. Sometimes I get the feeling, Doris, that my older sisters don't want me to make it."

"Oh, Sarah! Now, that's really paranoid! I've taken your stuff ahead of so many other pieces! And I've taken heat for that. Some women wanted to know who you were that you were getting so much space here. They haven't seen you around, you know, at any of the demonstrations. Do you really want to sit there and tell me I'm holding you back? I've been protecting you."

"Who complained to you?"

"Oh, fuck it! It doesn't matter. I don't have time to argue with you. I've got a splitting headache, and we haven't even done the arts layout. Would you mind?"

Over the weekend, while I was writing up my Millstein interview, Doris called me.

"What's this I hear about you going to work for *The Newspaper*?"

"I don't know. What did you hear?"

"It's all over the newsroom up there that you had lunch with Ron Millstein and he told a few people he was going to hire you. I thought you were supposed to be doing an interview for us."

"I was, Doris. It's all bullshit. He just wanted to buy me off, hold a carrot in front of me."

"A carrot! You mean you'd actually consider it? Double-cross us . . ."

"Of course not, Doris! I'm putting it all in the story. The man's not to be believed."

"Then why did he tell Jenny Locke he was going to hire you?"

"He told Jenny Locke? Why did he do that?"

"That's what I'm asking you. She's furious. She just about blew my ear out."

"Oh, he's probably trying to make her stop talking to me, just to fuck up the piece. Maybe he isn't as dumb as I thought."

"When can I see the piece?"

"Monday."

"Can you get it to me tomorrow? I'll be in the office all afternoon."

"I'll try, Doris."

"You'd better do more than try."

So hire me, I wanted to say. I really was strapped.

My job with the East 118th Street Block Association never had paid that much, and it was costing me a lot to live like a sixties person. The rents in the Village were humongous and so was the price of grass. What I had managed to save since college had gone to the lawyer who kept me out of jail after the incident that got me fired from the block association job.

It hadn't been much of a job, really. I ran an after-school program for the culturally deprived in a little storefront between Second and Third avenues, right next to the numbers joint run by the Italian named Sal who was such good friends with the local police. He was also good friends with Jesus and Fredo, my two Neighborhood Youth Corps assistants, who used to disappear on me every afternoon around three-thirty, when the number came out and the bettors had to be paid. They were not bad kids, and running numbers on a block like that was sort of equal to selling fire insurance in Four Corners, Mass. It meant people trusted you, vaguely, and were willing to invest in a small way in your product. The numbers running would never have brought any trouble for the boys if it hadn't been for certain other high-risk undertakings of theirs and my own profound ignorance of the culture of the culturally deprived.

What happened was that Jesus and Fredo came to see me at the storefront one day a good hour before the program was supposed to start, and they told me they had to quit right away on the spot. They didn't want to give me any reasons, but I wheedled it out of them that there had been an immaculate conception on the block which scared them shitless, and they wanted to get away and think about it for a while, let the meaning of the miracle sort of recede into focus, from the distance of Brooklyn, where Fredo's cousins lived. They wanted to know if they could have their jobs back when they got over the terror. I told them not to be so silly and superstitious, that I would talk to the pregnant girl and find out who the father was, just to prove to them that it was no miracle and they shouldn't be afraid. Understandably, the girl wouldn't talk to me. Her mother had locked her in and set up a little shrine outside her room, with flowers and a statue of the Virgin and a glass of holy water that had been blessed by the Pentecostal radio priest. I did some research, though, among the other East 118th Street teenagers, and I learned that Jesus and Fredo had often gone star-watching with the girl on the roof of an abandoned building on East 117th Street and that exactly one month before the girl, whose name was Angelica, had felt her first wave of morning nausea, the three of them had seen a huge meteorite and taken it as a sign. How else could Angelica have conceived through Handi-Wrap? Jesus and Fredo disappeared before I could explain it to them, because Angelica's father, a merchant seaman who did not believe in miracles, arrived home and said he was going to kill the two astrologers and sell his daughter to an Arab he knew in Cartagena. Angelica's father had to go back to sea before he could commit murder, and Jesus and Fredo showed up at work the day after he left. They were not good friends anymore. Confinement seemed to have made them despise one another, and I had a hell of a time with them, trying to keep them from fighting, while all around us the little culturally deprived children were dyeing their hair with the finger paints.

The underlying conflict, I soon learned, concerned the paternity of Angelica's child. My two helpers had each decided during their exile that a real man would offer to marry the mother of his child. They both stood on their dignity about this and spouted some things they had read in pamphlets I had given them about the rights of Latinos to determine their own destiny. But who was the father of the child? They were ready to decide in battle, but finally I persuaded them that Angelica should make the choice. I said that a woman would know such a thing, that a woman could tell when she looked at a man whether his child was in her belly. The two little fornicators believed me. But Angelica, who had been lying in bed reading her horoscope for the year and some articles in *Redbook* about birth control, multiple orgasms, and the salaries that "new" women were making downtown, answered both proposals with "You're kidding." She showed me a prediction that she would come into a financial windfall and get a new boyfriend in October. She later enrolled in the city's high school for pregnant mothers (from which, incidentally, she graduated with honors, describing herself in the yearbook as "Presidential Aspirant").

Jesus and Fredo fell into depression and swore their undying brotherly love for one another. They took a new interest in Sal and were often longer away from the storefront, causing me disciplinary problems with the play dough and the creative building blocks.

One day my two helpers brought two female helpers with them. The girls were younger than Angelica, and they giggled a lot. They adored Jesus and Fredo, who left them minding the children with me for whole afternoons but still collected their Neighborhood Youth Corps checks on time, promising to take the girls dancing on Saturday night. I would notice the boys nuzzling up to their girlfriends in hallways when I passed by in the evening. There was a knowingness about the way they stroked the girls' hips, an assured tautness in their faces when they moved in close for the good-night kiss.

"How many of the girls on this block use Handi-Wrap for birth control?" I asked the boys one day when I caught them alone.

They pretended I had been speaking to the alternate-side-of-the-street-parking sign. Finally Fredo turned his back to me and said, "They all do. What's it to you?"

I said maybe there would be another star-watching tragedy; perhaps the two of them could start a little counseling group to stop this

**17**

from happening. They said, "Sheeeyit!" in unison and dug their hands in their pockets in the manner of teenagers whose sense of etiquette has been severely offended.

"Suit yourselves," I said.

A few days later, Jesus approached me as Fredo practiced his right jab against the storefront poster.

"How cou' we get the information, like?" he asked. "For that teen counseling thing? You got any books?"

I spent the next Saturday perusing the bookstores for tasteful sex education volumes, and I found three that I thought were sufficiently low key while also not heavy on technical vocabulary. They were illustrated naturally enough, but all that the kids on 118th Street had to do to see sexual organs was commission the tallest among them to buy a copy of *Screw* magazine from a news dealer. These were not innocent kids. Ignorant, maybe. But a pencil-drawn erection was not something they had never seen. The schoolyard wall on 119th Street had crude line drawings of the very thing.

I gave them the books on a Monday. They testified at the arraignment Saturday morning that they never had held any meetings but had merely passed the books around among the teenage girls on the block. They were charged, like myself, with corrupting the morals of minors, a charge Judge Reel threw out immediately after I had agreed to pay my lawyer two thousand dollars. However, there was the matter of the numbers slips discovered on the persons of Jesus and Fredo at the time of their arrests.

They were given six months probation each. All charges were dropped against me. My two helpers had to go to Brooklyn permanently, though, and the board of directors of the block association, all parents from the block, fired me with, as the courts say, extreme prejudice.

I remember how hard it was to look at the faces of those board members while they were examining the textbooks. I would have cried, except that they all looked so embarrassed.

The day I left the storefront, Eduardo Rivera, Fredo's uncle, came by to get the keys.

"What you gonna do now?" he asked me. "You been one damn fool."

"Yeah," I said. "I don't know what I'm gonna do. Go home and take a bath, I guess."

"You need a husban'," he said. "You goine home to your folks?"

"No," I said.

"Why not?"

**18**

"Oh, I can't live with them."

"You need someone looks after you. You're some mixed-up kine of lady. Your folks know you los' your job?"

"Not yet."

"How you gonna make ends meet? You know, pay the lan'lord?"

"How about welfare?" I said brightly.

"You got a education, Harvards!" he said, horrified.

"Listen, my parents will help me out if I'm really stuck," I said. "Don't worry about me, Mr. Rivera. I'm just sorry I made such a mess of this . . . this . . ."

"Forget it," he said.

"Well," I said, "here are the keys."

He took them. I looked around the grimy little room with its splintered small children's desks for which I had filled out seventeen Board of Education application forms. The posters of Martin Luther King and Cesar Chavez were curling at the corners. Dr. King's large liquid eyes were focused on the unseeable, but Chavez was looking right at me, mournfully, with all the pains of the strikes, the hunger fasts, the nights in jail, the beatings, murders, rains of spit and vitriol endured, and for what, he seemed to be asking me, imploring me, accusing me—while also forgiving me the way only an accusing martyr can forgive—for what did I lead my people through all those sufferings, if it was going to mean girls like you would be sent among our little virgins bringing copies of *Sex Made Simple, What Is Love?* and *Before You Try It: The Teen's Guide to Reproductive Choice?*

"Well, adios," I said to Mr. Rivera.

"I better walk you to the subway," he said. "Some people on the block is pretty mad you got Jesus and Fredo in trouble."

He walked me there, and he bought himself a token so he could stand with me on the platform until the train came. We couldn't think of what to say to one another. Everywhere I looked, I saw "Fuck" and "Pussy" scrawled on the pillars and the billboards. "I eat pussy" was written across the teeth of the big smiling brown man of the Rheingold Cerveza poster, while under his chin a pedant had written, "He sucks cock."

Mr. Rivera stepped from left foot to right foot as if trying to keep warm. But it wasn't cold in the station. We were in the January thaw just then.

"It's really warm," I said.

"Yeah, real warm," he said.

After about a million years, the train came.

**19**

"You take care now, you hear?" he said.

"Thanks, Mr. Rivera," I said.

Across from me, all the way home, the Ex-Lax poster asked me, "How can you feel pretty when you're constipated?"

# IV

*The Evil Eye* was just down the street from my apartment building on Christopher Street, but it never would have occurred to me to go in there with my tale of woe. I went to the Poor Mouth, where I had friends who were also nostalgic for the sixties and used to drink a lot of cheap wine while they remarked how nothing was happening anymore.

Peter O'Feeny was in the bar the night I got fired. He had seniority in the place, and everybody liked him, though he lorded it over them all, because he was a safely ruined man. A poet who had not published a stanza in the last five years, he would drink with anyone. He taught a course at the New School and was adored by his students, who used to bring their girlfriends into the bar to meet him, in the full trust that he could not steal anybody's girl. It was to Peter that I told my tale of woe, and he said I should put it in writing. I had nothing else to do the next day, so I took up Peter's suggestion.

I brought the piece to the bar. Peter said he liked it, and he put it in his pocket, promising to take it to *The Evil Eye*. About three weeks later, he remembered it and gave it to Lars. Lars gave it to Doris with a note at the top saying: "This looks like it's been dragged all over town. I've read too many of these. What do you think?" Doris called me soon thereafter. She liked the piece but thought it should be rewritten and I should "spell out the connections between specific incidents and issues that women can relate to in general." The instruction was not helpful, and in the end Doris had to make the connections herself, inserting a few strident paragraphs about the corporate conspiracy to keep poor women ignorant of their biological functions and the inherent sexism in popular horoscopes.

"I see Doris made you put some clit into it," Peter said to me

**20**

the next time I appeared in the bar. But I got a few letters of praise from women, and Planned Parenthood put me on its mailing list. One person wrote me a note with an enclosed leaflet about Egyptian astrology. "What is your sign?" she asked. "I'd like to meet you." The note was signed "Aurora."

Then Doris sent me to cover a feminist teach-in, and I became a regular correspondent on the beat, writing about women like the Faulkner character who believed in "rights for women, as long as women would let her dictate what was right for them." (Doris didn't think that was apt. She cut it out of my piece on the New Vogue for Trashing Betty Friedan.)

I was getting paid $150 per story. My rent was $300 a month, so there was a shortfall, as the mayor used to say in Washington. And the shortfall had been growing over the months that I wrote for the *Eye*. My parents had been sending me money and writing me worried letters, which I suppose put me in a sort of sixties situation, but I had nothing to show for it—no truncheon scars, no Venceremos Brigade T-shirts, not even an arrest record to speak of. All I got in the East 118th Street pornography raid was a station house summons.

By the time of that lunch with Ron Millstein, I was so poor I had gone through all the pockets of all my coats and blue jeans to find the change for the subway fare and back. My good clothes were in the dry cleaners downstairs and had been there for three months because I didn't have the spare forty dollars to get them out.

I wished I had played harder on Lars's sympathies. However, I wrote the piece about Ron and handed it in on Sunday evening without a word of complaint to Doris. She was smoking Gauloises and looked as though she couldn't take much interpersonal contact. She glanced at the first page, blew out a huge Frenchy cloud, and exclaimed:

"I don't *believe* this! Did he really *say* this?"

"Yes," I said.

"Well, I don't have time to read it all now. I'm sure it's fine. I'll call you tomorrow," she said, withdrawing into her smoky gloom.

She claimed later that she had been going through a crisis with her ex-husband that night and had been additionally saddled with the music section of the paper, as the music editor had locked himself in a studio somewhere on Houston Street with a sudden inspiration for a sound poem. In any case, Lars called me the next morning to ask where my story was.

"I gave it to Doris last night," I said.

"She can't find it," he said. "Do you have a copy?"

"Doris always makes a copy."

"I think you're going to have to write it again," he said. "Can you get it done by six?"

"Are you going to pay me double?"

"Look, if you don't want the piece to run, Sarah . . ."

"Okay, okay, I'll do it again."

I had started reassembling the thing from my notes when the telephone rang.

"Is this Sarah Makepeace?" said a crisp female voice.

"Yes."

"Hold on for Mr. Millstein."

Perhaps a thief had stolen my article and spirited it up to him? I braced myself.

"Hello, Sarah. This is Ron."

"Hi, Ron."

"Gee, I enjoyed our lunch last week. I was telling Sondra what a good lunch we had. Have you finished your piece yet? I want you to come up here today and meet a few people. Can you make it for lunch? What are you saying about me? Whatever you do, don't call me rotund. Gil wants to meet you. He's free at twelve-thirty. On the dot. We don't keep Village time up here, ho ho! So I'll see you at twelve, right?"

"Mr. Millstein, I don't think—"

"Call me Ron, for god's sake! It's bad enough my name's Millstein. I don't have to hear it all the time."

"Ron, I don't think it would be appropriate for us to, um, be discussing a job, um, when I'm writing about you."

"I don't want to know what you're writing about me! I know you'll be fair. Listen, I promise not to talk about your article at all. I want to hire you. Gil thinks you've got potential. He's read your stuff, you know. That Betty Friedan piece was great! You really stuck it to those bitches. And I told Gil what you said about strong women, you know, not wounding a man's pride."

"But, Ron, you said—"

"You'll be up here at twelve, right? You know where the *Newspaper* building is."

"Yes, but—"

"You've got plenty of time. 'Bye."

# V

Months later, people told me they had not been able to figure out why Ron wanted to hire me. I hadn't done anything of note. I wasn't *known*. I did not fit the mold. And say I had been about to trash him in *The Evil Eye*—that wouldn't have been anything new. *The Evil Eye* tried to do in *The Newspaper* every other week, and nobody paid much attention. Readers who believed what the *Eye* said about *The Newspaper* wanting to ship all the blacks and Puerto Ricans down to Mississippi in boxcars with packed lunches of pigs' knuckles and cuchifritos would have believed that before they read it in the *Eye*. Ron didn't have an image to protect with *Eye* readers, if you see what I mean, and most people on *The Newspaper* couldn't figure out why he had even talked to me in the first place.

Not that they knew who I was when I came into the newsroom. I came in there dressed in a nicely faded blue work shirt and tiered blue cotton skirt of which I was quite fond but which to others looked peculiarly droopy and dated, like an old hippie hand-down, the castoff of some groupie's beloved idol, maybe, what Joan Baez could have given to the Freedom Democratic Party store on Bleecker Street after she got tired of singing "There but for fortune go you or I" in it. And I was wearing flat-heeled sandals, which you didn't *do*, high or low class, around Times Square since the platform shoe came in. "I had you pegged as somebody's nerdy daughter, Swope's kid from Swarthmore who plays the violin and sings madrigals: 'Ooouv me this life it paineth,'" one of my friends later told me. "I thought you were about eighteen years old." Most people didn't take notice of me for at least five minutes, the length of time it took a rumor to get to the back of the newsroom and halt the luncheon calls for a deep analysis and interpretation. "That's Sarah Makepeace from *The Evil Eye*," the word presently got around. "I hear her old man's got a piece of the company. Those whores would hire anybody! Look at Ron pouring on the charm."

Ron was sitting in the center of the enormous room, wheeling around on his mobile chair, introducing me to everybody within earshot, which meant copy editors and all his various assistants, who sat around the two huge desks called Dayside and Nightside with clipboards in front of them and forty-three buttons on each of the three or four telephones they all seemed to have, which rang often and were not answered. I got a confused but very gratifying impression that they were all not answering their phones out of politeness to me. They were jacketless to a man and had their shirt sleeves rolled up to midforearm the way newspapermen always did in the movies, but they did not talk too fast or speak out of the sides of their mouths like the old movie journalists. In fact, they seemed rather shy and waited for Ron to call their names before looking up to smile at me.

The room extended for hundreds of feet, with rows of desks going back to the far wall north of Ron's own. Other clusters of desks sat south of his, bunched together as if for work teams. Ron pointed out the main geographical bodies:

"That's Foreign over there, and that's National, and you see Sports over there in the corner. That's my old love. And then you see that guy by the fountain with Marco? That's mean Vic Veblen, the photo editor. He's a perfectionist. And you see all those desks out there? Those are my troops. Watch this."

He rolled to starboard, catching a short-necked microphone by the throat, and he nearly totaled his secretary before he came to a halt against Nightside.

"AKELROYD!" he called, amplified and grinning. "AKELROYD, GET UP HERE ON THE DOUBLE!"

A man in the fourth row of reporters' desks got up languidly, too languidly to have been heeding the urgent command. He walked not straight up to Ron's desk but the long way around, past some cubbyholes I took to be mailboxes. He paused by these, reached for the contents of one and sorted slowly through the envelopes. I looked out over the desks again, searching for Akelroyd. Ron, meanwhile, had picked up a telephone receiver and was speaking into it while simultaneously spearing sheets of paper from his desktop upon the two spikes to his left.

The man who had gone for his mail appeared at Ron's right.

"Yes?" he said. "You called me?"

Ron raised his left hand to indicate that he had heard and could not yet answer. Into the phone, he was saying:

"But I told you we were holding it for Sunday, Maureen, because it will get better play on Sunday, and you have to weigh the urgency against the news slot. Yes, Sondra got the invitation. Didn't she call you? I'm sure she'll be calling you to accept. She loves fashion shows. You shouldn't do this to me, Maureen. I can't afford it.

Yes, I know that, and the paper knows what a good friend you are, Maureen, Mrs. Kleinfreude believes in the zoo. Yes, yes . . ."

Akelroyd shrugged and turned away, starting back toward his desk.

"Just a minute!" Ron cupped the phone. "Vin!" he called. "Wait a minute, Vin!"

Akelroyd turned slowly.

"Mrs. Heller—Maureen—I'll have to call you back," Ron said into the phone.

Akelroyd moved a step closer. He raised his eyebrows.

"Vinnie, I wanted to introduce you. You're one of our stars," Ron said.

Akelroyd's shoulders shifted perceptibly and his eyebrows relaxed. "To whom do I have the pleasure?" he asked, looking at me for the first time. He put a hand to the middle button of his jacket, and I noticed then that reporters wore suits while copy editors wore unpressed slacks and shirts.

"This is Sarah Makepeace from *The Evil Eye*," Ron said. "Sarah, this is Vincent Akelroyd, our city columnist. He won the Meyer Berger Award this year, you know. He's one of our best writers."

"Some people do not lump me with the aggregate," Akelroyd said. "Are you doing a piece about this place? Going to tell the Village youngsters how the adults function? Don't quote me. I wouldn't want you to strain yourself with the spelling of my name."

"Ho ho! Vincent's not as bad as he sounds! Are you, Vin? He can teach you the ropes, Sarah."

"I beg your pardon. Are we giving tutorials to the underground press now?"

"Sarah's coming to work for us," Ron said. "We need some new blood around here." He winked at me with one whole side of his face.

"*She's* coming to— What have you *written?*" Akelroyd asked apoplectically.

"Actually, I'm working on a story about *The Newspaper's* policies toward women," I said.

"Well, we don't have a position on clitoral orgasm," Akelroyd said. "And you may quote me on that. Do you know how to spell 'clitoral'?"

"Ho ho ho ho ho!" Ron laughed. "Vincent is terrible, absolutely terrible! Don't you love it?"

"May I take my leave of you, sir? I am lunching with the governor."

**25**

"Today?" Ron said, making a sudden grab for his clipboard. "I thought that was tomorrow."

"Today," said Akelroyd.

"Where? Why didn't you remind me? I've got to tell Photo. See, Willie's got 'Guv' down here for Tuesday. God *damn* it! *Willie!*" Ron yelled, and one of the shirt-sleeved men along Dayside got whiplash coming to attention in a seated position. "God *damn* it, Vin! I wanted you to talk to Greg. He's got questions. We need a response on the MTA thing, and you have to ask about his meeting with Kennedy. Damn it, Willie, *where is Greg?*" Ron showed his teeth.

"Greg's in Albany," said the one answering to Willie, hopelessly, rubbing his neck.

"This is for the column, Ron, remember? We discussed this on Friday," said Akelroyd. "I write a col-*umn*. I do not do leg-*work*. Greg can ask his own puerile ques-*tions*."

"Where are you meeting him?" Ron asked.

Vincent cast cold eyes on me.

"It's all right. She won't tell the goddman *Star, god damn it!* You should have *looked after this!* Am I supposed to tell *everybody everything* around here?"

Ron's face was purple. *Now* he was going to have a heart attack.

"We are meeting in the '21' Club," said Akelroyd, enunciating as if his tongue and teeth were his fingertips and they were holding a distasteful object prior to release over a garbage can.

"The '21' Club. Did you hear that, Willie?" Ron said. "Are you awake now? God, I'm surrounded by *idiots!* Tell Vic it's '21,' and put Guv down on the possibles. Good, Vin. Thanks. Now, Sarah, let's go see Gil."

That was where he really trapped me, Ron did, because he had Gilbert Foley all primed to meet this incredible Radcliffe girl who had worked on the *Crimson* and served on five hundred different academic restructuring committees and graduated with highest honors while still keeping her social conscience intact, which meant she had eschewed the easy and obvious career ladder lowered flat on the ground for her upon graduation day to instead sacrifice herself for the good of humanity in the slums, where she had single-handedly prevented massive riots. Where did Ron learn about my work in the slums? That question obsessed me, I remember, as I sat listening to Foley in his dim-lighted office of browns and soft grays, because it was the only fact he had got right, the bare nugget of it anyway, other than the Radcliffe girl designation, but that last had so often served to distort my perceived image that it couldn't count as a fact.

I mean, a word like "Radcliffe" has evocative powers like the word "red," and right away it can cause misinterpretation, such as occurs when you say "The lady in red," instead of "the lady in the long dress," which would make you see a different woman in your mind altogether. "So you're a 'Cliffie," men used to say to me in the Poor Mouth before I knew enough not to have a background, "a real 'Cliffie," they'd say, while I saw their eyes glisten with horny expectation. *I've never fucked a Radcliffe girl,* they would be thinking, though they wouldn't tell me that until later and then only if they made it into the sack with me, which took them hours, sometimes weeks, since they mistook me for an intellectual and wanted first to argue with me about the biblical symbolism in Faulkner's novels or Mailer's grasp of the meaning of time. One man, an African journalist with a Cambridge accent—Cambridge, England, that is—treated me to three hours of refined speculation on the subject of Virgil's military inaccuracies before he realized I had not read Virgil. He said then that it was lonely for an African in New York, and he sighed when he paid the bill. He didn't even want to seduce me, white as I was, and blond, sort of.

Older people weren't too subtle about showing what Radcliffe meant to them, either. There was this patron of the East 118th Street Block Association who used to come up there once in a blue moon to watch me teaching the little culturally you-know-whats how to suck the handle end of a Magic Marker if they must suck. "Saree, Lester stole my *pur*ple!" was the degree of need I serviced, and S. Millicent Forsythe thought it was "just fantastic" the way I did it. He kept saying I should come by "for a bite one Sunday when my children are in town." I eventually got the invitation and went, expecting to be bored out of my skull hearing how fantastic I was, while the Forsythe children checked their watches and calculated how much longer they'd have to sit around the living room making Dad feel good about the trust fund he'd set up for them. One of them did, the daughter. I saw her checking her watch several times. She had a job as a securities analyst and I guess was indifferent about the trust fund. But the son, S. Millicent, Jr., had a heck of a good time, or so he said later when we went out on a date arranged by his father and the conversation stopped cold. The old man was a good talker, it had turned out, so the Sunday lunch had not been boring. But the date was. S. Millicent, Jr., didn't know what to say to me after he had said his father thought the work I did was "just fantastic."

Ellie and I used to talk about the Radcliffe syndrome a whole lot when we first got out. She was going to Columbia Law School and living with me in a cockroach breeding station on Carmine Street, one of those quaint old apartments that had never been painted since day one. She said her professors had this attitude about her which made them want to ask her all the hard questions, and it was driving her crazy, which, incidentally, is why she went to see Roger the shrink, and fell in love with him when she said, "Well, first of all, I went to Radcliffe," and he said, "So?" Ellie thought her professors hated her and that it was only because she had gone to Radcliffe. "They say it to me all the time—they say, 'Surely our Radcliffe graduate will enlighten us on this point,' and, 'What is a class action, Miss Bliss? Would you call Radcliffe girls a class of litigants?'" One professor didn't call her by her name. He called her "Radcliffe."

But it was, as I said, even worse with the younger men, who we knew had the terrors underneath it all that we were smarter than them ("they," of course, but 'Cliffies learned not to be too socially grammatical) and would display our smarts in front of a whole bunch of people when they had an arm around us and weren't paying attention, and that right then a handsome, pipe-smoking novelist would ask, from the far side of the room so everybody could hear: "What do you think of Ellie's argument? Do you agree that Watergate was a reenactment of the Reformation?" and when the poor guy couldn't do much but shrug, then the novelist would ask, "How do you keep up with this girl?" preliminarily to fetching us a drink. Young men thought we were going to humiliate them, and there was only one way to sort of alchemize our IQs down to size, namely, fucking our brains out, an expression most popular with the sorts who went after us. If they could get that Radcliffe cunt around their BU or City College or Amherst or Stanford or Texas State or Brandeis, or St. John's University, Stony Brook, Southern Illinois, or Christ, even Harvard cock, and make it beg and squeeze and slime until it couldn't hardly stand it anymore, and if then BU City College Amherst Stanford Texas State Brandeis St. John's University Stony Brook Southern Illinois or again Harvard (where we were said to be statistically, like, smarter, chosen from a smaller, more elite brain pool than the boys') could just ram that Radcliffe vagina home to a huge mind-fucking orgasm, then they had us, they had had us, and things would equal out.

But to older men, we looked like good prospects for breeding grandchildren who could go to Harvard.

28

"Listen," Ron said to me just before we went into Foley's office. "I had to tell him a little white lie about you. I had to tell him you're on staff at the *Eye*. It's practically true anyway, and I did it for your sake, so don't let me down, kid. This is your chance!"

"A little white lie" was something of a gargantuan understatement, as I soon learned, hearing Foley praise me to the skies, call me "a moral standard-bearer," "a quiet achiever," "one of the best of your generation," and so on. He said I was the sort of woman they had been searching for high and low, and he wondered why I had failed to come to his attention when I was on the *Crimson*—I shot Ron a panicked look here. Ron shook his head quiveringly and then smiled toward Foley, who was continuing to list my great attributes, saying it had all been for the best that I didn't go straight from the *Crimson* to *The Newspaper*, "because you buried yourself in that tragic, noble legacy left to us by John Kennedy and have come away enriched with a perspective on life we don't get much of a handle on around here." Buried in a legacy? Handle on a perspective? Were the man's metaphors kind of haywire, or was I simply unable to connect? That scene in the newsroom had *started* to put me off my stride, and then coming unprepared and next to totally unwitting into this darkened room for a job "interview" with the most powerful man in journalism, who was apparently telling me I had the job—not me, though, but somebody Ron had invented for him to believe was me, sitting there in the half light dressed like Joan Baez used to dress—had got me *completely* off my stride. I was too embarrassed to speak. I mean, think what it would have done to Ron for me to speak up, clear my throat, say, "Um, Mr. Foley, I'm afraid there's been a large misunderstanding here. Your man Ron here has just told you a whopping number of lies about me, and furthermore, I don't want to work here. I don't wish to work here. It isn't my *scene*, see, I am not able to visualize myself in this setting. . . ."

"At Guild minimum," Gilbert Foley was saying, "which I think is now about—Ron, help me out on this—about twenty-one thou."

"That's right," said Ron. "You hit it on the button."

"And so it would have to be, at the beginning, at that level, I'm afraid," Foley said, stretching his legs up onto his desk while I gripped the sides of my chair and began to obsess about how Ron had found out I'd worked in the slums, which couldn't have been from reading my *Eye* story, since if it had been, he would never have thought I was a *Newspaper* type of person. Did *The Newspaper* call up the FBI on me? They might be inaccurate enough. I did

**29**

have an arrest record. Could they get my Freedom of Information Act file? Was I feeling dizzy, or was it just the light? Why did Foley keep his office so dark?

Then Ron said he had to leave us for a minute, and I got really scared. Up to then, I had felt a sort of secondary responsibility, but when he left, I suddenly felt as though *I* had told those lies, and at the same time I became aware that I had to pee really desperately.

Foley, too, seemed more uncomfortable now. He had a thin, what you might call epicene face and it seemed to be growing thinner. He had long bony hands which he kept holding together like a man at prayer. Presently he stood up, put his fingertips to his chin and began to pace back and forth in front of me.

"Now, I don't quite know how to put this to you," he said, "but there is one thing that worries me, one slight hesitation I have about you. It's your association with, ah . . . I can't fit it into the larger picture—the *Crimson,* summa cum laude, the mayor's task force on crime . . ."

God! Ron had told another whopper!

"You see, Sarah," he said, now resting one buttock on his desk, "we have a very great public trust here, and the people we hire— well, they're not merely talented. We hire the best talent in the country—no, the world. But we don't want talent alone. Some of the most gifted writers I know are people I wouldn't hire. Because we want—well, I don't know how else to put it—we want character. We don't want people using the paper for their own petty or even not so petty interests." His voice was becoming singsongy, like the voice of my high school guidance counselor.

"We cannot permit," Foley went on, "any member of our staff to abuse the trust of our readers. We cannot allow it. There is nothing I frown upon more severely than the hint of a special interest in our news columns, be they the interests of one or two or of, indeed, one hundred thousand people. We look after the interests of *all* the people, we look after their *best* interests. I think it was Thomas Jefferson who said that an informed electorate is the best guardian of democracy, and that is in sum what we are, the guardians of democracy. Some people have compared us to the Church. I think it was Liebling who used that metaphor first. He meant it unflatteringly. As you know, he was an embittered atheist and fellow traveler. He was wrong about us, but we took it as a compliment, because we would like to think of ourselves as the secular equivalent of the Church. You know, Sarah, when I walk through those gates in the morning sometimes I say to myself, You are the editor of *THE*

*Newspaper*, and I feel such a mixture of pride and deep humility that I can scarcely find words for it. There *are* no words for it, because the feeling is spiritual, as if hands had truly been laid on my head by my predecessor to deliver a force of compassionate courage into my being. Yes, Henry Bolinger was probably the greatest editor this paper ever had, and I will always feel humble in his shoes. Sarah, I want my reporters to feel as he felt about this newspaper and as I feel and as we all feel: that we are privileged to have been called into service here. And I know there are frustrations and rivalries and often days when I myself can't seem to see clearly through all the sturm and drang of the world. But if you work for us, you *are* privileged, you *are* one of history's elite, and no matter how difficult it may seem at times, no matter how taxing and wearing, no matter how deeply discouraging it may be to hear the Agnews and the Mark Rudds and all stripes of political or philosophical bullies trying to bend *The Newspaper* to their needs—and there are pressures; you cannot begin to know the pressures people try to bring to bear on us all—despite all this, you can be firm, you can be steadfast, you can hold to the trust we have in you as long as you have it in us, because there is only one boss here, there is only one commander, and it is not really I, it is the plain, unvarnished message of our motto, 'The Truth Is Our Business.' And so you see, what I am trying to express, Sarah, *is* a form of creed. And you must believe in it to work here. You simply will not be happy here, nor we with you, unless you feel passionate about the truth."

Maybe if I hadn't had to pee so badly, I would have cleared the air right then, but I thought that if I confessed for Ron, there would be rather a long discussion. I couldn't possibly have sat through it.

"Mr. Foley—" I was going to ask to be excused.

"I'm not quite finished, Sarah. I must ask you this: Do you think that your association with *The* ah, *Evil Eye* would make it difficult for you to feel comfortable here, to, ah, adjust? I don't fault *The Evil Eye* for what it tries to be. The new journalism has contributed a fresh voice, and it is always a healthy thing to see a new, young newspaper on the stands of this city. But as you are, I am sure, aware, there is a *difference* between the standards of that, ah, Greenwich Village weekly and our own. Tell me, do you think you could learn to write in the third person?"

"I did it all through college," I said weakly, meaning in my college term papers.

"Ah, yes, the *Crimson*, of course. I would love to see your clips from there sometime. Perhaps Ron—"

At the sound of his name, Ron came charging into the room, barking:

"Gil, Gil, Gil, Gil, Gil! The city's folding again! We're going to need ten more columns! Sorry, Sarah, but this can't wait. City Hall just called, and the mayor's going live on Channel 13 at 2:00. Ford told the city to drop dead, and that's exactly what's going to happen! They're closing the zoo! We need the go-ahead for the ten columns right away. I'm sorry, Sarah."

"That's quite all right, Ron. Sarah and I have finished our little chat, haven't we, Sarah? Unless you have any questions."

"N-no!" I said, getting up unsteadily. I was dying!

"Okay," said Ron. "Listen, Sarah, I'm going to be a little late for lunch, so you just go out and find Willie. He'll show you around."

I found the ladies' room first. There I heard a conversation which in the circumstances seemed one of the sweetest little dialogues I had ever heard. It went like this:

"I think it was the sangría. They put so much sugar in it. But can you believe it? Four fucking pounds in one night! I think I'll start smoking again."

"You should come jogging with me."

"You don't lose weight jogging. Didn't you read Lilly's piece about that? Women don't lose weight jogging. So I don't see the point."

"Oh, shit! That's the third one of these things that came unglued! Five bucks down the drain again. I think they put them together with spit. That's what I think."

"Where'd you get that skirt?"

"Same place I got this crummy barrette. Bendel's."

"Bendel's is a rip-off. How much?"

"I shouldn't have bought it."

"It looks great on you. Greg was giving you the eye yesterday."

"Greg's an ass man. It flatters my ass."

"How much was it?"

"One hundred and twenty-five. Sumpin like that."

"They suckered you."

"I know."

"Well, you do look good in it. Where do you want to go?"

"I don't know. You wanta try the Greek's?"

"No. All those wimpy Culture people go there. How about Joe Allen's?"

"Okay."

"I saw Al Pacino in there last week. He didn't stay. Too crowded.

32

He was all by himself. Looked sort of wasted, I wanted to help him out."

They giggled, and I heard their footsteps recede. As they went out, the ex-smoker asked, "What's Ron so excited about?"

"Probably the zoo, because Mrs. Heller's . . ." and that's all I heard.


# VI

Along with four of his "idiots," Ron took me to the Petit Enfant again, and he held forth again, nearly uninterrupted, with his unexpurgated gush of free associations, while the copy editors or assistant metropolitan editors or special features men—I couldn't keep track of their titles—all ordered themselves numerous drinks and once in a while said, "You're quite right there, Ron," or, "You're not wrong there, Ron," or, "Good point, Ron," or, "Really?" which last I guessed came when Ron wasn't telling them something they didn't already know. But they enjoyed themselves. I could see they were enjoying themselves, having a lunch on the boss, ordering filet mignon and spécialité de la maison ($15) with three different kinds of wines and a couple of flambé desserts. This time I had decided to pay attention to how Ron managed to eat his food while talking non-stop, but there wasn't much to it. He just ate very, very fast, and when he did actually have to pause, take a drink or something, one of the "idiots" said, "You're quite right there, Ron," or dragged out a "Reeeally?" with an added "Hmmm"—a high-register, now-that-you-put-it-that-way "Hmmm," though, not a deep, skeptical, sardonic "Hmm," which would have cast him in the role of nay-sayer or detached thinker. Those guys were on their toes, and there wasn't much room for side conversation, with the chorus line constantly on call.

Once when Ron was launched into a long explanation of the city's financial crisis, and the "Reallys" were coming faster than the "Good point, Ron"s, the man sitting next to me—I was two down from Ron—asked me quietly where I was from, and I began to tell him about Four Corners, Mass., in what I thought was entertaining piss-on-your-origins fashion, thinking he was an all-right guy because he was chuckling through his nose and snorting in all the right places, until he suddenly, right in the middle of my description of Millard Bone, the stone-deaf town cop and taxi driver, clutched my wrist and said, "Sarah, you'll want to hear this."

"Absolutely unreadable!" Ron was saying. "Absolutely unreadable! We had to give it to the rewrite bank, and Flicker will bear me out on this"—"Absolutely, Ron," said the man next to me—"Jenny threw conniptions. Really got hysterical. I think she's cracking up."

"Ron could be right," said a man across from me who had horn-rimmed glasses and a little goatee. He looked like a scared little psychiatrist whose id had collapsed. Later I learned he was a senior copy editor.

"*Could* be right! Ron's being kind!" said the one called Willie, who now seemed to have a pain in his back and was drinking Bloody Marys.

"You see, Sarah," Ron went on, "I didn't want to tell you this for your article because I don't like to hurt my staff, but you're one of us now, you're part of the family. Jenny Locke is really going through a terrible slump. She's writing the most god-awful stuff. You haven't seen a by-line of hers in—correct me if I'm wrong, boys—oh, three months."

"Wasn't there one last—"

"Quite right there, Ron," said the goatee.

"We frankly don't know what to do about her. We've tried her on Fashion. We've tried her in the courts. We had her on General Assignment, thinking that she'd find her own pace there, but *that* was a disaster. What we went through with the Police Department!" He put his hand to his forehead. "Remember that one, Jess?"

"Yes," said the man next to me.

"Jenny filed a com*plaint* against a police officer for *sex*ist re-*marks!* My god! She went out on a simple sniper story and got embroiled in an argument with this poor cop who was trying to keep her from getting shot, and the next thing we knew, we had the commissioner calling us, the com*mis*sioner! Wanting to know what *The Newspaper* thought it was doing, sending out nuts to cover emergency situations. Well, he called her a psycho, if I'm not wrong,"

"You're not wrong, Ron," said three editors.

"He was not mincing his words. He said Jenny would have been arrested and taken to Bellevue if Public Affairs hadn't had a man on the scene. So you see, Sarah, it is no joking matter, this Feminist

**34**

Faction, and you would be cutting your own throat if you had any-thing to do with them."

"Cutting your own throat," said Willie.

"That's what happened to Susan," said Ron. "Of course, I never should have promoted her. You should have stopped me. All of you should have—"

"Is that Susan Braithwaite?" I asked, and they rolled their eyes affirmatively. "Didn't she do that series on Harlem? That was a very good series."

"You should have seen the raw copy," said the goatee. "It looked like a zombie had written it and then let his cat walk all over it."

"Zombie! Cat walk all over it! Ho ho ho!" Ron chortled. "You see, Sarah, now you're learning the secrets of the newspaper busi-ness. Now, you're *not* to repeat that. Is she, boys? The blacks are even more sensitive than the women. Zombie! Pass me the blanc de blanc. It's a little young, don't you think? Too fruity. We'll have to tell Jacques. Yes, Sarah, you've got a great deal to learn about what goes into a great newspaper, a really great newspaper—the crème de la crème of American journalism, I call it."

"Well put, Ron," said Willie.

"What you read in the morning is a far cry from what we see when it comes hot from the typewriter. You oughta see the way Greg Swenson spells! Phooweeet!" he whistled. "We give him early copy deadline every day just so we'll have time to clean up the evidence of his crimes against the English language, ho ho ho! I like that! Crimes against the English language, ho ho ho!"

The editors went, "Ho ho ho!"

"But Greg's a good man, good reporter, *great* reporter!"

"You're right there, Ron," said the man next to me.

"We have some of the *greatest* reporters in the world on our newspaper, Sarah. Gil and I have assembled a staff of unparalleled professionals. Why, when I go to cocktail parties, I can't stop talking about them. People won't *let* me stop talking about them. I wish they would, really. I wish sometimes I could walk into a room and *not* be known as Ron Millstein, metropolitan editor of *THE Newspa-per*. They never give me any peace. And you will find this, too, Sarah, when your by-line is known. Steve Figland was just saying to me— I had a little talk with Steve, and I think it did him a world of good. I told him, 'Steve, I know what's wrong with you, because, Steve,' I said, 'I can remember when I wrote that novel.' You didn't know I wrote a novel, did you, Sarah? Never sold very much.

Maybe you remember the title, *At the Crossroads of the World*. Sold about three thousand copies, which for a first novel was in those days quite respectable—1959—and if I may say so enjoyed a brief succès d'estime—"

"It is a *very* good book," said Willie. "He was compared to Algren."

"And so I said to Steve, I said, 'I know what's wrong with you, Steve,' I said. 'You've got a masterpiece complex.' And you know, his face lit up. It was like watching the sun come out. He couldn't stop thanking me. I think he's going to be all right now. But it takes, you know, Sarah, it takes a good psychologist to deal with a sensitive man like Steve. You know, I think Steve is one of the most intelligent people on our staff," he said to all and sundry.

"Really?" said the goatee.

"Hmmm," said the man next to me, and I thought I perceived a shifting of buttocks all around.

"Do you know he used to be the talk of the town?" Ron went on. "Why, it used to be that I couldn't go to a cocktail party without hearing his name! When he did that interview with Christina Onassis? *Everybody* was talking about it, just *everybody*. And I want the same thing to happen to you, Sarah. I want to hear your name on everybody's lips. It *will* happen. I just know it. I have a gut feeling about you, Sarah, that you're going to be a star."

The "idiots" all fingered their forks and looked shy.

# VII

No one believes me when I tell them that I never actually accepted the *Newspaper* job, never said the words "I accept" to Ron Millstein or Gilbert P. Foley. By the time we came back from that second lunch, it was simply a foregone conclusion that I had been hired, and the story of how had gone through several editions of the newsroom grapevine. I was simultaneously alleged to be related to the publisher, an honors graduate of the John F. Kennedy School of Public Administration at Harvard, and a dumb pushover of a woman who would serve as Ron's foil against the Feminist Faction, the first of a series to come.

Nor can people believe that I tried to get Lars to reconsider putting me on staff at *The Evil Eye*. That very afternoon, fresh from the lunch, I called Lars with sincere, no, desperate longing to get my clothes out of the dry cleaners. I thought, stupidly, that *The Newspaper*'s by then firm offer might make me look like a better prospect down at the *Eye*.

"You fucking sneak!" Lars said. "Now I know why you didn't want to write that story. You won't ever write another story for us again!"

"But, Lars, I *wrote* it! Ask Doris! Listen, I'll write it for you again."

"Doris doesn't even want to talk to you. She said what you did is the dirtiest thing anyone's ever done to her. You *used* us."

"Lars, didn't you hear me? I said I'd write the thing *again* for you."

"You're the one who's having a hearing problem. I told you you'll never write for us again. You belong on *The Newspaper*. You're their *type*."

That really hurt. Because even though I hadn't calculated one step of my dealings with Ron, even though I knew deep down in my heart I was a sixties person and belonged on the *Eye*, where people still thought the sixties were, oh, viable, like, *alive* as an idea for the way things ought to be, with everyone overcoming everything through song and marijuana, with no one caring how much money he made or whether he got tenure or famous enough to be a People, as long as he got laid and had enough Dylan records—even though I believed in that vision of things and would have been perfectly comfortable believing in it on fifteen thousand a year as a staff writer for the *Eye*, there was a little kernel of guilt in me, a little voice that said: Maybe you aren't cut out for it. I mean, I wanted to be a sixties person, but the sixties people didn't seem to want me. They weren't very sixtiesish anymore, Doris talking about how you had to earn your position in the Movement and blaming me for a fuck-up she had made, which come to think of it was an old-fashioned fifties rat-race sort of thing to do and not a hell of a lot different from Ron's telling lies about my accomplishments to make me look like a fantastic catch, a good company acquisition, as his *types* would put it. No, I wasn't his type, no siree. But then, I wasn't Doris's type, either. So what type was I?

Before I could answer that question for myself, the *Newspaper* job was a fait accompli, and I didn't have anything else. It was twenty-one thousand a year or zero. Minus zero, actually. There were a few bills coming in, things I couldn't leave at the cleaners, so to speak.

I never actually did say, "I accept." But I didn't say no. And Ron simply assumed that he had bought me, lock, stock, and "fresh pair of eyes," as he called me in the first few weeks of my employ.

*The Evil Eye* never found the story I'd done about him, and during my second week on *The Newspaper,* the *Eye* put me in its press gossip column, made me sound like a real shit, said outright that I'd killed my own story just to get the *Newspaper* job. I could see I was going to be on the *Eye*'s next Christmas list of People's Enemies. Ron loved it. He just loved it. He would take me for drinks in Sardi's with a couple of the shirt-sleeved members of his chorus line, and he would say, "I'm proud of you, Sarah, I really am. You have caught on faster than anyone I ever hired." Then he'd get a little looped, and he'd prop his enormous haunches onto a stool and beckon to me to lean in close so he could talk low. "You can tell me," he'd say. "Did you really do that for me? Did you kill that story?"

"They lost it, Ron. I told you that," I would repeat.

"Will you ever show it to me? I'd like to see what you said about me."

"I don't have a copy," I would say.

"Come on, Sarah, just give me a hint."

"I said that you were an unreconstructed male chauvinist. And that you tried to bribe me with a job offer."

"Ho ho ho ho ho! Bribe you with a job offer! Oh, that's good!" he would bellow, forgetting the confidentiality of the theme. "Doesn't she have a great sense of humor, boys!"

And the underlings would grin and say yes.

As for my catching on fast—well, that was debatable. The first day I had an assignment, I got lost on the QB train when I should have been on the RR and missed a news conference of the Puerto Rican Parade Committee while I was trying to find my way back from Coney Island. Jess Flicker, the Nightside editor and the man who had paid such slender attention to my description of Four Corners, succinctly told me I had "really blown it."

A man from the Puerto Rican Parade Committee called Ron's office to say that blood might flow in the streets this summer if the press continued to ignore the legitimate claims of the Puerto Rican community.

"Oh, crap!" Ron said loyally. "We don't have to take that. We did the parade last year. I'm *glad* you missed the news conference, Sarah. It serves them right."

Flicker, who heard this little pronouncement, sort of winced at me from behind Ron's back.

I went slumping back to my desk, where my deskmate, Greg Swenson, gleefully waited.

"Hear you took the wrong subway," he said. "Couple more fuck-ups like that and you'll be out on your ass."

"News travels fast around here," I said.

"You've got enemies," Greg said. "Jenny Locke has a lot of friends."

Jenny would not speak to me. Her desk was, conveniently for me, way in the back of the room, while mine was six rows away from the City Desk, as both Dayside and Nightside were called. Ron sat at Dayside but he had jurisdiction over both divisions of editors. He and his immediate assistants gave out the assignments and kept a list of running stories, which eventually went to Jess Flicker for space allotment and close reading. Nobody liked Jess because of the close reading part.

When a reporter was ready to write a story, he would show a summary of it to Jess, who might then suggest it was ass-backwards and should start with the murders by, not the arrest of, say, a deadly black window washer who killed white women in high-rises. Jess would give the writer an exact space to write to, in a lingo of copy desk monosyllables, a "buck" being a column, a "half buck" being of course half a column, and so on through various permutations of journalistic form, all of which I might think I had learned until a new one suddenly was sprung on me—"Give us a D head, kid"—to keep me feeling green and stupid the way copy editors seemed to want all reporters to feel. Everybody had to get his summary approved and be given a space allotment at the same time every afternoon, so there was a lineup at Jess's desk at rush hour, and it made him as irritable as a subway token clerk. This was the hour when I might find myself in line behind Jenny Locke and be compelled to witness how diligently she was not talking to me. She even left the line sometimes if she saw me coming, going off to stand by the Photo Desk and rap a little with mean Vic Veblen, who had the hots for her and was, during the first few months, unable to coordinate photographers to go along on my assignments. She was standing nearby the night Jess first said to me, "Sarah, what's your lead?" And she heard me say, "What's a lead?" I know, because I heard her say, "Oh, Jesus!" before Jess yelled, "Aaaaaaggghhhh!"

But in the early days, I was not always aware of what meant what, and a number of insults were wasted on me. I did not know that mean Vic Veblen had the hots for Jenny or that *The Newspaper*'s inability to find a photographer to accompany me had any significance interpersonally, was a statement to me and about me, not the mere motiveless result of poor coordination. I did not know that certain copy editors hated Ron's guts and sometimes edited his favorite reporters with the passionate venom of ill-paid and passed-over prison guards left momentarily alone with the warden's chosen cons. Nor did I know that Willard Dixby, the national editor, was engaged in a life-or-death struggle with Ron Millstein which had caused *The Newspaper* to predict on alternate days that the Democratic convention was going to be held in Los Angeles, that it was going to be held in New York, no, that it *was* going to be held in Los Angeles, as each day the National or City Desk had the story. Willard Dixby was introduced to me sometime during my first week at *The Newspaper* and said to me in his thickly Southern accent, "Weyall, Miz Makepeace, I don't expect you will fahnd us veree interesting. We don't inveyent news here." He looked me up and down then, smirking as if waiting for me to protest, but later Greg told me he had probably been trying to convey a wordless horror for the way I dressed.

*The Newspaper* was what you would call seething with enmities and rivalries, and the waters boiled and flowed every which way, and everything that happened there washed over everyone from some hidden hot spring or other of unspent revenge. There was no such thing as an out-of-context isolated newsroom event. Everything had a context, and all the contexts squeezed up against one another and could make a person thoroughly confused. When the copy editors crossed your commas out, people made an interpretation of your standing vis-à-vis Ron and of Ron's standing vis-à-vis Dixby and of both their standings in the eyes of Gil Foley and of the publisher in the great beyond. If the photographers were more than usually cranky, surmise was made that mean Vic Veblen had made another hopeless pass at Jenny, and if the photographers were more than usually nongrumpy, surmise was made that Veblen had made it into Jenny's pants, although how far was debatable and subsidiary theories evolved therefrom concerning the indomitability of a hopeless lover's hopes.

There were interpretations made of the seating arrangements, which in the old days had been according to seniority but which lately had been juggled around a lot and seemed to mean various things at various times. There were many interpretations made of the tones of voice and the hand gestures Ron used when he made assignments, and the number of times he said each would be a front-page story. If Ron so much as raised his eyebrows during an editorial meeting, the men around him took this to mean he disapproved. But did he disapprove of what he'd had for lunch? Of Willie's new button-down shirt? Of the actual story under discussion? Or was his mind quite on the story under discussion? Was he maybe worrying about a story mentioned ten minutes back, about which he had said, "But what's the lead?" Or was he thinking something *deep*, like that Jess Flicker had sounded pretty negative yesterday during the upstairs luncheon with the publisher and might be defecting to Dixby?

Everybody had a history of remembered betrayals and injustices going way, way back to the day they were hired. I had never been in a place that had so much history clogging up the works. Not even Four Corners, which was three hundred years old, had such a heavy feeling of history, because people moved in and out of the town in good sprightly American fashion and brought new dullnesses to it while the old dullnesses moved ten miles away or went to California and sent no letters back. *The Newspaper* seemed almost *un*-American, it was so laden with the ancient memories of people who had started out life there and knew nothing else.

They did not distinguish, either, between newsroom history and the history of the globe, because to them it was all personal, there was a direct link between what happened to them and what happened to the President of the United States, not in the civics-book way that all Americans were supposed to be tied to their elected representatives, but in a hot frenetic newsroom symbiosis which connected their veins to the circulation of the biggest newsmaker in the land. And so election night 1948 was not merely the night Harry Truman got elected. It was the night Eddie Schwartz lost his wife, because that night everyone in the newsroom had to stay up all night *waiting* for Harry Truman to get elected, and to pass the hours they played poker, a game Eddie was then so good at he won five hundred dollars, no mean sum in those days, after which he decided to go home early and surprise the missus with an armful of gifts.

I know if Harry Truman hadn't been elected after such a long and wearying count, my early days on *The Newspaper* wouldn't have been half so tolerable, because Eddie wouldn't have been such a loner and wouldn't, probably, have taken the time to explain all these things to me, starting with what a lead was.

## VIII

My next assignment, after I proved I could not find my way around the BMT, was the weather story. Ron had heard on the radio that the day might be a record high.

"Sarah," he said, "this is your chance to really capture the mood of the city, make us *feel* the whole town coming into summer. I want to know how the shoppers hold their packages in the heat and how cabdrivers stand it, what little old ladies do on the top floor without air conditioning, and—and see whether the mayor takes his shirt off. They're on an energy-saving program down at City Hall, you know. Well, I don't have to tell you! You read *The Newspaper!* Oh, Sarah, I envy you! Going out with a fresh pair of eyes! I can remember—"

"Ron, uh, Ron—" Willie Crespi tried to butt in. By now I knew that Willie was his chief assistant.

"Let me see. I think my first assignment was the Leaky murder case—yes, yes, I'm sure that was it! What a rich case! With millions at stake and several high-society suspects, her children and her nephews, and the maid—they all hated her. She'd been poisoned—"

"Ron, Ron, I hate to interrupt, but—" Willie tried again.

"Just a minute, Willie!" Ron said sharply. "Can't you see I'm *busy?*"

Willie said, "I'll have to call you back, Clarence," into a phone and looked sour.

"Well, I forget whether that was the day they actually cracked the case; probably wouldn't have been, because Holcomb himself would have gone down. You're too young to remember Holcomb Molding, the great courtroom reporter."

"Ron, this can't wait!" said Willie.

"Oh, what is it, Willie? Go on, Sarah. Get me a front-page weather story," Ron said. "Good luck!"

"Wait a minute, Sarah," Willie said. "Ron, she's got to help out

42

Foreign. They need someone to cover for them with the Japanese prime minister."

"Well, Sarah doesn't have to worry about that," Ron said, smiling. "Go on, Sarah."

"But, Ron, we don't have anyone else!" I heard Willie saying as I went out.

The day was glorious, not too hot at all, but brilliant and breezy, full of soft spring smells. I walked west on Forty-eighth Street swinging my arms and whistling, happy until I reached Eighth Avenue. I suddenly could not think what to do next. I stood still in the sun. Where might the old ladies on the top floors be? I stood and stood.

"Nice day," said Freddie the news clerk, passing me on his way in to work. That embarrassed me into opening my notebook. I made one inscription: "Prostitutes sucking soda through straws."

"Hey, there! Ain't I seen you someplace before?" said a tall black man with a shaven head who had planted himself in front of me. "In auditions, wasn't it? Yeah, sure, you were in that gang for *Chorus Line*. You get the part?"

"No," I said, "no, you must be mistaken. I'm a reporter."

Across the street I could read the double marquee: *Deep Throat* plus *Nurses Night Out*.

"A reporter, eh? Yeah, wow, that's it! I seen you on Channel 5."

"No. I work for *The Newspaper*. I'm on assignment now, actually. What do you think of the weather?"

I held my pen poised.

"Is this a interview? You wanta put me in the paper? What paper you say you're from?"

"Yes. *The Newspaper*. Yes, I'm interviewing you."

"Well, put down that my cousin's a producer. You ever hear of a movie called *Shut Eyes*? Low-budget flick. Had some distribution problems. Hollywood shit, you know."

"Oh, well, thanks," I said, closing my notebook, beginning to walk.

"Hey, wait!" he said, stepping around in front of me again. "You ain't aks me nothin'."

"What's your name?" I asked, opening the notebook again.

He cleared his throat. "Lessee. Put down Eldridge Jones. I got to think, see, 'cause I use a stage name."

He cleared his throat again. I showed him what I'd written.

"Did I spell it right?"

"Oh, yeah, yeah," he said quickly. "What's this about?" He

**43**

seemed to be watching someone across the avenue behind me.

"The weather. I'm writing a story about what a hot day it is. It may be a record high."

"It ain't hot. It's juuuss right."

"Thank you," I said, jotting that down.

"Is that all you're gonna aks me?"

"Yes. Oh, well, maybe you could tell me what you do for a living."

"What I do? For a living?"

"Yes. So people know what kind of a person you are."

"Uh, put down actor—yeah, I'm a actor. Right."

"Have you been in any well-known plays or movies? Things people would recognize? Are you in anything right now?"

"Uh, I am presently unemployed. But I did have a part in *Shut Eyes*."

"What's the name of your cousin's company?"

"The name? Er, look, I'll catch you later. I got to run," he said. And with that he went walking swiftly off up the avenue, slipped into a doorway, and was gone.

I decided to cross to the other side of Eighth and walk north toward the park. I had gone a couple of blocks when another man fell into stride beside me.

"Miss," he whispered. From the corner of my eye he looked like a young toughie. I stretched my pace and set my mouth.

"Miss!" he whispered more urgently, loping along with me. I went faster. He went faster. I started to run, heard a car horn, wheels, and felt a hand clasp my arm and yank me backward.

"You get away from me!" I said as I fell against him.

"Hey, hey! Take it easy," he said quietly. "I'm a cop. You almost got yourself killed. Didn't you see the light?"

I looked at him. He was smiling and holding his hands palms up to show he would not hurt me. Behind him a plate-glass windowful of bare-breasted women looked at me mockingly. I felt my heart beating hard.

"I scared you," he said. "I'm sorry. I work undercover in this area. I have to look the part."

"Wow!" I said. "You really scared me."

"I saw you talking to Batman. I had to find out what he said to you. What did he say to you?"

"Batman," I said. "Batman? What—what—"

"Look, you don't look too good. Why don't we go in the deli. I'll buy you a cup of coffee."

**44**

I just stood there. I was feeling spaced. He looked like a young Mafia character. Anybody could say he was an undercover cop. Around here.

"I'll even show you my badge," he said, smiling as though he felt sort of weird himself.

"Well, just for a minute," I said. "I'm in a hurry. But I think I need a cigarette."

"Come on. I'll buy you a pack."

We went into Seymour's Deli a little way up the avenue. There was a prostitute sitting at the counter, but she didn't seem to be awake. Her wig was askew, and she leaned on one elbow. Her elbow was the only part of her body that hadn't gone slack. Seymour's was otherwise deserted. The grease and dust on the windows screened the light from outside. The cigarette machine didn't work.

"I'll buy you a cup of coffee," he said. "Sit down."

I went to a booth in the back. He leaned on the counter, waiting for the coffee. The old man, Seymour, I guess, wasn't too quick, so it took a while. My friend was watching the street and the droopy prostitute. He was wearing tight jeans and a ghastly shiny green shirt which was unbuttoned halfway down his unhairy chest. Three gaudy gold chains helped to complete the image of young Italian punk. But maybe it was his saying he was a cop, I don't know: something didn't work about his "cover." There was an attitude in his chin and a curve of his posture, his butt stuck out just a shade too much, as though he was used to wearing all those cop gadgets on his hips. Of course, I had never had much to do with cops except at demonstrations, when they put on their killer silence, and that one time in East Harlem, when a fat old sergeant took me to the precinct house, apologizing to me the whole way: "You'll get off, you know, it's a go-through-the-motions situation. We gotta work with this community."

The young cop slopped my coffee into the saucer as he set it down.

"Ooops, sorreee," he said, "I no mean to do that," mimicking Puerto Rican English.

"It's okay," I said. "What do I owe you?"

"We'll get to that," he said. "The coffee's on me."

He took a sip of his own and went, "Aack!" and practically dropped the cup into the saucer, splashing coffee onto the tabletop. "Shit!" he said, then looked up at me, grinning stupidly. He slid out of the booth again to grab some napkins from the counter. This time he moved like a boy in a hurry, with the quick grace that scoops up

**45**

a grounder. But I only watched him out of the corner of my eye. To keep from embarrassing him more, I looked at my coffee cup, sipped from it.

As he sat down again, dabbing at the spilled coffee, I said, "It's not that bad."

"You don't have to be nice," he said. "I didn't make it."

He had dark brown eyes and thick dark eyelashes, but god, the green shirt was awful! It looked all wrong on him.

"Are you really a cop?" I said.

"'Fraid so," he said, reaching into a back pocket. He produced a wallet and opened it to show the badge. Underneath it was a nameplate.

"Kevin Mondavi," I said. "That's an unusual—"

"Irish mother, Guinea father. What's your name?"

"Sarah Makepeace."

"Sounds like Cotton Mather or something. Don't tell me your folks came over on the *Mayflower*."

"I think they came around 1640."

"You're not from New York, obviously. Let me guess. I'd say"—he squinted—"I'd say Connecticut. Greenwich, Connecticut."

"God, no! Nowhere near. I'm from Massachusetts."

"Where? Boston?"

"Nope. You never heard of it. Four Corners, Mass. Population one thousand six. I went to college in Boston."

Why had I said that?

"So you went to Radcliffe, am I right?"

"'Fraid so," I said. "But we shouldn't be shooting the breeze here. I've got to get going. What was it you wanted to ask me?"

"They call you 'Cliffies, right?"

There it was, the glistening look. Why should a cop be immune? I should have known.

"Yes, they do," I said briskly. "Listen, I've got a deadline."

"I *thought* you were a reporter. You with *The Times*?"

"No, *The Newspaper*."

"Why were you interviewing Batman?"

"That's what you call . . . ? He said his name was Eldridge Jones."

"Eldridge Jones. That's a new one. That may just come in handy, Sarah. That may come in very handy."

"Why do you call him Batman?"

"'Cause he's big, bad, and black, and flees de scene on big black wings."

"He seemed pretty harmless—"

"His real name's Joe Brewster, and he's not harmless. He picks up runaways, girls who don't know their way around, tells 'em he's gonna put them in his cousin's movies."

"But that's not—"

"Then he rapes them and cuts them up."

"Oooh! Why don't you arrest him?" I shivered.

"There's never been a witness who could stick it through to the trial. See, he picks on pretty pathetic types, girls who are on their way to becoming prosses. You're not really his usual kind of victim. A 'Cliffie. Why'd you talk to him?"

"I didn't pick him. He picked me. But then I thought I might as well put him in my story."

"What kind of a story is that?"

"I'm doing a story about the weather."

"About the weather. That's a story? The weather's just the weather. What's the news in the weather?"

"My boss said it might be a record high." I looked at his watch. It was noon. Only six hours to deadline! "Listen, I'd better get going," I said. "I've got to find some old ladies living on the top floor without air conditioning."

"Try Brooklyn. There's lots of old ladies over there without air conditioning."

"I don't know my way around Brooklyn."

"No, I don't guess you do. How long have you been at *The Newspaper?*"

"A week. But this is my first assignment—well, my first *real* assignment."

"Now I get it," he said, nodding, looking sort of sympathetic.

"Get what?" I asked, wishing I hadn't told him it was my first.

"Oh, just the way you looked out there on the street talking to Batman. You oughta write about Batman."

"I don't have time—"

"Not today. I mean when you have the time. Somebody should write about him. He's got a rap sheet a mile long, but no convictions."

"Rap sheet?"

"You are green. That means arrest record."

"So you *can* arrest him."

"Sure, we can arrest him, but he gets out after a couple of days."

"I don't understand. If you have the evidence—"

"I told you. The girls don't stick it out. We had one, but her

**47**

credibility was weak. The judge decided not to believe her. Threw the case out after three months. She had become a prostitute by then anyway, and her pimp didn't want her going to court."

"Gee, that's too bad."

"Maybe I could get her to talk to you, if you promised not to use her name. She thinks I'm a bouncer. Doesn't know I'm a cop. How can I get in touch with you?"

"Just call *The Newspaper*."

"You don't have a home phone? You living with somebody?"

"Maybe I should call you," I said, looking at his watch again.

"You can't right now," he said. "Nobody calls me at Women Alive. Well, listen, maybe you're not interested in the story."

"My phone's listed. I'm in the Village. Look, I've really got to go now. Thanks for the coffee."

"Don't mention it," he said. He grabbed my wrist as I was getting up and leaned forward to speak very quietly. "If you see me on the street around here, don't recognize me, okay? If you forget, call me Bubba."

I giggled, but I was a little thrilled. A real undercover cop, after all, trusting me. Where did he keep his gun?

"*Where do you keep your gun?*" I whispered.

"You better get going, lady," he said in a normal voice. "The weather might change."

He released my arm and did not follow me out of Seymour's Deli. I walked north toward the park. A couple of blocks up the avenue, I saw the Women Alive sign. "Topless" was written all over the windows, "Topless," "Topless." Two prostitutes in hot pants were standing in the doorway, pouting into the sun. I heard thumping music as I passed them. Business did not seem to be coming their way. Maybe it was the weather. Should I ask them? I turned around. One of the prostitutes looked me up and down haughtily, stuck out her chin, and turned her back to me. I lost heart.

I wandered up through the park and found myself heading toward the polar bear's cage. He was swimming back and forth in his tiny pool, looking the way an imprisoned soul ought to look on a fine spring day. He'd dive under, hit the side, come up nose first, give a shove, and float backward with his front paws tucked up and his nose sticking straight up into the air, then *whoosh*, he'd dive again, come up nose first at the far wall and repeat the same backward tucked-up glide across the pool. I got interested in the mechanics. I couldn't see how he did it, really, when he was so enormous and the pool so small. I must have watched him for twenty minutes, without taking a note.

One-fifteen. Oh, Jesus, I had to interview *somebody*.

So I started in. I found a rich kid's nanny reading *Psycho*, a chauffeur from the Costa Rican consulate eating yogurt, a secretary from the Bloomingdale's credit department doing the *Evening Star* crossword puzzle, a bunch of teenagers from Queens doing nothing, a whole lot of bums and shopping bag ladies, a CBS mailroom clerk, a guy who said he wrote Gothic novels but never worked in the daytime—he was doing T'ai Chi exercises—and a reporter from the *Morning Chronicle* out doing the weather story for her city desk, who gave me the best quote of the day: "When a nice day in New York is news, that means my boss just read another book about growth in the sunbelt." I came across a class of third graders going insane trying to sketch a tree, and a Greek hot dog vendor who couldn't say anything in English beyond, "Feepty cens, sebeny-five, on-yuns, no on-yuns, orrrench, dolla-twenny-five, Coke, dieyaecola, no speak." I counted sixty-two bicyclists, twenty-nine runners, and seventeen transistor radios.

The quotes were not much. "Lovely day." "Smells like summer." "Nice day." "Smells like spring." But my notebook was getting a nice thick flexible feel, like a college spiral toward the end of term, and I thought I'd go find a phone to give Ron a rundown.

Well, if you've ever noticed, there aren't any phone booths on Fifth Avenue along the park. This must be because Jackie Onassis and the others who live along there don't like pay telephone users lurking around. I must have spent a half hour finding out, walking down Fifth Avenue, pricing the clothes on the women in silk dresses and little slivers of shoes, watching taxis emit red-cheeked, silver-haired men, getting resentful when they did not turn around to help their sleek young wives step out behind them but let the doormen do it. I decided they must be awful in bed.

I finally went into the Pierre and found a phone booth that smelled of lilac.

"Hello, *Newspaper*, City Desk," said an unfamiliar voice.

"Hi, this is Sarah Makepeace. Could I speak to Ron?"

"Sarah who?"

"Sarah Makepeace."

"Oh, yeah. Hi, Sarah. Freddie here. Ron's in a meeting. But Willie's been looking for you. You shoulda called in."

"I should? Nobody said—"

"Here's Willie."

"Hello, Sarah. Where've you been? Your summary was due an hour ago. Are you ready to write? Is it a record high?"

"Gee, I don't know. How, um, how do I find that out?"

"You call the Weather Bureau. You know how to do that?"

"Sure, sure, Willie. Um—"

"Where are you?"

"At the Hotel Pierre."

"What are you doing there? You're on Weather!"

"I'm using the phone. There aren't any phones in the park."

"You went to Central Park? God, what a cliché! Well, get back in here, Sarah. Your story's due in half an hour."

"Half an hour! I thought the deadline was six."

"Weather's down for early copy. That's four-thirty."

I took a cab. It got stuck in a traffic jam five blocks from the office. I ran the rest of the way.

"Get your summary to Jess right away," Willie said.

I typed out a page of quotes from my notebook and dashed up to Jess Flicker's desk.

"Sarah, this isn't really a summary. What's your lead?"

"What's a lead?"

That's when Jenny Locke said, "Oh, Jesus!" in the background, and Jess yelled, "Aaaaaaggghhhh!"

Jess recovered instantly, though, and asked me bitingly:

"Sarah, was it or was it not a record high?"

"Um, oh, I'll find out right away. I just thought you wanted the summary—"

"Go find out and write me a summary and put that in the lead!"

I ran back to my desk and dialed the weather: "Clear tonight and tomorrow. Winds southeast at five to ten miles an hour. Barometric pressure—"

"MAKEPEACE. SARAH MAKEPEACE." I heard my name over the loudspeaker. Ron's voice.

I dashed up to his desk.

"Hi, Sarah. Got your weather story done?" Ron asked, smiling.

"Um, no, Ron. I just got back."

"Was it a record high?" Willie asked.

"I don't know, Willie. The weather recording doesn't say."

"You called the weather recording! Jesus Christ, Sarah, don't you know *any*thing? I told you to call the Weather *Bureau*. That's where they *make* the recordings. They'll tell you if it's a record high."

"Never mind that, never mind that," said Ron. "I've got an *even better* story for you, Sarah. I'm going to make you an instant foreign correspondent. You are going to cover the Japanese prime minister's speech at the Hilton."

"But, Ron—" said Willie.

"This is important!" Ron said. "Sarah, you'll have to go right away. The prime minister's leaving the building right now."

"What building?" I asked.

"This building," said Ron. "Get downstairs right away."

"But what—"

"Just stick with him till he's finished his speech, then call Foreign. Go ahead. And good luck."

By the time I got downstairs, the prime minister's motorcade had motored off. I hailed a cab to the Hilton. The lobby was filled with a bunch of men with white labels pasted on their coats: "Veterinarians Association of North America." I went around getting lost among the escalators and different elevator banks until I found a bellhop, who said all the "ballroom functions" were listed on the second floor. Then I got on an elevator that didn't stop on the second floor.

Finally I found the registration desk, and there a nice woman told me the prime minister's speech would be in the Marie Antoinette Ballroom at seven o'clock.

But *The Newspaper*'s deadline was at six. Besides, where was the prime minister?

I called Foreign. Got a clerk named Oliver Weed.

"Mishiyoko's down at the World Trade Center," he said. "You're supposed to be on assassination watch, is that it?"

"I don't know. Ron said I was just supposed to follow him and cover the speech. Listen, Oliver, I don't know the first thing about Japanese-American trade agreements."

"I thought they were going to send Figland. We've got security clearance for Figland," he said.

"Well, maybe you should tell Ron, because I'm *supposed* to be writing the weather story, and—"

"I'll see if I can get you clearance. Gimme your press card number, Social Security number, date and place of birth."

I did as he asked, and he kept me on hold while he called somewhere.

"Okay, Sarah," he said ten minutes later. "You just stay there and cover the speech. Let us know if he deviates from the text."

"That's all you want to know?"

"That's all we want to know. Unless, of course, he gets shot, in which case you luck into a by-line."

About an hour and a half later, the prime minister's black limousines pulled into the Hilton driveway. I saw what looked like Secret Service men open the door of one, so I figured he must be the little man with the Charlie Chan smile who got out first. This mistake was corrected when a gang of photographers and TV crews pressed forward around a taller Oriental with a pencil mustache. They surrounded him and moved in a clot through the lobby. I thought I ought to shove in there among them to see the shot when it was fired.

But a giant grabbed me by the throat and yanked me backward. "Hey!" I said. "I'm press."

"Wear your press card," said the giant, who had a little hearing aid in his ear.

Then I perceived that all the other press people wore their press cards on dog chains.

To tell the truth, I was out of sight of that prime minister clear up to the Marie Antoinette Ballroom, and I was mighty grateful nobody shot him. On my way into the ballroom, I was grabbed again by two Secret Service men. They said I wasn't down on the list.

"We've got a Steven Figland here. You aren't going to tell us you're Steven Figland."

"I showed you my press card. Look, call the Foreign Desk of *The Newspaper*. They'll tell you. They said they cleared me."

In the end, they decided just to frisk me and search my purse, which they hadn't done to all the other people going into the banquet, who weren't press, who weren't anything but people rich enough to pay for the dinner, business VIPs, I guessed. Why I had to look like a potential assassin seemed sort of arbitrary, because I had started to dress the part of *Newspaper* reporter, unless they could sense it in me that I smoked grass and had performed fellatio in the Widener Library stacks. I mean, it didn't *show*.

But at last I got inside the ballroom and found the press table and my own shiny press kit with the speech inside and a few glossies of Mishiyoko, as well as a free copy of Japan Airlines' magazine with a cover story about a "Geisha Disco." Mishiyoko spoke in Japanese. There was simultaneous translation, though, by a young woman who appeared to be reading from the same text we had. We wouldn't have known whether he deviated, if he did deviate, at all. Nevertheless, I tried to listen carefully to the translator, despite the buzz of conversation at the press table.

"Who're you with?" whispered a plump young man with a walrus mustache, sitting to my right.

"*The Newspaper*," I whispered back.

"What's your name?"

"Sarah Makepeace."

"Sarah what?"

"Makepeace."

"How long you been there?"

"Listen, I'm trying to hear the speech."

"Fuck the speech. Your guy Buttonweiser had it yesterday. Relax."

We didn't actually see the beginning of the ruckus. Walrus Face said afterwards there's always a lapse like that when something strange and sudden happens and you're there. He calls it the I-don't-believe-this-is-happening syndrome.

We heard a roar and then a crash, glasses breaking, silver tinkling, and then a hushed rustle going through the room like the sound of everyone taking in breath. And then we saw the group. Five tall young men in tuxedos holding their overturned table in front of them as a shield, while they yelled: "*Killer! Killer! Killer! Mishiyoko's killing Tokyo! Mishiyoko's killing Tokyo!*"

They threw eggs at the podium and went on chanting as Secret Service men pounced on Mishiyoko, slamming him to the floor of the dais. A couple of Secret Service men caught eggs smack against their cheeks, while from everywhere more of them broke forth through the oh-my-god-stuttering banqueters. They charged for the chanters, crushing feet, pulling shoulders out of sockets, pushing through the dinner guests like upright Russian swimmers doing a freestyle through a solid sea of Muscovites. I heard quite a few "Ow!"s and "My leg!"s from the ocean waves before the Secret Service men reached the five chanters, and then there was a confusion of shouts, limbs, mad-looking eyes, grunts, and the five young men were on the ground getting kicked if they so much as wriggled, and they got kicked quite a bit.

The dinner guests were by now talking excitedly to one another, so that it was hard to hear what one fool protester yelled as he was yanked up onto his feet, handcuffed, and hauled away, but it sounded like:

"We are the Red River Army! We oppose all forms of industrial pollution, ow! And killers of the earth! We will not stop here! We will rise up in every city where the people are choking on the capitalist roomph! We will kill the killers of the earth! We wiooop—"

**53**

There a Secret Service man squashed an egg into the young man's mouth.

"Jesus!" I said to Walrus Face. "What happens now?"

"Now we try to kill a few people to get to the phones. Race you!"

But I followed him, because he seemed to be able to make the waters part in front of him. I did admire the way he elbowed his way through. Alas for me, he became a gentleman at the phones and secured me one before he got one for himself. I'd been counting on eavesdropping before I called Foreign.

Oliver Weed was a sweetie, though, and he sort of coached me along. He said I'd have to dictate on the spot. No time to compose my thoughts. No nothing. Shoot. So I did. He typed as I talked.

"Very good, Sarah," he said. "Is this the first time you've done a quick feed?"

"It's the first time I've done anything."

"You're a pro," he said. "Now go back and find out whether there's going to be any statement from the prime minister or the leader of that business group. And see if you can find out who those guys were. Then call me back. Don't be long. We're past deadline."

Walrus had disappeared. I caught sight of him again in the ball-room, taking notes over near the dais. I worked my way over there. Walrus was interviewing the head of the Chamber of Commerce.

"Shocked, I would say," I heard. "Shocked and distressed that he was subjected to such a childish spectacle. And that we want to extend our deepest apologies to Japan."

"Do you have any idea what that group was? Progressive Labor? Socialist Workers?" Walrus asked.

"I never saw them before in my life," said the Chamber of Commerce chairman.

"Okay," said Walrus. "Find out anything?" he asked me.

"No," I said.

"It's a bitch this happened," he said. "I was going to ask you to buy me a drink. Dick McCarthy's the name. UPI. See you."

He went off, and then I felt really lost. I asked a Secret Service man whether the prime minister would be issuing a statement.

"Shut up!" he said, and put his finger to his earpiece.

On my way out, I heard someone calling, "Sarah, Sarah!"

I saw S. Millicent Forsythe waving.

"I *thought* it was you!" he said when I got near. "Why, how delightful to see you, Sarah! Whatever brings you here? I was so sorry about that, ah, problem you had with the block association. I hope you found another job."

"Yes," I said. "How are you? Wasn't that something!"

"It was quite frightening, quite frightening. But what are you doing here? Did you know those boys?"

"I was going to ask you that, because I'm covering—"

"I can't understand it. That was Junior's table. But he didn't come. At least, I don't think he did. Did you see him?"

"No. You mean Millicent Junior? That was his table? Where those protesters sat?"

"Well, it was the Forsythe Foundation table. I can't understand it. I am most distressed!"

I made a note now.

"You're not writing— Sarah, are you reporting this?"

"Yes, I'm covering it for *The Newspaper*."

"Oh, dear! This could be very awkward."

"Maybe if we could find Junior, he might know how those people—"

"Oh, I'm sure he doesn't know. Junior wouldn't— He's a sensible boy. *You* know him. He wouldn't— They were supposed to be young people from the foundations. We've been trying to get more young people involved. Oh, dear!"

"I'd better go call my office," I said. "It's past deadline."

"I wish you wouldn't. But then, I suppose you must. Oh, this is so awful! Gil Foley's a friend of mine. Do you think that would help?"

Some people shoved between us. I waved at him.

"Gotta run, Mr. Forsythe," I said.

I beat it to the phone. Weed loved the Forsythe Foundation bit.

"How'd you find that out, Sarah?" he asked.

"Luck," I said.

"Good reporters are always lucky," he said. "Listen, Ron wants to talk to you. You're on the front page, kid. Buttonweiser's inside, following your jump. Serves the lazy slob right. I'll switch you to Metro."

"Hi, there, Scoop," Ron said. "Didn't I tell you I'd get you on the front page?"

"Yes, Ron, you did. Somebody must have told you about the Red River Army."

"The what? Sarah, I am a lit-tle concerned, I have to tell you, that you didn't get your weather story done. You didn't tell me it was a record high. The *Morning Chronicle* just came up, and it's all over the front page."

"Gosh, Ron, I didn't know—"

"Well, come on back in and write it for us for second edition, and I'll forgive you."

When I got back to the office, Oliver Weed came up to me, all excited. The cops had the names of the Red River Army boys, and there were new developments coming in quarter-hourly.

"Can you do a couple of inserts, Sarah?" he asked.

"No, no, no, no, no!" said Ron. "Give it to rewrite. Sarah's tied up."

I was given half an hour to write the weather story. I would have made it, except that Jess Flicker came back to my desk and argued with me over the "goddamn polar bear in the lead," made me rewrite it, then came back and argued again, said I couldn't quote a fucking *Morning Chronicle* reporter in the third paragraph or anywhere else in a *Newspaper* story, for shit's sake, didn't I know the *rules?*

Ron went home somewhere in the middle of my labors, and the last page of my story got to the copy desk five minutes late. The polar bear never got in.

As I was walking out, I heard Flicker saying loudly, "Boys, I think we've got another Figland on our hands."

# IX

It was ten-thirty by the time I got home, and I should have been exhausted, but I wasn't. I was all keyed up, jumping around my little two-room pad, banging into things, talking to the TV, saying, "Sarah, you're a pro!" checking into the icebox and back out again, bopping down to Smiler's to buy a beer and the Smiler's specialty shrimp salad on rye, bopping up past the newsstand, seeing no second edition yet, thumping up my stairs thinking about the polar bear, dancing around with my sandwich, dropping shrimp juice on the floor, saying, "Flicker, you're a fuckhead!" and thinking about that polar bear some more, wishing I could call the zoo night watchman, ask, "Is he still swimming across that pool with his nose in the air?"

I called up Ellie. She was writing a big brief. "What's the matter with you?" she asked me, didn't wait for the answer. "Is that *Eye* story true?" she asked. "Did you really get hired that way?" Didn't wait for the answer then, either. Hung up fast.

After that I calmed down a little. But only a little. I thought of going to the Poor Mouth and thought of not going to the Poor Mouth. What if Doris was in there? I didn't want to see Doris, not for a while.

If you've ever been stuck alone in New York at night with no one to talk to and no place to go and feeling all hepped up and talky and jumpy, then you know that's when the vibes of the city really get to you, when you can *hear* all that life outside whooshing and whizzing up and down all the streets, and you know everybody else is out there having a fine, fine time. Up in Harlem folks are bouncing along in their funky new vines, lights are flashing, cabs are racing everywhere, slinky ladies stepping out, Sardi's fills with a roar, bums are getting it on with the wine, night is syncopated over Times Square, and the air in the Village is all lifting with the aspirated feeling of the sounds from the bars. *Everybody's* out there, everybody except you! New York doesn't ever want you to stand still; you can feel, when you listen, how she shifts and she moves and she just goddamn belly dances all through the night, asking you to come on out and let her try to turn you *on!*

I couldn't stand it. I was starting to feel sorry for the Statue of Liberty that she had to statue it out all alone in the middle of the harbor, looking at all those lights.

When my telephone rang, I jumped three feet in the air.

"What are you doing?" said a man's voice, and in my state I could see the guy holding on to his dong, while he got ready to say, "I was looking in the phone book and I saw your name, *puff, puff,* Make—peace."

"Who's this?" I asked sharply.

"It's me. Kevin."

"Kevin?"

"Mondavi."

"Oh, Kevin the cop. Hi."

"What are you doing?"

"Oh, farting around. Why? What's up?"

"I'm in your neighborhood."

"Oh."

"Oh, she says."

"What am I supposed to say?"

"What happened to your story?"

"It's in the second edition. What time do they put it on the stands? Do you know?"

"Should be out by now. What'd you do? Miss your deadline?"

"I got diverted to the Foreign Desk. They needed somebody to watch the Japanese prime minister, see if he got shot."

"I heard some hippies jumped him at the Hilton. You see that?"

"The Red River Army. They threw eggs at him."

"Eggs, that's original."

"Well, this was an ecology group. I s'pose they wanted something biodegradable."

"Getting cynical already, eh? I thought you were a Save the Earth type. Are you going to invite me up?"

"We-ell . . ."

"I'd ask you out for a drink, only I'm a little short on cash. Tell you what. I'll bring you the paper."

"Okay, but don't get the wrong idea."

"What wrong idea?"

"You know."

"Look, I've got a lot of ideas in my head. I mean, any one of 'em could be wrong. I've got ideas about Democrats, Republicans, Communists, fags—"

"Kevin, I just don't want you to come up here expecting me to hop into bed with you."

"Sarah, I just met you this morning. I don't know what kind of *person* you are. I'm not ready to *give* myself yet. Look, I'm cool. I just need to talk to somebody who doesn't call me Bubba. I need to unwind."

"Sorry, I only wanted you to understand—"

*"Please deposit five cents for the next five minutes or your call will be interrupted."*

"Thirty Christopher, right."

"Yes, 3-B."

The phone went dead.

Scarcely a minute later, my buzzer rang, and he came bounding up my stairs and tapped on my door. I opened it and stood back to make room for him, but he didn't come in right away. He leaned on the doorframe, looking as though he might be reconsidering, might be about to turn around. I was reconsidering myself, thinking maybe we should go out. My apartment was so small, and he looked so different now, softer and needful, but more handsome too. He looked as though he had had a shower and now felt kind of silly about it, as though he was afraid I might think he had taken a lot of trouble preparing to drop in on me, which wouldn't have fit with the casualness of the phone call. He had on a clean white T-shirt and the tight jeans and a nicely faded levi jacket that might have been calculated to appeal to a girl who lived in the Village. I guess his butt still stuck out, but I couldn't tell from my vantage point. He really looked nice, and he stood there hesitating as though he was afraid of something, not meeting my eyes very much, so that I was able to stare at him, examine him freely while he weighed whatever it was he was weighing, how much of a fool he'd end up feeling, maybe. He had this suppressed smile on his lips which made the lines around his mouth look sensual and at the same time gave him a pent-up, suffering air, as though often he had had to stop himself from saying things right there at the last stopping point, at the corners of his lips. How hard it must be to be a cop, I thought.

And then he said, "Your second edition wasn't out yet I hope I can keep my hands off you," and stepped inside and took a seat way over in the corner by the windows, and I felt palpably disappointed. I knew I'd better be careful if he was going to have that effect, so I sat down on the hard dining room chair, my one dining room chair, and positioned myself behind the dining room table—dining room and living room were of a piece in my place, the little kitchen was at my back—and we began to talk. I opened a bottle of wine and poured us each some while he was telling me about the veterinarians who had found their way to Women Alive and got drunk there and stood up and barked like dogs at the girls doing topless bottomless dances ("Bottomless too? They allow that?" I asked. "Oh, yeah!" he said. "Everything goes.") on the stage. He said he had had to throw out a guy who started biting the girls, and I waited for him to go on, but he stopped then and asked me about my day. It came pouring out of me in a fast breathless patter, and we drank more wine, and I talked and talked while he watched me from the corner. I can't remember what I said, too much anyway, because it was he who had said he needed to unwind. But he was smiling at me all the time, and I couldn't stop, I was so jumpy. I think I even told him sort of what I had thought after the Secret Service men searched my purse, not exactly that I *had* committed fellatio in the Widener stacks but that they might think I was the sort of girl who *would*, and somehow it got around to the real thing that was bothering me, how I felt I shouldn't really be on *The Newspaper*, how it looked to my friends like a sellout and maybe it was.

"You oughta try working for the Police Department sometime,"

Kevin said. "Everybody's gotta compromise. What are you gonna do? Go turn tricks?"

That made me feel worse but sort of reassured too, as though I had a partner in the business of difficult wrong turns. It gave me a surge of pity for him that he was a cop.

"Do you have a boyfriend?" he asked me once, and I thought then he might be planning to make a move. "There is this guy," I said. There was. A rock group manager who was not often in town and then didn't talk much or seem to care about me after we'd had sex. But I didn't tell Kevin this, only that I was seeing the guy off and on. The men situation was pretty fluid, I sort of hinted, because people were going through a phase of—well, experimental isolation, a kind of free-floating phase. The wine seemed to be going to my head, and I could feel myself forming large thoughts about urban angst in the seventies, and I had started to get shivery with excitement, listening to myself, waiting for that front page, wondering would he make a move. My limbs were still jumpy and I could feel it on my skin, how much I wanted him to touch me.

Finally he stood up.

"I've got an idea," he said.

Oh!

"Let's go get the paper," he said.

"Oh, yes! Let's!" I said. Would he leave then?

We walked into Sheridan Square. I held my arms by the elbows.

"You're awfully quiet all of a sudden," he said. "You afraid they killed your story?"

"Gee, would they?" I said, and then I *was* afraid to look at the paper. He looked.

"There you are," he said. "Right at the top. They spelled your name right."

"Holy shit!" I said happily. The headline looked enormous:

## PROTESTERS THROW EGGS
## AT MISHIYOKO BANQUET

Forsythe Foundation Used
As Front, Red River Army
Five Arrested in Hilton

*By Sarah Makepeace*

"Congratulations, Flash," Kevin said. "Come on. I'll walk you home."

God, he really was as good as his word! Planning to leave me at the door. How could I tell him I had changed my mind? I must have talked too much. He didn't like me anymore.

"I think my weather story's in there too," I said. He was carrying the paper.

"Where?" he said, opening it to the index.

"Probably on the city page," I said.

He handed me the paper. I opened it to the city page. There was my name again, under CITY BASKS IN RECORD SUN.

"Record sun. That's a queer idea," I said, closing the pages.

"Wait," said Kevin. "I want to read it."

I opened the paper again, and half the innards fell to the sidewalk. Kevin scooped them up.

"We'd better read this upstairs," he said solemnly.

He went behind me up the stairs. I went fast. At the door, I fumbled with my keys. What if he didn't like my writing?

We spread the paper on my table and read side by side: "A group of militants stood up during the Japanese prime minister's speech to the chamber of commerce . . . eggs thrown toward the podium . . . Forsythe Foundation used . . . incident embarrassed . . . caused the minister to cut short . . . five arrests . . ."

I wasn't reading very carefully. I knew the thing by heart anyway. I could smell Kevin. A soapy smell.

"You're famous," he said. "Looks fine." He turned to the city page while I pretended to have an itch on my upper arm and then stuck a couple of fingers into my left armpit. I hadn't had a shower since the night before. Yep. Sweaty. Maybe that was why he hadn't—but then he put an arm around my shoulders in a sort of palsy, light way, letting his hand dangle loose as if I was a buddy.

"New Yorkers took to the park yesterday by foot, by wheel, and by perambulator to bask in the bright sun of the warmest May 12 ever recorded here," I read, now seeing how flat and unoriginal it sounded.

"I had a much better beginning," I said. "I had this thing about the polar bear getting homesick for the tundra and trying to dive through the earth—"

But I stopped talking then, because Kevin was looking at me in a strange mocking way with his eyebrows raised and the suppressed smile.

"Still feel like a sellout?" he said, and then he moved around a little away from me and his hand slipped over to my neck.

"I, uh, don't know," I said, not looking straight at him. ("Sexual attraction usually begins with a warm tingly feeling in the lower

**61**

abdomen in girls," *Sex Made Simple* had said.) I couldn't breathe. Kevin put his other hand on my waist. My heart started to beat faster, and I thought: *If he kisses me, and I put my arms up, he will definitely smell,* and then my waist squeezed in on itself and made something happen to the unspecified center of me, and I thought of saying to Doris Munster, "The thing about orgasms, Doris, is that you never know quite where they do get started," and my cheeks felt hot. What was he waiting for? Suddenly he let his arms drop and stepped back. "Damn it!" he said.

"What's wrong?" I said.

"Well, you said . . . I promised." He folded his arms and scrunched up his shoulders, squinting at me.

("The boy is usually the one who makes the first move, but there are no rules about this," *Before You Try It* advised. "Girls should realize that boys are human and worry about their pimples too.")

"Don't you ever break your promises?" I said. What a stupid thing to say! I meant—

"Well, shit," he said, and he grabbed me fast and kissed me crookedly and unzipped the back of my dress just like that, and I said, "Maybe we shouldn't," and he kissed me again, and my heart beat fast, and my dress was coming off my shoulders. "Kevin," I said. "Where's your bed?" he said, but he had already figured out it was through the door near the windows. He pulled me by the wrist into the bedroom, and in there my dress fell off. He lost his balance and we both fell onto the bed. He got on top of me with his clothes on. I heard a siren outside going *blip blip* and felt a panicky fear that it was his partner, coming to pick him up.

"What's that?" I said.

"What?"

"That siren."

"A siren? I didn't hear it."

"Oh," I said.

"Why don't you relax," he said, putting his mouth where *What Is Love?* said girls should be touched in Phase Two of lovemaking. (*Before You Try It* had it under Part Three: "Petting.") I thought I would die before we got through that part, but eventually Kevin got my undies off and then kicked off his jeans and something thumped hard on the floor and the wastebasket fell over, but we took no notice of the sound. Kevin's bare hairless chest felt lovely and hot and smooth against my bare hairless chest, and I guess mine felt good to him too, because he forgot about Phase Three and went straight into Phase Four and I was glad and had begun to really get

**62**

into it with him when he clutched me hard and came, leaving me with a feeling like the unsung highest note of "Aaaaaall my triaaaaaa-als, Lord" pent up in my womb.

I must have sighed pretty hard, because he said, "I thought you were ready. I'm sorry."

"Oh, that's okay. I'll get over it in a minute."

"I'm really sorry," he said. "I don't usually do that."

"It's really okay," I said. "I'll just keep you up all night."

"I can't stay all night," he said.

"Oh," I said.

"I wish I could," he said.

Then neither of us said anything for a while.

"You wouldn't have any grass," he said.

"Now, is that a question a cop ought to ask a girl when he's just taken advantage of her?"

"So I took advantage of you, did I? You were too drunk to know what you were doing, is that it?"

"I do have grass, Kevin, but you are an officer of the law."

"It's just an ACD now. Nobody gets hit for a little joint anymore."

"What do you mean, ACD?"

"Adjourned in contemplation of dismissal. That's what the DAs do in all the little pot arrests. You should know about that. It's down on your sheet."

"You looked up my arrest record?" I said, getting up on one elbow.

"Sure," he said. I could see him grinning in the dark. "Down for a morals charge. What'd you do? Try to turn a trick?"

"God damn!" I said, sitting up. "You think I'd do something like that? Jesus, Kevin!"

"Shhh! Shhh! You'll wake up the neighbors."

"My neighbors don't come home until four in the morning. Kevin, where did you get the idea I was arrested for prostitution? It was for corrupting the morals of minors. Jesus! Turning a trick! You've spent too much time in Times Square."

"Yeah."

"Do you like it? Working undercover?"

"How many men have you been to bed with?"

"Oh, a few," I said in a high small voice.

"Get your grass."

"I don't know if I want to get high with you."

"You just went to bed with me!"

"That's different. Getting high is—is—"

"Getting high is getting high. Look, I was only kidding about that arrest thing, honest. I figured you turned down some cop in the Two Six, and he stuck you with a summons. It happens."

"It does?"

"Sure. Cops do bad things. You know that. You've read about the Knapp Commission. Get your grass."

So I got up all naked and rolled us a joint, a big fat messy one on account of my rolling it in the dark, which I told him would protect me from his future testimony and him from mine, should I decide to report him, as we could each say to the judge we couldn't actually say we had seen beyond a reasonable doubt the nature of the substance, only smelled it.

While we were smoking the thing, he asked me about the circumstances of the corrupting-morals-of-minors charge, and I told him the whole story about Jesus and Fredo and Angelica and the sex books.

"The cop who arrested you, did he put cuffs on you?" Kevin asked, idly touching a nipple.

"No," I said. "He was a nice old guy. Very fat. He couldn't be very good at chasing bad guys. He kept apologizing to me while we walked to the precinct."

"I would have," Kevin said. "I would have put you in cuffs."

And then he grabbed my wrists and held them together while he kissed me long and slow, and I closed my eyes and could see him arresting me. I shivered. He let my wrists go and gently pushed me back against the pillow, and then he did something that wasn't in any of the teenage sex books but which, if it had been, would have been listed in the *Before You Try It* chapter called "Probably Not Yet." *What Is Love?* would have put it in the Glossary of Terms. *Sex Made Simple* might have stuck it in the Personal Taste section of the chapter on Compatibility.

"Oh, Kevin, please!" I moaned finally, prompting him to skip to the semifinal phase, or what was for him the semifinal phase but was for me a series of Phase Fives during which I kept imagining him booking me in the station house and leading me to a quiet cell in the back, while unaccountably Joan Baez could be heard singing from the detectives' room upstairs, "The Niiiiiiight they brought old Dixie down."

"I think I'm falling in love with you," I said when Kevin had finally fallen off me, exhausted.

"It's not a good time to make a judgment like that," he said.

"Are you seeing a shrink?" I said.

"How did you know that? What time is it?"

"How should I know? Why do you need a shrink? You don't strike me as repressed."

"Don't you have a watch?"

"Call the time. What's the matter? The wife waiting to hear from you?"

He stood up, turned on the light, and called the time number. Then he dialed another number and asked for an extension. He seemed to be searching the room meanwhile. He was picking things up, looking under the bed, and frowning.

"Hi," he said into the phone. Then he sighed deeply. "I know, I know," he said. "I wasn't watching the time. I told you this job I'm on isn't exactly nine to five. . . . Okay. . . . Okay. . . . Let's talk about it later. Don't start that, Helen. Look, I'm tired. I've had a long day. I'll pick you up at Emergency in twenty minutes. 'Bye."

He hung up and searched around for his clothes, assiduously not looking at me.

"You're married," I said. "I might have known."

"You didn't ask," he said. "Listen, did you see what happened to my gun?"

"It's just my luck. Getting stoned with a cop." I was feeling sort of proud, actually. Could Doris Munster do that many—

"Sarah, get the fuck up and help me find my gun," Kevin said curtly.

I got up and looked around in the covers. Then I remembered that thump on the floor and the wastebasket falling. I picked up the wastebasket. It felt sort of heavy. I scraped around in the papers and cigarette butts.

"Sarah, what are you—" he said, but then I fished out a heavy square-shaped leather wallet.

"Is this it?" I said, starting to open the flap. Kevin quickly grabbed it from me and clucked his tongue at me.

"It doesn't look big enough to be a gun," I said.

"You want to see it? Okay, don't touch." He pulled it partway out of the case so I could see the little square handle and part of the barrel.

"Have you ever shot it?" I asked.

"Nah," he said. "Not this one."

I shivered. He shoved the thing into his back pocket.

"Have you ever shot anyone?" I asked.

He shook his head and sucked in air through his nose. Doris never had a man like this.

"Well, Sarah, it's been—"

"Aren't you still stoned? Won't your wife notice?"

He walked out into the other room. I followed him. He opened the apartment door. I stood there watching him with my arms folded, naked.

"It's been what?" I said.

He turned around in the doorway.

"You never heard of Kevin Mondavi, did you?" he said.

"I guess I never heard of Kevin Mondavi," I said.

"Good girl. I'll call you."

# X

It must have been about four o'clock when Kevin left. The telephone woke me at the ungodly hour of nine. Freddie, the clerk, said Ron wanted me instantly at a five-alarm fire at West Tenth and Hudson.

"Looks like suspicious origins," Freddie said.

"What's Ron doing at a fire?" I asked.

"Ron? Ron's at home listening to the radio," said Freddie. "What's the matter with you?"

I needed time to think. I had lost all my shoes. There was an empty wine bottle on my table. I turned on my radio, heard the Berlin Chorale Singers singing "*Wachet auf, ruft uns die Stimme.*" When I bent down to look for my shoes, my head spun. I could not see anything under the bed. Perhaps a little snooze, I thought, letting my head sink onto yesterday's clothes.

The telephone woke me again.

"Hello," I said, now seeing the colony of shoes under the bed.

"Sarah? Sarah, what are you doing writing about the Japanese prime minister? You don't know anything about Japan!"

"Oh, hi, Dad."

"Sarah, that's exactly what's wrong with *The Newspaper*. They shouldn't let a neophyte like you do an assignment of such—"

"Dad, I don't have time to talk."

"I'm going to write a letter, Sarah."

"About my story? Dad, how could you—"

"It is all the more important when my own daughter is involved. It is a matter of principle, Sarah."

, "Please don't do that, Dad! There're lots of other things you can complain about. Why don't you write about pollution in Japan?"

"It is the height of hypocrisy for the nation that dropped the atom bomb to heap scorn—"

"Dad, I don't have time to *talk!* Do whatever you *want!*" I shouted, and hung up.

At least he got me so pissed off that I was out of the house in a jiffy. I could see the smoke from the fire. The air smelled of it too. Sticky hot air.

But the blaze was out when I reached Hudson Street. The firemen were hosing down the smoking shell of the building, and a huge crowd of young men stood around watching the firemen, wading in the water, festively calling to one another, flirting, wiggling their shoulders, enjoying the mood of someone else's disaster.

I found the fireman in charge, a Chief McFarland, and I stood in water a foot deep, taking notes. He was not a talkative man.

"Was anybody hurt?" I asked.

"No casualties, no. The building was vacant at the time of occurrence. We had negative manpower threat. Speakin' off the record, no attributes to me, our biggest problem was controlling the spectators. Always is down here. You can see for yourself, it's wall-to-wall faggots. They appear to like fires."

"What about, um, what caused it?"

"Undetermined," he said.

There wasn't anything more to it, so I went ambling off looking for a coffee shop. My hours were supposed to be eleven to seven. I had finished with the fire at five past ten.

I got to the office at five past eleven.

"Where have you been, Sarah?" Ron said as soon as I set foot in the newsroom. "We've been looking for you all morning!"

"Freddie said I was supposed to do that fire at Tenth and Hudson."

"That was hours ago! Listen, you've missed the press conference now, so you're going to have to fill in with phone calls."

"There was a press conference about the fire?"

"Of course not, Sarah! I'm talking about the Red River Army. Didn't Willie tell you?"

"No."

"Well, never mind. I want you to call the police commissioner right away. He's issued a statement about the Red River Army. Get cracking!"

"What about the fire?"

"Make that a City Short. But do it later, Sarah. This is much more important! You're going to be on the front page again."

"Good! Oh, Ron, did you notice how hot it is? I think it's going to be another record high today."

"We had that *yesterday*, Sarah. Go call the commissioner."

The Police Department put me onto Deputy Commissioner Dalrymple. He told me I should have been at the news conference.

"How long you been at the paper, Sarah?" he asked.

"A week," I said.

"Oh, brother! Why didn't they give this to Eddie Schwartz?"

"Don't ask me. Look, can I talk to the commissioner?"

"The commissioner's tied up. Well, we'd better make the best of it. Take this down," he said, "but no attribution." He said I could say "sources close to the commissioner" had learned that the Red River Army had been operating "underground" for the last year, "infiltrating various foundations" and "preparing for terrorist activities." He said there was "information" that a "cadre" had met at an environmental conference in Cambridge, Mass., the previous November. There were possible tie-ins to "Cuban spies."

"You mean to spy on foundations?" I said.

"Oh, god!" said Dalrymple.

"Sarah, Sarah!" Ron said to me, looming over my desk.

"I'm on the phone!" I said.

"Who're you talking to?"

"Just a minute," I said to Dalrymple. "Somebody named Dalrymple," I said.

"That's the PR guy," said Ron. "I want you to talk to the commissioner. We've just learned there's a Cuban angle in this."

"Dalrymple just said that, Ron, but I don't understand. Why would the Cubans want to spy on our foundations?"

"Oh, Sarah! Don't be so stupid! Ask him if there's a grand jury investigation."

"Um, Mr. Dalrymple, my boss wants to know whether there's a grand jury investigation."

"I couldn't discuss that," Dalrymple said. "Is Ron there? Could I talk to him?"

"He's gone back to his desk," I said. "Look, I'm a little confused. Maybe if you tell me again. What was this group planning to do?"

"We are not at liberty to discuss anything that goes before a grand jury."

"Does that mean there is one?"

"Draw your own conclusions."

"You're doing a grand jury investigation of Cuban spies infiltrating foundations?"

"You're not a bad reporter," said Dalrymple.

"I still don't understand what the point would be, um, for the Cubans."

"Look, I'll give you this. But you didn't get it from me. One of the Hilton defendants has expressed strong sympathies for the Castro regime."

"Strong sympathies? Is that a crime?"

"I can't go any further than that, Sarah. And you didn't get it from me."

"SARAH MAKEPEACE!" Ron called over the loudspeaker.

"'Bye," said Dalrymple.

"SARAH!" Ron called again.

I hurried up to his desk.

"Sarah, Sarah, I want a summary on this right away. And I want the Cuban thing in the lead," Ron said, looking at the clock.

"I don't know, um, how to describe it, Ron. I mean, the Cuban thing."

"Do I have to tell you how to write your lead? It's a Cuban spy ring!"

I dashed back to my desk and wrote a lead saying that the Police Department was conducting a grand jury investigation into a Cuban spy ring that had infiltrated American foundations. Ron took it from me and went running off somewhere. My telephone rang. Greg Swenson, my deskmate, picked it up as I was running back to my desk.

"S. Millicent Forsythe, kid. Be good to him. He's an asshole buddy of Gil's," said Greg, handing me the phone.

"Hello, Mr. Forsythe," I said. "How did you know I was on the Red River Army story again?"

"You're doing another story? Sarah, I thought I told you not to mention the foundation. The police have been here. They've got a subpoena for Junior."

"A subpoena. Wow! Did they arrest him?"

"Junior is not here. Look, Sarah, this is all a ridiculous boys' lark. You've got to explain to your editors. I heard there was a news conference. Were you there?"

"No. Where's Junior?"

"Junior called me this morning. He's very embarrassed. He thought there were only going to be signs. He was not aware that there would be eggs. There was only one boy who brought them."

"So Junior knew those people, the Red River Army?"

"No, no, he didn't. And there *is* no Red River Army. It was all a joke. Maybe I should talk to Gil about it."

"Well, why don't you just tell me what really happened. I'm supposed to be doing a story about the grand jury investigation. The Police Department says they were Cuban spies, Mr. Forsythe, trying to infiltrate the foundations."

"Cuban spies! Why, that's sheer fantasy! They hadn't even met each other until last night. They're all actors."

"Actors?"

"Yes. I told the police. They were hired. I don't know who hired them, and Junior doesn't know. One of them wore a Ché Guevara T-shirt. Is that what the commissioner— Oh, this is too ridiculous. I'm going to have to call Gil."

"Well, maybe you should. My boss is pretty excited about this."

"All right, Sarah. Thank you. Who's your boss?"

"Ron Millstein."

I hung up and wrote a summary about the fire.

As I gave it to Flicker, I saw Ron coming back to his desk.

"Ron, listen. S. Millicent Forsythe called me," I said.

"Sarah, how could you write a lead like this?" Ron said angrily. "How could you say the Police Department is conducting a grand jury investigation! The district *attorney's* office does grand juries! You embarrassed me, Sarah. Gil has lost confidence in this story."

"Well, I'm beginning to lose confidence in it myself, Ron," I said. "Mr. Forsythe just told me the Red River Army is a joke, that they're all actors, that somebody hired them—"

"Sarah, of *course* Millicent Forsythe is going to shoot down the story! I'm surprised at you! Don't you know he has an image to protect? Now go back to your desk and *write that story!*"

I went slumping back to my desk. Greg Swenson had his feet up on his typewriter and he was humming a little tune. I sat down next to him and moaned:

"What am I going to do?"

"What's the matter, kid?" Greg asked.

I explained.

"Don't do anything," said Greg.

"But Ron said to write—"

"Forsythe said he was gonna call Gil, right?"

"Yes."

"So take a powder."

"What?"

"Disappear for an hour."

I went to the ladies' room and did the crossword puzzle. I didn't stay for an hour. When I came out, Willie Crespi was calling my name over the loudspeaker.

"Yes?" I said, presenting myself at Dayside.

"Sarah, where have you been? Ron is very upset with you," Willie said, glaring up at me from between his hunched shoulders.

"I was in the ladies' room," I said innocently.

"How long— Listen, Ron wants to know why you didn't tell him this was just a boys' lark. You can't do this sort of thing, Sarah. S. Millicent Forsythe spoke to Gil, and Ron was made to look very, well, uninformed."

"Where's Ron? I *told* him—"

"Ron's at lunch. Your story's been killed. Ron's very disappointed in you, Sarah. You should have sensed there was something wrong with the story. This isn't *The Evil Eye.*" Willie narrowed his eyes when he said "*Evil Eye.*" Then he sneered, "Why would Cuban spies want to infiltrate foundations?"

"Willie, that's what I asked Dalrymple!"

"We were going to put that story on the front page, top of the fold, Sarah. Gil was angry," Willie said. "Gil does *not* like *The Newspaper* to be used, even by the Police Department."

"Willie, I *told* Forsythe to go ahead and call Gil!" I pleaded.

"*You* told Forsythe to call Gil? Why the hell did you do that?"

"Well, I didn't know what to believe, and Ron wouldn't listen—"

"Sarah, don't you ever, ever go over Ron's head, do you hear me? Don't *ever* do that! I'm telling you for your own good. Ron's your only rabbi on this paper. You come to us if you have a problem. Don't *ever* go to Gil. Is that clear?"

"Gee—"

"I'm sure Ron will forgive you this time because you're new, but—"

"MAKEPEACE!"

Jess Flicker was calling me over the loudspeaker from the next desk. Willie waved me off.

**71**

"Where's your fire summary?" Flicker asked.

"I gave it to you."

"We can't find it. Was it a big fire?"

"It was out when I got there."

"Was anybody hurt?"

"No. It was just a big Village crowd scene."

"Okay. Make it a City Short. Put in the crowd."

I went back to my desk.

"MAKEPEACE!" came the call again.

This time it was Freddie on Dayside.

"Call came in for you up here. You want to take it here?"

"Who is it?"

"I dunno. He says he's a friend."

I took the phone from Freddie.

"Hello, Flash. You busy Saturday night?"

"Oh, hi, Kevin. No, I'm not, but what about your— Wait a minute. Can you call me back on my extension?"

"You call me. I'm in a phone booth. I've got a tip for you on that Red River Army thing."

I called him back from my desk.

"Who've you been talking to? Your phone's been busy all day," he said.

"I've been chasing phantom Cuban spies."

"That's all bullshit."

"I know. But why would your commissioner hold a press conference about bullshit?"

"That's his job. He puts out the bullshit, we get more money. The big thing is conspiracies right now. They're trying to glom onto federal grant money. Interstate conspiracies. The feds don't like it. You know any federal agents?"

"No. Anyway, my story's been killed."

"What story?"

"About the Cuban spies."

"Things are looking up! *The Newspaper*'s getting honest. Listen, the Red River Army is really Crazies for Hire. One of my buddies in Manhattan North told me. He pulled the sheets on the five defendants—well, only two of 'em have sheets. They were arrested last December for throwing pies at the mayor and Barry Farber. Remember? It was at that 'I Love New York' special on Broadway."

"I remember."

"Well, those two were working for an outfit called Crazies for Hire. They're in the phone book. You can call them up. What they

72

do is take a fee, hire themselves out to cause trouble for people who want trouble caused. But they don't say in advance what they're going to do. It's pretty smart. Their clients can't be brought into it. They're all unemployed actors. They don't do any violent stuff. That bit with the eggs is abut as violent as they get."

"They're really in the phone book?"

"Yeah."

"Wait a minute. Can you hold on?"

"Okay. But hurry."

"Greg, quick! Where's a phone book?" I asked. Greg pointed to the shelf beside my desk. I took the book onto my lap and found Crazies for Hire. "Is this it, Kevin? At 97 Carmine Street?"

"Yeah."

"How do they get away with it? Listing themselves."

"The DA's trying to nail them. But most of the time, the people they attack are people everybody wants to attack, so the DA's been reluctant to, like, hit them too hard. Look, everybody wants to see the mayor get a pie in his face."

"What about the people who hired them at the Hilton? Wouldn't they be guilty of something?"

"Crazies for Hire never tell who they're working for."

"You're sure they did the thing at the Hilton?"

"My buddy says two of 'em definitely did. The other three are in Actors Equity. Their lawyer said so at the arraignment."

"Where did the commissioner get the Cuban spies thing?"

"Beats me. It's stupid. He'll have the feds crawling all over him."

"Anyway, my story's been killed."

"Yeah, but this is the real story. Call up Crazies for Hire. See what they say."

"I think I will. Hey, thanks, Kevin."

"What about Saturday?"

"I haven't thought that far ahead."

"Don't make a date."

"Kevin, what about your wife?"

"My wife's fine."

"Well, don't you think it's sort of unwise for us to—"

"Very unwise."

"So maybe we shouldn't—"

"Listen, I'm gonna be a very wise old man. I want to see you Saturday night."

"Okay," I said weakly.

After I'd hung up, I saw Greg Swenson looking at me with pensive interest. He must have heard every word.

I noticed that it was three-fifteen. I called Crazies for Hire.

"Cuban spy ring," said a cheery voice.

"Hello, is this Crazies for Hire?" I said.

"What number did you dial?"

"This *is* Crazies for Hire at 97 Carmine Street, isn't it?"

"If that's what it says in the phone book."

"I'm Sarah Makepeace from *The Newspaper*. Could I speak to your, um, leader?"

"I'm the only one in the office, Sarah. Call me Tonto. What can I do for you?"

"I just want to know whether you have a comment about your five, um, employees who were arrested at the Hilton last night."

"We don't have employees per se. We work strictly on a commission basis."

"How much do you charge?"

"It depends. Our base fee is five hundred dollars. But we usually negotiate each assignment separately. Legal costs are additional."

"How much did you charge for the Hilton thing?"

"We don't keep accounts."

"Well, how much would you charge me if I wanted something similar?"

"Oh, we never tell you what you're going to get."

"Tonto, I heard that a guy named S. Millicent Forsythe, Jr., hired your outfit for the Hilton dinner. He's pretty rich."

"We never reveal the names of our clients. But it's true, we do charge rich guys more. How rich would that guy be?"

"Several million."

"Well, if we were hired by a millionaire—I'm not saying we ever have been, but if we were—we would charge a thousand dollars a head."

"That's a thousand for each of the, um, actors or a thousand for each person hit with an egg or a pie?"

"A thousand for each therapist."

"Therapist? I thought you were actors."

"We are incorporated as a group therapy clinic. We're nonprofit, you see."

"Are you putting me on?"

"I could be. Then again, I could not be."

"Tonto, it was five people from your outfit who were arrested last night, right?"

74

"Yes, those *were* our people. But today is a new day. The Secret Service broke three of Wallaby's ribs."

"Who's Wallaby?"

"Wallaby's just Wallaby."

"I take it nobody uses his real name on the job."

"Real is a relative concept, Sarah, if that is your true name."

"Tonto, was one of your people wearing a Ché Guevara T-shirt?"

"I have to go now, Sarah. It was nice talking to you."

"Wait, Tonto! I need to know how your group got started. Whose idea was it? Are you all actors?"

"Just put down that we are all Scorpios, Sarah, and we—oh, yes, we got our training watching the Watergate hearings. Toodle oo."

"MAKEPEACE!" Flicker called me. "WE NEED YOUR CITY SHORT."

I typed it out quickly and brought it up to him. I saw that Ron was back at his desk.

"Ron, Ron!" I said. "I've found out the *real* story about that Hilton thing."

"Hey, what is this, Sarah?" Flicker said loudly. "You can't use a quote like this! 'Wall-to-wall faggots'! Shit!"

"Let me see that," Ron said grumpily, holding out his arm.

Flicker handed me my City Short. I carried it over to Ron. Ron read it, shaking his head, saying, "Oh, no, no, no! *No*, no, no!"

"Listen, Ron," I said, "the people who did the Hilton eggs business are a weird group called Crazies for Hire. I just interviewed one of them over the phone. They're listed in the phone book, Ron. Remember when the mayor got a pie in his face—"

"Sarah, we do *not* quote every stupid thing that is said to us! And this is anonymous, an *anonymous* fireman saying, 'Wall-to-wall faggots.' Really, Sarah!" Ron said.

"I didn't get his first name. But did you hear what I was saying about the Hilton thing?"

"We are not running any more stories on that Hilton incident. We had it in the paper this morning," Ron said.

"Maybe we ought to have something," said Flicker, who had walked over to Ron's desk.

"Gil does not want that story running tonight," Ron said. "Sarah knows that." He glared at me.

"Okay," said Flicker, "but this is a new development."

"I am not going to argue it with Gil again!" Ron said.

Flicker stood there.

"Oh, do a D head, Sarah!" Ron snapped. "But do not mention the Forsythe Foundation."

"What," I asked Greg Swenson, "is a D head?"

"Four paragraphs, thereabouts. Is that all they gave you?"

"Yes."

"Well, hurry up and do it. I'll buy you a drink."

Greg took me to the upstairs bar at Sardi's. I did not last long. After two drinks I pleaded exhaustion, went home, and fell asleep without eating anything. The telephone, once again, woke me up.

"Hello, Sarah. Jess here."

"What time is it?"

"Nine o'clock. Were you asleep?"

"Umm."

"Can't take the pace, eh? Wake up. The *Chronicle*'s got a big spread on Crazies for Hire. I hope you saved your notes. I'm going to pass you over to Luddle on rewrite.

# XI

The others subsequently told me that Luddle flunked out of Alcoholics Anonymous because of me, but I don't know if that is true. I felt bad about him anyway, because he had big droopy pouches under his eyes and would be reading poetry at his desk when I called in, and he would get so confused by my dictation. But in the beginning, everybody at *The Newspaper* seemed confused to me, Ron most of all. Ron couldn't remember what he'd said from one moment to the next. He was always telling people they'd be on the front page and then telling Willie two minutes later to kill their stories or have them write D heads. He switched tacks five hundred times a day, and then at the last minute, before the five o'clock front page meeting with Gil, he'd shout, "Why didn't somebody tell me this? Suing her doctor because she had quintuplets! It's a first! Why didn't somebody tell me, god damn it! You idiots, it's on the wires! Get me Figland!" And he'd send Figland and four other people out at ten past five, and they'd all call back in to dictate to Luddle at twenty minutes past deadline, with Ron shouting in the background, "Where's Figland? Who sent Figland out?"

Ron forgot about his little tiff with me right away, but he forgot also that I needed instruction, or maybe he forgot that his lies about me *were* lies. In any case, I was left to learn by the sink-or-swim method while he was off shouting at his idiots, and every once in a while he absentmindedly patted me on the back or called me "a great reporter" in front of his underlings, who all knew better but humored him in the rush, since nothing so irrelevant as my qualifications mattered against the significance of the approaching deadline. In their heart of hearts, I know, the underlings were appalled at my ignorance and suffered agonies of cognitive dissonance while reading my copy. I heard them sighing, gasping, swearing, emitting groans, and calling for Freddie's aspirin supply as they labored to make sense of what I had done to the names of famous people. Not only did I misspell their names, I mixed up their positions. I confused state with federal courts and couldn't tell plaintiffs from defendants, and I demoted several congressmen to the status of city councilmen or once in a while unwittingly promoted a state senator to the U.S. Senate. Poor Luddle wasn't the only one who suffered from my efforts in the first few weeks. One night in early June, Jess Flicker pounded his fist on the Nightside desk so hard (also hitting the bull's eye of my reference to the Board of Estimate as "the Board of Education") that he broke a knuckle.

After that, I made an earnest vow to learn what it was I was supposed to be doing, and I started hanging out with the other reporters, asking them things about their techniques. They seemed shy about it or something, as if sharing basic skills was against the rules. They were much happier talking about the seating arrangements in the newsroom or about how smug Willard Dixby was looking lately or about what a lamentable mess Vic Veblen was making of things with Jenny. If I asked them direct questions, they usually turned to each other to ask where they should eat lunch. I did find after a while that I could pick up a little of the lore of the business if I didn't say anything, if I just sidled over to them and listened in. But it wasn't the sort of lore that revealed techniques. It was personal stuff about what incompetent assholes the editors were, functional illiterates mostly, with "tin ears" for quotes. They called each other incompetents too, behind each other's backs. They did this most often behind Vincent Akelroyd's back, said he was a "talentless toady" and "too stupid to get writer's block." Everybody who didn't have a story on the front page regularly said that those who did had written "hype jobs," "crap," "puff pieces," "bullshit," "City Hall handouts," or simply "lies." And they said that the "key political strategist" so often quoted in Greg Swenson's analytical pieces was really the governor's foot doctor, while Susan Braithwaite's "numerous sources in the black community" were her mother and her husband. They said Vincent Akelroyd didn't have any sources at all, but made up his quotes and faked whole interviews with Liv Ullmann, who was too nice to complain.

It made me feel better about being such a fuck-up myself, hearing what they said about the editors, but then I started wondering what they said about me when my back was turned, and it got so I was afraid to walk away from a group of reporters. Pretty soon it felt like high school, like standing around in the hall with the In crowd watching the nerds go by.

I started to have trouble deciding who I should learn from, and at the same time I started finding it difficult to, like, suspend disbelief when I read *The Newspaper*. The prose still sounded authoritative to me, but its authority began to seem like a trick. I mean, "a key political strategist in the governor's inner circle" sounded pretty impressive if you didn't know it was the governor's foot doctor. But I knew, and I knew that the guy who wrote the phrase was a hokey-looking pip-squeak with a gap between his front teeth and a degree in Media Ecology from City College night school. How could I believe what Greg wrote when he let me overhear him asking the governor's press secretary whether Greg's latest *Newspaper* story on the governor's budget strategy was *true?*

I liked Greg. No one could dislike a man so eager to hide how short he was. He had a short-guy swagger, and his head was too big for his body, which made him seem smaller. When he smiled, his gap teeth made him look like a hayseed. He wore thick-heeled shoes and dressed very fancily in tailored suits and wide silk ties. But when he stood up and grinned, the total effect was pitiable; he looked like a boy on his first high school prom date telegraphing his keen desire to be taken for a spiffy man about town as he prepared to step on your toes. Women were soft on him, and I heard that Jenny Locke had had a "big thing" about him, maybe still did.

I liked Ron too, I have to tell you, though in my mind he was beginning to resemble Mr. Potash, the fat, hysterical music teacher who conducted the raggle-taggle Regional High School orchestra. Liking people at *The Newspaper* wasn't hard to do when you saw them close up and under pressure, messing up left and right. But it was just this seeing them close up and under pressure that had started to undermine my faith in *The Newspaper*'s authority. Besides, *The Newspaper* had hired *me!*

The better I got to know the place, the more hokey and familiar everyone became. Willie Crespi, with his bent back and perpetual open-mouthed inability to second-guess Ron fast enough, started to look to me like the hang-jawed, hunchbacked law student who taught my Radcliffe composition class and couldn't think of a thing to say about Shakespeare after he'd used up "profound." Steve Figland seemed the spitting image of a gangly, loony caseworker I had come across in East Harlem, trying to convert Angelica's mother to Judaism. Jess Flicker, although lean-cheeked and driven, swore like a truckdriver and reminded me of the Four Corners town drunk in a mean sober mood. Susan Braithwaite could have been one of the ageless black goody-goodies in high school or at Radcliffe, always well groomed, always punctual and sexy in the tight-assed, cock-teasing way of girls who did everything but. Jenny Locke was the only one who seemed without reference to anything outside New York, but she was a familiar type nonetheless, even had the same facial expressions as Doris Munster, the nobody-fucks-me-over set to her mouth and eyes. She was a little hard-edge, a bit past her prime, but very attractive in her hauteur. Eddie Schwartz was like a familiar imaginary figure to me, but that was because he seemed so much the archetype of an aging newsman, which was something I knew only from movies about reporters in the thirties and forties. He wore an old fedora at all times and used "dese" and "dose" when he felt like it; his favorite expression was "Fuck daht!" He had committed himself to learning ancient Greek on the rewrite bank to show up Luddle, who only read Andrew Marvell.

Eddie is the one who finally managed to get me invited along for lunch with the others. I had been eavesdropping on a conversation about Willie Crespi's wife's stupid remarks at some cocktail party where the publisher's wife had been stranded with her, and I heard Akelroyd say, "How did Flicker break his hand?" and there was an awkward pause, so I turned around toward the group—I had been pretending to look up Times Square on the subway map—intending to confess, but Greg said hurriedly, "Where will it be today, folks? Il Penseroso or the Fleur-de-Lis?"

I wandered away then, so as not to be left stranded when they all walked off. But Eddie, who knew how Flicker had broken his knuckle, said, "Sarah, you ever been to dis French joint the Fleur-de-Lis?"

"No," I said. "It sounds expensive. But don't let me stop you. I've got early copy—"

"Fuck daht!" said Eddie. "This is editorial lunch day. We got all afternoon."

And the others chimed in, "Come on, Sarah"; "Sarah's never been to the Fleur"; "We gotta break in Sarah," and so on, sounding at last as though they meant to make me one of them. Jenny said she had just remembered a lunch date, and Akelroyd said he was going to the editorial lunch. So the gang that first time was Steve, Greg, Eddie, Susan, and me.

I felt so happy being included that I forgot not to ask questions about technique. The luncheon conversation went like this:

"Let's have California. Gleason wrote about this great Zinfandel. Let's order a couple of bottles."

"Shit, Figland, the California's a rip-off! If you knew anything about wines, you'd know that. Even Sarah here knows California's a rip-off. Tell him, Sarah."

"Do they serve California wines in French restaurants?"

"You see, Steve, you dummy! Even Sarah knows that. Let's take the Chateau Simard."

"Are you paying?"

"What do you mean, am I paying? This is dutch, you big schmuck! You getting hit for alimony this week, or what?"

"Every week. I wish I'd never seen that woman."

"No, you just shouldn't have married her. So it's the Simard."

"Well, I don't care. I'm not drinking."

"Susan, you give me a pain in the ass. We take you to the best French restaurant in the Times Square *quartier*, and you're not drinking."

"I can't. I've gained five ponds. Even with jogging."

"You look luscious. What are you worried about?"

"I just got this fantastic pair of silk pants. At that place in Brooklyn Heights? Fifty percent off. They're a teensy bit tight."

"We'll take the Chateau Simard."

"Steve, I really liked your story on the new therapy. How did you get that man to talk about his impotence? That was really moving."

"He quoted himself, ha ha! Figland, when are you going to take me to your tennis store?"

"Anytime you say, Swenson. Any Saturday."

"You know I can't do it on Saturday. I'm stuck with the kids."

"You should check out this store in Brooklyn Heights, Sarah. You like silk pants? You should. You're skinny. Très Chic, it's called.

**80**

It's on the corner of Montague and—oh, shit, I forgot exactly. But you can just ask once you get there."

"Do you live in Brooklyn?"

"Me? I live in Harlem!"

"That's right. I think Ron told me. Does it help, living in the neighborhood? I mean, to get pieces. That one about the lady whose son died of an overdose—did you know her before you did the piece? How did you find out all that stuff about her boyfriends?"

"What are you girls talking about?"

"We're not *girls*, Greg."

"Cunts, then!"

"Fuck daht! Greg don't know how to talk to broads. Sarah, honey, you gotta help me pick a horse today. I need your luck today."

"You're buying a horse?"

"I wanta propose a toast—"

"Nah, bettin', sweetheart. Coupla two-dollah bets at OTB."

"—to Willie Crespi."

"What's with you, Figland?"

"To Willie!"

"To Willie!"

"Willie!"

"Willie's going into the hospital. He's got curvature of the spine. They're gonna put him in traction."

"He needs traction on his gray cells."

"He sure had a rag on today."

"Willie's always got a rag on."

"What does that mean—a rag on?"

"Susan, tell the little girl from the Village about the menstrual cycle."

"You've got a lot to learn, Sarah."

"I know, Greg. For instance, maybe you can tell me how you got that story about Bella Abzug's staff defections. You must have had her office wired."

"Look here, Sarah. See, here's the names. Wadda you think? You like Comin' Up Roses? Or waddabout Black Beauty?"

"Oh, Black Beauty, I guess. Greg, how did you get that story?"

"That's for me to know and you to find out."

"Greg never tells anybody how he gets his stories. Don't feel bad. Eddie, I got to talk to you. Superman wants me to buy a new car. Listen, Eddie! You still plugged into that Volvo dealer?"

"I haven't talked to him in about a year, Susan, but I don't think he'd be a problem. He loves me forever, he says."

"Eddie wrote a piece during the gas shortage, you know, said Volvos get great mileage."

An hour passed this way. In the ladies' room, Susan asked me how I came to work for *The Newspaper*. But then she asked whether her ass was getting too fat, and the other question was forgotten. When we came back to the table, Eddie was gone, and Steve and Greg were talking about a new summer intern on the city desk.

"What a piece! I hear she goes to Sarah Lawrence. Akelroyd's already putting the move on. I think I'll head him off."

"You stay away from her, Swenson. She's a nice girl, very sensitive."

"I thought you were living with somebody, Figland. Listen, I'm willing to share a Sarah Lawrence girl. We'll take her out to lunch together. How's that?"

"You won't get to first base, Swenson. She's a virgin."

"Who told you that?"

"She did. She heard Ron talking to me about the piece on new life styles. But I shouldn't have told you. She doesn't want it known. They're ashamed of being virgins now—isn't that terrible!"

"Fuck it. At Sarah Lawrence they've gotta be emotionally re-tarded. Shit! You ruined my day, Figland. I can't take a virgin."

"You're so full of shit, Swenson! You wouldn't get to first base."

"Will you two stop that? Let's get the check. I have to split."

"Relax, Susan. Ron won't be back for another hour."

"I have to do my expense accounts."

"Yeah, me too. I'm six months behind."

"Six months! How can you remember—"

"He doesn't remember. He makes it up. They don't ask for receipts unless you spend over twenty-five dollars in one sitting. All my lunches cost between twenty-three seventy-five and twenty-four ninety."

"You charge your own lunch?"

"Strictly with sources, stupid. Sarah, don't you know anything?"

Greg showed me his expense form later in the week. He had charged the Fleur-de-Lis lunch to the paper, putting down the mayor's press secretary as his luncheon guest. He advised me to fill out my forms every Friday, because "budget types like regularity."

"How do you get away with it, Greg?" I asked.

"Who's gonna worry about a lousy twenty-four fifty-six? Listen, that's cheap. You gotta always make it so it looks like you're down to-the-penny accurate, see. Why would a guy lie about six pennies?"

"What if the mayor's press secretary finds out?"

"You think he's gonna fuck me over?"

"No, I guess not. But I can't—"

"Of course you can't, stupid! You can't use anybody yet! All you got is taxis."

And so I was broken in. After that, I did become one of them, at least in a lunch-eating sense. But taking the many hours to eat lunch with them did not bring me any closer to understanding how they did their jobs. When they weren't talking about food or clothes or cars or getting laid, they bitched about Akelroyd, the front page stories, and the editors, and before long I became aware—though I still had not learned how to get to City Hall on the subway or who knew what was what down there—that the rivalry between the National Desk and the City Desk knew no bounds and that this was the underlying drama of all the other craziness in the newsroom.

The rivalry was really only between Ron and Dixby, but it involved everybody else and could extend around the globe to Peking and beyond. As a matter of fact, Ron and Dixby had had a battle royal when Nixon went to China, with Ron arguing that two or three of his top reporters ought to go along to report on urban living under Chinese communism and Dixby arguing that five or ten of his top reporters ought to get the White-House-in-absentia angle, which made Ron up his ante to five or ten reporters to match National. The Foreign Desk already had three reporters poised for the trip, men who had been studying Chinese for the previous half century and waiting for this historic moment to crown their careers. Clarence Swope, the mild-mannered foreign editor who had come to *The Newspaper* from *Worldview Quarterly,* was not equal to the fight, and so one of his China experts got bumped for Vincent Akelroyd and a second of them was made to do legwork in the Peking Palace of Justice for a National Desk man who wrote the Life in China series. The bumped China scholar resigned from *The Newspaper* with a broken heart and sought to mend it in the CIA, where, some said, he was able to have Vincent Akelroyd listed as a possible "enemy agent," which made Akelroyd's stock go way up eventually, although at first it made Gil nervous. The tentative "enemy agent" listing was publicly revealed during the post-Watergate disclosures of government spying on private citizens. Akelroyd then got himself on several talk shows, where he quickly elevated himself to membership on Nixon's Enemies List and won a book contract and the metropolitan column in *The Newspaper*.

My lunchmates said the Peking episode had signaled Clarence Swope's decline. It revealed he was not tough enough, not a fighter, and when word got around that a man on his level was not a fighter, his authority drifted away from him mysteriously, like the popularity of a movie star who is rumored to be happily married for too many years. This ephemeral process was nonetheless real and potent, my sources said, and soon Clarence Swope was having difficulty getting the man in Rio to rouse himself from his beach pallet to go look for revolutions in the Brazilian hinterland. The Paris bureau chief began taking off afternoons to go to the movies, and the man in Bonn assigned himself to spend a month in Amsterdam a week before two national news weeklies had the German chancellor on the cover.

By the time I got to the paper, everybody knew, in the ineluctable way that everybody around an office knows the exact coordinates of bosses' fates, Clarence Swope was on his way out. He wasn't even playing in the hot competition of the five o'clock front page story conference, much less during the rest of the twenty-four hours, when both Ron and Dixby were hatching devious schemes to foil each other, steal each other's sources and best reporters and access to Gil Foley. Ron had the edge over Dixby in personal intimacy with Foley, and he did not hesitate to call the editor at his home at four in the morning, when he knew Foley would be glad to talk to someone, anyone, who was awake. Ron also frequently invited the Foleys to dinner and shamelessly called Foley his "best friend" and "the only man I've ever loved."

Willard Dixby could not bring himself to make such declarations, but he flattered Foley in his own fashion, courting him at lunch with quotations from Catullus and Petrarch and Cicero—Akelroyd had heard him do this—used in such a way as to imply that Foley was one of history's greats. Foley liked Dixby's extravagant Southern drawl and his richly hyperbolic praise. But no one knew how deep this liking went, because Dixby's real attraction, his ace in the hole with Foley, was his friendship with the young publisher William James Kleinfreude III. Dixby could let it drop into the conversation once in a while that he had yesterday told "Bill" what he was today telling Foley, and that was enough.

Dixby had come to *The Newspaper* through Kleinfreude. It was after the publisher had gone on a tour of *The Newspaper*'s Southern holdings, one of which Dixby was then running, a smallish daily in Greensboro, North Carolina. The two men had hit it off immediately. Dixby took Kleinfreude on a bar crawl with some local coeds. The publisher came back up North telling everyone Willard

Dixby was the best newsman in the country. About a week later, Dixby showed up in the newsroom and was made assistant to the national editor. I don't know what happened to that poor guy. Dixby took over his job six months later, which was about four years before I got to *The Newspaper*, and ever since then, Gilbert Foley had been afraid to pose Ron's name for the job of editor, even though he wanted to, or told Ron he wanted to, before he retired.

I couldn't understand this part of the story. I asked Greg why Foley didn't just speak up, if that was what he wanted to do.

"Don't be stupid, Sarah!" Greg said. "Gil's gotta know Kleinfreude's gonna say yes before he asks. There's no asking again."

"Why not?" I asked. Greg said if I didn't know, he couldn't explain.

Eddie Schwartz said he thought Foley was beginning to have his doubts about Ron and might be secretly drifting toward Dixby. There were certain signs. The City Desk expense budget had been cut, and Ron's private office had been painted after Dixby's. Eddie said the Feminist Faction was an embarrassment to the paper and Foley probably thought Ron should never have allowed it to be formed. No one on the national staff had joined it. Then, too, Ron had seemed more nervous lately about stories that the publisher's mother read. Eddie said he had made Figland rewrite a piece on penthouse gardening six times and had assigned Eddie to do a three-column feature on the cancer-causing ingredients in canned dog food. Mrs. Kleinfreude kept a large penthouse garden, and she loved small dogs. She had sent Eddie a note of praise for his dog food exposé. When Eddie showed it to Ron, Ron said he was going to put the piece up for a Pulitzer nomination.

But meanwhile Dixby was said to be growing ever closer to the publisher through methods that had worked in Greensboro, and Ron was growing more frantic. Ron had got it into his head that the showdown would come at the Democratic convention in August, and because he had got that into his head, Dixby had also, or so everybody concluded from the intensely wary way he regarded Ron's intense interest in the convention. Dixby had already reserved sixty rooms at the Hotel St. Regis for convention week. Ron had asked the Democratic National Committee to give sixty press credentials to the City Cesk. *The Newspaper* usually got convention credentials for only forty reporters. Something had to give. Eddie said we should all arrange to be on vacation at convention time, because the newsroom was going to be "like a lot of hot shit between two fans."

# XII

Of course, in the beginning all that stuff about Ron and Dixby and Foley and the publisher went in one ear and out the other. My mind was too full of worries about my own situation to make room for matters of such distant meaning. If I had not crammed for exams at Radcliffe, I would have been scared I was losing my mind. Too much detail stuffed into the brain during a short space of time can make you temporarily insane, I had discovered one day after a grueling Shakespeare exam (preceded by forty-eight hours' sleepless drilling in the beauteous iambics), when I'd emerged wearing my nightgown over my blue jeans and was dispossessed of the memory of the route back to my dorm. Similar lapses would overtake me now as I rode back uptown from the State Comptroller's Office for Auditing New York City with my lap buried under five pounds of freshly minted audit reports that told, in a language alien to English majors, the story of New York's indebtedness. Or perhaps it was not the words so much as the ungraspable vastness of a two-billion-dollar debt that kept eluding me. I would sit on the jiggling train with the comptroller's summary report on top of the pile, reading his statistical jargon with such doomed and hopeless concentration that I would fail to notice the Times Square stop or indeed Columbus Circle, and ride all the way to Seventy-second Street, with my eyes moving over and over the same paragraph, which contained a riddle about the union pension funds and the "moratorium" on city bonds. During the return ride, I would begin to write my own tentative summary of the comptroller's summary, and the word "comptroller" would come out "controller" and would later be pounced on by Jess Flicker and his Mafia of copy editors, who would all then fail to notice I had written "indebtedness" where I should have written "indemnification."

I really was hopeless on the fiscal stories, and my confusion one night over a certain Sanitation Department cost productiveness analysis was so complete that when the telephone on my desk rang, I did not hear it. Or rather did not locate it as a thing in my range of reality until Greg yelled:

"Sarah, pick up your stupid phone!"

I stuck the receiver between my left shoulder and my left ear and continued typing, while a voice said:

"Sarah, is that you?"

"Umm," I said.

"Kevin here," he said.

"Kevin who?" I said.

"Whadda you mean, Kevin who? Knock off the fucking typing, you bitch!"

He promptly hung up on me, and I saw that I had written: "Sanitation Defartment man hours."

"MAKEPEACE, ARE YOU WRITING FOR TONIGHT OR WHAT?" Flicker yelled over the loudspeaker.

It wasn't yet "night" as normal people think of the interval, but "night" in the newspaper sense, that time approaching deadline when the next morning's edition would be "put to bed." I suppose the clock said six, and outside the building the streets were still brilliant with June sunlight. But we sat under fluorescent lights at that hour, writing "yesterday" every time we referred to today, one of the many cheating illusions we kept up to make our readers feel as though the voice that spoke to them under our by-lines was right there and up to the minute, not fourteen hours' distance away. Around me were the sounds of the many other feverish participants in the collective sham, pounding away at typewriters and swearing in the adrenalated din which was the only sound in the world that could cure Steve Figland's writer's block.

My telephone rang again, and as I picked it up, Flicker appeared wild-eyed at my desk, shouting, "Sarah, where's your next take?"

"Who's that creep?" Kevin shouted in my other ear, and next found himself talking to Flicker on my phone while I resumed typing.

"He says," Flicker told me, a sort of bemused calm settling over him for a moment, "he will see you Saturday night."

Flicker put down the phone, looked at the page in my typewriter, ripped it off the roller, and ran back with it to his desk.

"Sanitation Defartment" appeared twice in *The Newspaper* the next morning.

Kevin called me later that evening to ask whether I was seeing another man named Kevin. Of course, I wasn't, but it took me a while to persuade him of that. People outside *The Newspaper* didn't understand what happened to us in the newsroom.

But then, I didn't need a psychologist to tell me what it meant when I didn't recognize Kevin's voice on the phone. It *was* weird, even by newsroom standards. I knew his voice. But Kevin wasn't in my *plans*. I mean, I didn't have plans for myself, actually. I had worries about not having plans, and he figured very largely in what I wasn't planning, if you follow me.

I hadn't expected to hear from him again after that first night of unrecapturable sex, most especially not after he called his wife from my house. When he did phone me the next day to reserve Saturday night that first week, I was so frantic about the Red River Army story going wrong and so grateful for his cop knowledge that I passed up the opportunity to point out our spiritual incompatibility. Asking about his wife was not the point, but at the time it did not seem appropriate to get him into an in-depth discussion of his *values* or his being a cop, since all we had had was a one-night stand. And I was sure that a two-night stand was all he had in mind, that he wanted to come back only one more time to be able to tell the boys in the station house that there was a woman he could make have four orgasms in a row. It was the sort of thing a man might not want to boast about unless he had made it happen more than once, had, so to speak, tested the mechanism. I could understand that. If there had been a station house for me to go boast in where I could be sure it would get back to Doris Munster, I wouldn't have minded letting it out that I had had four orgasms in one sitting, or whatever you called a single session of sex. Maybe the number was five. I couldn't be sure. This competitiveness in the area of orgasms was something new to me, and I was a little ashamed of it, though not enough to stop gloating inwardly over my newly discovered potential. Don't forget that *The Evil Eye* had branded me as a Judas of the Women's Movement, and even before that, Doris had come down on me with her righteous rap about earning my stripes in the struggle. Well, orgasms were pretty central to the whole gestalt of feminism. Why shouldn't I pin a little medal on myself?

On the other hand, Kevin was a cop and so a priori wrong for Movement sexual partnership, a tainted vehicle for my liberation, tainted in so many ways I couldn't list them all, but the sum total of them filling me with shame and self-loathing at least equal to the pleasure of the orgasms. Every Sunday morning I would promise myself that I would not see him again, and every Saturday afternoon I thought I should tell him to his face, and then when he came through the door I thought I should tell him later, but when he put his arms out to me I thought: *This may be our last time, he could be shot,* and took his warm crooked kiss and was lost.

I really mean lost. He made me feel out of kilter with myself,

88

and I was sure I would never have gone to bed with him in the first place if I had not suffered the series of shocks that began with my arrest in East Harlem and was continuing daily with the many detonations of the newsroom. All these shocks I blamed somehow on the Women's Movement, because without the Movement, I would never have tried to circulate sex books among the virgins of East 118th Street and so would never have met Ron Millstein or been hired by *The Newspaper*, with no place else to go, and it was the nerve-racking *Newspaper* job that had shaken my screws loose so badly that I betrayed all my counterculture idols in the arms of a cop. No self-respecting sixties lover could knowingly go to bed with a cop and still have the same *inner definition* as a Flower Child. But then, my whole inner definition perhaps went out the window when I heard Gilbert Foley say twenty-one thousand a year, and now it was becoming a regular thing that Kevin would reserve my Saturday nights while I would keep thinking each one should be the last and meanwhile he would keep thinking each one should be the last because he was also not without self-doubts, and we were both growing fonder of one another than he or I or his psychotherapist thought we ought to be.

Kevin's therapist, amazingly enough, provided the first real bridge between us, while also adding to my catalogue of worries. Kevin said he had been startled when I guessed from one remark that he was seeing a head doctor. He would not have been had he known how steeped I was in the language of shrinks and of those shrunken, how it was a dead giveaway to me to hear the word "judgment" in connection with the process of falling in love. But he didn't know that then, and my guess made him think I must be really insightful. That, not my proud parade of orgasms, was what had made him want to see me again. Multiple orgasms, he unkindly told me during a late-night intermission, were very common among women a little older than I. The topic did not much interest him. Dr. Festniss did.

The opportunity to discuss Dr. Festniss with someone other than his wife was a thing he had been yearning for for months before he spotted me taking notes on the remarks of a Times Square rapist, although he did not then connect me with the yearning. He said the sight of me in my bright yellow dress at first only filled him with dread for the future of his Women Alive investigation, because from a distance I looked as young and stupid as any rape-baiting college girl out doing a sociology paper on Times Square might look. He thought if I were killed it would cause a summer-long disruption of routine in the precinct, because nice white girls' murders always did. He and his partners would be forced to abandon their three-year struggle to nail the mobsters who owned Women Alive, and twenty other topless joints, and half the state of New Jersey, to search for my killer, who would never be found. After he had walked up to me, and seen that I wasn't "half bad-looking" or so young, he had decided to try to pick me up. He lost his nerve, he said, when he heard I had gone to Radcliffe. Somebody had told him Radcliffe girls don't like sex! He really had asked for my phone number just in case Batman's most recent victim would talk to me. There was no other reason—then.

But he had at least eight more hours in Women Alive that day, and the place made him terribly horny. He wasn't sleeping with his wife, and he dared not risk making it with one of the whores in Women Alive, though they often offered their bodies as "tips" for the little favors he did for them—the six-packs of beer and the cigarette cartons he brought them between their "acts." "You've got no idea how hard it is to find a nice broad in my work," he said. So he had recently gone back to the habits of his boyhood, sneaking miserable time with himself in the bathroom, while making dutiful observations of his fantasies all the while for Dr. Festniss's edification.

"You looked too skinny," he said on our third Saturday night. "That dress doesn't do much for you." But I was the first "reasonable" broad he had met in a year, he told me tactlessly, having picked up the habit of tactless honesty in his sessions with the doctor. So it might have been Jenny Locke or Susan Braithwaite who caught his eye or lovely Flicka Poinsby, yes, and Flicka was stricken enough, downcast enough, to have gone to Seymour's Deli with him. She was gorgeous and shapely, I thought jealously, as I listened to him telling me how slowly my own flat-chested body had worked its way into his desires. Not until he finished work had he actually thought of coming downtown to see me. He had showered at the precinct, but he always did that after work. He had showered and called a friend in night court to see whether I had an arrest record. *Then* he got the hots for me.

I was right in thinking he had come for a one-night stand and right in perceiving that he had reconsidered in the doorway. It was still going to be a one-night stand until I guessed about the therapist. Kevin hadn't told anyone except his wife that he was going to Dr. Festniss, and she alternately said she didn't want to hear a thing about his therapy and tried to pry out of him every single thing he said about her in the doctor's office. She was the one who had sug gested that he go to Dr. Festniss in the first place, because Kevin couldn't figure out what to do about his marriage. But the doctor didn't think the marriage was Kevin's problem. The doctor wouldn't say what he thought Kevin's problem *was*, though, and Kevin spent the therapy sessions in a guessing game, asking Dr. Festniss, "Am I getting warm? Am I getting warm?" each time he came up with a new theory about himself.

"I think I've got Approach-Avoidance Syndrome," he told me during our fourth Saturday night together.

"Where'd you get that idea? Are you reading psych books?"

"Well, this one. It's supposed to be the basic Psych One text-book. They use it at John Jay."

Kevin was studying management techniques at John Jay College of Criminal Justice.

"And you're reading the chapter on Approach-Avoidance Syndrome," I said.

"I finished it a couple of weeks ago."

"Why don't you read about hysterical paralysis? That would help you out with Dr. Festniss. You could just lie there in his office and say nothing at all."

"I've read about that. It doesn't apply. It's a women's disease."

"Well, then try the chapter on paranoid schizophrenia."

"Come on, Sarah!"

"No shit, Kevin. You might discover that Dr. Festniss doesn't *want* you to reach a decision about your marriage, not ever, that he only wants to rob you blind for the next fifty years and torment you with secret techniques to make you hear voices telling you to kill your wife, which will drive you really crazy, see, and you'll have to make more appointments with Dr. Festniss and pay more money and hear more voices until you get so crazy and destitute that your wife runs off with a rich doctor—with Dr. Festniss!"

"Dr. Festniss thinks you're threatened by my treatment," Kevin said, licking the lobe of the ear that had failed to recognize his voice on the phone.

"Dr. Festniss didn't go to school all those years for nothing. I'm threatened by the whole idea of you—your gun, your handcuffs, your wife, your John Jay College of Criminal Justice classes, not to mention the guy who charges you fifty dollars an hour to ask you what it's like to go to bed with me!"

"He doesn't ask me. I happen to think it's relevant information."

If you think Kevin didn't talk like a cop, you don't know what cops were getting into at that time in New York. I didn't know until

I heard Kevin going on about his "anomie" and his "existential con-fusion." And he said he wasn't the only one who talked like that. He said there were plenty of cops taking graduate courses, turning into these squad car intellectuals who debated the "relevance" of the criminal justice system for the "urban underclass." They weren't the dumbbell Officer Krupke types anymore, who'd hit you over the head and ask questions later. They were tormented, sensitive men, to hear Kevin tell it, and they saw themselves as "guardians of a disintegrating social order." They were getting too well educated to fit the image I had of them as bigoted Northern rednecks who would bash my head in for shouting "Peace now!" Kevin said they were no longer gung ho on the Vietnam War, which was a dead issue any-way, and that plenty of them smoked pot and liked the Beatles and could talk jive just as well as the hippest Harlem purse snatcher, and he said they were all fucked up about what they were doing, and lots of them went to shrinks.

Not that he talked about Dr. Festniss in Midtown South, his precinct, which was why he had to talk to me about him, and mess up my mind with all his revelations of vulnerability, of uncoplike humanity and just downright lovable fucked-upness of a kind I could understand, making me possibly close to thinking I'd like to live with him, a mind-blowing incongruity I did not need at that time, with all the other disturbances to my equilibrium. And so I attacked Dr. Festniss, who should have been able to keep Kevin together, cop-whole, not let him fumble around in the dark with me, looking for his own inner definition. And Kevin liked my attacks on Dr. Festniss because he secretly hated the doctor's interminable refusal to tell him what was wrong with him, and it really looked as though Kevin's therapy might be causing us to fall in love.

I had this fantasy that I was going to meet Dr. Festniss one night at a dinner party at Roger and Ellie's house, only he wasn't going to realize I was the Sarah his patient was banging every Saturday night, and so he would tell the assembled group all about me and my resistance to his patient's therapy while I was sitting right there, and he'd come up with a theory that all cops were latent homosex-uals who had to find women of probably similar psychic makeup who could perform acts of hysterically exaggerated sexual response in a mutual symbiosis of compensation behavior. "But what does she do to resist you, this girlfriend?" one of the dinner guests would ask. "She cracks dumb jokes, mocks the process," he would say, at which point Ellie and Roger would steal their eyes over to me, and Ellie would ask Dr. Festniss, "What does she do for a living?"

"She's a newspaper reporter," Dr. Festniss would say, and Ellie would elbow Roger, and Roger would pompously clear his throat before turning to me to say, "Perhaps you can shed some light on this case, Sarah."

# XIII

Roger and Ellie had indeed held such dinner parties for all their shrink friends, and the shrink friends all talked about their patients' love affairs and helped each other diagnose them.

Roger and Ellie had made a smug marriage out of their psychiatric connection, and they now saw psychiatry as no mere tool for aiding the sick but as the holy grail itself, the salvation of the world. Roger thought that everybody should be given psychotherapy as automatically as children were taught to read in the "developed nations." He had submitted a lengthy paper on this subject to *Worldview Quarterly*. *Worldview*, I was happy to learn, rejected the manuscript. But Roger didn't let this discourage him. He said Freud's ideas, too, had been very unpopular in the beginning.

At his dinner parties, Roger liked to impress his guests with his penetrating psychoanalytic insights about world leaders, whose infancies he said he could deduce from studying their pictures in *Time* magazine, and he usually had a new one figured out at each dinner party. Idi Amin came in for a heavy diagnosis, as did Henry Kissinger and the ever-fascinating Richard Nixon. I always enjoyed asking Roger what had gone wrong with Nixon's therapy. It was Roger's contention that psychotherapy for world leaders could prevent wars and—you name it—clear up international trade disputes, stop cannibalism, anti-Semitism, totalitarianism, anything big enough for the Einstein dinner table. But Roger couldn't make up his mind about Nixon, about whether he had or had not been properly analyzed. Sometimes he said recognizing Red China had been "a transcendent victory over paranoia," but other times he said Nixon's doctor was a "neurotic quack," or the Plumbers would never have been hired. The neurotic quack bit was risky around me,

**93**

though, as it gave me the opening to ask who should analyze the analysts in his ideal world and whether people in it would have to get certificates of sanity to vote and so on.

Roger wasn't such a bad guy. He was just a little nuts, and he played the role of doctor to the hilt, stroking his beard, crinkling up his eyes, and asking "How do you feel about that?" when you'd just said it was raining outside. If he hadn't married my best friend, I don't think I would have minded him at all. But his influence on Ellie was awful.

Back when we were in college, Ellie was a spunky radical. She gave speeches for SDS. She was bright and very up on radical literature, able to throw in the Hegelian stuff, dialectical materialism, and the capitalist menace, but she had this tough Brooklyn manner that made the abstractions seem vivid, and she used the word "motherfucker" as noun, verb, adjective, and adverb. She had real gusto. When I met her there wasn't a Harvard dean who did not tremble before her hot, quick, staccato declarations. She was one of the most effective SDS speakers on campus, in spite of the painful way her voice came through an amplifying system. But the cool, handsome preppies at Columbia Law School didn't like her rough Brooklyn style, and then Roger got hold of her and began to mold her into something else. She told me he had made her aware of her "repressed femininity," and she soon began speaking more slowly and without the "motherfucker"s. After she moved in with Roger and finished law school, she went to work for the Legal Aid Society, where at first she had to be prodded to speak loudly enough for the judges to hear her. By the time I took the job on *The Newspaper*, she had converted completely to Roger's beliefs and was enrolled in night classes in psychology at the New School for Social Research.

It happened that my third week at *The Newspaper* coincided with her decision to start pleading all her Legal Aid clients not guilty by reason of insanity. Most of her clients were young blacks and Puerto Ricans, like Jesus and Fredo, for whom crime was an admired form of self-realization. They resented being called insane. They all asked to have Ellie removed from their cases, though this was not done at first, but eventually the judges and the Legal Aid higher-ups began to wonder why *all* of Ellie Einstein's clients were insane. The administrative judge called the head of Legal Aid to ask whether he had created a bureau for insanity pleas. Ellie was summoned and given a stern warning. She ignored it, continued to plead her clients insane, and found that the judges now listened to her clients when they asked to have "this weirdo" removed from their cases. In two days, Ellie lost all her clients. She was called in again and given a final warning.

Both Ellie and Roger had called me on deadline every day of the week until Friday. Each day I had said I couldn't talk. Finally, on Friday morning after she got her final warning, Ellie caught me in a moment of relative calm.

She wanted me to write about her.

"I am forcing them to recognize that the so-called crime problem is a mental health problem, Sarah. This is important!"

"I can't write about it, Ellie."

"Why not? You're not afraid to, are you, Sarah? You're not intimidated because I told you about the administrative judge? *You* worked with sociopaths. You *know* I'm right!"

"If I write it, Ellie, everybody will think you're crazy. *I* think you're crazy."

"Crazy! You're calling *me* crazy!" she uttered, in a tone reminiscent of the old loudmouthed Ellie. "You are the most messed up person I know. Doris Munster told me what you did to her."

"Look, Ellie, I just think you're going about this in a crazy way. You can't expect— How do you know Doris?"

"Never mind how I know Doris. I'm going to lose my job, Sarah, and you don't care. You don't have any loyalty!"

"Wait a minute. I want to know how you know Doris, Ellie."

"It doesn't matter. I shouldn't have mentioned her."

"God, is she in your therapy group?"

Roger, who had of course cured her, always pointed out that the therapy group was part of Ellie's training in psychiatry.

"Sarah, I don't want to go into that. I shouldn't have—"

"That means I'm right. Oh, shit! What does Doris talk about? Does she think Oedipus was a woman?"

"Sarah, you know, you always give yourself away with those stupid jokes. You deny everything that is happening to you with a joke. You're not getting any younger, you know."

"What does that have to do with anything?"

"Roger says, and I agree with him, that ever since you got fired because of that stupid thing you did in East Harlem, you've been avoiding the guilt about it, and that's *dangerous*, Sarah. You can't go running away from yourself like this."

"Ellie, my boss is calling me," I said, and he truly was.

"Are you going to write about this situation, Sarah?"

"I told you, Ellie—"

"Because if you don't, it's criminal negligence, just criminal negligence, letting these sick people go to jail—"

"Ellie, calm down."

"Calm down. You want me to calm down when I'm about to lose my job because I'm doing my job? It's a fucking catch-22, Sarah. The system is crazy, but when you say that, people say you're crazy. Don't you *see?*"

"Yes, I see, Ellie, but I don't think you're going about tackling it in the right way."

"What is the right way? What about your stupid fucking sex books in East Harlem? What about that, huh? You wrote about that. You can write about it when it's *you* who's up against the system. But not when it's me! What's happened to you, Sarah? You used to care about the poor. Maybe Doris Munster is right about you. You sold out, you know that? You fucking sold out. And you'll pay for it. Roger says you're so guilty you can't stand yourself, and that's why you're avoiding me."

"Listen, Ellie, my boss is having fits," I said, although actually Ron seemed already to have forgotten about me. "I'm sorry if I upset you. I shouldn't have called you crazy. But listen, you don't like your job down there, anyway—"

"That's not the point—"

"So why not let Roger support you for a while?"

"Boy, have you changed!"

Not as much as you have, sister, I wanted to say, but she had hung up. She was really going bananas. Still, I shouldn't have called her crazy. I didn't mind her calling me a sellout. It kind of cleared the air. But having Ellie and Doris in the same therapy group! *That* could be trouble. Ellie knew that I had never worked on the *Crimson.* And now she was very mad at me. If only I hadn't called her crazy! Doris talked to Jenny. What if it got back to Jenny somehow that I hadn't worked on the *Crimson?* All because my roommate had to go marry that nerdy shrink who didn't like my cracks about Richard Nixon's therapy being such a big success.

You can begin to see why I liked to plant doubts in Kevin's mind about the goodwill of Dr. Festniss. The doctor was quite right in discerning the tones of a threatened person in my pillow talk. I was threatened with diagnosis from all sides!

The queer thing, meanwhile, was that each time somebody dumped on me for taking the *Newspaper* job, I got a little less negative with myself about the job, just like the way I seemed to want Kevin more each time I heard that Dr. Festniss disapproved of our being together too regularly.

My father had started calling me up about three times a week to tell me to quit *The Newspaper*, and he kept threatening to write a letter to the editor about me. He was the only one of all the people I knew who might have benefited from a bit of psychotherapy, as he had absolutely zilch insight into himself. He didn't know he was emotionally arrested, in a permanent state of adolescence. He didn't know people in Four Corners called him "Mister Makenoise" or that Noah and I used to warn our friends before we brought them home just to say they agreed with him, no matter what he said, since otherwise we'd never get away from the dinner table. My father was to pacifism what Roger was to psychiatry, and he had a few hundred other subjects up his sleeve when he ran out of steam on the subject of war—he had the CIA, the State Department, the FBI, the presidential seal, the congressional frank, chemical fertilizers, the Republican party, Christmas cards, nuclear power plants, reconstituted orange juice, Mormons, lipstick, Burger Kings, the Warren Commission, the automobile, amusement parks, AT&T, lawyers, funeral homes, insurance companies, x-rays, TV dinners, TV, Texans, winter road-salting, air conditioning, Hollywood, the Standard Oil Company, and the Four Corners town selectmen, all of which my father opposed in some form or fashion, his usual being the letters to Gilbert P. Foley, letters that had presumably been going to the bottom of the pile somewhere deep in the recesses of the *Newspaper* building for thirty years.

Surely Gilbert Foley couldn't be reading all his mail. Surely he couldn't have yet connected me with the man who wrote: "Sirs: I call your attention to a very grave situation in the state of Massachusetts which has gone unnoticed by your correspondents but which is apparent to any alert citizen who stands sentinel on his democratic rights, namely, the Massachusetts Health Commissioner's arbitrary ruling on water fluoridation. Gentlemen, it amounts to fluoridation without representation. . . ." Dad was not a right-winger, but he agreed with the right-wingers on the fluoridation issue and several other of his obsessions, as if in the twilight of his mind there lurked certain Jungian universals of the fear of chemistry which a right-wing Mormon could feel at home with. My brother and I might have killed him a few times after what he said about our teachers in school board meetings, but he stood only five feet two in his stocking feet, so it wouldn't have been a fair homicide. Noah and I were both tall. Dad said this proved he was tall in his genes too, and had had his growth stunted by the Dr. Meeker's Health Tonic his mother had forced him to drink as a boy, and perhaps this was so. In any case, Dr. Meeker's Health Tonic had started his chemophobia.

A psychiatrist could have argued that Noah committed symbolic patricide when he chose a career in organic chemistry and that my going to work for *The Newspaper* was also doing abstract violence to my father, the five-foot-two King Laius of Four Corners, Mass., but I thought only Noah could be blamed. He had *chosen* his calling. Mine had chosen me, and I was as helpless and overwhelmed by it as a little cork on the high seas. I did wish Dad could understand that. Because the more he badgered me, the longer he kept at me to quit *The Newspaper,* the more I wanted to resist him. This *was* crazy, but the harder Dad pushed me to quit, the more reasonable it seemed to me that I should stay. And if in the beginning I just took it day by day, not really committed to it in my heart of hearts, not really believing Ron when he said I had the makings of a great reporter, pretty soon I was telling myself I might actually get the hang of it, I might *become* a great reporter, which might not be such a bad thing, since great reporters could make lots of money off the movie rights to their lives. It was all very well for my father to be a purist on his inherited money, but he didn't have enough to support me in any zone of my sixties zeitgeist like Aspen or Greenwich Village. "You could live very cheaply in Four Corners, you know, Sarah," he had actually suggested during our last argument. Live in Four Corners! Me? After I struggled so hard to get out of it? Wild horses couldn't keep me there! How would I get laid in Four Corners? Who would I get high with? It was unthinkable that I should go *live* there!

But when Dad put it to me so plainly as, like, the *alternative* to working for *The Newspaper,* I suddenly knew I *wanted* to work for *The Newspaper,* that there was no better place to be working, because every day on the job something new could happen, I might meet a new man or discover a new Watergate and make millions on the subsidiary rights and be free to live anywhere, anywhere but Four Corners! The thing with Kevin wouldn't last forever, I told myself, and I had to look after my future. If only Ellie, Roger, Kevin, Dr. Festniss, Doris Munster, or my father did not ruin it for me.

But I nearly ruined it myself, as things turned out, with a slight misreading of a budget line in one of those state comptroller's audit reports I hefted uptown on a sultry June morning.

# XIV

The report was called "Unrealized Capital Increments in the New York City Eleemosynary Trusts," which could be translated: "Money the city has been sitting on." I wrote this and got into a heated discussion with the copy editors about the difference between a wit and a wise guy. They changed "Money the city has been sitting on" to "Unspent interest in city capital trust fund accounts." In any case, the report listed one hundred fifty charitable trusts that rich people had given to the city over the years to support various weird or worthy things, such as the room full of books about tobacco in the Public Library, the water plume in the East River, the Central Park Zoo, the collection of jawbones in the Museum of Natural History, and the weekly Hungarian culture hour on WNYC. The state comptroller had discovered that the interest in these trust accounts had been erroneously frozen by the city comptroller since the beginning of the city's fiscal crisis, thus for over a year. In that time, the trust funds had been accumulating interest, which in some cases amounted to millions of dollars. All the rich people's wills stipulated that the interest was to be spent yearly. The state comptroller said the city comptroller had violated his fiduciary trust in freezing the money, an understandable abuse of authority in those early days of near-default when it looked as though city bond holders might try to foreclose on the very bricks of City Hall. By some fluke in the law, though, the trust funds were exempt from city bond holders' claims.

My story simply explained what was in the state comptroller's report, and not once did I type the word "controller" where I meant "comptroller." I thought I had done a letter-perfect job. The next morning I got phone calls from the head of the Hungarian Cultural Union and from the chairman of the board of the Metropolitan Museum, both of whom thanked me for "saving" their outfits.

Ron summoned me up to his desk to pat me on the back. He said the story showed professional polish.

"It was upbeat, Sarah," he said. "We need more stories like that. We need to show people that this city isn't dying. Nobody's going to kill New York City, not while I'm the city editor of this paper!"

"Good point, Ron," Willie Crespi said. "Ron made that point to the publisher's mother this morning," Willie told me, nodding and firming his lips.

"I did, actually," Ron said. "And it was because of your story, Sarah. Mrs. Kleinfreude called me to tell me how much she liked it, and we both agreed there should be more upbeat news in the paper. She was very, very pleased, Sarah. Mrs. Kleinfreude thinks you saved the Central Park Zoo. You know, that's one of her great loves."

"You handled her beautifully, Ron," said Willie. "You really did. You should have heard him, Sarah. He was superb! I don't know how he gets away with it. Calling Mrs. Kleinfreude the queen of the jungle—"

"Oh, ho ho! She knew I was teasing!"

"That's why Ron is such a great city editor, because he has just the right touch with her. Frankly, Sarah, just between us and the four walls, Mrs. Kleinfreude goes a bit overboard about the zoo sometimes, and it does take someone with Ron's delicacy and tact to let her know in a gentle way that we have other things to cover, that we have a mission. Ron always puts it that way: we have a mission—"

"Mission, hell! I love this city! And so does Mrs. Kleinfreude," Ron exploded. "This morning she told me she was having a love affair with New York. Don't we all feel that way?"

"I couldn't have put it better," Willie said.

"You love New York, don't you, Sarah?" Ron asked me.

"Usually," I said.

"Oh, you love it all the time. That's why I hired you," he said. "I knew you couldn't be making a living on *The Evil Eye*, so why would you be staying around if you didn't love it here?"

"Exactly!" Willie said, grinning at me from between his hunched shoulders. The hospital stay had done nothing for him.

"Why don't we have a story about the zoo?" Ron said. "There should be a follow-up on the trust funds, and everybody likes the zoo. Sarah, call up the mayor's office and get them to tell you they won't be closing the zoo. We'll lead with the announcement. Yes, this could be a front-page story, an upbeat front-page story! And call Mrs. Heller, Sarah. And go up to the zoo and get some mothers and children to say how glad they are."

"Great idea, Ron!" Willie said.

"Get cracking, Sarah," Ron said.

I had no idea who Mrs. Heller was, but Greg quickly warned me that she was head of the zoo committee and "Mrs. Kleinfreude's best friend."

Vincent Akelroyd came stomping to his desk, which was two rows ahead of ours. He pulled out his chair so violently that it banged against the desk behind him.

"Vincent's upset," Greg said.

"What's wrong, Vinnie?" I called to him.

Akelroyd did not answer immediately. He threw open the top of his desk with a tremendous bang. We all had similar flip-top desks which were rigged with springs and levers that made the typewriter bounce up into place as the top was shoved down into a slot behind it. The rigging was dangerous and could take off a finger if one did not approach it with respect. To slam it around as Akelroyd had just done was a form of reckless abandon not usually seen in the newsroom until close to deadline.

"God damn!" he yelled.

"What's the matter, Vincent?" Greg asked him.

"Mushbrains," Akelroyd muttered through clenched teeth. "They are all mushbrains!"

"They must've killed his column," said Greg. "What'd you do, Vinnie, try to slip in another of those confessions-of-a-call-girl pieces? Vinnie thinks he's the Anthony Burgess of Times Square, Sarah."

"You are going to be out of business, Swenson," Vinnie said. He swung around in his chair. "There is no room for your *scandale* reportage in an *up*beat newspaper."

"Yeah, Ron's on a kick about being upbeat," I told Greg. "He asked me whether I loved New York."

"So? Write one of your columns about Liv Ullmann, Vinnie," Greg said loudly. "She loves New York."

"You asshole! Wait till Ron gets hold of you today," Vinnie said darkly. "How can you stand sitting next to him, Sarah? Does he ask you how to spell?"

My telephone rang. Akelroyd raised his eyebrows to show bored unconcern.

"The truth is our business," I said. "Makepeace here."

"Hello, Sarah, this is Jack Sharfblick. You remember, we met yesterday?"

"Oh, yes, of course I remember. You wrote the eleemosynary report. That was a good report. I could understand it."

"You wrote a nice story, Sarah. The boss was very pleased."

"I'm glad to hear that. You wanta tell my boss?"

"Uh, well, Sarah, actually there was one little thing I thought you might want to correct the next time you write about my area."

"Oh, what?"

"It was just a little thing, but I think you transposed a couple of figures. Well, one figure in that agate list at the end—you know, where you listed all the trust beneficiaries beside the dollar amounts of the increments?"

"Yes?"

"Well, you see where you've got the Central Park Zoo? Maybe you corrected this in the last edition, but anyway, you put ten million beside the zoo in my edition. Do you see it?"

"Yes, but—"

"I think you must have been looking at the Metropolitan figure when you typed that, because you typed ten million beside the zoo."

"Yes, I see, I did. But I've got ten million beside the Met too."

"I know. That's correct. It's just the zoo figure. That should be ten thousand."

"Oh."

"I'm sure it was just a typo," he said soothingly. "But I thought you'd want to know—for the record."

"Gee, thanks, Jack," I said.

"I just thought you'd want to know."

"*Now* what am I gonna do!" I cried as I hung up. Of all the mother-loving one hundred fifty figures to get wrong, I pick Mrs. Kleinfreude's zoo fund!

"What's the matter, sweetie?" Greg asked, cupping his own phone.

"Oh, nothing," I said. "I just messed up so badly I think I'll have to resign."

Greg told someone named Alex that he'd call him back.

I explained what I'd done.

"Yeah, you messed up good," he said. "Listen, you better just tell Ron what happened. He won't like it."

"He'll fire me."

"Don't be stupid! He can't fire you. He'll lose face with the Feminist Faction if he does that."

"I'm going to resign."

"Don't do that, Sarah. I'm telling you, Ron will just hit the ceiling and then maybe he'll put you on rewrite for a while."

"With Luddle?"

"Luddle's okay. Go on, tell him."

I walked over to the City Desk. Ron was on the phone, chatting away in high good humor. I stood near him trying to invent a convincing excuse.

"Oh, god, yes!" Ron was saying. "And that whipped cream! Positively obscene! Obscene!"

A memory of my father composing his letter on canned whipped cream flashed before my inward eye, and I had a sudden vision of the pile of his letters being dumped on Ron's desk by Freddie—

"Hi, Sarah. Can I help you?" Willie asked me. "Shouldn't you be going up to the zoo?"

"I have to talk to Ron," I said.

"Ron's busy," Willie said.

"Sarah, Sarah," Ron said, "this is Mrs. Heller. I'll let you talk to her. She's very excited about your story, Sarah. Maureen, she's standing right beside me," he said into the phone. "I'll put her on."

"Hello, Mrs. Heller," I said hopelessly.

"Hello, Sarah! I hope you're free for lunch. I've just been singing your praises to Ron. That was a wonderful story you did, dear!"

"Well, there was a slight problem with it, um, a typo, Mrs. Heller, which—"

"Oh, you can tell me all about it over lunch, Sarah, dear. Have you ever been to '21'?"

"No."

"Good, then it will be an adventure for you. Can you meet me there in half an hour?"

"Um, well, I'm supposed to go to the zoo—"

"Does she want to meet you?" Ron said. "Don't worry about the zoo!"

"Yes, for lunch," I said to Ron.

"Oh, don't worry about the zoo," he said. "This is *much* more important! Mrs. Heller comes first."

"Well, Ron says you come first," I said into the phone. Ron nodded and grinned.

"Yes, he's terribly frightened of me," said Mrs. Heller. "Isn't it wonderful!"

"Right, Mrs. Heller," I said.

"Call me Maureen, dear."

"By the way, where is the '21' Club?"

Ron shook his head so fast his chins quivered.

"You sweet child!" Mrs. Heller trilled. "It's on Fifty-second Street between Fifth and Sixth. You can't miss it. You'll see ghastly statuettes of jockeys out front. Ta ta!"

"Sarah, Sarah, don't hang up!" Ron pleaded, reaching for the phone. But it was too late.

"Call her back! Freddie! Willie! How could you hang up like that, Sarah?"

"Ron," I said, "could I have a word with you, in private?"

"I don't have time, Sarah!" he snapped. "Can't you see I'm busy? Hurry up, Freddie!"

"The line's busy," Freddie said.

"Now you see what you've done, Sarah!" Ron shouted. "She called me, and you hang up!"

"Ron, I've really got to talk to you—"

"You'd better get to work, Sarah," Willie said, standing up to walk around behind Ron's simmering rotundity. Willie put his arm through mine and led me away.

"Leave him alone, Sarah. He'll get over it," Willie said. "What did you want to tell him?"

"Well, there was this typo in my story, Willie, which—well, typing a hundred fifty names and figures—"

"A typo! Jesus, Sarah, I'm glad you told me first. You're really going to have to learn to live with typos, Sarah. We have our priorities here."

I gave up then. I went to "21" cursing myself for my cowardice. When I arrived, I felt even worse. Mrs. Heller's kindly old face was radiant with the mistaken belief that her zoo had been saved.

"This will be fun, dear," she said. "We can celebrate. They make the best Bloody Marys here! Why don't we get a table upstairs. Then we can really talk."

When we were seated in a dark alcove with our Bloody Marys, Mrs. Heller raised her glass.

"Cheers!" she said, compelling me to do likewise.

"Now tell me," she said, "how long have you been at the paper, dear?"

"About a month."

"And do you like it? Well, you can't know that yet. Tell me what you think of Ron."

"It's a little hard to say. I've never met anyone like him before."

"Where are you from, Sarah?"

"A little town called Four Corners in southwestern Massachusetts."

"Near Great Barrington, isn't it? Yes, I know the town. Charming name. What does your father do?"

"He doesn't do anything, um, professionally. He writes lots of letters."

"Writes letters? He sounds odd."

"Actually he is odd. I mean, he's a very good citizen, you know, concerned with— Actually, Mrs. H—I mean, Maureen, my father is a crank."

"How delightful! But how does he make a living?"

"He inherited money from his father."

"Of course! Makepeace is an old banking name. And how did you come to work for *The Newspaper*, Sarah? You must be very clever."

"No—no, it was sort of an accident. I met Ron on a story I was doing for *The Evil Eye*, and he decided to hire me. Ron's like that, I guess—impetuous."

"Ron? Ron is quite insane, dear. Surely you know that!"

"Well, he's scatterbrained."

"Oh, this is terrible of me, getting you to talk about your boss. I forget what it's like to be under the thumb of . . . of . . . I am really quite spoiled. I've been filthy rich all my life, and I do try to make up for it a little, but I have often wished I had grown up without any money and learned to get by on my wits. You were very wise to get away from your family, dear. This is such a wonderful time for young women! Oh, I wish I were your age! Don't go getting married now and spoil it all. You can have such fun on *The Newspaper!*"

"I have to tell you I made an awful mistake in my story, and I don't think I will *be* on *The Newspaper* when Ron finds out!"

"I *know* about your mistake, dear! Don't be silly. Come, let's have another Bloody Mary. They're too delicious."

"You know? But the zoo, it won't—"

"That mistake is a little godsend for us. Where is that waiter? I always forget how slow they are upstairs. They get used to leaving men alone with their mistresses up here. Yoooohooo!" she called.

A waiter popped into view. She signaled for another round.

"There," she said, turning her happy gaze on me. "Now, what was I saying?"

"About the mistake."

"Oh, yes! I noticed it right away, you see, because of course I know how much interest we've got in that trust account. But I had an idea the mayor's office might not know. I called there this morning, and my little hunch was right. They haven't even *looked* at those trust accounts. So I told the young man who does cultural affairs—what's his name?—I told him we would sue if the money wasn't released right away, and he assured me there would be no need for a suit. They don't want any lawsuits on this, you see, Sarah, because there are too many little agencies just poised with their lawyers waiting to sue, but everyone has been afraid of how it would look, the bad public relations, suing the bankrupt city, you know, for the jawbone collection when they've been laying off policemen. Ah, his name's Albert Keene, the mayor's assistant for Cultural Affairs. He assured me that the money would go out today."

"But it's not there, the ten million," I said. "When he calls the bank, he'll find out."

"He won't call the bank. He will ask Budget to send us a check for perhaps the first five million. I think he said it would be five million."

"But where will he get it?"

"They have a general fund. Even with all those controls, they have plenty of loose money. We are going to get that check. And five million, Sarah, is going to save the zoo!"

"But eventually they'll find out. You'll have to pay it back or something."

"Sarah, dear, the mayor got a huge amount of negative mail when he announced he was going to close the zoo. I know exactly how much mail he got. Every schoolchild in the city sent him a letter. The mayor is not going to ask us to pay him back. He'll go to the Board of Estimate when the mistake is discovered, and they will quietly authorize an appropriation through the Parks Department budget."

"They can't do that anymore. The Financial Control Board—"

"The Control Board will approve it too. They are all politicians, my dear. No one who wants to survive in politics in this town will be caught dead hurting the zoo."

"But the mayor already—"

"He's learned his lesson. Believe me, Sarah. I have worked with politicians all my life. Shall we order lunch? They have wonderful steak tartare here, so good on a muggy day! Would you like to try it?"

But I did not believe her, and my appetite was spoiled by the gloomy, guilty knowledge that I would have to wreck her scheme later on. It was bad enough that I had made a huge error, but then to be drawn into a conspiracy to plunder the city by virtue of it—oh, I felt awful! Mrs. Heller was so happy! She didn't seem to have any morality at all. I almost envied her. She was babbling on about her days in Albany. I gathered her husband had been a big politician up there. She reminisced about how he had fooled the press, and she said Ron had been such an eager reporter, he printed anything Reginald Heller said to him on a slow news day.

"I think if Reggie had told Ron he made the grass grow on a Saturday afternoon, Ron would have written it," she said, "Saturday's such a slow news day—I'm sure you know. One weekend Reggie told Ron a shocking lie about how he single-handedly stopped the war between the Gallos and the Profacis. You're too young to remember that era, dear, but when my husband was governor—"

God, her husband was the late Governor Reginald Heller! And I had been about to ask her what her husband did!

"—in broad daylight all over Brooklyn, a ghastly business!" she was saying. "Of course, Reggie didn't have a thing to do with stopping it, not a *thing*. But he knew when the truce came because of the wiretaps, and he shamelessly told Ron he had negotiated it. I was afraid someone would contradict him, but Reggie told me no one would dare to.

"He said, 'You think Joe Profaci's going to call up Ron Millstein?' If Reggie could only see what his exclusives did for Ron's career! I think he would be pleased. He liked Ron. Do you like him, Sarah?"

"Yes, I guess I do," I said.

"That's good," she said. "You wouldn't want to work for a man you didn't like. Especially not a man like Ron. So impossible! Some people have difficulty with him, you know. The publisher thinks he's way too fat."

She insisted on paying for the lunch, which was against the rules at *The Newspaper* and another burden on my conscience as I walked back down through the sultry air, planning to tell all to Ron and then resign. Ron should know that the zoo committee was trying to pull a fast one on the city. At least I could come clean on that before I left for god knows what. Waiting on tables? What if I mixed up numbers there too? Anyway, I positively was not cut out for dealing with the high and the mighty. How could you ever know when they were lying?

Strengthened by the Bloody Marys, I marched straight up to Ron.

"Hello, Sarah," he said pleasantly. "We have some great pictures of the zoo. How'd your lunch go?"

"Ron," I said, "I have to talk to you right now. In your office."

"There isn't time, Sarah. You have to write your story. We have a statement from the mayor's office. It's on your desk."

"A statement from the mayor's office?"

"Yes. Simon announced he's not closing the zoo, and the zoo committee is getting a check for five million this afternoon."

"We have to *stop* this!"

"Stop what? What's the matter with you?"

"Ron, could we *please* go into your office? I want to talk to you alone!"

He would not sit down in there. He heard me out standing up.

". . . And so you see, Ron," I finished up, "it's all a huge mistake, one mistake on top of another. The zoo is not saved. I think I should resign."

"But the zoo *is* saved!" he said. "Don't be silly! I wouldn't think of letting you resign! I forbid you to resign!"

"But, Ron! The whole thing is my fault. It's a gigantic fraud on the taxpayers."

"Don't be so neurotic, Sarah! You're exaggerating. Besides, the taxpayers want that zoo. There was a huge letter campaign. Relax, Sarah. I shouldn't have snapped at you this morning. I'm sorry about that. There, I apologized. Do you feel better?"

"Well, I still feel terrible about the zoo. Everyone's going to be so disappointed. Mrs. Kleinfreude—"

"What are you talking about? The zoo's getting five million dollars."

"But I just explained—"

"I know what you explained, and you're never to tell anyone what you just told me, understand?"

"You mean you don't want me to write the true story?"

"Of course I want you to write the *true* story, Sarah! What Mrs. Heller told you was *off the record!* I'm sure I told you that before you went out to lunch. We never print off-the-record material. Never. Mrs. Heller never talks on the record. So forget what you heard. We have it on the record that the zoo is getting a check for five million dollars."

It turned out that the mayor's office had discovered my error after Mrs. Heller's call that morning. The mayor, however, had indeed been looking for a way to reverse himself on the zoo, and the promise to Mrs. Heller became the excuse. He found an extra five million in the Parks Department budget and gleefully took all the credit himself, thereby upstaging the state comptroller and getting his picture on the front page of *The Newspaper*. It showed him holding hands with Patty Cake the gorilla. My story ran under the picture.

No more was said by Ron or by me about the near fraud we committed, but from that day forward, Ron began to seem a little wary of me. He still occasionally invited me to go for a drink at Sardi's and called me "a great reporter" in front of the idiots, but now when he thought of it, on his second drink, he would screw up his eyes and say to me, "I can't believe you didn't know where the '21' Club is."

# XV

Then, unaccountably, Ron sent me down to City Hall. A man in the bureau was going on vacation. I say unaccountably because Ron had plenty of other, more experienced hands to choose from on the Metro staff and because Greg Swenson, who claimed never to be taken by surprise by anything Ron did, nearly ran over his new squash racquet when he heard the news.

"Ron's sending *you* to City *Hall?*" he said, rising in his chair and wildly bugging out his eyes. His chair rolled around over the flimsy cardboard box from Taiwan Traders.

"Look what you made me do!" he said. He leaped to one side and scooped up the box, hurriedly ripping it open. Seeing the racquet was unharmed, he kissed it. Then he sat down again, holding the beloved object on his lap.

"You can't leave me, Sarah," he said in his normal voice. "We haven't gone to bed yet." He gave me his gap-toothed smile.

"It's only for five weeks, Greg. Somebody's going on vacation."

"Who is?"

"Someone named Norman."

"Not Norman Kroll? The swing man. Jesus, Sarah, he's been there for thirty years! You can't fill in for him! Why didn't Ron pick

**109**

somebody who's been there before, knows the ropes? I mean, Sarah, no offense, kid, but you'll be a disaster. What the hell is Ron doing? He can't send me because Lipschitz hates my guts. But Eddie or Steve or even Jenny's good at that stuff."

"Who's Lipschitz?"

"Who's Lipschitz? You don't know who Lipschitz is? Clive 'Turd Face' Lipschitz? He's the fucking bureau chief, Sarah!"

"Oh, that's right! I've seen his by-line."

"Get this, Akelroyd!" Greg called to the columnist, who was just then emerging from the men's room. "Ace Makepeace here is going to City Hall."

"You don't say!" Vinnie uttered. "Well, that's another thumb in Jenny's eye."

"Oh, sure, *that's* it!" Greg said.

"I don't see how—" I said.

"Because Jenny would be the natural one. She's done City Hall lots of times. Spent a year there, didn't she, Vin? For once you said something sensible, you pompous fart. Ron's gotta send a woman. It's gotta be that."

Actually, Ron had another reason for sending me to City Hall, but none of us guessed it then. Everyone assumed he was sticking it to Jenny. She was working at a desk in the back row of the rewrite "bank," the dunce seat of the room, typing up the Health Department's dirty-restaurants list. She was ostensibly being humbled, but the set of her jaw suggested there might be a flaw in the process. She had not spoken directly to me in the five weeks since I'd come to the paper. She had endurance. Though the others said she was prepared to forgive me if I should cross over to the Feminist Faction. She would always forgive a convert. I felt bad about her typing the dirty-restaurants list. Everybody said she was a top-grade reporter who didn't deserve the punishment she was getting, even though she could also be a pain in the ass and a first-class cunt, a metaphorical confusion that confused no one who had crossed her. It was ludicrous to think of me being somehow pitted against her. Yet people did see us as rivals. When people said Jenny was being discriminated against, they then looked at me accusingly, as if to say I was being discriminated for. Even Vincent Akelroyd, who thought feminism was the advance guard of Orwell's Anti-Sex Brigade, said Jenny's talents were being wasted, and he was not shy about telling me everyone thought my talents were being severely strained.

My reputation had preceded me down to City Hall, and an unfortunate little episode which occurred just after I arrived served to

**110**

confirm what the bureau chief had already heard about me. He did not tell me this in so many words, but he didn't have to. His treatment of me spoke volumes.

I arrived on a sunny Tuesday morning around ten-thirty. The mayor was then holding a press conference in the Blue Room. At the same time, the City Council was meeting in its chambers upstairs. The city comptroller was simultaneously releasing a lengthy report on overspending in the Parks Department, and angry cabdrivers were "demonstrating" with their cabs in the parking lot out front.

The press room was empty. It smelled of stale cigar smoke, but there were no windows of easy access that would open, as two huge air conditioners filled the bottom windows and all was sealed tight around them. They appeared to be merely circulating the dead air in the room. I thought I could see an upper window that might open. It was very high up, and to reach it I had to climb atop the nearest desk, bring a chair up with me, and stand on top of that. I had just managed to find the window latch with my fingertips when I heard voices, quick footsteps, and a man yelling:

"What are you doing? Jesus Christ! That's my desk! You're gonna fall!"

I'm sure if he hadn't yelled at me I would have been perfectly all right, but the yelling startled me and seemed to upset the molecules holding the chair in its delicate balance on the desk. I could feel myself slowly teetering. There was only one thing to do. It was grab the window frame or certain death. I grabbed the window frame. The chair fell over, and there I was, dangling by my fingers over the *Morning Chronicle*'s word processor.

"Help her, somebody!" I heard. "Squirt, we need you! C'mere. Quick!"

Then: "Okay, lady, now don't panic and don't kick your feet. Now, Squirt here is gonna let you stand on his shoulders."

I felt a hand on my left ankle, then the welcome shoulder underfoot. I brought my right foot down where I thought the other shoulder ought to be.

Very carefully, hand-walking down the window, I crouched lower and lower until I could grasp the person's head with my hands, and in a confusion of skirt, shoulders, swear words, and somebody's clicking camera shutter, I was brought trembling to the ground.

"What the hell were you tryin' to do? Commit suicide from the first floor of City Hall?" said a little man with thick-lensed glasses,

**111**

who introduced himself as Miltie Clendenon of the *Morning Chronicle*. He had been supervising the rescue.

"Oh, I ruined your shirt!" I said to my rescuer, Squirt, a very tall young man who was vigorously brushing off his shoulders. "I was trying to open a window."

"It's okay," he said dully.

"Those windows don't open," said Miltie. "Who are you, anyway?"

"Sorry, I should have told you. I'm Sarah Makepeace. I'm here to replace Norman Kroll while he's on vacation."

"Things are lookin' up, boys," Miltie said. "We got a trapeze artist for a roommate."

"Where is Clive Lipschitz?" I asked.

"Over there," Miltie said.

He pointed to a balding man in a pink seersucker suit who had materialized at a desk in the far corner, and was already talking on the phone.

"Where's Norman's desk?" I asked.

"Under the picture of His Former Honor Mayor Lindsley," Miltie said, doing a little two-step, then extending his hand toward a cartoon drawing of John Lindsay with straw hat and cane. "You never been here before?"

"No," I said.

"It helps if you take up smokin' cigars," he said, smiling as he brought his own unlit butt to his mouth. "I hope you like it here, Sarah. You got off to a good start."

"Thanks," I said.

I walked over to Lipschitz's corner of the room.

"Hi," I said.

He frowned at me and lifted up a finger to indicate silence. By now there were two other men at the desks beside his. One was a short, intense-looking, dark-haired young man whom I'd seen lunching alone with Willie Crespi. The other was a gray-haired, red-faced man whom I'd never seen before. Like Lipschitz, he was talking on the telephone. The younger man was typing.

"Hi," I said to him. "I'm Sarah Makepeace. Ron sent me here to fill in for Norman."

"Oh, hi, Sarah," he said without turning his head. "Can't talk to you now. Doing a summary."

Thinking I ought to read the city news, I opened my copy of *The Newspaper* to Lipschitz's piece about "rollbacks" in the Office of

Management and Budget. As I could not understand it, I commenced to the editorials, skimmed them, and then turned to a feature on the sheepherders of Tasmania, read all of it, then flipped to the crossword puzzle, and had spent a good twenty minutes trying to think of Romeo's last words before I looked up and perceived that Clive Lipschitz was no longer on the phone. He was typing.

"Hi, Clive," I said, standing near his desk. "I'm Sarah Makepeace, at your service."

"Hi, Sarah," he said, tossing me a quick squint. "I don't have time to talk to you now."

"Fine," I said. "I'll be right here."

I sat at Norman's desk all day. Clive filed his story. Then he rushed out of the room, stayed away an hour, rushed back in, and filed another story. The younger man, who eventually told me his name was Nick Pankhurst, went out for a two-hour lunch with a source, came back, called the office, dictated a summary, and then went uptown to write his story in the newsroom.

The older man, who introduced himself to me as "Drehner here," filed one story before lunch, went out for an hour, came back, put his feet up on the desk, polished off the whole crossword puzzle in twenty minutes, and then whiled away the rest of the afternoon smoking cigars and playing cards with Miltie.

At the end of the day, Clive Lipschitz rushed out, saying a hurried "See you tomorrow, folks" over his shoulder.

The next day went similarly. The *Newspaper* men scarcely talked to me. Clive was polite but he did not ask me to do anything. He worked terribly hard. He seemed to be doing the work of two men, while the other two in the bureau were doing about the average load. The three of them consulted each other in the morning and then each worked alone.

The third day was the same. No one asked me to do anything.

I got the message by then, so on the fourth day I brought in a copy of *Lolita* and was content. The next Monday I brought in *War and Peace*, just to see what Clive would say when he saw it. But he either didn't notice or thought I might presume too much interest if he commented, and I ended up having to pretend to read the bloody thing, which I had already read, and I was very annoyed with myself for not having brought a contingency book. The following day I brought *The Choirboys*, a book Kevin had said cops hated. I could see why when I got to the cop who thought he was going crazy all the time.

**113**

The day after that, Wednesday of my second City Hall week, I told Clive I wanted to go uptown after lunch to pick up my paycheck. He shrugged.

I was approaching the thrilling denouement of *The Choirboys* as I turned the corner into the newsroom, the book open in my hand.

"What are you doing, reading novels now?" I heard Ron ask.

"Oh, hi, Ron. It's a good book. Good subway reading," I said quickly.

"Come in here. I want to talk to you," he said, beckoning toward his private office.

I followed him in. He sat down on one of the two facing couches, and I warily sat down opposite.

"What's happened to you? I haven't seen a thing by you in two weeks," he said.

"Maybe you should ask Clive Lipschitz, Ron."

"I'm asking you, Sarah. What's the matter? You were doing so well. Is something bothering you? You're not getting writer's block, are you? You're not thinking of doing a novel?"

"No, Ron. I'm just not getting any assignments."

"No assignments? What do you mean? You're sitting in for Kroll. He covers the City Council and the Board of Estimate."

"I think Lipschitz wishes you had consulted him before you selected Kroll's replacement, Ron," I said.

"That's nonsense! Clive has been begging me for help. You women are too sensitive! I'm sure he's delighted to have you, Sarah. Show him what you can do. Show some initiative. Go out and find your own stories."

"I don't think you understand the situation, Ron. Clive doesn't *want* me writing stories."

"Don't be ridiculous! You think a bureau chief doesn't want his staff writing stories? Why, that's crazy, Sarah! That's paranoid! Nobody on this paper thinks that way."

The image of Jenny sitting motionless at her desk rose to mind.

"Okay, Ron," I said. "I'll try to come up with something."

"That's what I like to hear!" Ron said warmly. "Go out and get us a scoop, Sarah. I want to see your name in the paper. I want to hear people talking about you."

The next day I went exploring around City Hall. I wandered upstairs, looking for the City Council chambers. A policeman saw me trying to open a pair of enormous doors.

"It's locked, miss," he said.

"Where's the City Council?" I asked.

**114**

"They're in recess," he said. "You might find one or two of them in their room downstairs."

I found a big room downstairs filled with desks, but there was no one in it. I wandered out and heard the sound of typing coming from a room off to the right. The door was open. I walked through. The front room here, obviously a receptionist's office, was unoccupied. But someone had seen me come in.

"Yes? Can I help you?" a woman called.

I passed through into another room. Here a young woman was seated at a big desk piled high with official-looking documents. She was turned sideways, typing. She wore gold-rimmed glasses and had a queer headband across her forehead, like an Indian or hippie maiden. She went on typing.

I cleared my throat.

"Hi," I said. "I'm supposed to be looking for a story. You got any hot scandals for me?"

"Just that the mayor's gone on the blink again. Who are you?" she said, turning to look at me.

"Sarah Makepeace. Sorry, I'm with—"

"*The Newspaper*. I heard about you."

"Are you a City Council, um, person?"

"Oh, no! I work for the Council president. My name's Laura Dasher. There's not much going on right now, unless you want to write about Golden Age Week. But I already gave Clive our release on that."

"This is Golden Age Week?"

"Yes. They're having a big festival at Coney Island, crowning the queen of the grandmothers or something. They all have a good time."

"What did you mean about the mayor going on the blink?"

"Well, it's not really anything new. Nobody knows where he is."

"Oh."

"He was supposed to be at the Golden Age festival, but he didn't show."

"That seems unwise. For a man who wants to get reelected."

"I don't think Simon wants to get reelected. This isn't the first time."

"First time he skipped out on the Golden Age festival?"

"Oh, *that* doesn't matter! Half the politicians skip it. The thing isn't big enough. But he's been gone for a day and a half, as far as I can tell. I've been trying to get him to sign some bills. *I* was supposed to leave for vacation this morning."

**115**

"What bills?"

"Nothing you'd care about. Just some street name changes and a restructuring of the Human Resources Administration."

"That sounds important."

"It's just on paper. No bodies get moved around. It means the city can qualify for new federal funds in law enforcement. How do you like Room 9?"

"Room 9?"

"I thought you were in the press room."

"Yes, for a few weeks."

"Well, that's what they call it. Didn't you see the number on the door?"

"No."

"It helps if you keep your eyes open around here." She seemed sort of irritated.

"Well, I guess I shouldn't be keeping you," I said.

"Be my guest," she said. "I'm just waiting for the mayor to get back."

"Where do you think he is?"

"Beats me. I told you this isn't the first time. Lester Simon's gone AWOL before."

"What did you say? AWOL?"

"Absent without leave—you know."

"Oh, I'm sure somebody knows where he is."

"You want to bet? Try asking a few people down at the other end of the hall. I'll bet you five dollars—no, *ten* dollars—they all give you different answers."

"Sarah, where the hell have you been?" Lipschitz said, suddenly appearing in the doorway. "I've been looking all over for you!"

"Oh, hi, Clive," I said. "I guess you know Laura—"

"Of course I know Laura!" he said quickly, waving a hand at her. "Come on, Sarah. I have something for you right now."

"Well, 'bye, Laura," I said. "Have a nice vacation. Where are you going?"

"New Hampshire. I'll probably be eaten alive. Blackfly season."

"Sarah!" Clive said from the hallway.

"I'm coming, I'm coming," I said, wishing I had made him wait longer.

"What the hell were you doing in there?" he asked me huffily. "Pankhurst is covering the City Council."

"I was just looking for a tip. Laura told me something interesting, Clive."

**116**

"Laura doesn't know anything! Why didn't you check in with me first? You were supposed to check in at ten."

"Laura says the mayor is AWOL, like, not to be found."

"Sarah, Laura happens to be working for Stanley Greenblass, who happens to be planning to run for mayor next year. You think you can trust anything she says about Lester Simon? You have to know the angles down here. Now, I've got a story that's just right for you," he said, handing me a press release on the noon ceremony to be held that day in the City Hall parking lot. The Greek archbishop was going to bless the hot dog carts.

"Gee, Clive," I said. "Ron told me to look for a scoop."

"I talked to Ron this morning," Clive said wearily. "He thinks this is a perfectly good assignment for you. You can write a nice color piece. If I had time, I'd do it myself."

"Okay, Clive."

At noon, the parking lot was a hot, silvery sea of vending carts, and Marco Fellini, a potbellied photographer whom I had seen previously only from a distance, dashing across the newsroom, stood beside me cursing his luck.

"Whadda crap sto-ree!" he said. "Whadda nothin' story! Look at these poor bastards! On a day like this they could be makin' money."

The hot dog vendors stood by their carts in their Sunday best, and they did look woebegone. The temperature must have been about ninety-six, and they were all wearing dark suits. But they had the stoic posture of Christian martyrs, and when the archbishop finally appeared on the steps of City Hall in his long black robe, they all knelt by their carts on the torrid pavement.

The archbishop began chanting in Greek. An altar boy rang little bells to punctuate his strange incantation. In the middle of the ceremony, a group of politicians came out of City Hall, talking loudly to one another and drowning out the voice of the archbishop.

"Look at those turkeys, will ya?" Marco said. "They come out here and practically knock over the priest, trying to show how much of a shit they give about the Greeks. Whose idea was this anyway?"

"That's a good question, Marco. I think I'll ask the mayor's people."

"Where's the mayor? He comes to all these things."

"You've done other things like this?"

"All the time. It's all crap."

"The mayor maybe doesn't think church and state ceremonies should mix."

"Bullshit! I told you he comes to all of 'em."

"Marco, could you tell me something honestly? I heard—somebody told me that your boss Vic Veblen won't assign photographers to do stories with me because he's in love with Jenny Locke. Is that true?"

"Vic? Vic's married. Jenny sure ain't in love with him."

"Being married doesn't seem to have a bearing on the office romances."

"It's none of my business. I love my wife—my ex-wife she is."

"That's nice."

"How long you been down here, Sarah?"

"About a week."

"You married?"

"No."

"Never get divorced, Sarah. Aah, here goes. Now they're gonna sing."

The vendors all broke into a vigorous, haunting song of Eastern, faintly Russian flavor.

"What are they singing?" I asked Marco.

"The hymn to the hot dog, stupid!"

After the ceremony, I interviewed a few of the vendors, but the interviews were difficult, as their English was not fluent, and when I asked where they were from, each of them said, "Astoria, America, USA," and did not seem to understand me when I said, "But in Greece, where? Before Astoria, where?"

*"They're afraid of Immigration,"* Marco whispered to me.

Still, I managed to write three pages on the event. These were ultimately condensed into a caption to go under Marco's picture.

After that day, I had plenty of work to do. Ron had obviously ordered Clive to give me assignments. Clive had obviously decided to interpret the order in his own way. Everything he gave me was what Marco would call a crap story, a nothing story, and usually became a picture caption or a D head, if it got into the paper at all. I did ribbon cuttings, lunches at the Citizens Budget Commission, tree plantings, proclamations for Secretaries' Week, Clean Streets Week, Puerto Rican Parade Day, Turkish Independence Day, Fashion Avenue Day (formerly Garment District Day), and Dental Hygiene Day. Some of the proclamations were read on the steps of City Hall by the mayor, who appeared in the flesh, hale, hearty, and glad-handed enough to make me think Laura Dasher had indulged in wishful thinking when she said he did not want to run again.

Two weeks went by in this way, with me writing picture captions and D heads too small to rate a by-line. When Operation Sail happened, Lipschitz assigned himself to the mayor's launch and dispatched me to the disaster control room in the basement of the Municipal Building, a promising post, I thought, because many tragedies had been predicted for the huge event. But alas for me, only two people and one tugboat dalmation fell into the water, and none drowned. The disaster control room was as dull as an air raid shelter on Armistice Day, and you couldn't get any duller than that except maybe in Four Corners, Mass., on a Sunday afternoon when the town drunk and the town cop and my father were all asleep.

On the Tuesday after Operation Sail, Lipschitz became magnanimous. He assigned me to go aboard one of the tall ships docked at South Street Seaport. So I was out all morning and did not return to Room 9 until after lunch.

"You took your own sweet time!" Clive sneered at me when I came in. "Call Margaret right away."

"Who's Margaret?"

He did not answer. He handed me a slip of paper with an extension on it. At least I figured out it was a *Newspaper* extension. I dialed.

"Editor's office," said a whispery voice.

"Oh, I think this is a mistake," I said.

"Who's calling, please?"

"Sarah Makepeace, but I think I have the wrong number."

"Oh, Sarah, I'm glad you were able to get back to me. There's still time. Mr. Foley would like to see you this afternoon. Could you get here by three?"

"Mr. Foley wants to see *me?*"

"Yes, this afternoon. Can you make it by three?"

"I guess—well, yes," I said, noticing the time was two-fifteen.

"Excellent," she said. "I'll put you down, then."

"Margaret, if it's about the *Crim*—"

But she had already hung up. Clive, I could see, was pretending to read his notebook while cocking an ear in my direction.

"I wonder why Gil wants to see me," I said to no one in particular.

"It isn't usually for a social chat," Clive said without looking up.

"Well, see you later, Clive," I said.

"Don't count on it," he said gleefully.

# XVI

Clive, I should explain, had never bothered to give me a phone message before this. All the bureau's phones had buttons on them for all the lines, and Clive answered all calls that came in when he was at his desk. If I was sitting right there and a call came in for me, he would tell me curtly to pick up. But if I wasn't there, he told whoever was calling he'd let me know and then never did.

He was perfectly friendly or at least cordial with the people who called me, so they did not suspect he was the problem. They suspected me. For my father, it wasn't much of an insult. He was used to me rebuffing him, and he had staying power. He just called me more often at home. But for Ellie and Kevin, it was disastrous. Ellie had been fired, and Roger had quickly realized he couldn't have her staying at home all day—his office was in their house—so he was nagging her to get another job. She was in a terrible state. She thought Roger didn't love her anymore, and she thought I didn't want to be her friend anymore. Luckily I ran into her at the Sheridan Square newsstand one night when I was out looking for my latest D head, and she screamed at me and then burst into tears, and our friendship was saved.

But Kevin, who since the time I had failed to recognize his voice on the phone had been obsessed with the idea that I knew another man named Kevin, really suffered at the hands—or rather voice—of Clive Lipschitz. Clive had a demonic ability to pick up the signals of a caller's emotional frequency, and I don't doubt that he gave back to Kevin in a ho-ho, man-to-man sort of way the signals that he was sharing more than my telephone with me. Kevin envisioned him as a square-jawed, flashy-toothed handsome brute of a fellow like the correspondents he saw on television, and he took to dropping in on me unannounced at midnight on the days he had left messages with Clive. He looked haunted. He was getting dark circles under his eyes, and he had started smoking my cigarettes. He was racked by jealousy.

"Take your clothes off!" he would say tersely as he walked through my door, not "Hello," or "How was your day?" Sometimes he said, "Who gave you that nightgown? Take it off!" when that applied. Then he would walk around me, searching me up and down for telltale bruises or bite marks as he asked me a hundred questions about where I'd been that day.

"Where were you at ten-thirty? That guy said you hadn't come in yet! Where were you? Did you sleep late? Were you out last night?"

"I was on the steps of City Hall watching the Girl Scouts present the mayor with a big ugly apple. Kevin, I *told* you Clive doesn't give me my messages."

"What's this? What . . . is . . . this?" he might ask as he discovered his own signature upon my thigh.

"You bit me there. Don't you remember?"

"That was last week! This looks fresh."

He suffered badly. When he wasn't suspecting me of carrying on with Clive Lipschitz, he fell back on the fantasy of the second Kevin, and his detailed interrogations did not relieve him at all. They yielded up more names of men.

"Miltie Clendenon? You had lunch with him *again?* I don't want you eating lunch with him. Why can't you eat lunch with one of the girl reporters?" he'd say.

"There aren't any other *girl* reporters in Room 9. Kevin, stop this!" I'd say.

But he wouldn't stop until he had worked himself up into such a frenzy of imaginings that he was completely wild for me. He became a sex fiend. He made love to me on the floor and on the table and on the couch and in the shower. He couldn't get enough of me. He would exhaust himself in these storms of jealous passion and sometimes slept so soundly afterwards that I had to shake him awake when it was time for him to call his wife. I couldn't talk sense with him at all until he had been asleep next to me for an hour.

Then once or twice I tried asking him what Dr. Festniss said about his jealous delusions.

"He wouldn't understand," Kevin said. "He's Jewish."

"You mean you haven't told him?"

"Not too much, no."

"I don't get it, Kevin. You've finally got something really crazy going on, and you've been seeing this shrink for—what is it? A year? A year and a half? And you won't *tell* him about it?"

"Two years."

"Did you ever get like this with your wife?"

"Helen? She wouldn't look at another man."

"Does she know about us?"

"No, I don't think so."

"What would she do if she did find out?"

"I don't know. Kick me out, maybe."

And where would he go then? Kevin's parents lived in upstate New York. His brother, who was a cop in Nassau County, had five kids and a wife who was a Jehovah's Witness. Kevin hadn't been out to see them since his sister-in-law tried to make him subscribe to *The Witness* three Christmases past.

This topic of the hypothetical moment when Kevin's wife found out about us had come up the night before I got the call from Margaret. As I rode uptown on the subway, trying to think what I should say to Gil Foley when he confronted me with the fact that I had never worked on the *Crimson*, I saw a young black man step on the train, weeping inconsolably. He was carrying a shabby suitcase, tied round its bulging middle by a leather belt. Tears were dripping down his cheeks in two long rivulets, and he was sniffing and catching his breath in little sobs.

Where would Kevin go if she kicked him out? How could I stand having him there every night, giving me the third degree? Or would she kick him out? She might make him promise never to see me again, I thought, feeling a stitch in my heart. And I'd have no job, no Kevin, no nothing. And then, wouldn't you know it, a Jehovah's Witness who just happened to be riding on that train got up to hand the weeping man a copy of *The Witness*, and he wailed more loudly than before, and I imagined Kevin appearing at my door with a suitcase, weeping, and I cursed Clive Lipschitz darkly.

# XVII

I had not spoken with Gil Foley since the day he told me I was hired. He seldom walked through the newsroom, and when he did, he held himself aloof from the people he passed, literally held himself by the right elbow with his left arm crossed behind his back, and he allowed himself no eye contact with anyone below top editorial rank and never stopped to talk with Ron or Dixby if there was anyone else near them. On those rare outings he looked like a tall, thin bird, a crane or an egret, because his shoulders were so narrow and his chin was so sharp and the back of his jacket tufted out like a tail under his left arm, while his thin chest swelled strangely forward. I thought it was a queer way for an editor to carry himself in front of his staff, but I had no experience with editors, and certainly Foley's carriage worked, if what it was intended to do was keep everybody at a distance. No one spoke to him when he walked by, not even when his coattails brushed a piece of copy paper off the top of a reporter's desk.

Ron said Foley was naturally shy and had cultivated his shyness as a policy, believing he should not permit himself to fall into chummy camaraderie with people he might have to fire or send to Warsaw. He had come by his belief the hard way, after trying to make friends with select reporters in the early years of his editorship. He had gone drinking with them at Sardi's and dined in their homes and accompanied them on their assignments. But Ron said they couldn't forget he was boss, even when Foley had forgotten, and the air of the drinking sessions had always been charged with hidden calculations, sometimes not so well hidden by the third round.

"He could never let himself get drunk with them," Ron told me. "One night he had one too many and promised two men the same job in the Paris bureau. Of course, then he had to send someone else, and the other two never forgave him. One quit and went to work for the *Wall Street Journal* and the other guy went to American Express. Both were men he had thought of as his friends. They hurt his feelings, being so false, and then quitting! There's nothing that hurts Gil more than having a good man quit this newspaper.

"But he learned after that not to get too close. They were always asking him to send them to Paris. It was a strain. He used to say to me, 'Why doesn't anybody want to go to London?'

"If Gil ever asks you what your ambition is, Sarah, say you want to go to London. That will really impress him."

I couldn't tell, when Ron offered these treacherous little confidences about Gil Foley's character, whether he was just showing off or sincerely ratting on the man or doing both at once. Ron's motives seemed so mixed so much of the time that no one could read him clearly—except on the subject of Willard Dixby, about which he never wavered. But it was dangerous to be so indiscreet about Gil with the likes of me, dangerous for someone on Ron's level anyway. And I thought that might mean it was true that Ron was on his way out. He didn't act like a man who was in control of his career. Everybody said that to run *The Newspaper* you had to be very cool, very controlled. They hated Gil because he was so cool

**123**

and controlled, but they said Gil had what it takes.

How Ron, the irrepressible extrovert, could be the friend of a man who walked through life as if it were a tomb was one of the few mysteries about Ron. Although, considering that his great "friend" held the power to make him the next editor, there was a possible explanation. Ron could have a little more control than we thought he did. Then again, Foley might himself be on his way out now. It would be just like Ron to cling to a friend in the power structure who was falling out of the structure. Anyway, how good a friend could he still be to Ron, if Ron had had to lie to him to get me hired?

Foley had the power to fire me, in any case. And what I needed to know right now was whether those lies about me were sticking. The only person who could tell me was Ron. Five minutes before my scheduled doom, I searched the newsroom for his round form. He was nowhere to be seen. Oh, how I wished I could summon him! Ron would know what I should do. Ron might even have a fresh set of lies for me. We were just *kidding* about the *Crimson*. That "typo" of the zoo funds was intentional and for a higher cause. Where *was* Ron? Did he know Gil wanted to see me? Wouldn't Gil have told him—ah, but not if Gil knew Ron had lied. He wouldn't want Ron to warn me.

I squared my shoulders and headed off toward Foley's office, dreading each step that brought me there.

"Hello, Sarah! My, you're prompt!" Margaret said sweetly. "He's on the phone. It will only be a minute."

Actually, I waited an hour, and in that time I suffered such remorse that I knew it would be a good thing to be fired. After all, the lies were mine if I had lived with them. How could I have let them stick this long?

"He's ready now, Sarah," Margaret finally said, startling me out of a frowning contemplation of life as a waitress.

The light in Foley's office was so dim that I could not see anything at first.

"Hello, Sarah," he said in a noncommittal tone. "Please sit down."

I squintingly made out a chair near the wall and walked toward it.

"Oh, sit here, why don't you," Foley said. My eyes followed his voice. A chair near his desk took shape, and I guessed he meant that. As I sat down, the blindness seemed to pass, and I could see him sitting behind his desk. He had his hands in the prayerful position in front of his face.

"How are you, Sarah?" he said. "Ron tells me you're working like a tiger."

This was not what I had expected. And yet if you're going to fire a person, you might at first flatter, I thought. He could keep me here for half an hour, give me his spiel about the passion for the truth, and then—

"Listen, Gil," I said. "I think I know why you called me in here, and I can save you the trouble—"

"Yes?" he said.

"I was very surprised when you hired me, because—"

"Yes, it was a departure for us, taking someone from *The Evil Eye*, but you came with good credentials, Sarah. Your *Crimson* background—"

"Well, that's not true, Mr. Foley, as I'm sure you've discovered, because I—I—"

His eyes were closed. He was sitting there in that semidarkness with his hands in front of his mouth, and his eyes were closed.

"I really have a lot to learn!" I blurted.

"Yes, you have, Sarah," he said, opening his eyes. "I'm glad to hear you say as much. If you're aware, then that is half the battle, don't you think? If you can be self-critical?"

"I don't know, Mr. Foley, er, Gil. I seem to make a lot of typos, which—you know—at the time, you don't know you're making them, no matter how self-critical—"

"Oh, typos!" he said with a chuckle. "I'm afraid I still type with two fingers. You don't type with two fingers, do you, Sarah?"

"No."

"No one does anymore. It's become an anachronism, like the newspaper extra and shoeshine boys. We used to have a shoeshine boy in this building. He was a newshound himself, liked to go out with the police reporters. There were so many police reporters! His name was Sammy. We called him Sambo. It was a form of endearment then. His favorite story was the Leaky murder case. He kept all the clippings. He had boxes of them! There were so many papers then, you know—"

At that moment there was a tap on Foley's door and it opened, dazzling our eyes with sunlight and letting Freddie and two workmen come tromping in with a large cardboard box. Margaret walked in behind the trio.

"Oh, Mr. Foley," she said, "I hope you don't mind! You said as soon as it came—"

"This is it, then?" Foley said, as the workmen began tearing off the cardboard.

"Yes," said Margaret.

"Careful!" he said to the workmen, who had just ripped the box violently.

"Be careful!" Freddie echoed.

Sawdust spilled out onto the rug, and a large round blue surface became visible. The workmen dug into the box and more sawdust spilled out. Slowly, with exaggerated care, they pulled out the treasure, flakes of sawdust falling all around. It was a large globe attached to a heavy brass stand. They set it on the floor with gingerly caution. One of the workmen gave the globe a little flick with his fingers. It spun slowly and glinted as it turned.

"Turn on your desk light, Mr. Foley," Margaret said.

He switched it on.

The globe was enormous, about four feet in diameter.

"It's so beautiful!" Margaret said. "Oh, it's exquisite! It was hand-painted in Holland," she said to me. "The finest Dutch enamel."

Freddie and the workmen retreated with the cardboard box, but Margaret stayed behind, clasping her hands, looking rapt.

"The blue is a little garish," Foley said, "don't you think, Sarah?"

"I like it. The oceans we had in school were always so pale."

"Thank you, Margaret," Foley said.

Margaret backed out of the room and closed the door behind her.

"Look at those names," Foley said, now turning the globe himself. "London. Paris. Vienna. Tripoli. Baghdad. Leningrad. Peking. Bangkok. Saigon. Hong Kong. Tokyo. Fiji." He sighed. "I always wanted to file a story from Zanzibar. Of course, that's gone now."

"It is?" I said.

"Yes, it's part of Tanzania and Zambia now. Nothing will ever sound as exotic as Zanzibar. Would you like a drink, Sarah?"

"What?" I said. I really thought I had not heard him correctly.

"I said, would you like a drink? I could use a little pick-me-up. This time of the day. What would you like?"

He stood up and walked toward the wall, which buckled in on itself under his hand, revealing a small icebox and a liquor shelf behind.

"Oh, a beer, maybe," I said.

"Don't have beer," he said. "Could I interest you in a nice cold vodka tonic?"

"Sure," I said.

Neither of us said anything for a little while. I shifted my feet. The ice clinked into the glasses.

"Oh, yes, Sambo was a real newshound," Foley eventually resumed. "He knew more cops than most of us did, and he could be a real help on a story. He went along with me a couple of times when I was starting out on general assignment. 'Be sure to ask about the motive, now, Gil,' he'd say. 'And don't forget to ask was there forced entry. That be the key, right there. Lets you know if the murderer knew his victim!' Ah, good old Sambo! If he'd been born forty years later, he would have been a reporter on this paper," Foley said, walking over to hand me my drink. "But I think if he'd had a choice, he would have gone to work for the *Chronicle*."

Foley sat down behind his desk again and raised his glass to me. "Cheers," he said.

"Cheers," I said, suddenly wondering whether I should have accepted the drink. Perhaps he had put no liquor in his own glass?

"Ah, then, I like to think he's up in Tabloid Heaven right now, reporting on the follies of us all. Dear old Sambo! He did love murders! . . . Do you ever think about the afterlife, Sarah?"

"No, I don't. I wasn't raised in any religion."

"When you get older you will. We all do. Ponder the imponderable."

"Um, Mr. Foley, could I ask you something? Did you have something specific you wanted to . . ."

"I'm getting to that, Sarah. Naturally, I wouldn't call you in here without a very specific purpose. But it's a matter of some delicacy, Sarah, and I want to put it in context for you. I want you to understand. You might not like what I'm going to have to say to you, and I've found that when people don't like what they hear, they sometimes don't hear it. But I think you're intelligent. You want to do well here. I'm not wrong, am I?"

"N-no," I said.

"When I asked Margaret to call you in here, Sarah, I meant to be very brief with you. I felt you should know better than to have— well, Sarah, I wasn't in a patient mood, and I was forgetting about your time on *The Evil Eye* and how that might have instilled in you a certain love of irreverence for its own sake, which is, of course, the appeal of the *Eye* with its young audience. But I have had time to think about it, Sarah, and I want to be fair to you, I want to give you

**127**

a chance to think about it, about how serious you are in wanting to stay here, because if you aren't serious, then there's no point in our talking," he said, pausing to take a swallow from his drink.

"But I think you are serious, Sarah, I think you want to be one of us, you want to be a seeker of the truth. But there are many kinds of truths, many versions, and what we do here is to select, we use our judgment to present the fairest, most objective and intelligent version of the truth as we know it."

He stopped here, took a long quaff of his drink, and turned to look at his new globe.

"If it's about the zoo, Mr. Foley . . ." I said.

"And I'm glad this globe arrived when you were here, Sarah, because it can serve to bring home my point to you," he said. "Look at it. Imagine yourself an astronaut looking at this beautiful blue orb. Try to distance yourself from this room, this little patch of land in the middle of New York City. You see New York City here? It's a little dot, one small dot."

"Yes, I see," I said obediently.

"This is not just a New York paper, Sarah. This is the greatest paper in the world! I know that sounds boastful, grandiose, but I'm not boasting. I am speaking the plain truth. Our people are all over this globe. They are the watchdogs of the world. What they write affects everyone, everyone! I mean it. We are more important than the United Nations. Sometimes I think we are more important than the President of the United States. . . . Would you like a refresher?" he asked abruptly.

"Oh, no! I haven't finished this," I said.

He rose to replenish his own drink, and I now wondered nervously whether I should have been drinking faster.

"Do you know what it's like to run this paper?" he called to me from the liquor cabinet.

"No," I said helpfully.

"Of course you don't. You can't. You can't begin to understand how it feels to sit in my chair." He came back to sit in it. "The responsibility! The terrible responsibility! And always wondering whether we are right, whether we *are* getting the truth. Because people look to us, Sarah, they look to us for the answers. They want us to make the world seem comprehensible to them. We have to filter the unsorted detritus of reality, and we have a moral force, Sarah, yes, a moral force, not just in our editorials but in the judgments we use in writing stories, in the placement we give them, the emphasis, in what we say and what we do not say. And I am the final arbiter of that, Sarah; the buck stops with me. I decide what goes into *The Newspaper*, into every column inch of it, and if you don't think I agonize over every inch, every sentence, every *word* . . . Why do you think I can't sleep at night? I'm famous for lying awake, surely you know that. And do you know what I think about when I'm lying awake? I think of the whole earth. I turn it in my mind, I ask myself how well we're covering every city, every nation, every last piece of dust. Sometimes, Sarah, I seem to be able to feel the lugubrious turning of the earth, to actually feel it as I lie there in bed. Do you know how that feels? It feels lonelier than God! Do you know there are people who are planning to steal my garbage?" he said climactically.

This remark was so odd that I put my glass up to my mouth to cover my confusion and suddenly downed the rest of my drink.

"But I am digressing, Sarah," Foley said. "Let me get you another drink."

I noticed that his glass was nearly empty again.

"Just a small one, Mr. Foley," I said.

"Some people here call me Gil," he said, taking my glass. "I can never decide what's appropriate." He walked to the bar and, while pouring fresh drinks, suddenly asked:

"Sarah, how do you feel about homosexuality?" But then he said, "It doesn't matter. You don't have to tell me how you feel. *The Newspaper* doesn't have feelings about it. *The Newspaper* is not for or against homosexuality. It is simply a part of the life around us, like the theater, like subway graffiti. I'm sure you've seen our fine pieces on the Gay Rights Movement. We cover it as a serious— which we believe it to be—a serious political movement."

Here he handed me my glass again, amply filled. He walked to his chair with an ease I had not seen before.

"But, Sarah, I'm sure I don't have to tell you that this is a sensitive area. Homosexuals are still very sensitive about their status in society—like women, actually. And we do not wish to offend them unnecessarily, just as we do not wish to offend women unnecessarily, I might add. Do you follow me, Sarah?"

"I think so, Mr. Foley."

"Good, then you probably don't need to be told that you cannot quote a fireman—even if he said it to you for quotation—using a pejorative to describe homosexuals who are watching a fire, a crude pejorative. If you are writing a story about homosexuality *in* the Fire Department and the attitudes and departmental rules that are pertinent, *then* you might be allowed to quote a fireman on the subject.

**129**

But not in a story about a fire, Sarah, where it looks like a gratuitous swipe at homosexuality per se. And I don't think you need to be told that we don't use certain words in *The Newspaper* which might be appropriate for *The Evil Eye*—"

"Oh, I know, I know!" I said gushily. "I wrote that my first week here, Mr. Foley, and I'm sure I wouldn't make that mistake again."

"I'm sure you wouldn't, Sarah. But I did want to let you know that I see everything you write, and this did—this did concern me. Perhaps you ought to tack up a little sign on the side of your desk with that old saying: 'When in doubt, leave it out.' That can be a pretty good guide, you know."

"Yes, I've heard the copy editors say that."

"Well, I'm pleased to see you taking this, ah, little scolding so well, Sarah. Some of our reporters do find it difficult to take criticism. I'm glad you're mature enough to accept it. How are you liking it here? Are you enjoying yourself? Your parents must be proud of you."

"Oh, yes! It's very interesting, very interesting. I can't really compare it to anything else I've done."

"Oh, but the *Crimson*, of course, gave you some experience. I imagine this is very different from *The Evil Eye*, though, isn't it?"

"Yes, very different."

"What do your friends on the *Eye* say about your working here? Are they envious?"

"I haven't actually talked to, um, my friends on the *Eye* lately."

"Quite a few of them have applied for jobs here, you know. Well, I'm sure you know about that."

"Oh, who?"

"Quite a few. Doris somebody applied recently. And that poet, what's his name? O'Feeny, I think. Of course, we can't use a poet!"

"You mean Doris Munster and Peter O'Feeny?"

"Yes, that sounds right. How well do you know them, Sarah?"

"I don't know Doris very well. Peter's a nice guy. Very bright. But I never heard him say he was interested in journalism."

"It's a strange paper, *The Evil Eye*. Very uneven. I mean, they've done some outstanding things. Your pieces were quite good. But when they sink, they hit rock bottom. This business of going through famous people's garbage—"

"Oh, they just do that with rock stars and people like that. It's campy journalism."

"Have you seen today's issue?"

"No, actually."

"They have announced they are going to publish the contents of the garbage they claim to be collecting from the homes of prominent editors around town."

"Editors. That's sort of off—"

"Sarah, we recycle our garbage. Lily and I do it as a matter of principle. Surely, the *Eye* approves and wouldn't want—"

"The *Eye* does all kinds of crazy things."

"I'm a bit concerned about this, Sarah. If you were to talk to them—"

"I don't have any influence with the people on the *Eye*, Mr. Foley. They think I sold out to come here. They think I trashed an exposé of sexist practices."

"I read that ridiculous item, yes—yes, they do seem to have it in for you. Envy, you know, Sarah, is a terrible thing. We all have that burden to bear here, being unjustly accused by people who want our jobs."

"Oh, I don't think I've made enough of a splash to attract the sort of hostility—well, to make anybody envious."

"Don't say that, Sarah! You *have* made a splash! Ron tells me Maureen Heller can't stop talking about you. Ron has high hopes for you. And so do I. I would like to see you in Washington someday. Washington, hell! Paris! You would like to go to Paris someday, wouldn't you, Sarah?"

"Or—London," I said recklessly. I took a big gulp of my "refresher," left untasted until now. It seemed to be three-fourths vodka.

"What a sensible girl you are! I feel I can trust you, Sarah. I'm sure you can talk sense into Lars Shield. I'm sure he would listen to you. How would he like it if I read his garbage, printed it?"

"He might, actually, like it," I said, taking another large swallow of my drink. It went down in a cool-warm silky glide.

"Yes, yes, I guess he might," Foley said pensively. "I do find that sort of rummaging in private trash distasteful. It is an invasion of privacy, don't you agree?"

"Yes, I guess."

A buzzer sounded on his desk.

"Ah, well, Sarah," Foley said, "there's Margaret reminding me that time marches on. I did enjoy chatting with you. We must do it again."

He reached for my glass, half full though it was, and I let it go.

He threw his and mine into his wastebasket. They were plastic.

"Oh, do tell Margaret I'm ready for the front page, will you, Sarah?"

"Yes," I said, rising.

"Oh, and if you were to speak to Lars Shield, you might tell him I find it odd to be under, ah, assault by a staff that is asking to come into my employ. What if he were to discover in my garbage the letters from his own employees? Would he, ah, report that?"

"I told you, Mr. Foley, I haven't been talking to him lately."

"Of course, you're not to tell him about our little talk here, Sarah. I'm sure I don't have to tell you, but I wouldn't want you to discuss our talk with anyone. So it's just between us, understood?"

"Oh, yes, Mr. Foley, I wouldn't think of it," I said, feeling a little woozy.

I walked out into the bright light again and swung rather wide around the corner toward the City Desk.

"Oh, Sarah!" Margaret called behind me.

I turned my head, feeling my cheeks burn with the heat of the vodka.

"Oh, yes, Margaret. He said to tell you he's ready for the front page."

"He wanted you to have this," she said, handing me a copy of *The Evil Eye*.

# XVIII

Not fired! Not fired! Not anywhere near to being fired. My heart swelled with good feelings for all the earnest toilers in the newsroom. Their little frowns of concentration looked now so endearing, so childlike. I wished they could all go have drinks with the editor and learn that he wasn't such a formidable guy, that he could be human and miserable like the rest of them, that he could get paranoid about his garbage. It would help their morale, and his too. Everybody should relax more, take life a little easier. This living from deadline to deadline was a crazy way to exist. Look at Jess Flicker over there, trying to scratch himself under his cast. Breaking a knuckle, for Christ's sake, over a minuscule mix-up of titles! I could see him yelling at Steve Figland right now. Next he would burst a blood vessel. It wasn't worth it. Poor Jess! I should put in a good word for him the next time I had drinks with Gil, tell Gil he was working too hard. Why not, if Gil was going to use me as a sounding board? I might even put in a good word for Jenny Locke. I could divorce myself from silly resentments. I *would* put in a good word for her, at the right time, when Gil was consulting me about the Women's Movement. In fact, I should have a position ready on that, in case he called me in suddenly again. He had taken me by surprise this time. I hadn't said enough, hadn't begun to tell him what was wrong with *The Newspaper,* how disorganized it was, how terribly slapdash. Did he know Ron changed his mind every five minutes? How much did Gil know? If he was so badly misinformed about me, it was possible he was misinformed about a lot of things. He might not *know* the nuclear deterrent theory had serious flaws. If he didn't know, and he was running the most important newspaper in the world, then shouldn't I tell him, wasn't I morally obligated? How to put it to him the right way . . . Gil, can you honestly say you'd rather be dead than red?

After some time, I am not sure how long, I noticed Willard Dixby's lizard eyes looking at me from the middle distance. I smiled at him. The slits of his eyes seemed to narrow slightly, as if he suspected a vile Metro Desk plot. In my grand mood, I pitied him the knotted psyche which held him prisoner, apart from human warmth. I moved smilingly toward my end of the room, passing the slavish, pen-chewing copy editors and coming around a pillar to spot Ron's large round back. For once, he was sitting still, reading something on his desk. Delightful, impossible Ron! I knew he would be glad to see me. *He* did not hold himself back from warm human feelings!

"Hello, Ron, old buddy!" I said, coming to stand beside him.

"Sarah, what are you doing here?" he said.

"Me? I work here!"

"You're supposed to be in City Hall."

"Ah, but I was summoned away from that palace of pleasure, Ron—"

"What's the matter with you? Are you drunk?"

"Drunk with happiness!"

"Well, don't bother me now. I've got to go to the front page meeting."

"Yes, I know. You should enjoy it. Gil seems to be in a good mood."

"You were in with Gil? What were you doing with Gil? Sarah,

you shouldn't go see Gil without telling me!"

"I looked for you, Ron, but you weren't around. I just got summoned today, this afternoon—"

"I can't talk to you now, Sarah. But don't go away! I want to see you as soon as we're finished," he said, heaving himself out of his chair and bounding off toward Gil's office.

There was no chance that I should escape after that, in any case, as Jess Flicker had spotted me and wished to know what had happened to my tall-ship feature. His ailing hand seemed to be itching very badly under the cast. This did not tend to smooth communications between us. I said I had forgotten about the piece, due to a summons from the editor. Jess said that was the lamest excuse since Steve Figland called in sick with housewife's knee, and then he ordered three-quarters of a column on the double, slugged "Ship."

"You know how to spell 'ship,' don't you, Sarah?" he jeered, while scratching his cast.

Only when I sat down to write the story did I wonder how much vodka Gil had put into my drinks. I seemed to have writer's block, yet great thoughts were right on the verge of my mind. I smoked a few cigarettes and tried to think how I could get the word "imponderable" into the lead. "When pondering the imponderable," I wrote, then ripped the page out and crumpled it as I'd seen Akelroyd do. Perhaps another word, the sea as a symbol of the unknowable, no, of infinity, no, of adventure, no, infinity. This didn't seem to be helping me. Maybe I should focus on the ship. Yes, the ship could be a ghost from the past, yet not a ghost—it was real. A relic. No, too dead-sounding. How about a vestige? Another crumpled paper bit the dust. I lit a cigarette again and stared off into the distance, dreaming Gil Foley and I were together, composing an editorial called Pondering the Imponderable. . . .

"Sarah, I want to see you this minute!" Ron snapped. He had appeared from nowhere, with a glowering lip.

"But, Ron, I have to do this story," I protested.

"What story?"

"A feature on a tall ship."

"I'm sick of tall ships. Who told you to do that? Forget it."

"You'd better tell Jess. He's expecting—"

"Come with me!" he said. He sped off toward his office. I followed, feeling perplexed and put upon. As he reached his office door, he flung it open, then turned to yell, "Willie, tell Jess Sarah's story's been killed!"

He sat down heavily on his favorite couch, and I sat down in one of the green chairs. Then he stood up and put his hands in his pockets and wiggled them there, fluttering his trouser legs.

"Now, Sarah, I told you to dig for stories," he said. "What have you been doing? I haven't seen your name in the paper for a month!"

"I've been writing stories, Ron," I said. "I just haven't been getting by-lines. They all turn out to be picture captions and D heads."

"I don't want you to disappoint me, Sarah. I stuck my neck out for you, you know. Gil didn't want me to hire you."

"Well, Gil just told me you were—"

"And that's another thing, Sarah. You must *never* go to see Gil without telling me! Is that clear?"

"Yes, Ron. But you weren't—"

"Now, I want you to tell me everything you discussed with him," he said, sitting down hard on the couch again. "Because if you made a false move, Sarah, it could be very serious."

"Gil wanted to—at least I think he wanted to explain to me what the paper's policy was on homosexuality."

"Homosexuality?" said Ron, and his eyes got very big. "But you're not—Sarah, are you—why didn't you—how did Gil—Sarah, you should have *told* me!"

"Ron, it was because of the City Short I wrote, you know, way back when I was starting, when I quoted the fireman saying 'wall-to-wall faggots.'"

"Oh, *that!*" said Ron, showing tremendous relief. But an instant later he collected his features into a stern look and held up one finger. "Yes, that was a stupid thing to do, Sarah," he said. "I told you about that."

"I know, Ron. Anyway, that was what Gil wanted to talk to me about."

"Just that? It wasn't worth his time. He must have had some other reason for calling you in, Sarah. Think. What else did he say to you?"

"He talked about how lonely it was to be editor, all the responsibility, the worry."

"Yes?"

"Well, that's about it."

"I don't understand. Gil called you in to discuss a phrase in a City Short and then told you how lonely he was? It doesn't make sense."

"Maybe he just wanted to get to know me a little better," I said wisely. "And I think he likes to unwind sometimes, have a drink with a reporter."

"Gil doesn't drink with reporters. I told you that!"

"I guess he made an exception today."

"You *are* drunk, then!"

"I only had one and a half drinks, Ron."

"One and a half! Sarah, Gil must have had a reason. I want you to think very hard. Try to remember everything he said."

"Well, he did seem a little worried about something *The Evil Eye* had written, but he asked me not to mention it, Ron, to anyone."

"Sarah, you can tell me! I'm his best friend!" Ron said, smiling as if the sun had just come out in the dusky Grand Central of his brain.

"It wasn't anything important, Ron. I think Gil just gets a little paranoid about the *Eye*, about the things they write about him, you know, calling him the patsy of the Establishment and all. It's silly, because he *is* the Establishment."

"What specifically was he worried about, Sarah?"

"Please, Ron! He asked me not to tell anyone. I probably wasn't even supposed to tell you I saw him."

"Sarah, I don't know whether you realize how badly you're doing here. You're still on probation, you know, and quite a few of the copy editors don't think you should be kept on. If you blew it with Gil—"

"Probation? What's that?"

"We have a three-month probationary period for everyone here. Didn't you know that?"

"No."

"I've been defending you, Sarah. I think you've got potential. I would *like* to see you pass your probation. But you're going to have to try harder. You're going to have to come up with a scoop. Clive tells me you haven't come up with a single story on your own."

"That's not true! I got a tip a couple of weeks ago, and he wouldn't let me— Ron, Clive doesn't *want* me to get a scoop!"

"What was your tip?"

"Well, Clive said the source was not, um, to be trusted on the subject, but I don't know. She works for the Council president, and so Clive says any dirt on the mayor coming from her—"

"Dirt on the mayor? What was it?"

"Maybe it's not true, Ron. Anyway, it wouldn't be very upbeat, if it did turn out to be true."

"Sarah, for god's sake, what was it?"

"Well, this girl, uh, woman who works for Greenblass says that the mayor sometimes disappears, can't be found, like, for a whole day—goes AWOL was the way she put it."

"Where does he go? What do you mean, he can't be found? You mean his staff doesn't know where he is?"

"She said if you ask his staff where he is, they all give different answers."

"And what did Clive— That's incredible! It can't be true! I want that story, Sarah! I want you to get it in this week!"

"This is my last week in City Hall, Ron."

"I know; that's why you're going to have to work fast. Clive is too close to the mayor's people, Sarah. You should have seen that. You should have worked around him."

"But he's the bureau chief."

"You're going to have to learn to be more independent, Sarah. You must bring all your stories to me. We need this story. *You* need it! If you're going to get to the convention—"

"The convention! Ron, I'm not ready—"

"Of course you're ready. You'll have a fresh pair of eyes, Sarah. You'll be able— I didn't mean to be hard on you just now," he said, leaning forward and crinkling his eyes at me. "I'm only trying to help you. You know that, don't you, Sarah? I'm your rabbi. I defend you all the time. Yes, I do. I have told Jess you are going to be a *great* reporter. You have to be careful of Jess, Sarah. I'm your only real friend on this paper."

"Well, Jess knows, Ron, that I make mistakes."

"Everybody makes mistakes! Now listen. I want you to get that story on the mayor! What a story! What does he do? Where does he go?"

"I don't know if the story is true, of course."

"It *has* to be true. We need this story! We need it *this week!* I want it on my desk Friday morning."

"I hope I can get it."

"You'll get it. I *know* you'll get it! I don't want you to do anything else."

"What will I say to Clive? He covers the mayor, you know, and it might get sort of awkward with him, if he heard I was asking around. Anyway, he expects me to do all those D head things, the proclamations."

"Well, then, do some of those D head things. Go ahead and do Clive's assignments. You can work this on the side."

"I'll try."

"You'll have to do more than try, Sarah, because if you don't get this story, I'm not sure I can save your job. Jess isn't the only one who thinks you aren't working out. Willie has his doubts. Willie likes you. He really likes you. But he isn't sure you can take the pressure, Sarah. I've been telling him he's wrong. You're not going to disappoint me, are you, Sarah?"

"I hope not, Ron, but I do get a little worried, you know, when people think I worked on the *Crimson*. I worry that somebody might find out and tell Gil. Maybe we should tell Gil—"

"No, no, no, no, no! He wouldn't like that, Sarah. He wouldn't like that at all."

"It's just too bad he got the wrong impression—in the first place, I mean."

"Sarah, what is he worried about? You can tell me. You don't know Gil. I do. He's a strange man, a very complex man. He can sometimes turn on a person, someone he's confided in. For your own good, Sarah, you'd better tell me."

"You promise not to tell him I told you?"

"Of course I wouldn't tell him! This is between us!"

"Well, it was a thing he saw in the *Eye* today. They said they were going to be publishing things from the contents of the garbage of famous editors around town."

"He asked me whether we recycled our garbage!" Ron said.

The expression on his face was disturbing. He looked triumphant, yet guilty.

"Yes, he said he recycles his garbage," I said. "I think he was hoping I might be able to persuade them at the *Eye* that it was an invasion of privacy. But I told him I don't have any influence with them."

"Good thinking, Sarah. Yes, I don't think you should try to do anything. You let me handle it."

"But, Ron, you won't tell Gil I—"

"No, of course I won't breathe a word to Gil. Good girl, Sarah! You were right to tell me," he said, slapping his knees with satisfaction. He stood up.

I stood up too. Ron patted me on the back as we went out the door.

"You're going to be a *great* reporter, Sarah!" he said. "*I* know."

"*If* I can get that story," I said.

"Oh, ho ho, the story! Yes. When did I tell you to have it?"

"Friday."

"Maybe we can have lunch Friday," he said ambiguously.

# XIX

For the rest of the week, Clive kept me busy with his diddlyshit assignments, all of which seemed to be at outdoor functions, and the weather turned perversely hot and muggy as if it, too, were under the command of a resentful City Hall bureau chief, and so by Friday I was exhausted and unable to care very much that I might be in imminent danger of losing a job that required a body to stand around in ninety-nine-degree heat listening to people with wet armpits say they were "gratified to be here." I had made no progress on the story about the mayor, but Ron seemed to have forgotten about it, and my one source in a position to know, Deputy Police Commissioner Ed Dalrymple, told me, "The mayor can't disappear. There are bodyguards with him at all times. Somebody fed you a clinker."

When I left City Hall for the last time, all I took with me were the notebooks filled with "gratified to be here" quotes and the glossy paperback edition of *Trapeze Art for Beginners* that Miltie Clendenon gave me for a going-away present. "Take my advice. Get out of this business. Find yourself a nice husband," Miltie said to me as he walked me to the steps of City Hall. (Clive, telephonically preoccupied, had crooked a finger at me in farewell.) Miltie took the soggy cigar out of his mouth, wiped his lips with the back of his hand, and planted a loud damp kiss on my cheek.

"You'll do all right," he said. "You act dumber than you are. That's good. Yeah, you'll do all right," he repeated, returning the cigar to its rightful place. "Long as you understand Miltie's first law of thermodynamics."

"What's that, Miltie?" I asked.

"Shit floats," he said, grinning around the cigar.

I do think that Miltie genuinely would have liked to save me from journalism, but his *Morning Chronicle* weltanschauung could not offer me a substitute I would take. Miltie did not understand that since the sixties a nice husband was a contradiction in terms. I did not need a nice husband. I needed a swim. And that was exactly how I planned to suspend the weight of my existence, just as soon as I had picked up my paycheck. I thought I could slip in and out of the newsroom unnoticed in the Friday afternoon deadline rush and be floating on my back in the Leroy Street pool before anybody was the wiser.

The Leroy Street pool was no jewel of luxury. But it lay open to the sky between two quiet Village streets, and on a summer's evening, one could lie in its cloudy green water looking straight up at soundless airplanes passing across the blue. Local legend had it that Mayor Jimmy Walker's mistress had once lived on Leroy Street and that he had had a second name, St. Luke's Place, given to the street on her block to disguise her address. The second name was indeed there, attached to the same signposts that carried "Leroy Street," though the explanation seemed dubious. Trying to hide a mistress with a new street name made about as much sense as closing one's eyes to hide one's nakedness, a tactic that was actually not unknown at the pool, where in high summer bums often climbed the fence at night to take a bath and discovered themselves being observed in the ample street light near the deep end by a severe team of teen-aged body judges. There was definitely a carnal ghost lurking in the vicinity. On weekends, the pool attracted male homosexuals, who came tripping to it in clogs and high-heeled sandals. They stripped down to G-strings or skin-tight elastic trunks and rubbed themselves with fragrant oils, talking diets and dance classes and all the while flirting backward over their shoulders. Oh, yes, I had feelings about homosexuality! Those fags did things with their shoulders that women couldn't do anymore. How do you think I felt about them?

But in the early evenings during the week, just before it closed, the pool was often empty. That was when I liked to go there, to lie on my back in the easeful water, watching the silent airplanes and thinking lazily of the shy bums and the mayor's mistress.

How I longed for the pool that evening!

Even before I entered the newsroom, I could hear that the tone of its noise was wrong, and as soon as I passed through the open doorway, I could feel that the air conditioning was not working. I saw people squinting as if in a glare, but the lighting was the same as ever. They weren't squinting. They were wincing.

Ron was yelling: "Stop crying, stupid! Stop crying! Stop crying!"

I saw Susan Braithwaite sobbing into her hands not three feet away from him.

"FIGLAND, YOU'RE DOING SLAY, NOT FLOWERS!" I heard Jess say over the loudspeaker. "SCHWARTZ, YOU'RE DOING FLOWERS! GET THAT GODDAMN COPY MOVING!"

"FIGLAND, YOUR SLUG IS FIRE, NOT SLAY!" Willie Crespi rasped into the microphone.

"GOD DAMN IT, CRESPI, IT'S SLAY!" Jess's voice came back.

"*Sarah, where have you been?*" Ron shouted to me. "*Where's your story on the mayor?*"

Susan Braithwaite was left sobbing by the wayside.

"Look out," Eddie said to me under his breath as he dashed up to Nightside.

"*Sarah! Come here!*" Ron shouted, with his hands in fists.

I was ill prepared for this. Ron had not spoken one word to me since that "maybe we can have lunch." He had forgotten about lunch. I thought he had forgotten about the hot tip. It hadn't seemed to be the point of our little discussion, really, when you got right down to it. The point had *seemed* to be that Ron wanted to know what was bothering Gil. And once he'd wheedled that out of me, he hadn't seemed to care about the story about the mayor.

"*Sarah!*" he yelled again.

His face was very red, and as I got closer I saw that his shirt was wet, and he was sweating all down his neck and in droplets from his chin and nose.

"Do you have that story, Sarah? Are you ready to write it?" he asked in a calmer voice.

"The Police Department says it's not true, Ron, that it would be impossible," I said.

"You don't have it? You mean to say you don't *have* it?" His hands were forming fists again.

"N-no, Ron, not yet. I mean, I don't think it's true."

"And you waited until Friday afternoon to tell me this! Sarah Makepeace, this is the limit! *I never should have hired you! I should have known better than to hire a dumb, stupid New England goy!* That day you came in here wearing sandals and a workshirt, oh, goddamn son of a bitch, I should have known better, you can't even spell 'comptroller!' *You are so stupid!*" He yelled louder and louder and faster and faster and seemed to grow bigger as he yelled. He recited all my mistakes, *every single one of them*—every misspelling, every typo, every politician's title I got wrong. He went on and on. He did not care who heard. He did not care how many times he called me a dumb, stupid goy or repeated that I could not find my "goddamn way to the '21' Club." Once he said, "I should have known better than to hire a stupid shiksa who went to school with dairy farmers!"

And I don't mind saying I felt pretty stupid standing there. I couldn't speak. I couldn't think of what to say. My mind went absolutely blank. I don't know whether it was the shock of hearing him call me a goy or whether it was the detail of his memory or whether it was the accumulation of everything, his tremendous anger, but I could not speak. I was dumbfounded. I had never heard anything like it in my life. Every once in a while people did insult me for being a Wasp in New York, and Ellie had always had a love-hate thing about my ethnicity, but most of the time the insults were so mixed with envy that they hadn't felt like insults. Wasps were supposed to be ashamed of their bloodlines after the city fell out of love with John Lindsay, but nobody took that idea too seriously. In East Harlem, the teenage girls used to kind of stroke me as if I were a pretty horse, and they talked about how I had "good" hair. Most other places in the city, I didn't get stroked, but there were men who cared more that I was a Wasp than that I was a 'Cliffie. It had sort of bothered me to have such an impersonal thing work in my favor. But up to now, nobody had turned the thing around, held it personally against me that I was a Wasp. Believe it or not, I had never heard a Jew address me with such a blatant and hostile sense of racial superiority until Ron said "dumb, stupid New England goy." He really stumped me. What was I supposed to say back? I'm just as smart as you are, you pushy, conniving, loudmouthed Jew? It wouldn't sound right, and he knew it. It wouldn't sound on the same moral plane as "dumb, stupid New England goy" or "stupid shiksa who went to school with dairy farmers." It was horrible hearing a Jew insult me for my race, with all the wrongs of his history behind him stilling my tongue. I could not speak.

When he finally said, *"Get that story or stay all night!"* I did not at first realize that he was finished, and then I almost asked him, "What story?" because there were so many he had mentioned in his tirade against me. But I was led away by Willie Crespi then, and on my way to my desk I remembered which story Ron meant.

"Look out, kid," Greg said to me. "This is for real."

Very quickly and surreptitiously, he told me what had set Ron off.

About noon that day, there had been a memo posted on the city room bulletin board. The thing simply said that anyone desiring Democratic convention credentials should let the National Desk know by the end of the following Monday. The memo was not signed, and Greg said this meant it was not written by Gil Foley. It came from the National Desk. It meant Ron had learned in the most ignominious fashion that he had lost his competition with Willard Dixby for control of convention coverage, not only lost but had been cleaned out, routed, and publicly humiliated. Ron himself would have to apply to the National Desk for his personal convention credentials, and he would have no say about which of his own staff might be allowed to cover the convention. He could conceivably be shut out of the convention. That was within Dixby's power now. It was a prospect too awful to contemplate, that the city editor of *The Newspaper* might be shut out of the first presidential convention to be held in his hometown in fifty years. Ron had been finding it too awful to contemplate all afternoon.

"Ron's not in control of himself today," Greg said. "Watch out! He's looking at us. Pick up your phone. Look busy!"

I obeyed, and Greg picked up his phone.

"I thought he was never in control of himself," I said.

"You don't know Ron," Greg said.

"No, I don't think I do, or at least, I didn't. I didn't know he remembered things. He remembers everything I ever did wrong, Greg. *Everything!* Even things *I* forgot."

"Yeah, Ron's got a photographic memory."

"He remembers what people say, too. He's got total recall."

"Everybody knows that."

"But it doesn't jibe with the way he is usually, changing his mind all the time, forgetting what he said five minutes before."

"Sure it does."

"No, it doesn't, Greg. How could he be so scatterbrained and forgetful and have a perfect memory?"

"Because he's the boss, Sarah."

"I don't see how that explains it."

"How many city editors do you know?"

"They can't all be like Ron, Greg—"

Both our telephones went into the caterwauling off-the-hook sound, and we slammed them down at once.

"Tell you what," Greg said. "Dial me."

I did, and Greg picked up the phone and made a show of saying, "Hello, Alex!"

I said, "What you're saying is that he has too much on his mind even with that memory. Is that it, Greg?"

"He doesn't forget, Sarah. He only pretends to forget."

"But why?"

"It's his style. He doesn't like to say he's decided he made a bad assignment in the morning, so he pretends to forget it after lunch. Forgetting is good for all kinds of things. People can't get so mad at you if you fucked them over out of absentmindedness instead of bad will."

"But if everybody knows he's only pretending to forget, that he's really acting—"

"Don't call it acting. It's lying. Ron lies. He's a liar. Jesus! Haven't you caught on to that?"

"Um, well, every once in a while he has seemed—"

"Every once in a while! Shit, Ron lies all the time! Listen, when he was first made city editor, he went to a management training course and the instructor told him it's all right to lie to your staff about twenty percent of the time. Only Ron got it screwed up. He changed it to eighty percent. That's one time when his beautiful memory spazed out on him. He swears the guy said eighty percent of the time. Just ask him."

"I don't believe you."

"No, don't ask him. He'll lie to you. But I swear it's true. Ask Freddie. Freddie heard him talking about it."

"But he can't lie all the time, Greg. Nobody can. He'll get caught. It won't work."

"It's worked so far. I wonder how Dixby aced him out."

In Four Corners, people didn't lie very much. There wasn't much to lie about. I mean, the town had its share of adulteries and divorces and quiet alcoholics (the town drunk was only the most conspicuous), but none of them stayed secret very long. The place was too small, and everybody knew everybody else. It is very hard to get away with a lie in a small town, even a little lie, unless it has to do with something that happened to you before you moved to town, and happened in a place and a time that will never catch up with you. And if it does catch up with you, your past won't turn people against you nearly as fast as the lying about it, the latter being a sign of both cowardice and contempt for the level of sophistication in town.

Once, when I was about ten years old, a man named Cliff materialized on a bright Saturday morning, pumping gas at the Texaco station beside the Catholic church. He had a terrible purple-pink scar on his right cheek that didn't look real. It looked like something a makeup man would paste to the cheek of an actor playing an evil pirate or an unredeemed escaped convict who had an urge to kill nurses when they sang to themselves. But before the question could be hinted at, Cliff told everybody that the scar was the result of a racing accident. He would quickly add that he had sworn off car racing forever. Of course, this bit of information made him popular with the boys, and they started hanging out at the Texaco station after school to pester Cliff for more details of his racing days. Cliff couldn't resist talking about the Indianapolis 500 or at least letting it drop into the conversation once in a while before he said he'd sworn off forever. Before long, high school manhood was aroused and someone suggested a drag race. Cliff tried to get out of it, but the more he tried, the more the boys kept after him, and an awesome inevitability propelled him toward the full-moon of an April midnight when one hundred high school boys and girls who had seen *Rebel Without a Cause* perhaps three hundred times among them were gathered on the little hillocks at either side of Canaan Gap (the thrilling curve in the back road to Canaan where someone was killed about once every two years) and all of them hoping to see someone killed that night, preferably Cliff. The race course was a loop, with the start and finish at the gap, where everyone was watching. One of the boys had brought a .22 rifle as the starting gun. It did not make a very loud noise and did not sound at all like a gun going off, only like a loud smack. This was afterwards cited by those who would excuse Cliff's slow start. ("Real racers get used to real loud guns.") However, he not only started last but somehow started his car in reverse. He lost the race right there, but anyway, he got the car into drive and went forward and disappeared from sight, with all the teenagers cheering. They were sure Cliff had been clowning with the reverse gear trick and planned to come in way ahead of the other two. They waited the five minutes it took to do the loop at faster than the speed of light, and when they heard the distinct whining drone of an engine consuming itself, they cheered again. But Cliff's car did not appear first. The two rivals came first and crossed the finish line in a dead heat. The crowd waited and waited, but there was no sign of Cliff. Eventually they relinquished all hope of seeing the flaming crash, but they were not utterly disappointed. Their mood shifted from itchy excitement to mature and prideful solemnity, and they piled into the cars that had brought them there and drove off in somber procession around the loop, searching for the place where Cliff had killed himself.

They couldn't find him. Some people thought he might have taken a wrong turn and killed himself on another road, but that wasn't much help to the search party. The search had to be given up long before dawn, when the state police were sure to find the charred, mangled car and the corpse burned beyond all recognition. There was some debate about whether anyone should tell the police who the dead man was. This issue was never resolved, because

**145**

when the state police did find the car, it was in fine shape and there was no body in it. They found it in the little parking lot beside the Pawling, New York, railroad station.

No one ever heard from Cliff again, but about six months later our deaf town cop, who had lifted the one and only good fingerprint he ever got in his life from the steering wheel of that abandoned car, received confirmation from the FBI that our man Cliff the racing driver, also known as Wayne Butters, had come straight to Four Corners after his parole from Sing Sing, where he'd been doing three to ten on a forgery–grand larceny conviction. In prison, he had developed a very bad infection from a tooth abscess, which had required extensive surgery.

Cliff was the first real liar I ever came across, and he didn't make a big success of it, as you can see. Fred Beale, who owned the Texaco station, said he would have kept Cliff if he had told the truth about himself. And Fred probably would have. That was the trouble with Four Corners. It rewarded honesty to the point of absolute dullness.

The level of deceit I grew up with wouldn't have fooled a six-year-old. I heard lies like: "You'll be glad you walked to school in another ten years," and "Don't be silly! Of course they will grow, dear!" and "Divorce? Adam and I never thought of it." But these hardly counted as lies.

Then in high school, because of the sixties, my generation was encouraged to be open about everything. Sex was not taboo, nor was drinking. And marijuana was quietly tolerated. Our guidance counselor, the one with the singsongy voice, went to Esalen the summer after my sophomore year, and he came back all gushy and kissy and talking about "being honest about our feelings." He organized these groups where we were supposed to say just what was on our minds, and so the boys would say they were very horny, and the girls would say they were sick of school. Once I told the guidance counselor he was a wimp, and one of the boys said to him, "When you talk about loving everybody, it makes me hate everybody, especially you!"

I think the worst lie I told in all my adolescence was: "I'm doing my homework, Mother." And in college the practice of openness was so widespread that I ceased even hiding my marijuana cigarettes. It was a badge of our age, speaking the truth of our feelings, and older people had come to expect it from us by the time I got to Radcliffe, in the fall of '68 after all that craziness at Columbia. The let-it-all-hang-out code was already at least two years old, and anybody who didn't live by it was considered uptight and probably a lesbian or headed for a crack-up. I remember once Ellie was letting it all hang out with an assistant professor of English, telling him that Henry James "sucks" and "his characters never say anything but 'So there you are!' They're so fucking insipid—I mean, fuck!" And the assistant professor kind of blinked as though he was trying to change the picture inside his head or something, and then he said:

"If a rock concert is the apotheosis of all art to you, what sort of literature can you appreciate? 'Why don't we do it in the road?' rather says it all, doesn't it? It is your theme song, the ode to public fornication. To be quite, as you would put it, up front with you, Miss Bliss, you lack inner life, and that is why you find Henry James insipid. I pity you and all those who look to you for leadership. I sincerely do. You have no unspoken thoughts."

I guess he was basically right. I mean, there wasn't any such thing as the unspeakable in our lives. It meant that lying was kind of a dying art for the class of '72. When Watergate happened, we couldn't believe it.

I don't want to get too heavy about this. We weren't angels. We were just protected from having to learn guilt until we got out into the big world. You would have thought Ellie had learned some, with her Brooklyn street smarts, but she came from one of those defenseless families where everybody wore his heart on his sleeve. She actually didn't find out until law school that it wasn't always practical to say where you were coming from. In a way, she was a small-town girl too. I thought she had caught on (even though I didn't like it) when she started taking her cues from Roger, that "repressed femininity" business and all, but look where she was now, letting it all hang out in a new style.

I thought I had caught on after my big mistake in East Harlem, but Jesus Christ, look where I was! About to be out on the street again, like Ellie. We were a pair of *simpletons*, we two elite brain pool 'Cliffies!

You see, up to this point, I had thought that if a guy lies for you, it means he's your friend, he's in your corner. Ron had seemed to like me. But Ron had seemed to be so much that he wasn't. Wide-open Ron with his heart on both sleeves! The whole thing was a lie, a completely fake personality. He was a phenomenon of guile.

*"What are you doing, Sarah Makepeace? What in god's name are you doing? Where is that story?"* Ron's voice crashed through my speculations. I realized that I had been staring into space, and then his body came lumbering toward me.

"Ron! Ron! It's Sondra on the phone!" Willie called excitedly, trotting after him. "She's furious, Ron. You've forgotten you're giving a dinner party."

Ron stopped, slapped a hand to his forehead, and exclaimed, "Oy, veh!"

"You'd better go," Willie said gently.

"You should have reminded me, Willie!" Ron muttered. He tore back down the aisle, spoke into his phone for half a second, and tore out of the newsroom, muttering to himself as he went.

There was a collective sigh of relief. Ten minutes later, Willie dismissed us all. The Leroy Street pool had been closed for half an hour.

"Let's hear it for Sondra Millstein!" Greg said to all of us on the elevator.

"The poor broad!" said Eddie.

"I can't wait till Monday," said Susan.

"I know," I said morosely. "It's going to be awful."

# XX

There was one thing Ron had left out of his tirade against me. The *Crimson*. I figured I might be still hanging on by a thread with him if he was holding that little end of it for me. A very slender thread, though, since on Monday the story about the mayor wouldn't be any truer. I wished Monday would never come.

Saturday was hotter than all the days before, and my apartment wasn't air conditioned. My landlord catered to refugees of small towns who would put up with anything to live in Greenwich Village. The pair below me, two young men from Texas who had met and fallen in love in an unemployment office, had a bathtub in their kitchen. After Texas, a bathtub in the kitchen could seem downright friendly to a bona fide homosexual. Jim 'n' Jim (as they stenciled on their door) painted the bathtub black and gold and filled it with giant goldfish, and they were living happily ever after down there except when the cockroaches produced a new litter. When this happened, Texas banshee cries could be heard around the corner on Gay Street and the whole building reeked of Black Flag. The cockroaches would then skedaddle up to my apartment while their cousins slithered down to the first floor to listen to grand opera with the solitary figure in 1-A. I have no idea what he did for a living, but he must have been even more desperate to escape his hometown than I was, because he never complained about anything in the building, not even when the landlord left the heat off for a whole month one January for alleged "boiler readjustments." We didn't know what his name was. Jim 'n' Jim said the name on his mailbox, Ostreicher, had been there before he moved in. He had no visible means of support and he stayed in his apartment listening to records all day. He was terribly pale. Naturally, we called him the Phantom of the Opera.

Usually, his music woke me up on Saturday mornings, but this time the heat did it. Imagine getting fired and having to sit around in this heat, I remember thinking.

I called Ellie and tried to persuade her to join me at the pool.

"It's too hot," she said.

"That's the point," I said.

"Naah. The place will be too crowded. But thanks for asking, Sarah. You're the first person who's called me all week."

"How's the job-hunting?"

"Ask me another question."

"Had any good orgasms lately?"

"Sarah, you're really infantile."

"I think it's your duty, Ellie, as the wife of a psychiatrist—"

"Sarah, don't start that!"

"I've got a serious question for you."

"I'm not sure I want to hear it."

"How come men never have to have mastectomies?"

"Jesus, Sarah, won't you ever grow up? How do you know they don't have to?"

"You've got me there. I'm not up on the statistics. It could be there's a dramatic increase among fathers who share the parenting."

"Goodbye!"

"No, wait, Ellie—let's get together next week. I think I'll be fired on Monday."

"You're just saying that to make me feel better."

"I'm not. If I don't write this fairy tale about the disappearing mayor, my boss is going to fire me."

"The disappearing what?"

"The mayor. Somebody told me he walks off the job every once in a while and nobody can find him."

"Sounds like epilepsy."

"I thought it might be a little snort."

**149**

"Or intermittent autism. You could probably tell by examining his pupils."

"Great idea, Ellie! I'll hop right up to Gracie Mansion, shine a little flashlight in his eyes, and say, 'Sorry, Your Honor, just checking your whereabouts.'"

"You really think you're going to get fired?"

"Yeah."

"Why do you keep wanting people to reject you, Sarah?"

"You think I'm *trying* to get fired?"

"Not consciously—"

"Ellie, I didn't even try to get *hired* there, so— There is such a thing as a victim of circumstance, you know. Bricks do fall onto the heads of people who don't have a hidden brick-braining wish. And my boss is—is— Oh, Ellie, I wish you were studying astrophysics!"

"Yeah, I know. Roger says I'm getting aggressive again."

"For once, Roger and I agree."

"He says I've got confused gender identification. He says it's very common in depressed women with postgraduate degrees. Their id is female, but their ego is male."

"I take it back. Honestly, Ellie, why couldn't you have married a film-maker? How can you stand him analyzing you all the time? What does he say when you pop your blackheads? That it's a confusion of waste functions? Or maybe it's another symptom of gender confusion and of course yet one more of the infinite manifestations of penis envy—"

"Come on, Sarah! Roger wouldn't—"

"Can you imagine the insecurity of a man who goes around telling himself: All women envy me? Did Freud ever once suggest he could arouse penis envy in men? No, and we don't have to ask why, do we, Ellie? Nobody asked Mrs. Freud. I'm your friend, Ellie, so I won't ask you whether Roger ever worried he wasn't—"

"Sarah, stop it! Roger likes *you*. Why do you have to be so hostile to him after all this time? It's been over two years since we got married."

"That was a nice apartment."

"I've told you a million times that Roger would have paid half the rent until you found another roommate."

"I didn't want another roommate."

"He says you'll forgive him when you get married."

"I don't hold a grudge. I like this apartment better."

"Roger thinks you should come see us more. You want to come to dinner next week?"

"If Roger would stop being so fucking patronizing, Ellie, we might get along. Tell him he can stop feeling sorry for me. I like living alone. I'm having a good time."

"You're just about to get fired, and you're having a good time. You must have a new boyfriend."

"I'm surprised at you, Ellie. Where've you been? Men do not have to be the center of a woman's life anymore. Ask your buddy Doris Munster."

"All she talks about in group is her ex-husband."

"Really! Really? What does she say? What did he do to her? Did he beat her up? Cheat on her? Yeah, I bet he cheated on her. Who is he, Ellie? What's he doing now?"

"Just some guy named Jeff Munster. He lives in the city. I don't know what he does."

"Jeff Munster! So she didn't keep her own name! No shit!"

"I shouldn't have told you. We're not supposed to talk about what people say in group."

"So tell me some more. What's Doris's problem?"

"Who's your new boyfriend? Do I know him?"

"I don't know. You might."

"What's his name?"

"He doesn't want me to tell anybody."

"He's married?"

"Umm."

"Oh, Sarah!"

"I'd better get to the pool before every towel space is taken, Ellie. I'll talk to you next week."

But the cement beach beside the pool was nearly empty when I arrived. I picked a choice spot not too near or too far from the water. For two hours I was content, and my Simenon mystery became stained with thumbprints of suntan oil, clues to the murder of time. The embittered concierge was the most likely suspect, since she did the cooking for the building and the beautiful actress upstairs died of poisoning. But it was also pleasing to imagine a hidden monstrous character in the depths of the concierge's shy, walleyed husband. As the great detective sipped a calvados and considered which one was pretending not to know who took the rabbit stew upstairs, my elbows suddenly began to hurt me through the towel. I sat up. The pool had taken in half the population of the Village. A substantial other portion had found spaces around me. Children shrieked happily and tried to drown one another. Tired Village mothers sat with their feet in the water, looking martyred and apologetic in their faded bathing suits. An old Italian woman with hunched brown shoulders lay curled up on her towel in the fetal position, reading *Cosmopolitan*. Slender, skittish men lolled everywhere in their skimpy bikini trunks. I watched the pool and listened to the conversations behind me:

"Was she tripping? *Was* she *trip*ping! My dears, the bitch was just about in*vi*sible!"

". . . the advanced bar if it wasn't for that douchebag . . ."

". . . all the letters back, like he thought I was going to blackmail him. Can you imagine the tackiness of . . ."

"Have you seen *Amarcord?* That's much more commercial. Listen, they all sell out. Fellini's no different."

". . . three auditions this week. She was so depressed! She was dropping 'ludes, talking about how she was gonna quit dance . . ."

". . . playing for the bimbos, George, you can't survive . . ."

"This goon, you should have seen him! His neck was bigger than your waist. I got paranoid for a minute."

"You thought he was going to off you, Renato? You've really been smoking too much, man. That stuff is . . ."

"How can you say that? Why should there be two kinds of great? Mass appeal is always a sign of mediocrity."

"Do you honestly think *Last Year in Marienbad* was a good film?"

"You always bring that up, Philip. Can't you find another . . ."

"Come on, Renato! This is 1976. Things like that don't happen anymore!"

"God, I've gained so much weight since Alastair left me! It's horrible! I'll never let myself go like that again."

". . . more limited vision than, say, Bergman because Antonioni's reacting against extravagant sentimentality, and reactionaries tend to exclude . . ."

"Shit, John! What if he *is* elected?"

"Horrible! I'm so miserable I could kill him!"

". . . sentimentality of minimalism . . ."

"Ooh! Honeee! It is *so hot!*"

Here everyone laughed. When the conversation resumed, people spoke in whispers and the lowest of tones. Would Gilbert Foley ever have heard a conversation like that? Gilbert Foley probably never went to a city pool in his life. Ron said he was poor once, but Ron's credibility— the thought of Ron's credibility sent me into the pool. The swimmers had reached a critical mass. I got out again. This time a skinny man had his legs across my towel, a guy with pink plastic eyeshades and a black stretch bikini with a shocking-pink rose smack dab across his condensed private parts. Which one was he? The film freak? The dancer? The one whose lover wanted the letters back? Not the one who had gained weight. Probably the dancer. They called women douchebags.

"Excuse me," I said. "You're lying on my towel."

"Oh, I'm *so* sorry!" he said meekly, just like my mother.

Then I felt guilty. I wasn't what you would call a fanatical homophobe. I just thought there were too many fags in the Village. I thought some of them should be distributed out in Queens and Staten Island, out in Rockland County where Kevin lived, places that needed more weirdness in them to keep people from ODing on the neat lawns.

I headed back to my apartment to finish the Simenon novel. It turned out that the concierge had done it in the mistaken belief that her husband's playreading with the actress upstairs had been the real thing, heard through a heating vent in a downstairs hall bathroom. He: "I never dreamed this could happen! My life is beginning again." She: "If only you were free!"

It was still very hot, and I couldn't sleep. I felt as though the hours were creeping by in a horrible slow countdown until Monday morning. But Kevin was due to come by around eight that night, and for once I was looking forward to it without any reservations. I guess I had stopped conning myself that I would break things off between us. I only wanted him to get there fast. I wanted to see him charge through the door, hear him bark, "Take your clothes off!" and watch him remove the little gun from his belt to put it on my bookshelf before he came at me with his maniacal ardor. That was the one careful, deliberate thing he did—set the little gun aside on the bookshelf before he accosted me. It was like a little ritual of cops' implacability. It showed he could be really cool even when he was so excited. It made him sexy as all getout. The frisson of possibilities in that gun! My father hated guns, of course. I had been brought up to abhor them. But Dad was the kind of person who would have used a gun if he'd had one. Like Ron. There were certain similarities of temperament. I *had* to stop thinking about Ron.

But naturally I didn't stop thinking about Ron until I heard Kevin's tread on the stairs. Or was it Kevin's tread? He was climbing so slowly!

"Kevin!" I said, opening my door.

"Who did you think?" he said, but without the maniac's glint in his eye.

**153**

He walked past me, sighed, sat down on the chair in the corner, and said in a queer flat voice, "I need a cigarette."

## XXI

"She wants me to make up my mind," he said, now into his third double vodka and his sixth cigarette. "She says if I don't do it, she'll decide for me."

We were sitting in a secluded booth in Harvey's Saloon, a desolate bar on lower Seventh Avenue, about ten blocks from my apartment. The three other customers present, all seated at the bar, were talking in the low, gravelly voices of alcoholics. The bartender was missing a hand. He served up drinks with a prosthetic hook. We had wandered into the place on impulse, or perhaps because Kevin liked the look of it. Two minutes after he got to my house, he had suggested a little stroll "to buy some more cigarettes." The cigarettes in Harvey's were a dollar a pack.

"But maybe that's a good thing, Kevin," I responded. "Maybe you need a deadline."

"I can't take deadlines, not for something like this. And she knows it, the bitch! She's being a real hard-on. I think she suspects something."

"You mean about us? How can you be a bitch and a hard-on at the same time?"

"The last time she did this to me, she almost got me suspended. 'Course, that's what she wants—she wants me to quit the force. I couldn't sleep last time. You can't put a deadline on your emotions, pick a day on the calendar, mark it: Tuesday, stop loving her. You know how long this ambivalence has been with me? The day we got married, I was ready to take the limo to La Guardia—"

"Why should you stop loving her? Who said anything about that?"

"If I stopped loving her, I could move out."

"Why didn't you take the limo to La Guardia? Maybe if you can figure that out—"

"Because I hadda pick up Vito around the corner. I couldn't leave him stranded. Vito was my best man."

154

"You couldn't have thought about it very long."

"Whadda you mean? I thought about it all night, didn't sleep a wink. I still think about it. I figure Vito would have married her within six months."

"And?"

"And! Don't you see?"

"Then you wouldn't have felt guilty."

"I couldn't let her marry Vito! Vito's a slob."

"Kevin, sometimes I really can't understand why you come to see me. You're still in love with her."

"I'd go crazy if I didn't come to see you. Even the doc thinks I would. He says that a guy like me, who's got underdeveloped—who doesn't follow through with his fantasies, like it's probably necessary to act out my impulses—"

"Dr. Festniss approves of me now, does he?"

"—and then have the fantasies. This way it gets all out in the open, and we can see what we're dealing with, you know, get to the bottom of my ambivalence."

"Oh, shit! He's even worse when he does give an opinion."

"He doesn't, but I figured out what he thinks."

"And I'm the dose of medicine, is that it? Thanks a lot, Kevin. You're a real heartthrob."

"Maybe I'm in love with you, too. I don't know."

"If you don't, who does?"

"Hey, I'm sorry, Sarah! Look, you want me to take you home? I can get drunk by myself. I've done it a few times."

"Why do you have to get drunk? You know what happens to men when they get drunk."

"Look, you don't want to drink with me, I'm not gonna force you."

"Oh, Kevin! Don't make it sound like that! I was just looking forward to— I mean, you didn't even kiss me when you came in. You didn't even look at me."

"Here's lookin' at you," he said, grinning and holding up his glass. "How's life at the world's most boring newspaper?"

"Not boring. I think I'm going to be fired."

"Hey, Harvey!" Kevin called. "Bring this girl another wine. What makes you think you're going to be fired?"

"Somehow I don't think his name is Harvey."

"Okay, so *don't* tell me. What'd you do? Try to write something nice about cops?"

"It's what I didn't do. Oh, it's stupid! I never should have told

**155**

my boss about the tip. See, I got this tip that the mayor disappears every once in a while, and then I asked Dalrymple, and he said it couldn't happen—"

"Clean weenie, Dalrymple. You believe him?"

"Well, if anybody's in a position to know, he—"

"He's in a position to know, sure! He lied to you."

"You mean it's *true?*"

"I heard some guys in the precinct talking about it, very hush-hush. Nobody's supposed to know."

"Kevin, why didn't you tell me about this before? Where does the mayor go? How often does he go on the blink? My god, Kevin, do you know how big a story this could be?"

"Yeah. That's why it's so hush-hush. Look, I don't know anything about it, except the guys said somebody in the Village found him."

"When was that?"

"I forget. About a month ago, maybe."

"You've known for a month, and you didn't *tell* me?"

"There's lots of things I don't tell you."

"Oh, Kevin! Do you think you could find out more? It might mean my job."

"What about *my* job? I gotta think about that, you know. Nobody's supposed to know about this. Hey, Harvey, hit me again!" he called.

"What's the matter, Kevin? I've never seen you like this."

"I told you. She wants me to make up my mind."

"That's not really anything new. What did you do, read up on alcoholism? You should stop reading those books. They make you sick."

The bartender brought him a fresh drink.

"Is your name really Harvey?" I asked.

"Do you know how many people ask me that?" he said, and he went off without answering the question.

"I think I take after my Uncle Nick," Kevin said. "He was a manic depressive." He hung his head.

"Oh, so you're reading about manic depression."

"Dr. Festniss thinks I'm onto something. He got very interested last time when I told him about Uncle Nick."

"Eureka, Dr. Festniss looks interested! Five thousand dollars later he tells you you're onto something."

"The money is part of the therapy. It's not five thousand dollars, Sarah!"

156

"Add it up. Fifty an hour once a week for two years comes to five thousand two hundred dollars."

"He goes away for six weeks in the summer."

"Okay, so I'm a little over. Where does he go? No, let me guess. Martha's Vineyard."

"How did you know?"

"Oh, shit, he really *might* know Roger."

"Who's Roger?"

"I told you, he's my college roommate's husband. He always goes to the Vineyard in August. He's a shrink too."

But Kevin did not appear to be listening. He was scribbling on the table with his plastic drink stirrer.

"Damn!" he said presently. "Damn!"

"What is it?"

"You got it right. I *have* spent almost five thousand dollars on Festniss."

"Well, it's deductible."

"He owes it to me to tell me what to do."

"You deducted it, didn't you, Kevin?"

"It's nobody's business."

"Come on! The IRS doesn't show your tax returns to anybody! That's against the law."

"Huh! You're telling me? What do you think I do for a living?"

"Well, of course, you would know—"

"How easy it is to get someone's tax returns. Yeah."

"Ellie deducted Roger when she was living with him, because he was still her shrink."

"I bet you've got a lot of criminal associates," he said, grinning at me in the old way and rubbing his calf against mine.

"Let's go back to my place," I said softly, leaning toward him. He leaned forward too, and kissed me nuzzlingly. Then he pulled his head back a little and butted his forehead against mine. I had seen cows do this to each other in Four Corners when they were going out of heat.

"What's the matter, Kevin?" I said.

"I'm sorry, lady. You think I like being like this?"

"Being like what, Kevin?"

"Like Uncle Nick."

"Who is this Uncle Nick? You've never mentioned him before."

"Hey, Harvey!" Kevin yelled. "Hit me again!"

Then he said to me, "I don't say I'm exactly like him. He was

**157**

born in Calabria. He's the last one in the family born over there. My grandmother used to say the luck of Calabria stuck with him. He really had it rotten. Nothing worked out for him."

"That's supposed to make him a manic depressive? Bad luck?"

"No, no! It was the way he was, always up or down—way up or way down."

"I take it he's dead."

"Naah, he's alive. He's healthy as a horse now. What am I saying? He practically *is* a horse. He goes to the track every day, rain or shine."

"He sounds okay. Why are you worried about being like him if he's healthy as a horse?"

"You get to be eighty-five, you don't hafta worry about what you're gonna do with your life. It was before that he had the ups and downs."

"I tell you what. Let's go back to my house, and you can give me Uncle Nick's life story."

"When I was real small, I remember, he was into these get-rich-quick schemes. He would send away for pamphlets. Most of them just told you to be nice to everybody and smile all the time and think positive, but every once in a while he'd get a pamphlet that told him how to sell a product—you know, how to hype a ladies' face cream or perfume or hairbrushes—and Uncle Nick wanted to be a millionaire, but he didn't have a profession. Oh, he was smart. He used to say—"

"Kevin, why don't we go—"

"He used to say, 'This country was built on suckers. I'm a good American. I'm gonna build some more.' He thought Americans would buy anything because the lady next door had thirty pairs of shoes. She read in a magazine that it's better for your feet to keep changing your shoes. Uncle Nick thought if she believed that, he could make her believe that Charmante face cream would make her wrinkles go away. He sent away for the samples—those were free—and he sold them all to that lady. He was so excited! He was running up and down the street grabbing people by the arm and telling them to go in with him on this wonderful business he was gonna start. He was so excited! He hit on everybody in the family too. He said there was a money-back guarantee, that you couldn't miss. He must have collected about a thousand dollars from Pop and the other backers."

"They gave him the money?"

"Sure. This was his first big project, and Uncle Nick was so nice, so charming, everybody thought he was going to make them rich. When the boxes of Charmante came, he got all excited again, and he spent two whole days out selling. He sold the whole damn shipment in a week. Five hundred jars. The women really went for it, and everybody in the family was excited. They were all saying, 'Uncle Nick's gonna be a rich man! He's gonna buy us a big house in the country. Maybe he'll buy us a new car.' But a couple of weeks after he had sold all the jars and already sent for a new shipment, Aunt Rosie broke out in hives, and the doorbell rang, and she opens it, and there's a woman with hives, and pretty soon the doorbell rings again, and there's another woman with hives, looks like she got stung all over her face by a pack of bees. And then—"

"I think I can guess what happened to that business," I said. "But that doesn't prove he's a manic depressive."

"Oh, yeah? He went to bed for a month! He wouldn't eat. Aunt Rosie thought he was going to starve himself to death."

"I still don't see how you're supposed to be like him, Kevin."

"I said I wasn't exactly like him. But he was indecisive. After that fiasco with the Charmante face cream, he never could stick to anything. He got schemes again, but he had about five schemes going at once. He'd be selling some stupid perfume and he'd be betting on the horses and he'd be working in the basement on his inventions. Every time something went wrong, he'd drop everything and go to bed. And then a month or two later, he'd be back at the inventions and the horses and the door-to-door sales."

"What do you mean, inventions?"

"Crazy things he was making down in the basement. Once he made a windshield wiper and sunshade combination thing for cars that worked perfect except that when it was on, you couldn't see out of your car. Another time he made a chair that climbed stairs. Nobody ever saw that one work, but he swore to us the fucker carried him halfway up the stairs before he made some stupid move and fell over backwards and broke his collarbone. That's when the super exiled him from the basement."

"But how did he get along? How did he support his family?"

"There was only Aunt Rosie. They didn't have kids. I think my old man was the one who kept him going. Pop had a soft spot for Uncle Nick because Uncle Nick dropped out of college so Pop could go to high school. Pop always said if Uncle Nick had been able to finish college, he would have invented the atom bomb."

**159**

"Oh, brother!"

What was I to do? I sat there drinking with Kevin for another two hours, and my yearning for his body grew so cloying that I began to imagine myself marrying him, and I could see him taking my father by the arm, maybe nudging Dad's elbow to his gun, leading him across the room while he said, "I want you to meet my favorite uncle. This man is so smart, he could have invented the atom bomb!"

Kevin got so drunk he finally worked up his nerve to tell me that the Psych One chapter on manic depression said impotence was one of the common symptoms of the depressive cycle. When I walked him to his car (he said he had driven home in worse states), he called me his good buddy and said he wished I was his partner. Then he said all women sucked. Then he said he loved me and would kill any other man who laid hands on me, even though he was impotent and hated being a cop.

## XXII

When they fired me from the East 118th Street Block Association, the board of directors had a public hearing. I was invited to defend myself. Mr. Rivera was the judge. My accusers, Mr. and Mrs. Jorge Castro, the parents of two apricot-cheeked girls who had been caught red-handed with *What Is Love?* and *Before You Try It*, silently passed the books to him. This was a mere formality. Most of the board members had already seen the books. The illustration on page 28 of *What Is Love?* had clearly been perused by a coffee drinker, someone with a dirty thumb, a cigarette smoker, a person eating or cooking yellow rice, and someone who perhaps had a cold or an allergy. I don't know why I felt so sure that the viewers of page 28 were men, but I did know that East Harlem men were proud and at the same time sufficiently reticent to have had very few opportunities to compare their own erections to anyone else's. (It did trouble me that I had not summoned the courage to tell Jesus and Fredo that what page 28 showed was certainly on the large side of average. To this day I wonder whether the men of East 118th

Street are not suffering from the cruel comparison to a false ideal.) Whereas I felt equally certain that the viewers of page 41 in *Before You Try It* were women. The page was not smudged, but the top corner curled down as if it had been clutched between clean intent thumbs and forefingers many, many times. For that matter, the corner of the page opposite was also curled, over the text with the subheading "The Importance of Foreplay," for which the two drawings on page 41 were illustrations.

"Did you give these books to Jesus Cintron and Alfredo Vasquez and tell them to make sure all the girls on the block was to see them?" Mr. Rivera asked me.

"Yes," I said.

He polled the board.

"That's it," said Mr. Rivera. "You been fire."

So that is what I expected from *The Newspaper*. Something very cut and dried.

But no one approached me when I walked in Monday morning. Ron was on the telephone. Willie Crespi was playing with a bunch of rubber bands. Akelroyd had on his expression of haughty big-shit columnist. Greg was on the phone with Alex.

The only thing out of the ordinary at all happened when Jenny Locke passed my desk.

"Morning, Sarah!" she said with a wide, bright grin.

"What's going on? Jenny said hello to me," I said to Greg as I heard him slam down his phone.

"I don't have time to talk," he said, and he dashed off toward Dayside.

Willie Crespi soon walked over to me. His hands were tangled in rubber bands.

"What are you doing here, Sarah?" he asked.

"My City Hall stint is over," I said.

"Oh," he said. He opened his mouth as if to say something else, frowned, and then turned around and walked off.

Greg came dashing back to his desk. He was so frantic to roll a piece of copy paper into his typewriter that it took him three tries to get it straight.

"Slug it 'Endorse'!" Ron shouted, without the loudspeaker.

Greg squinted at the typewriter for a moment, then began typing in short, quick bursts. I walked around behind him to read his lead.

"Governor Feely has decided to indorse Senator George Love of

New Mexico in the presidential race," I read.

"Greg, you've got a typo," I said.

"Get the fuck off my back!" he grouched. "Go away! Don't bother me!"

It was a big story, even though no one could figure out which way the bigness fell. The governor was a singularly private man when it came to explaining his endorsements. Usually he didn't make them. He had a number of incongruous interests, such as Thomas Aquinas and belly dancers. If he hadn't been governor of New York, Feely might have fit in well as a college professor at Bennington or Sarah Lawrence, places where there was a lot of modern dance. It was so unusual for Governor Feely to make an endorsement and for a newspaper to find out about it in advance that Greg was very proud of his scoop.

Ron was too. Ron was preoccupied with the story all day. Once I tried to get his attention to tell him about what Kevin had told me, but he just didn't have ears for anyone except Greg.

As the day wore on, Ron's attention began to wear on Greg.

Ron came galumphing back to Greg's desk at noon.

"What does this mean, Greg?" he asked. "I want to know what the county leaders are saying."

Greg called a few county leaders, who all said they didn't know what it meant.

"What are Kennedy's people saying?" Ron asked at two o'clock.

Kennedy's people said the senator could not be reached. For deep background, they said they didn't know what it meant. They asked Greg what it meant.

"What does Love say about it?" Ron asked at three.

"Love isn't answering my phone calls," Greg said.

"What about your source?" Ron asked. "He's on Love's staff, isn't he? I told Gil he was on Love's staff."

"No, Ron. I told you I got this from a New York source," Greg said.

"How do we know it's true?" Ron said flightily.

"God damn it, Ron, I should walk out of here! I should just fucking walk out of here!" Greg said.

"Greg! Don't be so touchy!" Ron said, smiling sweetly. "I trust you. You *know* I trust you! But we always have to ask ourselves who's going to gain. I happen to know that the state committee is— a faction is leaning toward the National Desk, and—"

"Oh, for god's sake, Ron! What do you think this is? Some kind of Willard Darby setup? The story is *true*."

"All right, all right. I want a new summary for page one. And I want you to put the significance in the lead. Does this make Love a contender?"

"A con*tend*er! Shit, Ron, all he's got is New Mexico! You know how many people live in New Mexico?"

"But Udall and Muskie are tied. Neither one can get the first ballot."

"Yes, Ron, *I* was the one who told you that this morning. Remember?" Greg said. He sounded at his wits' end. "That's why this gives Love a little more bargaining power. He'll get the judges he wants and more money for his solar energy project."

"You tell me what it means in the new summary," Ron said, as though he had not heard what Greg had just said.

Greg cursed while he wrote the new summary, shouted, *"Copy!"* so that Freddie would pick it up, and then sat back to wait for what he knew would be the next rethinking of the editors.

At four-thirty Ron came waddling back to his desk.

"Listen, Greg," he said, "we're holding the story tonight. Gil wants someone to talk to Love."

"Holding the story! *How can you do that?"* Greg yelled, jumping up.

"It's an exclusive," Ron said. "No one else has it."

"But half the county leaders know it by now, and the rest will know by midnight. *Ron, you made me call them!* You think they're going to sit on it? You think they don't know any reporters?"

"Greg, I thought you protected your stories—"

"I *told* you, Ron, once you start calling on a thing like this—"

"All right, I'll try to change Gil's mind. But we've got to get more on the meaning of this, Greg. You keep working on it. You try Love again."

I heard Greg swearing to himself as Ron moved away. He dialed Alex. He spoke in very low tones. I only caught snatches of what he was saying. "Assholes here . . . credibility . . . Love is a yo-yo . . . Why won't he . . . Yeah, yeah, that's what I said . . . When has he ever made sense?"

At five o'clock Ron came back again.

"Greg, how do we know Love isn't a stalking horse for Kennedy?"

"How do we know Udall isn't? Or Muskie? We only know what we know, Ron."

"Have you talked to Kennedy?"

"He's not around. His people are just as puzzled as we are.

Look, Ron, the thinking in the party here is that this is strictly a Feely move, that it has nothing to do with any overall strategy. Feely wants his day in the sun, and he'll get it from this. If he had endorsed Udall or Muskie, they would have said, 'Get in line.' This way he's Love's most important backer."

"That's it!" Ron said. "Feely's day in the sun! Put that quote in the second graph."

"It's not a quote, Ron. Unless you want me to quote myself."

"Why not? You're a political insider," Ron said.

"You're the boss," Greg said icily.

He quoted himself as a "seasoned observer" in the second graph, and the story ran that night.

The next day, a lot of people called him from the Muskie and Udall camps to ask him what it meant. That day Love allowed himself to be photographed in the kitchen of his Taos summer home, where he was helping his wife, the crippled former Olympic champion, make bread.

"I love New York," was his only comment.

Nobody was bothering me, so I read *The Newspaper* and eavesdropped on Greg's conversations. Once Willie Crespi stopped by my desk and looked as though he was about to say something, but he didn't.

That afternoon a distraught police officer went berserk in Central Park and began shooting at transistor radios, while at the same time five hooded men hijacked the Statue of Liberty ferry, full of tourists, and said they would hold the vessel until the "captive nations" were free. Mayor Simon went out on a coast guard cutter to negotiate with them, and the lady suing her doctor for malpractice over the quintuplets appeared in court with all her babies and her unemployed husband. I was so happy eavesdropping on Greg that I did not notice the newsroom emptying out.

The next morning Greg spoke to me again.

"Here she is, the savior of the Central Park Zoo," he said as I sat down. "What are you working on now, Sarah?"

"Nothing much," I said.

"Ron didn't send you out yesterday, either," Greg said. "You know, he even sent Freddie out yesterday."

"He did?"

"Yes. Didn't you see? Is your probation up yet?"

"No. I've got another month to go. Greg, you don't think . . ."

"I think it looks bad."

164

"Yeah, me too. I wish I could get a scoop."

"Maybe you're not cut out for it, Sarah. Some people aren't. Maybe that's what Ron was trying to tell you on Friday."

"You think . . ."

"They don't usually fire people here. This place is very genteel. If the bosses insult you, you're expected to quit. Akelroyd's done it five times."

"Akelroyd's so self-important. Look, I don't feel insulted. I know I'm no good."

"You should quit, then."

"I need the bread. Where else would I work? If I try to do some kind of do-goody work, they'll find out about what happened to me in East Harlem, and that leaves my wonderful writing career. The only place that takes people who leave a job like this after two months is *The Evil Eye,* and they hate me."

"Try a newspaper in another city."

"Outside New York? Are you crazy?"

"Maybe I could get you a job with the Democratic State Committee. Would you like that?" he said kindly, showing his gap.

My telephone rang.

"Hello," I said. "The truth is our business."

"Don't tell me you are required to say that every time you answer the phone, Sarah!"

"Oh, hi, Dad! No, that's just for new employees, to give them company spirit."

"How can you lend yourself to—"

"Don't start that again, Dad. Not this morning."

"This morning it's more important than ever. Did you see the editorial on NATO?"

"No, I don't read the editorials. Most of us—"

"Sarah, it is that kind of willful ignorance which will lead mankind into World War Three! You must resign. You must!"

"But, Dad, I'm not connected with the editorial page."

"You cannot want to work a day longer for those *war criminals!*"

My other line started ringing.

"Could I put you on hold, Dad? I'll be right back," I said before he could answer.

"Hello. Makepeace here."

"Hi, Sarah, how was the pool?"

"It was wall to wall. A man with a pink rose over his cock spread his legs across my towel."

"Only a rose? Didn't people—"

"It was on his bathing suit. You know what, Ellie? I think they should bring back the sodomy laws."

"I told you it would be crowded."

"What's up? My father's on the other line."

"I can call back."

"No, I'll get rid of him. You hang on."

I switched to him again.

"Hi, Dad. Listen, I'd better take that call. Did you have anything else you wanted to tell me?"

"I am finally going to write a letter today, Sarah, saying that my daughter—"

"Oh, Dad! Can't you leave me alone!"

"I'm thinking of coming into the city. I may have to take action."

"Oh, god! Write a letter!"

"Letters accomplish nothing."

"Maybe we can talk about it this weekend."

"I've had enough talk—"

"Dad! It's *my* life!"

"I don't think you value it enough."

"Oh, for Christ's sake!"

"I warned you."

"Dad! What are you going to do?"

"I am going to save my daughter."

"How?"

"Goodbye, Sarah."

"Dad!" But he had hung up.

I switched back to Ellie.

"Me again," I said.

"How's your old man?"

"Worse than ever. Now he's threatening to take action quote unquote if I don't leave *The Newspaper*."

"What does that mean?"

"How should I know? Maybe he'll chain himself to the front gate."

"I always liked your old man."

"You didn't have him for a father."

"Listen, we're having a dinner party on Saturday. Can you come?"

"Saturday? Gee, Ellie, I'd love to, but I already have a date."

"So? Bring your date."

"I don't think I could do that."

166

"Why not?"

"I just don't think I'd like to bring him to a party full of psychiatrists."

"Is this your married guy?"

"Yeah."

"I thought so. People who feel guilty are always nervous around psychiatrists."

"It's not that, Ellie. Actually, I'm afraid he'd try to pump them all for a free diagnosis."

"He sounds awful. What are you doing with a guy like that, Sarah?"

"He's not awful, Ellie. He's wonderful. He's just kind of anxious about himself right now."

"The wife?"

"The whole thing."

"What's so wonderful about him? Where'd you meet him? I know. He must be great in bed."

"I didn't say anything about that."

"You said he was a mixed-up wonderful guy, so—"

"But I meant—"

"Sometimes I get jealous of you—"

"MAKEPEACE, SARAH!" came the sound of Ron's voice over the loudspeaker.

"Ellie, I'm being summoned," I told her.

"What if we switched it to Friday. Seven-thirty. Could you come then?"

"Okay."

"And you won't bring a man?"

"No. But please don't put me with Barry Ross again. If I have to hear him say, 'I can dig where you're coming from,' one more time, I think I'll give him a karate chop."

"Yeah, Barry's sort of a creep, isn't he. Poor guy!"

"*Sort* of! I think Barry went into psychoanalysis to make himself over in the image of Hugh Hefner."

"SARAH!" Ron called again.

"I'd better go, Ellie," I said.

"Okay. Oh, and if you hear anything about a job—"

"Yeah, in the unemployment office!"

"Oh, Sarah!"

"FOR THE LAST TIME, SARAH MAKEPEACE, GET UP HERE!"

"'Bye, Ellie," I said.

Ron's urgency gave me hope. It seemed to signify a sense of the

**167**

fleeting. Perhaps he had a hot assignment ready?

"At your service, Ron," I said, giving him a little salute.

"Sarah, sit down," he said coolly, all the urgency gone from his voice. I took the extra chair by his desk.

"Is this going to take long?" I asked, trying a tack of coolness myself.

"Why? You're not working on anything, are you?"

"Oh, yes, Ron, that story about the mayor, remember? You've been so busy, you probably forgot. I've got a good lead now—"

"Of course I haven't forgotten, Sarah. I've got Greg working on that story now. I don't want you working on it."

"Greg! But it was my tip! Ron, just give me another week. I've got a source, an inside source in the Police Department—"

"Sarah, this is not a weekly paper! That story could break any day now. Do you realize how long you've known about it?"

"Yes, but there's a cover-up, Ron."

"Sarah, you've known about that tip for weeks. Do you realize other papers could know about it by now?"

"Not from me. I didn't tell anybody about it, except you."

"I'm putting Greg on it."

"Oh, Ron!"

"I've already put him on it."

"Why didn't Greg say anything to me?"

"Greg's a great reporter. He knows how to protect his stories. I had been hoping you would learn from him, Sarah. That's why I put you next to him. But you don't seem—"

"Ron! Ron!" Willie interrupted, "Gil wants to see you right away!"

This didn't quite register with Ron. He paused. Then he started to say something else to me:

"In fact, Sarah, you should think seriously about whether you—"

That was as far as he got, though, because Willie actually shook him by the shoulder then, and as Ron was about to shove Willie's arm away angrily, Willie said:

"Ron, you've got to hear this. Gil's beside himself. He's talking about sabotage on the paper. I've never seen him so upset! It's bad, Ron, very bad. Something happened to National's hotel reservations. Willard's been in there accusing you, and Gil wants to see you right away."

"What hotel reservations? What are you talking about?" Ron asked Willie, and I caught Freddie rolling his eyes heavenward in disbelief.

"The reservations at the St. Regis!" Willie said. "Somebody canceled them all, somebody from *The Newspaper*. And now they're all booked to TV crews from Kansas City and Los Angeles! There isn't one free room in the whole city, you know, for convention week."

"How the hell did Dixby let that happen?" Ron said, looking rather showily shocked.

"He says he didn't," Willie said. "He says someone used his name. Ron, I'm *telling* you, Gil thinks it might have been someone from Metro!"

"Oh, but that's preposterous!" Ron said. "Why would we do a thing like that?"

But he looked kind of odd, as though he was trying not to smile.

"That's what I said to Gil," Willie said. "We all work for the same paper. But he knows, Ron, how you felt about the credentials."

"I don't think I should even answer this accusation," Ron said.

"Sarah, you'd better get back to your desk," Willie said.

"Sarah! Are you still here?" Ron turned to me. "You get back to your desk! And don't tell anybody about this, understand?"

"Who would I tell?" I said.

But everybody in the newsroom had noticed Willie's agitation.

"What's going on up there?" Greg asked me. Ron and Willie were standing up, talking heatedly to one another.

"You mean you don't know?" I said sneeringly.

"Don't be a cunt! Ron looks like he's gonna hit Willie."

Just then Ron put his arm over Willie's shoulders and the two of them walked off toward Gil's office.

"I guess you didn't call that one right," I said.

"What's eating you?" Greg said. "I was going to buy you lunch, but I think I'll take Jenny."

"I'm meeting a source, anyway," I said.

I was really hurt. Having Greg turn traitor was much worse than having Ron call me a dumb goy in front of everybody. I spent my whole lunch hour looking over my shoulder to see whether Greg was spying on me and trying to think how I could get back at him. The same prostitute was hanging by her elbow in Seymour's Deli. She saw me looking over my shoulder.

"Be cool, honey," she said. "Nothin's comin' down today."

Back in the newsroom that afternoon, Gil went on one of his walks through the aisles. I spotted his thin form in the far distance. Did he know Ron was trying to get me to quit? Only ten days before, he had told me I was working like a tiger. Did he want me to quit now, too? He *said* I was sensible.

Gil's heron-like form came nearer. He would pass right by my desk. I contrived to be stretching, standing up, turning around.

"Hello, Mr. Foley," I said. "That was bad luck about the hotel reservations."

The man's eyes did not move. His face showed no sign that he had heard a human voice. He walked on past me in his trance of authority.

"Sarah!" Greg said as soon as he was out of earshot. "You don't talk to Gil like that! Never! No one speaks to him in the newsroom."

"I don't care."

"What's the matter with you, Sarah? You can't take chances like that. You're in a very precarious position here, kid. You've gotta keep a low profile."

"Oh, come off it, Greg! You've been trying to get me to quit."

"What was that about the hotel reservations? What hotel reservations?" he asked.

"Why did you steal my story?"

"What story?"

"My story about the mayor."

"That was *your* story? No shit! Hey, Sarah, Ron didn't tell me that. He said he had it from a source of his."

"I don't know if I believe you."

"Oh, Sarah! If we can't trust each other!" He clasped his hands and looked very tragic.

"I still don't know if I believe you," I said.

"We should make love, Sarah. Then you would trust me," he said, and he smiled his hokey smile. "Hey, shit!" he said. "Did something happen to Dixby's hotel reservations?"

"You didn't hear it from me," I said.

"Oh, wow! Tell me what happened!" He bounced up and down on his chair.

"Somebody from *The Newspaper* used Dixby's name, and now all the rooms are booked to TV crews from out of town. Willie said Gil was calling it sabotage, and the finger points to Ron. Do you think Ron would do something dumb like that?"

"He's a genius!" Greg said.

He darted over to Eddie Schwartz's desk to tell him the news. Eddie came to me to confirm it. For the rest of the afternoon, reporters kept stopping by my desk to ask whether Ron had made the call to the St. Regis himself or got one of his idiots to do it. This kept me pleasantly diverted, and the editors were all in a dither among themselves anyway, so I got through the afternoon without being fired.

As I was leaving that night, I had to pass Vincent Akelroyd and a copy editor, but they were hotly absorbed in disagreement.

Just as I passed through the doorway, I heard Vinnie shouting, "I don't have to take this!"

He came running to the elevators, breathing hard.

We had to wait for a minute or so, and Willie came running out before an elevator stopped on our floor.

"Vinnie, you can't do this to us on deadline!" Willie pleaded. As an elevator door opened, he grabbed Vinnie by the arm.

"Let go! I'm quitting!" Akelroyd shrieked. He wrenched his arm loose and stepped into a crowd of secretaries. I stepped in with him.

"You'll be sorry!" we heard Willie say as the door closed.

"What are you going to do, Vinnie?" I asked him. The secretaries were all extremely silent.

"I shall never set foot in here again!" he said as the elevator door opened, and he strode furiously away, leaving the secretaries cooing like a flock of frightened birds.

# *XXIII*

I went into a slump when I got home. Things were getting so exciting at *The Newspaper*, I wanted to stay there more than ever. I tried to tell myself that *The Newspaper* wasn't a good place, that everybody was a schemer there, and it might be a compliment to me from the hidden moral order of the universe to get the boot from a man like Ron. Jesus! The way he looked when he got the "news" of the canceled hotel reservations! As if he had swallowed five hundred canaries—no, sixty hotel rooms! Really he looked as if there were a jackal living in his brain and at that moment it had hopped up and taken a peep out at the world through his greedy eyes. Maybe he was a genius. He had such tremendous talent for falsity. What the hell would he do next? I had to know. I had to *be* there to see! If only I could hang on until the convention!

Of course, I knew I wouldn't hang on until then, and I felt left out already. I felt awful. I should have been thinking about all the things Dad had been saying to me, all that stuff about how *The Newspaper* was going to get us into World War III. That might have made me feel better. Willie Crespi had once tried to persuade me that it was *The Newspaper* and not Pearl Harbor that got us into World War II. Maybe it was true. If you listened to Gil Foley, *The Newspaper* made the earth turn. What a bunch of weirdos! Dad had no idea! Eddie Schwartz said even the fashion editor got around to claiming it was *The Newspaper* that had persuaded Jackie to stop wearing pillbox hats. Good old Eddie. If Dad could have heard *his* stories, he would long since have chained himself to the front gate. Well, Dad would be glad when I got fired. Dad would say it was a compliment from eternal truth. But Dad wasn't *involved!*

Whereas I was hooked on the place. Let's face it, I was hooked on Ron, on the suspense his evil genius kept generating. And Dixby's too. People said Dixby was smart as a whip. They said he was evil, at least as evil as Ron. I took their word for it. And very soon now, these two evil guys were going to have it out with each other in a big way. I couldn't bear to think I wouldn't see the fight. Everybody said there was going to be a fight. Eddie was taking bets on who would come out on top after convention week. He said he was going to make more money than he had made on the Ali-Frazier match. He wasn't going to go on vacation! Nobody was going to go on vacation. They all wanted to *be there*.

I drank two beers and climbed into bed at nine-thirty, falling asleep as soon as my head hit the pillow. But my depression continued. I kept dreaming I was supposed to be somewhere, although I didn't know where. Then I was in a theater, and somebody told me I would be on stage that night. I hadn't learned my lines. Then I was in the wings studying the script, and along came the director. He snatched the script from my hands and shouted, "You should know this by now! You should know this by now!" The director was Ron. A buzzer signaled the time for my entrance, and I was pushed on stage. I could not remember one line. I could not remember what character I was playing! The buzzer sounded again. I opened my eyes. Someone was buzzing my apartment.

I turned on the light. It felt late, very late. Kevin never came by really late without calling first. Sometimes men from the street buzzed when they wanted to duck inside and hide. There was no intercom, so I always went to the front door to look when I didn't know who it was. The buzzing went on while I pulled on my jeans and groped around for a T-shirt. I ran downstairs in my bare feet, and there was Kevin, grinning at me through the glass. Oh, god,

**172**

he's drunk again, I thought, but when he kissed me in the foyer, wetly and pressingly, his breath tasted sweetly normal. He shoved me against the foyer wall, said, "I've got a present for you," and then put my hand down against his crotch. "Oh," I said, "Kevin, let's—" but he kissed me again, and while I was losing myself in his warm wet lips, he struggled with something in his back pocket. Help! He's not going to take the gun off right here! I thought. But then he pulled away from me and gave a little bow as he held out a folded wad of paper. "For my skinny little honey pie," he said.

"What is it?" I said.

"Take a look," he said.

I moved toward the shaft of light coming in from the street. Kevin stood behind me, putting his hands inside my T-shirt as I unfolded the paper. I saw "Confidential" and "Close-out Report."

"You're not wearing a bra," Kevin said.

"What is this, Kevin?" I said.

"Turn the page," he said.

I did, and I saw "Confidential" again, then "Missing Persons Report," a lot of dates and numbers, and below them a text beginning: "Mrs. Simon reports her husband was last seen on or about May 2 at 0700 hours. She states he entered limousine driven by Detective Archibald Trotsky at front entrance of mansion and waved to her from back seat. . . ."

"Kevin!" I said. "Kevin, you got it! You got it! Oh, I *love* you!"

I spun around to hug him, and he pulled me back into the shadow, where he mumbled about "another present" and brought my hand down to the same place, only now his fly was unzipped and his cock was exposed in a little fascist salute. Why does it remind me of a little fascist salute? I remember thinking as he closed my fingers around the hot silky skin. And then I did a quick psychoanalytic run-through of the details of this relationship—the gun, the strong arms, the undercover work in the sleaze pit of the free world. When I met this character, I thought he was a small-time gangster, I recalled. What would Roger Einstein make of me? I cursed Roger for the way he made me feel accountable to him. Was it possible Freud had been God in disguise, trying to scare us in a new way? Was I awake? Was I dreaming?

"Kevin!" I said loudly. "Are you out of your mind?" Because by then he had unzipped my pants. I wrenched myself free and bolted for the stairs.

"Come on," I said. "I want to read this thing." I ran up three steps at a time. He ran after me. I took the chair by my dining room table. He paced back and forth, saying, "Hurry up, Sarah," while I read.

What he had brought me were two documents, the Missing Persons report filed on the afternoon of May 5, when Eunice Simon reported her husband had been gone three days, and the one called "Close-out Report," which told how on May 6, Officer Francis Noonan of the Sixth Precinct had found the "subject" sleeping on a bench in Washington Square Park. The Missing Persons report, much the most interesting one, was unsigned and stamped "Confidential" five times on each page. After the bit about the mayor getting into the limousine, it went on to say:

> Detective Archibald Trotsky, subject's regular A.M. driver, accompanied Mrs. Simon to the commissioner's office. He was deposed separately, and in every respects his statement is consistent with hers.
>
> The detective said he does not converse with the mayor until they are south of 14th Street. Both Trotsky and Mrs. Simon stated this was done at the mayor's request. "He gets a little extra shut-eye on the way down," Trotsky stated. On the morning of May 2, the route was not FDR Drive, but Second Avenue. Alternate routes have been in use since the latest rash of bomb threats following mayor's refusal to grant parade permit to Bay of Pigs veterans. Detective Trotsky stopped for red light at 14th and Second. He states he looked in rearview mirror here but was not able to see mayor. He states this was not unusual. Mayor often lay down on back seat. Trotsky states he tapped plastic partition, then light changed and he proceeded several blocks, coming to a stop again at Houston Street, where light was again red. He states he opened partition here and called, "Your Honor," in a loud voice, repeated it several times, and finally turned around to look at back seat. It was empty. He took note of time, 0721 hours. He pulled through intersection and telephoned Gracie Mansion. He admits he is aware this was not police procedure but states the Gracie Mansion detail is committed to protecting mayor's privacy. Here he stated, "Seeing this wasn't the first time he took like a detour on us, I wasn't too worried about kidnapping." Trotsky cited lack of forced entry evidence also as indicating unlikelihood of kidnapping. He recalls he checked both back doors to see they were properly locked before leaving Gracie Mansion driveway. There was not a scratch on them, according to Trotsky. Forensic dusted for prints today, but due to delay in report of subject's disappearance, prints may not be of any significance, as chain of evidence was not secured.

Trotsky has been suspended without pay, pending a departmental hearing. He has been apprised of need for confidentiality. He has 17 years on the force, five departmental commendations, and reputation for dedicated service.

"Wow!" I exclaimed. "Kevin, this is dynamite! Wait till my boss hears this! Whatever happened to that guy Trotsky?"

"He's back on the job, but you won't see it in the report," Kevin said, nuzzling my neck. "Hurry up. You don't have to read every word."

I flipped to page two of the Missing Persons report.

"Look there where it says 'Classification,'" Kevin said, pointing to a little box in the middle of the page.

"So? How'm I supposed to know what that means? It says 30R. What's that? Walkie-talkie language? Simon's IQ?"

"Don't be stupid! It means he's a runaway and he's over thirty. That's the classification for derelicts."

"I can't belieeeve this, Kevin! I've gotta call my boss!" I said, jumping up.

"Wait," Kevin commanded, and he grabbed my wrist.

"No, really, Kevin, he just about fired me today."

"I thought you said he just about fired you last week."

"Yeah, but it was worse today," I said as my eyes skimmed the page. I flipped to the next page. "Jeepers!" I said, all swear words having left me. "I feel like Woodstein!" My eyes had fallen on the real nugget of the document, the section called "Prior Occurrences," wherein a bit of the strange life of Lester Simon was revealed. It said:

Subject's wife states her husband has disappeared on five prior occasions, but never for more than 20 hours. She states first occurrence was on or about June 25, 1974, when she and he were spending the weekend with their friends the Dr. Ignatius Nussbaums in Hollis Hills, Queens. She states mayor was sitting in backyard reading *The Godfather* in the shade of a red maple. She went into the house "for a few moments." When she returned to the yard, the mayor was gone. He reappeared approximately 19 hours later in the backyard, or about noon the next day. She states second and third occurrences happened in June and September of 1975 but is not sure of exact days. She said she would check diaries if legal accuracy is required. She states that on both occasions the mayor walked off grounds of Gracie Mansion late at night after telling her he was going out for a short walk. Both times he surfaced at the Tamawa Democratic Club in Greenwich Village the following day. On fourth occasion she states she did not know him to be missing first-hand but received calls from his aides at City Hall who wanted to know his whereabouts. She recalls this was around the time of the Sanitation Department layoffs in late 1975. She recalls her husband returned to Gracie Mansion at the usual time that day, around 2000 hours. Fifth prior disappearance was March 16 of this year. Subject was last seen at the Friendly Sons of St. Patrick dinner at approximately 2200 hours. He was next seen entering the St. Patrick's Day Parade at 55th Street 1400 hours March 17. He marched up Fifth Avenue in front of Rose of Tralee singers. This verified in press reports. At the time, press said Mayor Simon was feuding with Cardinal Cooke and thought this was reason for his not marching with dignitaries at front of parade. He took his usual place in reviewing stand.

Mrs. Simon states her husband has never explained whereabouts after the disappearances or reasons for same. She spoke very emphatically when denying that he returned smelling of liquor. Commissioner thought questions on this subject upset her. She also states she knows of no mental history in subject or his family, and she has seen no signs of mental impairment in him. Two Department psychiatrists were present and asked about symptoms. Mrs. Simon states she believes pressures are cause. States "fiscal crisis made Lester get bad headaches." His only explanation to her, she states, "I needed to be alone."

"Oh, Kevin!" I said. "I can't let this wait."

I stood up. He shrugged disgustedly, and I dashed into the bedroom, where the phone was. I dialed the City Desk. They took ages to answer. Finally, a strange voice said:

"City Desk."

"Hi, this is Sarah. Can you connect me with Ron?"

"What? Ron's not here."

"I know, but you can put me through to his house. He told me you could."

"Who is this?""

"Sarah Makepeace. *Please!* This is important!"

"Do I know you?"

"God damn it, I'm a reporter! Put me through to Ron."

"Listen, you want to interview Ron, you call his secretary tomorrow."

"Oh, *shit!* Is Luddle still there?"

"Yeah."

"Ask him who Sarah Makepeace is. He'll tell you."

The jerk went off to ask Luddle. Kevin smoked a cigarette in my bedroom doorway. He looked like Marlon Brando when he blew the smoke out, Marlon Brando in *A Streetcar Named Desire*.

"Luddle says he doesn't remember you," the jerk said.

"Oh, no!" I cried.

"Just kidding," the jerk said. "Look, this better be something big, or it's gonna be my neck."

"It is big," I said. "Don't worry. Ron won't mind."

But when I heard Ron's phone ringing, my heart started to beat fast. What if he did mind? The phone kept ringing, five, six times. Kevin came to sit beside me. He undid my pants again.

"Hello?" Ron finally answered. He sounded sleepy and cranky. Should I hang up? Kevin was pulling my pants down.

"Hello? Who's this?" Ron said suspiciously.

"Hello, Ron. Can you hear me, Ron?"

"Yes, what—"

"Good! This is Sarah. I went through the paper, so I didn't know whether the connection—"

"Hurry up!" whispered Kevin. He was now undressing himself.

"Sarah Makepeace?"

"Yes, Ron, who else would it be?"

"Don't you know what time it is, Sarah? It's close to *two in the morning!*"

"No, it isn't, Ron. I'm sure it's only around one."

"Are you drunk again, Sarah? What the hell are you doing calling me at this hour?"

"Ron, I've got the story about the mayor! It's incredible, absolutely incredible!"

"Greg's doing that story. I told you that, Sarah. I don't want you working on that story anymore. Wait a minute. Didn't you quit today?"

"No, Ron. Whatever gave you that idea?"

"You were seen walking out with Vinnie Akelroyd. I was told you both quit at the same time. It might not be such a bad—"

"Ron, I've got the Missing Persons report on the mayor. He was missing for four days in May and the report says he was missing five times before that. His wife told the police he was missing only after he'd been gone three days, and the Gracie Mansion cops were covering up too. And you know where they found him last time? Sleeping on a bench in Washington Square Park! *Ouch!*"

"What did you say you had? Don't shout at me, Sarah. Speak in a normal voice."

"I *said* I've got the confidential Police Department Missing Persons report on the mayor. *Ow!*"

"Sarah, my god, where did you *get* it! I *knew* you were a great reporter! I can smell it every time!"

"Let's say there are a lot of people working for the city who don't like cover-ups, Ron."

"*Why'd you tell him about the report?*" Kevin whispered, and only then did I realize why he had been twisting my arm.

"So you went to the Patrolmen's Benevolent Association," Ron said. "Very clever! Very clever, Sarah! You are really catching on. Now, listen, I want you to bring that report in as early as you can. Can you get to the office at nine?"

"I thought you wanted me to quit."

"You reporters are so paranoid! Can't you take a little teasing?"

"Greg told me you wanted me to quit. I can do that, you know. I can keep this report. Because my sources don't want it out of my hands, Ron. It's for background use only. I couldn't hand it over to Greg, you see. That would be violating a trust."

Kevin kissed my neck.

"I'm going to have to talk to Greg!" Ron said woundedly. "Did he really tell you I wanted you to quit? I thought better of Greg."

Kevin lifted me onto his lap and proceeded to try to force the issue.

"Well, that's what he told me, Ron," I said. "I figured it was because you gave him my story."

"I didn't give him your story, Sarah. I wouldn't do that!"

"But you said just now—and in the office today, you said—"

"I was trying to make you work harder. I often use that technique with my reporters. They call it creative tension, ho ho! Now I let you in on one of my little secrets. But you won't tell anybody, will you, Sarah?"

"No-nooo!"

"What's the matter, Sarah. Are you crying?"

"Oh, ho, no! No, I just thought I was going to drop the phone."

"You must be excited, landing a story like this! Aren't you excited, Sarah? You'll have the lead story on page one tomorrow!"

"You mean it? The story's mine?"

"I told you, it was always yours! Don't you believe me? I want you to be a star, Sarah. I want you to be as famous as Vincent Akelroyd!"

"Gee, Ron—"

"*Get off the phone!*" Kevin whispered.

"Absolutely! I'm very proud of you, Sarah. You've got what it takes. Tell me, does it say where Simon went in that report?"

"No, it doesn't, Ron. It says he just wanders off, and when he comes back he tells his wife, 'I needed to be alone.' But look, Ron, you probably want to get back to sleep."

"'I needed to be alone.' That's terrific! 'I needed to be alone.' Do you think he has problems relating to his wife? If he's under pressure all day, you know, some men are like that. When I want to be alone, I always take Sondra along. Well, I told you, I *love* women! I'm all for the Women's Movement personally, you know; that's why I hired you."

"Oh, really? Well, I don't want to keep you, Ron—"

"Have you talked to Jenny lately?"

"No, Ron."

"I thought I saw her stopping by your desk the other day."

"You probably saw her talking to Greg. Greg's a friend of hers."

"*Sarah!*" Kevin whispered murderously.

"Oh, Greg's not interested in her anymore," Ron said. "He told me he's sworn off her. Greg's got a lovely wife, you know, but I can't be a policeman about those things. Tell me, Sarah, you haven't heard anything about Jenny covering the convention, have you?"

"Gee, no," I said, rolling my eyes at Kevin, who was now lying back against the pillow.

"Let me know if you do, won't you? Of course, that's between us. I know I can trust you. I hear all kinds of rumors, you know, about everybody. You'd be surprised at the things I've heard about you and Greg! I don't pay any attention. But Jenny does harbor resentments. I think her judgment has gone haywire. I don't want her to make a bad mistake. Because Willard would just use her and then drop her. I'm sure you know what sort of a man he is."

"Yes, I've heard, Ron. I'll keep my ears open. But Jenny doesn't confide in me, you know. Listen, I'm sure you want to get your sleep—"

"I'm glad you're not like Jenny. She's so paranoid! She misinterprets everything I say! She's really a little crazy. Not like you. You understand me. You know how to take a joke."

"Gee, thanks, Ron. Well, good—"

"You know I didn't want you to quit, don't you, Sarah. A girl like you is one in a million!"

"Thanks, Ron. But I won't be worth much if I—"

**179**

"You don't mind me calling you a girl, do you?"

"It's awfully late, Ron."

"Then you *do* mind! To me you *are* a girl! I can't help it! Why is that sexist?"

"I don't mind, Ron, but I *do* have to get some sleep."

"Oh, yes, yes! We want you bright as a button tomorrow. You go *right* to sleep, now."

"Yes, Ron, I will. Good night, then."

"Good night, Sarah."

Kevin was stepping into his blue jeans.

"Kevin, you can't leave now!" I wailed.

"I shoulda left ten minutes ago. You never woulda noticed."

"Oh, please!"

"I'm going to find a broad who doesn't work for a newspaper."

"I had to call him, Kevin. He might have fired me first thing in the morning, before I could tell him I had the story."

"So? The guy sounds like a scumbag. He's ready to fire you until you've got a big story. Why do you want to work for him?"

"It's not him, it's—well, damn it, it's a good job!"

"You're starting to like it too much, you know that? Pretty soon you're gonna be one of those vultures that sticks a mike in the face of a guy who just got shot and says, 'How does it feel?'"

"Kevin, don't go!" I said so cravenly that he capitulated.

Alas, the long wait, the hour, his hurt feelings, and perhaps the intrusive worries about how I should word the lead of my story combined to upset the delicate mechanism of our timing, or maybe a little love moan which I uttered at an earlier point than usual (upon contemplation of the by-line Sarah Makepeace being read by the President of the United States) misinformed his capillaries, but whatever the cause, when he put his jeans on for the second time that night, the impending by-line on the front page of *The Newspaper* didn't seem very consoling.

"What happened to your impotence?" I asked him sadly.

"My cousin Tommy told me Uncle Nick was balling the super's wife down in the basement," he said. "That's why he got kicked out of his laboratory. It wasn't the crazy inventions, after all."

# XXIV

By morning I had recovered from the little tragedy of the night before, and as I walked from the subway station to the office, passing under the marquee that trumpeted *Naughty Nancy—The Sizzlingest Nurse in Sin City*, I was inspired with a vision of a pornographic soap opera starring myself. Called something like *The Sexy Scribe*, it would have subway poster ads showing me in the newsroom with a slinky dress pulled obscenely tight over my enormous but perky breasts, my hands on my hips, a slight frown tugging down one eyebrow while the other was arched, indicating a moment of high-pressure option-weighing. The text would say: "Sarah Makepeace, the most voluptuous reporter in Sin City, has only minutes to nail down the biggest story of the decade. Rex Ramrod, her hot-blooded police detective boyfriend, wants to use those minutes to cool his burning lust. He cannot wait! When Sarah sees him, her body turns to a quivering mass of Jell-O. No man before him has been able to bring her to such heights of pleasure! But she has a chance to break the biggest story since Watergate—if only she rushes to the hospital to catch the last words of 'Bugsy' Sapperstein, the cancer-stricken former chauffeur to Teamster leaders and Tammany Hall chieftains, a man so secretive he took the Fifth Amendment three thousand times in seventeen grand juries, so secretive in fact that he won't let on to the FBI whether he is still breathing! But Sapperstein has whispered to a nurse that he will tell all to Sarah and to Sarah alone. 'But hurry!' says Nurse Goshen. 'He has only minutes to live!' Rex Ramrod has just called from Heartbreak Hotel around the corner. 'Hurry, baby!' he says urgently. 'I've got thirty minutes before I go on the most dangerous undercover job of my life. I'm dying for you! This may be our last time!' Which will she choose, Rex Ramrod or the people's right to know?"

"What are you doing here?" Willie Crespi startled me at the elevators.

"Hasn't Ron told you?" I said, giving the elevator button a commanding push.

"Ron's got other things on his mind today," Willie said. "Do you know what time it is?"

**181**

"What other things? I just talked to him a few hours ago. He said I had the lead story of the day. He told me to come in at nine."

Willie sort of squinted at me as the elevator swooped us up to the third floor. When the doors opened, I bolted out into the lobby.

"Wait a minute, Miz Makepeace!" he called. "What is your big story?"

I told him.

"Why don't you do something with your hair?" he said, using his right thumbnail as a toothpick. "We are certainly not going to run that story unless you talk with the mayor."

"You think the mayor's going to tell me where he goes if he won't tell his own wife! What the hell is he going to say? 'I'm sorry. I'll never take another drink'? Or: 'I can't help it if I love Alphonse'? Think about it, Willie. He didn't tell his wife."

"I'll thank you not to tell me what to think about, thank you very much!" Willie huffed, and he strode quickly past me toward the newsroom. He called back over his shoulder, in pale imitation of Ron, "You're going to talk to the mayor or that story doesn't run!"

"Where's Ron?" I asked, skipping to catch up with him.

"You needn't concern yourself with that," he said. "You have some serious spade work to do, young lady!" He abruptly lurched toward Ron's private office, yanked the door open, and disappeared inside.

Wait till Ron gets here, I thought, and I went off whistling down the aisle, smiling at all the empty desks. I dialed City Hall and asked to speak to the mayor. I was told I must go through the press secretary, Mortimer Steele, who was not yet in. I left a message for him and sat back to consider how to break the news to Greg so as to inflict maximum humiliation.

My phone rang at five past ten.

"Makepeace here," I said, hoping to sound hardened by experience.

"Hello, Sarah, how are you? We miss you down here. Why are you making yourself so scarce?"

"Who's this?"

"Who's this, she says! You only worked next to me for five weeks. Women are so fickle!"

"Clive. Sorry. I didn't recognize the—" I wanted to say friendliness, but I let it hang. "How are you?" I said. "What's up?"

"I was hoping you could tell me that, Sarah. Mort called me. He's nervous about crossing jurisdictional lines, you know, and the mayor hasn't got much time to spare. What did you want to ask him? I'd be happy to put the question for you. I'll be seeing him in a couple of minutes myself."

"I'd probably better talk to him myself, Clive. I've got to write the thing."

"Suit yourself. What's it about?"

"Remember that tip I got from Laura Dasher about the mayor disappearing? I've confirmed it."

"Are you sure? Simon's people swear up and down—"

"I've got the Missing Persons report."

"Missing Persons report? What the hell—"

"The last time he disappeared, it was for several days. His wife finally went to the commissioner. They filed a regular Missing Persons report."

Clive exhaled in a descending whistle that sounded like a dud bomb.

"Those bastards," he said quietly. "They've been lying to me."

"I'm sure they didn't single you out, Clive. Dalrymple lied to me too."

"To you! Well, naturally— Okay, Sarah. Thanks for telling me. I'm going to let a few people have it in the neck. How'd you get the report, by the way? That was a real piece of work."

"Oh, I just got lucky."

"It pays to be female in this business, I always say."

"Listen, Clive, I'd appreciate it if you didn't tell people down there until tomorrow. I don't want it to get all over town that I have this story."

"Right, Sarah. Absolutely. Mum's the word."

That was an unlooked-for little bonus, Clive Lipschitz gnashing his teeth over my scoop. How quickly the tables had turned! "Hello, Sarah. We miss you down here." Bullshit! What about when he gloated over Foley's office calling me? Let him eat his heart out now. His favorite sources lied to him! Poor baby Clive. I fixed him.

Wait till Greg gets here, I thought gleefully. First I'll torture him. Then I'll tell him about Clive. Was that what Ron meant by "creative tension"? Creative malice, more like. When I was holding all the cards, I could really go for it.

How happily I schemed through the morning! I scarcely put a thought to Ron's absence. When the hour of eleven came around, it was not Ron I looked for each time someone came through the door, but Greg, crafty, double-dealing Greg.

"SARAH, COME UP HERE, PLEASE!" Willie Crespi's amplified voice sounded harshly.

I took my time about walking to Dayside. Willie was seated at Ron's desk. He was talking on the telephone and playing with the cord as if it were his own. He gestured to me to sit down.

"I think we can invite Walter and Barbara. We're in their league now," I heard him say. He smiled at me as if pleased to have an audience. He said, "Right, right," a couple of times, "Yes, Balducci's has them," and wound up with "Bye-bye, sweetheart," and a couple of kissing sounds. After he'd hung up, he played with the phone cord a bit longer. Then he straightened Ron's blotter.

"Sarah, how long have you been here?" he asked me without looking at me.

"You know, Willie."

"Don't be difficult, Sarah."

"Two months."

"Is it really that long? Still, for someone with so little experience, two months is nothing," he said, and he seemed to sink lower into his shoulders."

"It seems like about three years to me," I said.

"Yes, time does fly, doesn't it!" he said, inspecting his fingernails. "Well, after a while, Sarah, you will find that you can tell things by your nose. A good tip, for instance, is usually wrong. That's why we say, 'Never let the facts get in the way of a good story'—you know, in irony. Irony has its place. The best ironists have been newsmen of sorts. Swift and—and, well, Swift. He was the best. *Three Men in a Boat* may be one of the greatest pieces of irony ever written. Of course, he was an essayist. You majored in literature, didn't you, Sarah?"

"*Three Men in a Boat?*" I said quizzically. "I don't think—"

He cleared his throat. I wasn't helping him.

"Sarah, I'm not asking you to tell me where you got that document. I don't even want to know," he said reasonably. "The mayor has enemies, aahem, in the Police Department. You wouldn't know after two months. I'm not blaming you, Sarah. Even Woodward and Bernstein made mistakes."

He still wasn't looking at me. I didn't like his drift.

"Where's Ron?" I said tactlessly.

"Anyone could have made a mistake like this," he said, ignoring the question. "If Mrs. Simon forgot her husband was going to Puerto Rico and panicked and went to the commissioner, naturally it could look as though he *was* missing for those four days, and there *was* a report. Apparently what you have is what was written at the time, but of course it's been rescinded. It was all a mistake. I want you to give me the report, Sarah, because it's a libel. Whoever gave it to you committed a libel. You see, you don't know the libel laws yet, but just to circulate a false document can be . . . one. So you see, unfortunately once again the facts got in the way. And I'm sorry, Sarah. I know you were up late on this. Why don't you take the rest of the day off?"

"Are you trying to tell me the mayor went to Puerto Rico for four days and didn't call his wife, didn't call anybody, so they got so worried they had the police out looking for him? And what about those other times, Willie? What about the *five other times he disappeared?*"

"Young lady," he said, closing his eyes.

"Who have you been talking to?" I asked loudly. "Oh, *I* get it! Mort Steele called *you* back, didn't he? And he fed you that load of shit! His *job* is to tell lies for the mayor, Willie! Everybody knows that!"

"Don't you talk to me that way, you—you— You think I don't know— Mort Steele worked here *on this desk with me!*" he snarled, hunching toward me. "You're so ignorant, you don't even know Steele saved your ass! Do you know how it would have looked if we had run this story? You would have been finished, Sarah Makepeace, finished! You're in a very tenuous position here, you know! Your SDS conspiracy theories don't *wash* on a real newspaper!"

"Who said anything about SDS?"

"I don't have time to argue with you!" he said, turning his chair away. He stood up, backed away a couple of steps, yelled, "You bring me that report and take the day off! I don't want to see your face around here today!"

He sped toward Ron's private office.

"Where's Ron?" I said plaintively.

"You'd better do what Willie says," Freddie said quietly.

"Where's Ron?" I asked again.

"In deep trouble," Freddie said.

"Why? What happened?"

"Tell you later. Get that report," Freddie said.

I dragged myself back to my desk, feeling close to tears. At least Greg wasn't in yet. He didn't get the pleasure of seeing me lose my big story. What the hell was Willie talking about, SDS conspiracy theories? That was craziness. Complete craziness. I never got around to joining SDS. Ellie always said I was a counterculture freeloader.

I guess I sat there doing nothing for a while, because Freddie came back to remind me that Willie wanted "that report right away."

"Gee, I think I must have left it in my locker in the ladies' room," I said, suddenly remembering there was a Xerox machine in the morgue, and the ladies' room was in the same general direction. The report was actually in my purse.

Well, why not leak it to the *Eye?* Keep my options open.

I got held up at the machine. There was a clerk ahead of me copying all of Vincent Akelroyd's clips. He had asked for them to be sent to his home. This time he was letting the paper know he would not sit home sulking. He would look for another job.

As I copied the report, I considered what else I might leak to Lars. He loved inside dirt from *The Newspaper*.

But then when I walked back toward the newsroom, I heard an unmistakable ho ho ho. I heard applause. The staff was applauding. I came around a pillar and saw Ron's immense back. He looked more immense than ever because he was wearing a jacket and tie. As if *he* had been out looking for another job. He was holding up both thumbs and grinning down the long room. The reporters were still clapping. Willie Crespi was clapping too, very vigorously, but his smile looked queer.

I thought I should find out what was going on before I turned in the report. Greg, I saw with a sinking heart, had arrived in my absence and now stood beaming by his desk. How he would leer at me in triumph!

I walked toward my desk, fearing that any second I'd hear Willie calling me over the loudspeaker. As I went, I heard the distant babble of excited voices, which came closer quickly and passed me like a ripple on a smooth pond, and I made out first snatches of words like "detector test," and "passed his lie," and then "passed" again, and "lie" again, and finally the complete "Fucking passed his lie detector test!" spoken by Eddie Schwartz, who then said with the real voice of experience, "Well, if that don't beat all!"

"Hi, Sarah!" Greg said heartily. "You arrived just in time. Will you look at Willie's face, boys and girls? Is that a sickly smile or what?"

"Right on!" said Jenny, who had walked forward from her desk, the better to observe the scene.

186

"What's going on?" I asked.

"You know what Willie wanted me to do?" Greg said to no one in particular. "The putz wanted me to do a profile of Lindsay!"

"Nooo!" everybody said in chorus.

"Why did Ron take a lie detector test?" I tried again.

"Did you all hear that?" Greg said. "Sarah here wants to know why Ron took a lie detector test. What did they teach you at Raaaaydcliffe, Sarah? How to say, 'Do you take American Express?' in three languages?"

"Okay, so he wanted to prove he didn't cancel those hotel reservations, I suppose, but . . ."

"But what?" Greg said.

"But he did cancel them, didn't he? I mean, who else would have?"

"Who else indeed! The plot thickens!" Greg said.

"What matters is he passed," Jenny said.

"How did he *do* it, Greg? He probably lies every time he gives his name and address."

"Which makes him the perfect candidate for a lie detector test."

"What?"

"SARAH MAKEPEACE, WHERE'S YOUR SUMMARY?" Ron called over the loudspeaker.

"He's got you on a story already? He's amazing!" Greg said. "I guess that means he won't fire you today. Go to it, kid."

I ran to Dayside.

"Hi, Sarah! How's my ace reporter?" Ron said, flashing me a large expanse of teeth. He had such *big teeth!* "Did you come in at nine? Did she come in at nine, Willie?"

Willie had just picked up his phone and begun dialing fast.

"Uh, what's that, Ron?" he asked, letting his finger fall out of the dial.

"Oh, never mind!" Ron said. "It's almost twelve o'clock now. What the hell have you been doing all morning?" he asked me with cheerful gruffness. "Where's your summary? What does the mayor's office say?"

"Maybe you'd better ask Willie, Ron," I said.

"Don't be cute with me, Sarah. We've got to get moving on this. Look, I've got a meeting with Gil in forty-five minutes. I want to show him your summary. I told you this is going to lead the paper, Sarah. I was counting on you. Now, do you want to keep the assignment, or should I tell Greg—"

"Ron, Willie killed my story."

"Don't be silly, Sarah! Now, let's type up your summary right here. What will we say in the lead? What does the report say? Have you got a copy?"

"Right here," I said, handing him a fresh Xerox copy.

"Will you look at this! Oh boy, oh boy, oh boy! Look at it! 'Eunice Simon reported her husband missing at 1400 hours today in the office of Commissioner Rinkel.' Oh, boy! I don't think I've seen anything like this in my entire life on this paper! Well, that's not true—the Doomsday Report, but that was National's. Look at this! Prior Occurrences! 'On five prior occasions'! Ummm. Ummm. 'Reading *The Godfather* in the shade of a red maple'! Oh, Sarah! I could kiss you! I really could! And I will!"

He leaned forward and gave me a big smacker on the forehead.

"Now tell me quickly, what does City Hall say?" he asked.

"City Hall has not called me back, Ron."

"Well, damn it, why haven't you called them back? You have to keep after them! You have to be more aggressive, Sarah."

"I think City Hall called Willie back."

"But you're writing the story."

"Well, that's the thing. I didn't know if I would be writing it, Ron, or if there would be any story, because—"

"What are you talking about? Are you crazy? What are you saying? I go away from this place for one morning, and everybody falls apart! What's the matter with you?"

"I've been trying to tell you, Ron. Willie killed my story. He told me to take the rest of the day off."

"Killed the *story!* Willie, is that *true?*" Ron said, whipping his chair around toward his sinking deputy.

"No, of course not, Ron!" Willie said quickly, crinkling the corners of his eyes. "I just thought Sarah shouldn't be handling a story of such—such—well, involving a possible libel, because you know we've had trouble with her research before, Ron, her figures on the budget—"

"What are you talking about, libel! You can't libel the mayor!" Ron said.

"Uh, Ron, Mort Steele says the mayor was in Puerto Rico at the time of this, uh, so-called Missing Persons report, and the report has been rescinded, you see, so there's—"

"I don't believe that!" I said. "Mort Steele just made it up. Look, the police *know* the mayor was missing!"

"Ron," Willie said, "Sarah was going to ask the mayor about

some preposterous fiction, er, that he was seeing a man named Alphonse in secret, which is absolute fiction. I couldn't let her do that."

"I didn't say that, Willie!" I shouted. "You have twisted my words!"

"Shut up, you two!" Ron commanded. "I want to know who said the Missing Persons report was rescinded."

"Well, Mort told me for deep background, Ron," Willie said. "He said he didn't know the legal term, but it was his word—"

"Rescinded! Rescinded!" Ron chanted. "What kind of cockamamie talk is that? Look at this thing. It's got the mayor's wife giving evidence, for god's sake! No one can rescind a thing like this. Even if he *was* in Puerto Rico, *she* didn't know where he was. The *police commissioner* didn't know where he was. Since when does the mayor take a secret trip to Puerto Rico that starts when he ducks out of his car between Gracie Mansion and City Hall? For god's sake, Willie! Didn't you read this thing?"

"Sarah has been hiding it," Willie said sulkily.

"I am surrounded by idiots!" Ron shouted.

Willie reached for his rubber bands.

"Now, Sarah," Ron said to me, "you get on the phone with the mayor's office, and you tell them we're not buying their story. We're not buying it at all!"

"Okay, Ron," I said.

"And get me a summary in half an hour. Twenty minutes. I want early copy on this. The last page crosses my desk at four-thirty. You tell the mayor's office we're running this story tonight, whether or not we get a public statement from them. Get cracking!"

We did get a statement from the mayor—at 5:00 p.m., so I had to write the story over again. Still, I had a relatively easy time of it, relative to Marco Fellini. Ron sent him out three times to find the exact park bench the mayor had slept on, and when Marco finally just faked it and snapped any bench, Ron made him print a copy right away. Marco handed it to him still wet. Ron ripped the picture in two, shouting, "Not empty, you idiot! Get somebody lying on it! Do I have to tell you everything?" After the mayor's statement came in, it was clear that the facts were not going to ruin a good story, but Ron nearly did. He kept interrupting me every ten minutes. "Put in the red maple!" he yelled. "And *The Godfather!* Don't forget *The Godfather!*" Soon he was back again, telling me to call the Police Department psychiatrists who heard Mrs. Simon giving her deposition. Then he yelled, "What about Trotsky? We need a quote from

Trotsky!" Next he said the lead was too short. Then it was too long. I thought I'd never get the story written, but a sudden hiatus came at seven, when Ron was distracted by a sniper on the George Washington Bridge. He couldn't find anybody to send up there except Jenny, and he went running around yelling, "Where *is* everybody? Where *is* everybody?" until he finally had to send her. Later on, he lost my lead, which caused a frantic search of the copy desk at five minutes to front page deadline (eight-thirty). He abused Jess Flicker this time, shouting about "mismanagement" and "total incompetence." Jess turned Ron a stoical face, but a few minutes later, we noticed a commotion near Nightside, and three copy editors threw down their pencils in tandem and resigned on the spot. Jess strode over to Ron's desk to shout, "That's your fault!" Ron shouted, "Where's the goddamn lead?" and the two of them went on yelling at cross purposes, not understanding each other at all and not hearing Freddie, who was waving a sheet of paper around, shouting, "I found it! I found it!" This three-part aria might have gone on forever had not the diminutive but awesomely powerful production chief (the man who actually did have the power to say "Stop the presses!") thrust himself between Ron and Jess and shoved them apart at belly level. Seeing who was shoving, they became docile enough to perceive some things around them, and presently they heard one of Freddie's "I found it"s. Meanwhile, a bank chairman who did not realize the mayor had released a statement admitting to his strange disappearing act was making one last attempt to kill the story, telling Ron's secretary over the phone, "If this thing runs, it'll kill our federal loan negotiations. I wonder if Mr. Millstein is aware of what that will do to his career." However, Ron's secretary could not get her boss's attention. It was then 8:37 P.M. At 9:30, the first copies of the city edition came up to the newsroom and were passed out to the night rewrite men and me by Freddie's cousin Scazz, who looked like a weight lifter. His enormous palms left inky prints on the fresh copies. That and all subsequent editions of *The Newspaper* had in its lead column page one of July 15:

### SIMON ADMITS HE ABANDONS POST, HAS "THINK" SESSIONS ALONE IN WELFARE HOTELS

Eludes Bodyguards to "Be in Touch with Myself"; Council Chief Calls Him "AWOL Mayor"; Deputy Mayor Says Simon Seeks "Healthy Perspective"

*By Sarah Makepeace*

# XXV

That night I got all jumpy again, the way I had been the night after Mishiyoko got blitzed by Crazies for Hire. I wanted to see Kevin so badly! I even called Midtown South and asked for him, which he had told me never to do. His home phone wasn't listed, and he wouldn't give it to me. Anyway, I wouldn't have called there. The desk officer at Midtown South said it was Mondavi's day off, and did I want to leave a message? I said, "It isn't important," and hung up.

The next morning I awoke early and took a walk around the Village so I could watch people buying *The Newspaper*. I couldn't wait to get to the office. I didn't expect the President to call, but I expected the other reporters to stop by my desk and ask me how I got the story. That's what they had done to Greg the morning after he got the scoop on Freely's endorsement of Love. Behind Greg's back they had said his scoop was "nothing but a handout." But they all had wanted to know how he got it. Wouldn't they be ten times more envious of me?

So when I came strolling in at eleven, humming the tune of "Lay Lady Lay," I thought that the group gathered around Greg's desk were all waiting for me. That's because I didn't know what Greg had just found out.

I heard Jenny ask, "Greg, are you sure?"

"Am I ever wrong?" Greg said.

Nobody even noticed me sit down.

Now I can understand why, but back then I still didn't know the priorities of the profession well enough. I thought everybody was doing a number on me. Actually, Greg had just released a fresh news item, against which my scoop was not only dated but also insignificant. Greg had found out that Dixby had also volunteered to take a lie detector test, and most amazing, the test showed Dixby to be lying on the subject of the canceled hotel reservations! This called for the most trenchant analysis since Clarence Swope was hired. What could it mean? Well, certainly not what it seemed to mean. Everybody agreed to that. But what did it mean? No one believed Ron had not lied.

With the speed of hotshot journalists, they found the answer: The machine had failed. How could a machine substitute for a suspicious human brain? How would the Watergate story have broken if Woodward and Bernstein had been a polygraph machine? You couldn't get Robert Redford to play a polygraph machine. No machine could pick up the subtleties, the tiny inconsistencies, the minuscule inaccuracies of a really skilled human liar. Only the human cerebrum could do that. The machine had obviously failed.

"It's time we took another hard look at polygraphs," Steve Figland said, dangling a leg over the corner of Greg's desk.

"The hell it is, Figland!" said Greg. "You've got a death wish, you know that? God! That's all we need!"

"You'd be suspected of defection, Steve," Jenny said.

"Figland, you're unbelievable!" said Greg. "You're gonna walk right up there and tell Ron he should do a story telling the world how he beat the polygraph!"

"All right, all right, so it's not the right time," said Steve. "But it is a good idea. What the hell does *The Newspaper* want with a polygraph machine? Did you know we had one here?"

"Don't be stupid! They musta rented it," said Eddie. "Those things cost."

"No, it belongs to the paper," said Jenny.

"How do you know?" Greg asked.

"The woman who gives the tests told me. It belongs to the personnel office."

"Somebody should leak that to *The Evil Eye*," said Greg, sliding his eyes over toward me.

"I wonder why it worked with Dixby and not on Ron," said Susan.

"We don't know if it did work on Dixby," Greg said. "Besides, he could have been nervous."

"Those tests only work if the guy taking them is dumb enough to think they do," Eddie said. "Or if he has a conscience."

"So neither Ron nor Dixby—" Jenny said.

"Eddie's right," said Steve. "They're designed to measure guilt. But guilt can be manifested where it doesn't belong. I read about it. The subconscious sometimes responds to the wrong signals."

"Shit, Figland! You really were going to suggest a piece," Greg said.

"Maybe Ron hasn't got a subconscious," said Jenny.

"Everyone has a subconscious," said Steve. "Ron's just guilt-free."

"A guy without a subconscious would have murdered Dixby," said Eddie. "Ron hasn't laid a finger on him."

"Murder isn't as satisfying as beating a guy out of a job," said Greg.

"Yeah, a dead man wouldn't scream," said Jenny.

"I'd say Ron would kill if he thought he could get away with it," Susan put in.

"Naah!" Greg said. "I tell you, it wouldn't satisfy him. Ron's a sophisticated fighter."

"Well, whatever he is, he's an aberration," said Steve. "To be a Jew and feel no guilt!"

"Fuck daht!" said Eddie. "Ron's just a boss."

And just then, as if to illustrate Eddie's wisdom, Ron called out, "SCHWARTZ, ON THE DOUBLE!" over the loudspeaker. He soon called out, "FIGLAND, LOCKE, MAKEPEACE, GET UP HERE!" and we all looked at one another nervously.

But the matter at hand was a building collapse on Canal Street. The police wire had said twenty people were trapped in the rubble. Ron was all in a lather about it. He sent the four of us downtown with Marco Fellini. We took the subway, and Marco, lumbering behind us with his heavy camera bag bobbing against his potbelly, bitched to us as we ran ahead of him.

The collapsed building turned out to have been a tiny three-story walk-up that had housed only rats and a stray dog. The rats had fled the scene before we got there. The dog was yelping under an upside-down bathtub with old-fashioned lion's feet. A couple of firemen lifted the tub. The dog came slithering out. Marco snapped the great rescue. The dog was a mongrel with a lot of hair gone from its rump. It sidled over to one of the firemen and rubbed itself against his leg like a hungry cat.

"Scat!" said the fireman, kicking the dog away. "Ugly old dog!"

The dog whimpered and squeezed itself back under the bathtub. The firemen climbed onto their truck and drove off.

"Great story!" said Eddie. "Man bites dog."

"I got a good shot," said Marco. "Who's writing?"

"Forget it, Marco," said Jenny. "It's no story."

"It's a great picture," said Marco.

"What do we do now?" I asked. "Go back to the office?"

"Suit yourself," said Steve. "I know a fantastic Spanish restaurant on Morton Street."

"That's too far to walk," said Jenny.

"We can take a cab," Steve said. "You'll like it. It has limitless sangría, and there's flamenco music on the jukebox."

"What the hell? Let's see his little hole in the wall," said Eddie.

"Come on, Jenny. It might be a new one for the dirty-restaurants list."

"Wait a minute! What are you guys doing about this story?" Marco asked.

"What story?" said Eddie. "The dog's still under the bathtub."

"But my picture!" Marco pleaded.

"We're going to lunch, Marco. You wanta come along?" Eddie said kindly.

"Shit, I'd love to, but I'm on a diet. Left my yogurt back at the office. Besides, they don't take five in a cab. You guys go ahead. Maybe I'll catch a couple of weather shots. See you," Marco said, heading across Canal Street.

"Take your time!" Eddie called to him. "We'll be out for at least another hour and a half!"

"Right!" yelled Marco. And he gave the thumbs up sign.

By then Jenny had flagged down a cab. The three others climbed into the back, so I took the front seat. Eddie leaned forward to tell me that in cases like this, I should always make sure the photographer didn't get back to the paper much sooner than I did.

I was feeling pretty content. The others had included me—even with Jenny there—and the cabdriver had a copy of *The Newspaper* on the front seat, folded so my story was face up. I was sure they'd get around to talking about it at the restaurant.

But I was wrong. Steve monopolized the conversation. He got very talkative on the sangría and was remembering a girl he used to bring to the restaurant, somebody named Laura who played the flute and was "heartbreakingly beautiful" and "fantastic in bed." He said he might have left his second wife for her if she had been able to talk, that Leonard Bernstein and Pablo Casals were in love with her, but "they didn't know her, they had just looked at her." Steve said Laura drove him back into the arms of his wife. "Veronica was awful in the sack, just a disaster from beginning to end, but she was very articulate," Steve said. "Veronica had a doctorate in philosophy. You know I still miss her?"

At some point, Jenny's and my eyes met, and I thought we shared a flash of understanding. She looked terribly bored. But it was Eddie who hurt Steve's feelings in the end, saying he thought there was Welch's grape juice in the sangría. Steve ordered the check in a hurt, hurried tone before we'd cleaned our plates, and he went off to call Ron to let him know the emergency on Canal Street was over.

"Poor Steve," said Jenny listlessly. "Too bad he's so handsome."

**194**

"Why do you say that, Jenny? The guy's got enough working against him already," said Eddie.

"Because if he'd been born ugly, he'd have to finish that book to get women to go to bed with him."

"I wouldn't go to bed with him, book or no book," I said.

"Of course you wouldn't! None of *us* would," said Jenny.

"You broads are really something!" Eddie said. "You could make a guy long for the days of inequality. What the hell turns you on?"

Jenny sighed. I took a sip of my watered-down sangría and felt a stab of self-pity. Why couldn't I see Kevin whenever I needed him? Were they never going to talk about my story?

"Go ahead, Sarah, tell him," Jenny said. "What turns you on?"

"What turns me on? I guess, uh, understanding, a sense of humor, um, well, intelligence—"

"Bullshit!" said Jenny. "Understanding men aren't sexy at all!"

"Sarah," Steve interrupted, "Freddie says you've got an urgent message."

"What is it? Not the mayor? Did the mayor call?"

"What? It was a friend of yours. I didn't take the number. You'd better call the desk. Why would the mayor call you?"

That was the last straw. That was deliberate. They *were* doing a number on me.

My urgent message was from Mrs. Cintron, Jesus's mother, who was sitting in the office of a Legal Aid attorney, having hysterics.

"Djou gots to come down here, Sarah! Hesus neber been arrested before he met djou!" she said. "Djou a famous reporter now. Djou gots to speak for his characters. Hesus been frame!"

Of course, I went. *She* thought I was important.

# XXVI

Jesus and Fredo had been indicted on twenty-seven counts of grand larceny and one count of conspiracy to commit grand larceny. They had been arrested that morning along with a trio of hefty Italians, and the district attorney had held a news conference to announce the arrests had cracked a "Mafia stolen car ring." Jesus's Legal Aid attorney told Mrs. Cintron he didn't think he could get the bail figure down low enough to spring the boys, because there had been so much publicity about their Italian friends. He said if I would speak up for the boys, they might have an outside chance.

In the courtroom, Jesus and Fredo looked tiny sitting next to the three Italians. They weren't men I recognized from 118th Street. Fredo was holding onto his St. Christopher medal with his one free hand, and I saw him surreptitiously kissing it as the court clerk called out the case of *People* v. *Cintron, Monzone, Rastelli, Rastelli, and Vasquez.*

The Italians' lawyer spoke first. He was a flashy character from Brooklyn who seemed to make the assistant district attorney stutter. He said his clients could post $25,000 bail each within a couple of hours. The assistant DA said that was "ex-exactly" why he wanted the bail at $50,000. The judge left the bail at $50,000, and the flashy lawyer said his clients would post bail within a couple of hours.

I didn't hear the arguments over Jesus and Fredo's bail because the attorneys leaned right up against the bench. Mrs. Cintron blew Jesus a kiss and pointed to me. I saw Jesus elbow Fredo and they giggled. The judge looked over at me. Then the Legal Aid attorney, whose name was Mark Blossom, waved his arm at me in a come-here sign. I walked to the bench.

"You are Sarah Makepeace?" the judge asked me.

"Yes," I said. "I'd like to help these boys if I can. I'm sure it's all a mistake—"

"Shhh! You just answer questions," Mark Blossom whispered.

"You wrote that story about the mayor. A very interesting story," said the judge. "Of course, there's more to it than you were able to say. A man doesn't go to those hotels alone."

I opened my mouth, but Blossom put his finger to his lips.

"It's all right, Mr. Blossom. She can speak," said the judge.

"Gee," I said. "As far as I know, he was alone."

"Hmmm," said the judge. "Simon doesn't drink. I happen to know that. And no one would take a woman to a welfare hotel. People are drawing conclusions, you know. I expect *The Newspaper* knew they would. How's your man Mr. Crespi? Give him my regards. He once did a profile of me when I was sitting in Traffic Court."

"Oh, really? Well, I'll tell him you sent your regards, Your Honor."

"That was a most intriguing story. Most intriguing! How did you get it?"

"Um . . ."

"Oh, you needn't tell me today! Perhaps when we're better acquainted. You're new to *The Newspaper*, aren't you? I don't recall seeing your by-line before."

"I've been there two months," I said. Blossom seemed to twitch.

"Fine place. Outstanding newspaper. The very best. Now, I have told Mr. Blossom here that I would be willing to lower the bail for these boys and accept a surety bond cosigned by you. Mr. Blossom said you would be glad to do that because the boys are old students of yours. Is that correct?"

"Well, they—I mean, yes! And I would be happy to post—how much would the bond be?"

"Oh, let's make it ten thousand dollars each. I don't think the district attorney will go any lower than that," said the judge.

When we got out of the courtroom, I said to Blossom, "You know, I don't have any money."

"Not to worry," he said. "It's a paper transaction."

He led me over behind the courthouse to the office of Sy Shimmer, bail bondsman, and left me, with a "Gotta get back right away." Shimmer's office looked down-at-heel. But there were *New Yorkers* on the stained coffee table. Mr. Shimmer was reading something through a lorgnette. He had said, "Yes," to Blossom when we came in, and held up a hand. Then to me, "Be with you in a minute." I looked at *New Yorker* cartoons.

"Every day I meet new people," Mr. Shimmer said as he came around his desk to give me a handshake. "Today I meet a famous reporter. This is for twenty thousand dollars, am I right?"

"Well, two for ten thousand each. There are two people. Mr. Shimmer, I should tell you right away, I don't have twenty thousand dollars."

"Relax! Relax! Sit down," he said, going back to sit behind his desk. "You have an income, don't you? You work for *The Newspaper*, don't you? How much do you make?"

"Twenty-one thousand a year."

"Not like the television people, is it? I think it's a shame this country doesn't pay quality wages to quality people. Now, let me see. These two gentlemen got themselves mixed up with some big money—big money, am I right?"

"Oh, they're just boys! I thought fifteen-year-olds couldn't be charged as adults."

"They're not fifteen, Miss Makepeace. They're eighteen. No,

wait a minute. One of them is nineteen. Mr. Cintron."

"Nineteen?" I said weakly.

"Ah, perhaps I made a mistake. I was doing the arithmetic from date of birth. You would think a man of my business could do arithmetic, wouldn't you? Let me see. Yes, Jesus Cintron was nineteen last Friday. Fredo Vasquez will be nineteen in October. How long have you known these boys?"

"Almost four years."

"And they worked for you, am I right?"

"Yes, at the East 118th Street Block Association."

"That's good! They are lucky to have a friend like you, a person in such good standing. That's a court expression, you know, to be in good standing. How long have you been at *The Newspaper?*"

"Two months."

"And already you've brought down the mayor! You'll go far. Sign this one in two places, please, and put down the date and your Social Security number. Who's your favorite author, Miss Makepeace? Or do you like to be called Miz?"

"Favorite author? I have different ones at different times. I like Simenon."

"Ah, you have excellent taste, excellent taste! The French are the best. Such economy! *Le mot juste.* You know that phrase. 'The right word.' One more page and then we're done with Mr. Cintron. Have you done any writing yourself? I mean, apart from journalism."

"No," I said. "And I got into journalism by accident."

"Every great writer thinks he's not a writer. Gustave Flaubert—he's my favorite, that's why I was happy to hear you like the French—Flaubert was always doubting himself. Perhaps you will write a book someday."

"I don't think so."

"Now, these are the same forms for Mr. Vasquez. Again it's name, date, and Social Security number."

He watched me signing.

"You're not from New York, are you, Miz Makepeace? Where are you from?"

"Massachusetts."

"Not the Boston banking family, by any chance?"

"We're the poor relations."

"There!" he said. "Now, you know if your friends skip town, and god forbid they should, but if they do, we will forfeit the security right away. I suggest you get in touch with your bank or credit union right away."

"What security? I thought you said my job was enough."

"It's enough for me, but not for the insurance company. I am talking only if the boys abscond. I'm sure this won't happen, but just in case, it wouldn't hurt to have a talk with your bank, on the off-chance that you would need the five thousand dollars. The rest we've established you can manage in monthly payments."

"Five thousand dollars? Where did that come from?"

"I thought I explained to you. That's the security, the cash we've put up with the insurance company at this point. It's all on paper, of course, like an IOU. But should the boys skip . . ."

"I'm sure they won't skip," I said. My throat felt dry.

"With a friend like you behind them, I'm sure they won't. Here are your copies, Miz Makepeace," he said, handing me several papers. He rose slowly and came around his desk to walk me to the door. "Tell me," he said. "I'm just curious. Why would you bother with boys like this? Why are you doing this?"

"I'm not sure I know," I said.

"Another accident," he said. "Ah, but it gave me the pleasure of meeting you. For your sake I suppose I have to say I hope we don't meet again."

He gave me his hand once more.

"Have you read *Madame Bovary?* The greatest book ever written! I read it every year."

"No," I said.

"You remind me of my daughter," he said.

He let my hand go.

## XXVII

I was terribly late for the office. I had told Freddie I would be back by three. I ran across the street to the visitors entrance of the Tombs, where Mrs. Cintron was waiting. We showed the bail papers to a clerk.

"It's gonna take a while to locate these men," he said. "We got a lot of Cintrons and Vasquezes inside."

"Okay, Mrs. Cintron, I better run," I said.

"Djou gots to stay, Sarah!" she said. "Hesus told me he wanna see djou. He's gonna pay djou back, soon as he gets some money."

"We won't have to pay any money as long as he shows up in court."

"They promise him they pay his bails. Ees not right you pay his bails."

"Who promised him?"

"Djou know," she said quietly. Then she whispered, *"Rastellis."*

*"Oh, no!"* I whispered back. *"Tell him not to go near the Rastellis."*

"Eees not right you pay," she said solemnly.

"Mrs. Cintron, I didn't pay anything. All I did was sign some papers. If Jesus and Fredo show up in court, I'll never have to pay a cent. You make sure they show up on September eighth. Okay?"

"You nice lady," she said, clutching my hands.

"Thanks," I said. "Listen, I've really got to go. Tell the boys I'm sorry I couldn't wait. And don't forget, September eighth, Judge Fielding's courtroom."

"They gonna be there," said Mrs. Cintron, "eef I hab to kill them."

On the way uptown, I thought about what a nice man Sy Shimmer was, taking such a chance on Jesus and Fredo and me. Poor man, he shouldn't be in the bail bond business, reading *Madame Bovary* every year, contemplating *le mot juste* while he had to sit there watching people put down their Social Security numbers in his tattered old office. He did not seem to see himself as a bail bondsman the way, say, Gil Foley saw himself as the *Newspaper* editor. Mr. Shimmer seemed to see himself as a gentleman and a student of literature whose commercial dealings with humanity were repugnant to his inner being.

How lucky I was to have found him! Hadn't I got away from the life preferred by my own inner being? But this bail thing had brought me back again, closer to what I wanted to be.

Because seeing Jesus and Fredo in the courtroom had summoned up the old feelings in me, vague powerful feelings about the Cesar Chavez poster and the Martin Luther King poster, feelings I used to have on those nights when I got home from dodging play dough clumps and Ellie came home from the law library and we lit up a joint and put Joanie on the record player and talked about the summer of '68, the summer before college, when we had each separately watched the Democratic convention stoned with our parents, who didn't know we were stoned, and her parents had said what my parents had said, that the demonstrators were needlessly provocative, and in answer we had each walked out on them, not very far or for very long, since we were female and personally penniless and afraid of getting raped and cut up and left in plastic garbage bags along the New Jersey Turnpike, with which murderers felt such an affinity, although that fear had not deterred us from, separately and unsuccessfully, trying to lose our virginity before college, the best we could do in that blood-dimmed summer to assert youth's right to seek its own form of ruin. I don't mean all this went through my head in detail when I saw Jesus and Fredo sitting on the criminal bench next to the gargantuan Italians, but simply that they had evoked the state of mind from before, from the time when the way the world was was not my fault and when, with all hell breaking loose among the responsible adults, it had felt kind of noble to be a fucked up adolescent.

Of course, Jesus and Fredo probably saw me as the biggest kind of fool. Hadn't they lied to me about their ages in order to qualify for the Neighborhood Youth Corps salaries? But I didn't care! I forgave them. They deserved to lie. They were the oppressed, the suffering. What did it say in the law? Maximum feasible participation. Who could blame them for wanting in? Of course, they would think me a fool. But that was all right too. It kind of evened out our class differences. They might also skip bail. But I could take the risk. Anything to keep them from those Mafia characters, to save them from a life of crime!

The more I thought about it, the more likely it did seem that Jesus and Fredo would jump bail. Sy Shimmer must have thought it likely too. Why did he let me sign for them, when I didn't have any collateral? Was it a sort of literary gesture, allowing a fool the poetic license to live out her destiny? Well, I was grateful to him. He had helped me to buy back whatever it was I'd sold out in going to work for *The Newspaper*.

"Here I am!" I said to Ron, smiling with my full heart.

"Where the hell have you been?" he roared. "Why didn't you call in your summary?"

"Gee, didn't Freddie tell you? I had to go to court."

"Nobody tells me anything! What were you doing in court?"

"I had to post bail for a couple of kids from East Harlem," I said proudly.

"You're not supposed to go wandering off— Sarah, I don't want you bringing any of your East Harlem friends around here."

"Anyway, that story was a dud, Ron," I said.

"*I'm* the one who decides that!" Ron said. "Now listen, I want you to work as fast as you can. I want color, quotes, I want you to tell us the history of the building, who lived there, when it was built. And of course, you have to tell us why it fell down. And who were the people trapped inside. Hurry up! You haven't much time at all. How could you come back so late? The *Washington Post* wanted to interview you. I had to give them Greg."

"The *Washington Post*? What did they want?"

"How should I know? When can I have your summary?"

"But, Ron, that building collapse was nothing! It was a small building in the first place, and there weren't any people trapped in it. No one was living there. Even the rats were gone by the time we got there. There was one victim, a dog, which the firemen rescued from under a bathtub, but—"

"I know. Marco got a great picture, a front page picture!"

"Do you know what happened after he took the picture?"

"No. You're going to tell me. Now get to work."

"But we all agreed it wasn't a story. Didn't they tell you? Steve, Eddie, Jenny, and I—"

"Go write that story this minute!" Ron shouted. "Slug it 'Collapse.'"

Eddie overheard the order and helped me on the sly. He called the local precinct house, and he showed me the "rewrite man's bible," a telephone directory arranged in geographical order, which made it possible for me to call up stores and residents of the block where the building fell down. In the space of two hours, with Eddie helping, I put together a one-column story. The dog hadn't lived there. He belonged to a superintendent down the street. The building had been lived in by Russian Jews, Irish Catholics, Italian Catholics, and a conceptual artist named Casper Wyoming, who, as it turned out, had still been in residence at the time of the collapse but was out talking up his concepts at the Guggenheim when it happened. The guy in the hardware store across the street told me at five-thirty that the artist was putting up a sign in front of the rubble which said, "Building Collapse by Casper Wyoming."

Once Steve stopped by my desk and said, "You're not *doing* that story, are you?" in a tone of high contempt. Eddie went home before I was finished. Jenny had long since disappeared. Then Greg rushed off before I could ask him about the *Washington Post*. Even

Ron departed without saying another word to me.

As I was typing the last page of "Collapse" and sighing about the lonely evening ahead of me, my telephone rang.

"All right, you little rat! You scooped the shit out of us, but it won't happen again. What are you doing? Writing your Pulitzer Prize application? Hurry it up. I'm gonna buy you a drink."

"Miltie!" I said.

"Meet you in Sardi's in twenty minutes," Miltie Clendenon said, and he hung up.

# XXVIII

"God, it's great to see you, Miltie!" I said as I found him at a corner table in the upstairs bar. "I think everybody at *The Newspaper* hates me! Nobody said a word about my piece."

"You made 'em look bad, kid. What'd you expect? You made us all look bad." He gave me a sneering smile.

"I just got lucky."

"Got lucky, huh? What'd you do? Offer your slender body to that cop Noonan, the one who found the mayor? He's workin' the Gracie Mansion detail now, you know. But who'm I tellin'? Lemme get you drunk. What'll it be?"

"Oh, I guess a white wine," I said.

"Have a real drink!" Miltie said. "You deserve it."

"Okay. I'll have a vodka tonic."

Miltie fetched it from the bar because he said the waiters ignored *Morning Chronicle* men. When he returned, he asked me to give him a friendly warning the next time I got a scoop on the mayor.

"So I can make it for second edition," he said. "I wouldn't ask you to share an exclusive, but just so I can catch up by second edition. We went crazy last night. We had the mayor's statement, but they weren't saying any more at City Hall, and we didn't have the police report. Did you see my story? I had to quote *you!*"

"I'm sorry, Miltie. I didn't know."

"There you go, playing dumb again. Drink up. I'm paying."

He must have ordered me a double. It tasted like Foley's "refresher."

"I promise not to ask which cop you slept with, but you did sleep with a cop, didn't you? That's the only thing I can figure. A cop wouldn't give that report to his own mother."

"I can't stand cops, Miltie," I said. "They represent everything I abhor in capitalist, materialist American society."

"They're the best sources, kid. Besides, I thought cops were sexy. Fuck their politics!"

"Miltie, could we change the subject? How's your word processor? How's life in Room 9?"

"It's a little hard to change the subject when all I talked about all day was you. I hadda stick up for you quite a few times today, Sarah."

"Thanks, Miltie. You're a good guy. But you know I can't tell you where I got the story."

"Yeah, let's get drunk," he said, and he started waving for a waiter, though we were only halfway through our drinks.

"Was Clive mad?" I asked.

"Clive's a cool cat," said Miltie. "He made like he knew you were hot stuff all along. Being groomed by the bosses. But some of your other colleagues can't figure it out. I heard people saying you were a cunning strategist. One guy said you got fired but you pretended you didn't know it, and then you pulled this coup with Hizzoner."

"Who said I was fired?"

"I forget who. Was there some big blowup last week? Did Ron chew you out in front of everybody?"

"Yes, but—"

"That's when it was supposed to be. Well, whadda you know, he's comin' over here! Must be because you're with me."

The waiter took Miltie's order. He *had* made mine a double the first time. This time I asked for a weak one.

"Yeah, this guy—oh, I know who it was! Pankhurst. He said he heard the desk talking about it this week, how you were still coming to work, and they didn't know what to do. Nobody has ever done that before."

"But I *wasn't* fired!" I said, growing red in the face. "At least, I don't think I was. Do you think, now that Ron got his story— See, it was because he wanted that story. Oh, Miltie! I just agreed to cover somebody's bail for twenty thousand dollars today!"

"That's somebody, all right. How the hell did you get in with company like that?"

"Well, it's two somebodies, a couple of kids I used to work with in East Harlem. They got indicted with some Italians in a stolen-car ring."

"That mob case? You signed their surety bond?"

"Not for the Italians. Just the two boys."

"Who's the bail bondsman?"

"A very nice man named Sy Shimmer."

"You sure know how to pick 'em! I wish you'd asked me. Shimmer's been one step ahead of the DA for most of his life. He does all the small-time Mafia cases. Some people think he launders funny money."

"Well, it's too late now. I signed. And maybe I'm out of a job."

"Aw, shit! You're not out of any job! You're sitting pretty now. With that scoop! Bottoms up."

We finished our first drinks and went on to our second.

"You really think I don't have to worry?" I asked.

"I wish Clive could hear you say that. He thinks you're a female Machiavelli. He says you're the kind that would try to lure the publisher away from his wife, and if it didn't work, you'd charge sexual harassment. Clive thinks you're secretly in league with the Feminist Faction."

"What's wrong with him? Why does he think everybody's always got a plot going? Hasn't he heard of drift?"

"Listen, don't worry about it. If people wanta think you're smarter than you are, just let 'em. What's the harm?"

"I thought you thought it was better to have 'em think you're dumber than you are."

"Whatever works," said Miltie, smiling into his glass. "Chances are, whatever people think of you, it's not gonna be what you think of you—not around *The Newspaper*. Listen, when people in a normal line of work can't understand a person's behavior, they explain it in one of two ways. They say, *(a)* he grew up in a foreign country, or *(b)* he's crazy. But when people in the news business can't understand why a person does what she does, they think, *(a)* she knows something they don't know, and *(b)* she's gonna be the next managing editor."

"They wouldn't think a woman was going to be the next managing editor."

"No, I guess not quite yet. But wait a couple of years."

"Now they think she's planning to lure the publisher away from his wife."

"Have you ever met Kleinfreude? He's a charmer. You could drift in worse directions."

Miltie and I parted ways on Forty-fourth Street. Three blocks west or so, the sun was resting on the street like a fat orange water balloon. Two smaller fat orange water balloons flashed at me from Miltie's glasses.

"Keep your ears pricked," he said to me. "These things always come in bunches. And don't forget: Miltie gets a call in time for second edition. What are friends for?"

I should have realized that a man who had been in the newspaper business as long as Miltie Clendenon must possess certain oracular powers and that two bright orange suns glinting from his glasses could be a very freakish sign. But I felt no foreboding. Miltie tilted westward toward the big toy sun, and I moved eastward toward the Seventh Avenue moviegoers. Our session in Sardi's had filled me with such profound satisfaction that I did not want to walk too fast. Not since my brother's best friend from college, Phil Geswissen, a pure mathematician who could prove in numbers that the sun didn't exist, told me I had more "native intelligence" than Noah had I felt so deeply satisfied. No, not even then. For shortly after Phil had praised my mental powers, he grabbed for one of my underdeveloped breasts and tried to kiss me so ineptly as to make me doubt his ability to detect the native in anyone.

This time there was nothing to disturb the beautiful feeling in my soul. I could wander home at my leisure, letting Miltie's phrases repeat themselves in my head like exquisite musical themes. Talked about me all day long. Everyone speculating about my game plan. Thinking I outfoxed Ron! Called me a cunning strategist! Oh, how beautiful the city looked in the last light of day—the deep-blue sky, the sun shooting orange flames from the topmost windows, the bricks turning to red gold down all the side streets, and the whole bright panoply whirling by backward over the roof sheen of a pimp's Cadillac! Everyone had read my story! I made them look like fools! All the people who heard Flicker tell me how to spell "comptroller"! All the ones who heard Ron "firing" me! And all the people who saw me dangling from the window sash in Room 9! Oh, what happiness! Oh, women's liberation! Oh, wonderful rat race! I was the winner! Oh, fabulous, fabulous New York City! Phil Geswissen had not lied to me! I *was* smarter than Noah!

When I emerged from the subway in Sheridan Square, I imagined that all the homosexuals were happy too. They were out in force tonight, and as I walked up Christopher Street, through their milling and swarming bodies, I thought these were the winner homosexuals, the ones with the guts and talent to make it in New York. Make it in more ways than one, ho ho ho! But really, they and I were spiritual allies. We had more in common with each other than we had with the folks back home. Think of our wit and sophistication. They were the top men in cultural circles—fashion designers, actors, graphic artists, museum curators. Oh, but I mustn't stereotype. Some were no doubt boring stockbrokers. Accountants. Newspaper reporters. Cops. What a thought! Honestly, though, why should I begrudge them their fagginess? I liked Jim 'n' Jim. All three of us had suffered from the same suffocation of rural life, from the murderous feeling that there wasn't enough crime around. Jim 'n' Jim never even saw a fistfight until they got to Austin. Never saw other fags, either. Never saw a whole lot of them until they got to New York City, and then their eyes popped right out of their heads. The funny thing was, they felt the same way I did about too many of them crowding in on the Village. Even more so, maybe. They said the Village was being overrun by "street trade," the kind who, they almost hissed, "go to the trucks."

What did people *do* in the trucks? Oh, glory, what didn't they do! Just look at them out here tonight. They wanted *every*one to see that itch in their thighs. They were proud of it, proud of their horniness and proud of their scene. They owned Christopher Street. A man walked down here, he was going to get a look every two seconds, a look saying, "You want to fuck?" And anybody who showed disapproval would get the look saying, "You don't like it? Then fuck off!" Defiance was their way of life. They gave off defiance and sexual secretions from the same bodily glands, as though they had mixed sodomy with moxie and come out with the purest kind of sexual appeal this side of Eden. Talk about raunch! With their leather boots and tight-over-the-balls pants, with their mean metal things hooked onto belt loops—oooh, baby! there was one wearing metal studs on his nipples—with their hoots and shimmies and lewdly curled lips, they were the concentrated essence of raunch. They boasted about fist fucking! There was a guy who wrote for the *Eye* quoting them on the life in the trucks, lost dizzy nights longer than human endurance, places where people never knew each other's names. How did they keep it up night after night? Every

**207**

evening when I came home, I'd see the same ones out cruising, out looking for more, more, more, as though they could never be satisfied, were turned on all the time. They always gave off the feeling, even to me. I could feel myself getting turned on among them, walking that one block to my house. It was like walking through an invisible erotic steam made of the itchy expectation that they were about to break all rules.

No wonder the rest of America hates them, I thought. They give a contact high on the urge to sin. People don't like that. They don't want to be turned on by that throbbing vileness in the backs of trucks. And as I thought this, my own revulsion swelled with the familiar sickening Friday smell of their Caswell-Massey afterbath splash, and I took one step up my stoop and—*holy shit!*—remembered Friday night meant Ellie's and Roger's dinner! I had completely forgotten.

The time was now eight-twenty. Ellie had said seven-thirty. I had yet to shower and change. She was very precise about dinner parties. She was going to be furious.

---

# XXIX

---

But Ellie was so glad to see me, she couldn't get mad. She gave me a big hug when I arrived at ten to nine. Old friends are the best, I thought, and then she said:

"You're a celebrity, Sarah! Everybody's talking about your story. Oh, shit! I got lipstick on your cheek. Come on in Roger's bathroom and wipe it off. I want to tell you about Felix. He's dying to meet you! They're all dying to meet you."

Roger's bathroom was the one Roger and his patients used during working hours. His office, waiting room, and files took up the first floor of the three-story building, a redbrick Federal town house he had bought with the proceeds of many neuroses. He and Ellie lived on the second floor, and they rented the third to a *Rolling Stone* editor named Megan, who was supposed to be really hot stuff in her business and an intimate friend of about five hundred famous writers. Megan sometimes had late-night crises which required that she pour her heart out to Roger. She was a little strange. She once told Roger that Ellie had moved in with him because he lived opposite the house the Weathermen had accidentally blown up.

The first floor was the nicest. The waiting room opened out onto the back garden. But Roger refused to entertain in his place of work, so all the guests were upstairs now.

"Who's Felix?" I said. "Not another shrink, please!"

"Yes, but—"

"Oh, Ellie! I asked you for anything else. I'd take a child molester. What's with this lipstick, Ellie? It won't come off."

"Use soap, stupid! His name is Felix Lebwohl, and he runs my therapy group. He's really accepting."

"What does *that* mean, accepting? Ellie, this bathroom is too depressing. It's too clean. People must feel like they're in a hospital. Somebody should write on the wall."

"You'll see. Listen, if I wasn't married to Roger . . . Felix is gorgeous! He gets involved in things. He goes to political meetings. He goes jogging in the park. Sometimes he smokes a little dope. You'll like him a lot. He loves *The Newspaper.*"

"What's the hitch?"

"What do you mean, what's the hitch? Sarah, what are you *doing?* Stop that!"

I had written "FREE MEGAN" on the bathroom mirror with the bar of soap.

"Why isn't Felix married if he's such a great catch?"

"Since when have you decided being ummarried proves there's a problem? Sarah, wipe it off. She might see it."

"Megan's allowed to use Roger's bathroom now? Ellie, that's a bad sign," I said, slopping water onto my handiwork.

"Megan's in treatment with Roger. It's just for a little while. Roger wanted to prescribe Valium, and he has a strict rule: no drugs for people not in treatment. She had a very hard month. Hunter Thompson sent in a bag of blue pills instead of a piece."

"What was in the pills? Did you try any?"

"Megan flushed them down the john."

"Flushed pills from Hunter Thompson down the john! Megan is one sick lady."

"Shhh! She'll hear you. She's right upstairs."

"She's part of the dinner party?"

"Roger's been very worried about her. She's convinced all our phones are tapped."

"Who else have you got? Anybody I know?"

"You won't say *any*thing about Megan being in treatment now, will you, Sarah? Promise?"

"Of course I won't. Listen, she's probably a fantastic source. I have to consider that angle in all my human interchanges these days. What if she knows Marlon Brando's home phone number?"

"Are you still hung up on him? He's so fat, Sarah! Anyway, he's not a writer. Quick, I want to tell you about the others before we go upstairs. You know the Spissaks, don't you? Miles and Claudia. She's a sculptress, and he's the one who wrote that book *I Can, You Can.*"

"Oh, yeah, with the chinline beard. He says stay away from failures. I met them here last year. She asked us to pose for her study of roommates."

"Okay. Then there's John and Mona Treat. You haven't met them. John's a student at the analytic institute where Miles and Roger teach. Mona's a dancer, I think. And Herb and Wendy De-Vorak. Herb handled Roger's divorce, you know. *He* could give you a lot of scoops, because he's really plugged in. He's on the executive committee of the Bar Association. Wendy does transactional analysis. Don't ask me to explain it. But she's nice."

"Herb's the one you hope will find you a job, I take it."

"Don't say anything about that! He doesn't know I got fired."

"Who's Megan's man?"

"She's extra."

"That's what happens to people named Megan. You know, Ellie, I think Roger's wasting his time on her. I think anybody named Megan is doomed to get the short end of the stick in life. Hunter Thompson probably thinks so too. I bet he sent her uppers."

"Shhh!" Ellie said as she led the way up the stairs.

Roger came forward to kiss me. He took my hand in his and held it up as though we were about to commence an Elizabethan dance.

"This is our scoop artist," he said loudly. "What can I get you to drink?" he asked me.

"Oh, I guess a vodka tonic. Not too strong," I said.

I felt put on the spot. The others were all looking at me, except for one man, who stood at the far window, looking out at the garden. I started to follow Roger into the kitchen, but Ellie nabbed me and did the introductions, winding up with: "And that is Felix Lebwohl, peering out the window as if he wants to get away."

He turned around slowly. He was devilishly handsome, if somewhat clipped looking, like the man in the Hathaway shirt ads.

"I was just wishing we could all go into the garden," he said. "It's a beautiful evening."

"We'll be eating soon," said Ellie, "won't we, honey?"

Roger had emerged from the kitchen carrying my drink. Behind him came Megan, wiping her hands on an apron.

"There you are," he said. "Now, as soon as you've wet your throat, Sarah, you'll have to tell us how you got that story. Everyone wants to know."

"It came from the Police Department," said Herb. "The whole story was built around the Missing Persons report. Rinkel's trying to sink Simon."

"Is there more?" Wendy asked me. "Did you find out why Simon's been doing this?"

"No, I didn't. City Hall said yesterday there would be no further statements on it. The thing is, if he's the only one who knows why, then the secret's safe. Even his wife didn't know."

"Oh, come on!" said Herb.

"I believe it," said his wife. "It's a terrible time to be mayor."

"What's happened to the mayor?" asked Mona, the dancer, with a sudden worried look between her enormous eyes.

"You weren't listening, honey," her husband, John, said patronizingly. "They were talking about a story that was in *The Newspaper* this morning. It said that the mayor sometimes disappears and nobody knows where he is. She wrote the story." He looked at me. "I'm sure he's a schizophrenic. He's got Belinda's Syndrome."

"What's that?" I asked.

"That theory has been discredited, John," said Miles, who still had his chinline beard. "Belinda's Syndrome was probably just alcoholic lying."

"Belinda S. was a Chicago housewife who used to disappear for days at a time and then not remember where she was," John said. "She did indulge in alcohol, but ordinarily she was not subject to blackouts. At home she was a perfectly normal, sweet-tempered woman."

"She went to motels with strange men, they found out," Ellie said, "but she couldn't remember afterwards."

"Alcoholism is almost always a screen for schizophrenia," said John.

"I think that's putting it a little too strongly," Miles said. "We've seen teenage drinkers who are merely responding to group pressure."

"That's how my brother got into drugs," said Mona. "Everybody else was doing it."

"How old is your brother, Mona?" Miles asked.

"I think we should leave Geoff out of this discussion," John said.

"I'm not ashamed of him," said Mona. "He's kicked. He's been clean for two years. That's more than you can say for all those people you keep putting on Valium."

"Valium is *not* addictive! It is *not* addictive! You shouldn't get into areas like this, because you don't know what you're talking about—"

"Valium is, too, addictive. I read it in *The Newspaper*."

"Is that true?" Megan asked Roger.

"Anything is addictive to the addictive personality," Roger said soothingly, his eyes on the quarreling couple. "But as far as I know, Valium is not physically addictive. That is, it does not cause withdrawal symptoms. How did we get from the mayor to Valium?"

"What's your theory about Simon, Roger?" Felix asked. He had moved toward the center of the room, where people were seated on couches.

"I think it's depression," Roger said. "And there could be drinking."

"I think it's depression too," said Wendy. "But I maintain it's appropriate."

"Wendy's right. The poor man lives in a fishbowl," said Claudia, the sculptress.

"The pressures of fame," said Felix. "How do you find it?" he asked me quietly.

"Find what?"

"Being famous."

"I'm not famous!" I said falsely, thinking of Noah.

"Don't you think everybody's going to remember that Sarah Makepeace got that story?" he said, searching my face with his eyes. "It has nothing to do with you as a person, of course. Fame is a symbol of the father's power. I'm curious—has your attitude toward your father changed recently?"

"Not really. My father's—oh, you don't want to hear about my old man!"

"You find the subject disturbing?"

I was saved by the food. Roger called us all to the table, and while we were slurping gazpacho, he served up his latest public case study.

"Has anyone been following the conduct of our fair governor lately?" he began.

212

"Following in what way, Roger?" Felix asked. Apparently he was new to this gambit.

"Well, this endorsement of a joke candidate for President, for example, and the ages of his—"

"Love is not a joke candidate," Felix interrupted. "Haven't you seen the polls?"

"Oh, polls!" Roger exclaimed, shrugging so largely that he turned his soup spoon upside down and spilled gazpacho on the table.

"Love is ten points ahead of Udall," Felix said.

"We all know that Love is not going to get the nomination," Roger said. "Now, Feely's endorsement—"

"I like him," said Wendy. "He's cute."

"Wendy, really!" said her husband. "Wendy's grandmother marched down Fifth Avenue and was ostracized by her whole family so her granddaughter could vote for the cutest presidential candidate."

"I believe Governor Feely is undergoing a severe midlife crisis," Roger persevered. "I believe he is experiencing the phenomenon sometimes referred to as male menopause."

"My dear boy, Feely is only forty-two years old!" Miles interjected. "Don't you think that's a bit early for menopause? Anyway, I don't put much truck in that male menopause theory. I think it's wishful feminist thinking. A man does not have to lose his sexual powers or his attractiveness until he's into old age, and even then he can keep it up, if you will, with the right attitude. Even women can counteract the aging process with the right attitude. You should read my—"

"Oh, attitude, shmattitude!" said Claudia from three seats down. "I'm getting sick of all this attitude business. What's attitude going to do for a fifty-year-old woman? Miles has these twenty-year-olds falling all over him. 'Are you the one who wrote that wonderful book?'" she cooed. "'Oh, Dr. Spissak, you changed my life!' You think any twenty-year-old is going to throw himself at me—let alone a fifty-year-old! I think I should write a book and call it *He Can, She Can't!*"

"Now, Claudia," said Miles.

"You're a very attractive woman," Roger said quickly. "I'm sure women half your age have found it hard to adjust to having their husbands write best-sellers. But I'm glad you raised that point about older men and younger women. One of Feely's symptoms is his sudden craze for twenty-one-year-olds from the Midwest—"

"Twenty-one isn't too young!" said Felix.

"—and I think this shows an anxiety about his own decline which, coupled with the fact that his mother has moved into the mansion, indicates a deep concern for his manhood—"

"Didn't he go out with Miss Ohio?" Wendy said. "She was smashing!"

"Yes," said Miles, "and she's quite mature. Very bright too. She's studying theology."

"Miles was on the Carson show with her," said Claudia.

"And then there's the endorsement of Love," Roger said, appearing not to have heard any of the others. "I'm certain his mother didn't approve of that. She's a shrewd politician. So this is an act of rebellion too, which in a forty-two-year-old man often indicates latent homosexuality, the unresolved Oedipal situation being the source. Of course, that's also why he drinks."

"Oh, Roger, he's Irish!" said Wendy.

"How could he be a homosexual if he has children?" asked Mona.

"Mona, he said *latent!*" said John. "I wish you wouldn't—"

"And there's his paranoia," said Roger. "Remember when he accused the county leaders of plotting against him?"

"What does paranoia have to do with it?" asked Megan.

"It's true paranoia's a very common problem with homosexuals," said Miles.

"That doesn't mean all paranoids are homosexual," Roger said, smiling at Megan.

"Phew! That's a relief!" I said. "When I walk down my street I feel everybody's looking at me as though I don't belong there."

"Oh, Sarah!" said Ellie. "Sarah lives on Christopher Street," she explained to the others. "It's made her a homophobe."

"Darling, I wish you wouldn't use that word," said Roger. "Homosexuality is a character disorder, by whatever name you call it. It is not a mode of normal sexuality."

Everyone then tried to talk at once, vehemently challenging what Roger had just said. Wendy eventually made herself heard above the others.

"Does that mean Socrates had a character disorder?" she asked Roger. "Come on, Roger!"

"He committed suicide," Roger said feebly.

"When are we going to get to Nixon?" I said, feeling heady on the wine. "There's a paranoid for you!"

"Socrates committed suicide under duress," said Herb.

"Roger's well aware of his own limitations," Felix said. "He refers all his homosexual patients to me."

214

This shut Roger up nicely.

"Getting back to Feely"—Miles eventually spoke up—"I think it's very simple. He's getting over his divorce. He's acting out a bit, is all, with these young girls."

"Is Governor Feely a patient of yours?" Mona asked Roger.

"Oh, Mona!" her husband ejaculated. "If he was a patient, Roger couldn't talk about him!"

"Don't you listen to him, dear," Wendy said. "We talk about our patients all the time."

"Not by name," said Miles.

"No, not by name unless we all know him," said Wendy, "or unless he's a celebrity."

"Do you have any celebrity patients right now, Wendy?" I asked.

"That's not fair. You work for the press," said Herb.

"Well, just tell me one thing," I said. "Who's Woody Allen's analyst?"

"I'd like to know that myself," said Wendy. "I've never been able to find out. Do you know, Miles?"

"I don't think anyone does," Miles said. "It's a tribute to the canons of our trade."

"I heard it's a woman," said Ellie.

"It couldn't be a woman!" said John. "After all his hostile jokes about his mother?"

"I think it could be a woman," Roger ventured. "The length of the analysis—what is it? Fourteen years?"

"Where do you get all this information, Roger?" Wendy asked. "I didn't know half the stuff you told us about Feely."

"He reads a lot of newspapers," said Ellie. "Sometimes I think Roger should have been a reporter. He loves to know other people's secrets."

"What better profession than psychotherapy?" Roger asked her with a loving look.

"But it's too slow for you," said Ellie. "You like to know everything about a person right away. Besides, most of your patients aren't famous."

"They are all equally fascinating to me," said Roger grandly.

"After a while they are," said Wendy. "But in the beginning, the famous ones are much more interesting. I never fall asleep on them, either."

"You fall asleep during therapy sessions?" asked John. "My god! I'm so glad to hear that! I thought I was doing severe avoidance."

"I always nod off when they get into masturbation," said Wendy.

"I don't know why. That's why I record the sessions. Masturbation comes up a lot."

"Yes, I find that too," said Felix. "It's quite a recurrent theme."

"They think we want to know about it," said Miles. "They are trying to be good patients, tell us what they think we think is abnormal."

"How do you know what's wrong with people?" Mona asked Miles. "Some of John's patients don't seem to have anything wrong with them."

"Oh, Mona!" John moaned.

"That's a very good question," Miles said, and as soon as we had got up from the table, he took Mona away to a corner of one of the couches.

"Woody Allen's analyst is not a woman," Felix said to me in an undertone, standing close behind me.

"Wendy, did you hear that?" Herb called to his wife in a loud voice. She was standing across the room. "Felix here says that Woody Allen's analyst is not a woman!"

"Felix! You've been keeping something from us!" Wendy said. "Who is he?"

"That wasn't meant for public consumption," Felix said.

"Woody Allen's analyst is an old man," said Megan.

"Why've *you* been so quiet?" Wendy asked.

"Well, I'm not really sure," said Megan. "One of our photographers claims he overheard Woody saying the guy was an old man."

The inquiry finally stopped at that point, and people began to speak to one another in pairs and small clusters. Felix led me over to the window and tried to pump me about my family again. This didn't get him anywhere, so he asked about my friendship with Ellie.

"What about it?" I said uncooperatively.

"Well, has it suffered since she married Roger? He's hard to take, I think."

"Yeah. I thought you were a friend of his."

"Oh, I've known him for years. But she's the one I like. Ellie is in my training group. I gather you and she used to be very close. You were roommates in college?"

"That's right," I said, turning to look for an escape route.

"I think Roger's afraid you'll win her back," he said.

"What? Ellie and I aren't—"

"Roger is terribly afraid of homosexuality. He sent me another patient last week. In fact, you might be interested in this case. The man claims he was once intimate with Senator Love."

I turned back to face him.

"But isn't he supposed to be the perfect family man?"

"That doesn't preclude the other. The patient claims Love and he were lovers in Vietnam, before Love was married," Felix said, watching my face intently again.

"Well? What business is it of ours?" I said rudely.

"This man is afraid. He said he's been getting threats," Felix said.

"Do you think he's telling the truth?"

"Why don't we go to your place?" he said. "I don't want to discuss him here. I don't want people overhearing us."

What would you have done?

Ellie whispered to me, "What'd I tell you?" as I kissed her goodbye.

"You never told us how you got your story!" Roger said. "See if you can wheedle it out of her, Felix."

"I used my body, Roger," I said.

As Felix and I passed down the stairs, I heard Roger saying, "Why'd she say that? Why does she always get defensive with me, Ellie?"

# XXX

If only Felix hadn't acted so uncannily sure of himself! But he ruined everything with his repulsive confidence. From the moment we stepped out of the Einsteins' house, he laid claim to me as though I had been promised to him along with the after-dinner coffee. Men have a way of communicating how far they feel themselves to be in possession of you by their style of escorting you on a street where strangers can see. An offered elbow can still preserve a lady's reputation. It says if they are sleeping together, he is not advertising it. Hand holding betokens greater intimacy, though still not necessarily the greatest. An arm over the shoulders indicates he has recently seduced her or he has high hopes that seduction is imminent. An arm around her back with hand resting on her hip announces that the deed's been done. A hand buried in her back pocket says that it wasn't their first time. A hand pressing lightly against the small of her back tells the world he can steer her with the touch of his fingertips, i.e., she is his sensual slave.

Guess which one Felix Lebwohl used on me. He probably wasn't sure of anything under the surface. But his affect, as his therapist friends would say, was all sublime masculine assurance. When we were inside my door, he did not grab roughly or awkwardly, like a man who feared he was taking a risk. He coolly wrapped the fingers of his right hand around my left wrist. He held on firmly but at first did nothing else, and I tried to walk toward my dining table chair. He walked with me. I tried to tug my arm free without making too big a deal of it. He was standing beside me at the table. I started to sit down, but he clasped my other arm above the elbow and moved up against me, pinning me against the table. Then he tried to tip my chin up with the index finger of his left hand. I smelled an aftershave lotion. Not Caswell-Massey, but something very like. I turned my face to one side. He pressed harder with his finger. I felt a tickle in my windpipe and coughed convincingly, twisting away from him. He backed off.

"That wouldn't happen to you if you stopped smoking," he said.

"Ummm," I murmured, stepping over to the kitchen sink. "I know."

"I could have you off cigarettes in two weeks," he said, stepping across the distance between us to pat me on the back. "I have a foolproof method." He slipped his hand up to my neck. I turned around to draw myself a glass of water, drank some with my back to him, filled the glass again, and said with my back still to him:

"I don't want you to get the wrong idea, Felix. I have a boyfriend."

He came to lean against the sink beside me and folded his arms across his chest.

"Tell me about him," he said.

"Oh, it's complicated," I said.

"He's married?" said Felix.

"Ummm," I said.

"You don't strike me as the kind who would get into a masochistic situation like that. Although women of your status do frequently undermine themselves with men. That's why I asked you about your father earlier."

"Look, I might as well tell you, I don't like being psychoanalyzed."

"Yes, Roger said you were hostile to the profession. Why is that?"

He put his hand on my neck again.

"There you go: 'Why is that?' Look, Felix, I—"

He swung around to face me and pressed me against the sink. I leaned backward, holding my chin in. He had my arms pinned down.

"I find you very attractive," he said. "You have an innocent quality which is very special."

"You don't know me," I said.

"I would like to know you better. Why does that frighten you? Relax. I'm going to kiss you."

But he kissed my ear, because I turned my head away.

"Relax, Sarah," he said softly into my ear.

"But I don't *want* you to kiss me!" I said, and I twisted my body around.

"Why did you invite me up here?" he asked, moving away from me now, annoyed.

I sat down in my dining room chair and reached for a cigarette. "You said you wanted more privacy so we could talk about your patient," I said, lighting up.

"I wish you wouldn't smoke," he said. "In ten years you'll have breast cancer."

"Is that how you cure people of smoking? Appealing to reason?"

"Of course not!" he said. He smiled and sat down on the little couch next to Kevin's corner chair.

"Come on, Felix, tell me about your patient."

"I'll get to him," he said. "I want to know more about you."

I should have realized then that he wasn't going to deliver, but I mistook his moving to the couch as a sign that he was going to be a nice guy and give up trying to seduce me. His questions were nice. He dropped the doctory sharpness and spoke like a normal person making conversation. An hour passed while I talked about myself and he commented and gently prodded for more. Eventually I started yawning.

"Would you like to go to bed?" he said.

"Yes, I think I'd better," I said. "But you still haven't told me about your patient."

"I can tell you in the morning," he said.

"All right," I said, "but don't call too early."

He stood up as if to leave and I stood up but stayed near the chair. He walked toward me. I folded my arms. He stepped close to me and put his arms around me so that I was all bunched together. His eyes were shining.

"Felix, we went through this—" I started to say, and then he tried to kiss me again, and I turned my head.

"Sarah," he said, "you've made me wait a long time. I'm going to spend the night with you."

"No, you're not, Felix! Come on!" I said, and I shoved my elbows against him.

"What is the matter with you?" he said angrily, still holding me by the waist.

"There's nothing the matter with me. I'm just not attracted to you," I said.

"You should have told me that before," he said, letting me go.

"I thought it was obvious. I invited you up here to talk."

"A woman doesn't invite a man up to her apartment to talk. He doesn't expect her to. We're not children."

"You *said* you wanted to be alone with me to tell me about your patient."

"What did you want me to say? Should I have said I want to orgasm in your vagina?"

"Oh, god!" I said, reaching for my cigarettes.

"Look at you! You are really uptight."

"Listen, Felix, you weren't straight with me. You said—"

"I wasn't straight with *you!* That is sheer projection, Sarah. You weren't straight with *me!* You know I can't talk about my patients. I would have to get Renato's permission."

"Who's Renato?"

"Never mind!"

"Is he your patient? Why don't you ask him if he'll talk to me, then?"

"It's incredible. You invited me up here just to pump me, didn't you?"

"Look, you said—"

"I know what I said."

"I'm sorry if you misunderstood, Felix, but I misunderstood too."

"You didn't misunderstand," he said, moving toward the door. "I should have told you I was married! Goodbye!"

He slammed my door so violently that the peephole thing fell out. Felix's heavy tread could be heard all the way down the stairs. The front door opened and then closed with a big bang.

"Sarah? You all right?" called a voice from the second story.

"Yes, Jim," I called back. "Only my peephole thing fell off."

He came trotting up the stairs. He and his lover looked so much alike, with their shiny hair and their apologetic fag Wasp faces, that

I could only tell them apart by their difference in height. This was Jim the Shorter.

"What was that all abaaht? Have a fahgt with your boyfriend?" he asked in his soft Texas twang.

"No. I just met him tonight. I shouldn't have invited him up. I fell for his line. He's a psychiatrist and he said he wanted to tell me about a patient of his who had had an affair with a senator, a male patient."

"Which senator?"

"You won't spread it around?"

"Ah am the soul of discretion, honey. Lemme see if Ah can fix this theng," he said, picking up the peephole gadget.

"Senator Love."

"Senator Love? He's a doll! Who's his lover boy?"

"I didn't find out. Renato somebody."

"Renato's kind of a common name in the gay community. Whah'd this psahchahtrist slam your door so hard?"

"I told him I wasn't attracted to him."

"An he took it hard. You got a screwdrahver?"

"No," I said. "How about a knife?"

"Okay," said Jim. He put the peephole gadget in its hole in the door as I rummaged around for a suitable knife. He grunted as he worked.

"He really did a number on this theng," he said. "He must have been awful mad. You had him up here awhile. He got his hopes up."

"He's a creep."

"Whyd'you invaht him up here, then?"

"Well, in retrospect—"

"Yeah, you know better now. This theng is a mother!"

"If you can't fix it, just leave it, Jim."

But he kept struggling with it.

"Where's your nice-lookin' boyfriend?"

"At home with his wife."

"That's too bad. Ah'm sorry to hear that. Well, you'll find yourself the raght fellow one a these days. Maybe the boyfriend'll leave his wife for you. Ah stole Jim from two other people."

"You did? That must have been difficult."

"It wuz. Jim didn't used to like to put all his eggs in one basket. There you go. That oughta stay now," he said, patting the door.

"Thanks, Jim. You're a real sweetie."

"'Tweren't nothin'," he said, putting on a heavier drawl. "We

**221**

can't have you sittin' up here defenseless, with all that riffraff out in the street."

"The place was hopping tonight, wasn't it?"

"Honey, sometimes Ah almost want to go back to Woody Creek. But Ah guess between faggots and rednecks, Ah'll take faggots. G'night, Sarah. Sweet dreams."

"'Night, Jim. And thanks."

I went to bed thinking I'd sooner sleep with Jim the Shorter than with Felix Lebwohl. But for a long time I lay awake wondering about his patient, wondering if I should have tried harder to get the story. If Love was going to be a presidential candidate . . . But Felix was so repulsive! Still, a story that big . . . Oh, I couldn't have gone to bed with him. But then, there might have been a way to draw him out. Someone with more experience could have done it. Greg could have. Probably Jenny could have. Even a kiss. Greg Swenson definitely would have kissed a lady psychiatrist who repelled him for the sake of a hot tip on a presidential candidate. Shit, Greg probably would have let Felix Lebwohl kiss him! Why had I been so vehement? I should have been gentler, more artful. Kept him hoping longer. Stupid New England goy. I might as well face it. In the newspaper business I was going to be a flash in the pan, and I had already flashed.

## XXXI

At least I knew enough not to tell Ron about the new tip. After what he had put me through on the mayoral story, I didn't want to tell him anything that wasn't nailed down. That prick Felix could have been lying, for all I knew. Or his patient could have been lying. I let the thing drop from my mind, and for the next couple of weeks life sort of normalized. Kevin came by and noticed my peephole gadget was loose, and the explanation sent him into one of his jealous frenzies, which ended ecstatically. Ron was keyed up and sent me all over town looking for "bright" pieces of city life. We had lambent summer days and nights (Flicker said I was straining when I used "lambent" in a piece about ice cream parlors), and Dad was so busy with organic gardening that he left me alone.

Then all of a sudden, it was the week before the convention, and Ron was eerily calm. Convention delegates began arriving in the city and pronouncing it the Big Apple, and the National Desk's presidential campaign reporters made their appearance in the newsroom, thrusting their conceited chests out like so many Vincent Akelroyds, and Ron seemed unperturbed.

"He's really being a good sport," I said to Eddie.

"Who is?" Eddie asked as he licked the point of the pen he was using for his expense account form.

"Ron," I said. "Look at him. He's smiling at Jenny."

"I'm puttin' in for the cab down to Canal Street," said Eddie. "On that dog rescue."

"We took the subway."

"*You* took the subway!" Eddie said, shoving his hat back for emphasis.

"I think you should put more money on Dixby. Ron's giving up without a struggle," I said shrewdly.

"Stick around, kid," said Eddie. "Ron's got sumpin' up his sleeve."

"Like what?"

Eddie didn't answer, but that afternoon I think we found out what Ron had been waiting for. Dixby posted the names of the Metro reporters who had been selected to join the convention team. Freddie told me Ron had recommended Greg Swenson, Clive Lipschitz, Nick Pankhurst, three people from the Albany bureau, Eddie, and me. (He had claimed I was an "experienced" political reporter. This was the point of the City Hall stint.) Dixby's choices were: Steve Figland, Susan Braithwaite, Jenny Locke, and Vincent Akelroyd.

About two seconds after the memo went up, Ron's voice came thundering over the loudspeaker:

"SWENSON, GET UP HERE! ON THE DOUBLE, GOD DAMN IT! GET OFF THE PHONE!"

Two minutes later it was:

"EDDIE SCHWARTZ, GET UP HERE! EDDIE, WHERE ARE YOU?"

And two minutes after that:

"SARAH MAKEPEACE!"

As I arrived at his desk, Ron was waving his hands at Eddie and shouting, "Not for Thursday! I want this for tomorrow night! Get Marco! I want photos! This is going to be a spread! Go on, Eddie! What are you waiting for? Get Marco! I want a picture of every one of those hotels. Go on!"

Eddie ran off toward the photo lab, and Ron turned to me.

"Now, Sarah!" he said so rapidly that I almost jumped. "I want you to call up those radicals who threw eggs at the Japanese prime minister, and I want you to call up your friends on *The Evil Eye* and all the rest of your radical friends. I want you to tell us every protest that is planned, how many thousands are going to demonstrate. I want good quotes, Sarah, tell us what the disenchanted are saying, and talk to the police. I want to be able to tell people before it happens about the battle in the streets! This may be another Chicago!"

"You think so, Ron?" I said. "You think people would tell me in advance?"

"It's your *job* to *get* them to tell you, Sarah. Do I have to lead you by the hand? Get going! I want this by tomorrow night!"

In the end he let me take two days to do the story, because my first researches turned up only the news that Ralph Abernathy was going to bring poor people to demonstrate peacefully in front of the Garden. Ron wanted to know about radicals and violence, so I kept asking around, but people said that Watergate and the end of the war had taken the incentives away. Police Commissioner Rinkel said his "best intelligence" reported that a very small crowd was expected and there were no violent actions planned. None of the young activists still active quarreled with the commissioner's prediction. The head of the local branch of the NAACP, who was a veteran of the Movement from way back, said to me:

"The days of confrontation politics are over. We just want to be there as a presence."

I was disappointed, but I put the quote in my story.

When Ron saw the piece, he said, "Take that quote out! How does he know the days of confrontation politics are over?"

"It's just an opinion, Ron," I said. "But the guy has been arrested in forty different demonstrations."

"Take it out!" Ron commanded. "I don't want it in the story. You'll look very stupid if this turns out to be another Chicago '68!"

In retrospect, I think Ron had been hoping that his clean record on the lie detector test and Dixby's inexplicably tainted one might have caused Gil to take control of the convention credentials, in which case Ron's recommendations would have had more weight. But it was clear when Greg didn't get picked that Dixby was still in control and was sticking it to Ron. Greg really ought to have gone inside the Garden. He had the seniority. The governor's foot doctor was in the New York delegation. Greg would have been well plugged in. It was only meanness on Dixby's part to keep Greg out.

By Wednesday night, when I handed in my protestors story, we all knew that Ron's aversion for Willard Dixby was growing into an aversion for the entire Democratic convention. A great enmity is like a religious experience. The man who feels it can see his enemy everywhere. And now to Ron, the delegates, the hoteliers, the host committee, the Democratic National Committee, and even the button salesmen were taking on the face of his detested rival. The American flag became repugnant to him because it was being sold all over town in anticipation of the convention. Democracy itself looked to him like a weak and unjust system of government which the evil fates had fostered in the United States of America solely to provide a career opportunity for Willard S. Dixby.

You think I exaggerate? Wait till you hear the rest of this saga!

Ron got Eddie to write a piece about the declining quality of New York's famous hotels. See, after *The Newspaper* had lost its sixty rooms in the St. Regis, six other leading hotels had come forward with "emergency accommodations" for the National staff, and the St. Regis suddenly "found" ten unoccupied rooms for convention week. Ron ordered Eddie to find rich people who lived in the very hotels that had come to the rescue, and Eddie had no trouble getting them to say that things weren't what they used to be in luxury living.

Ron got Greg to do a story about the terrible strain the convention was putting on the New York City budget, and he leaned on one of the culture reporters to do a piece knocking the star system in convention coverage. Then he made Eddie do a piece about how the size of the press corps—8,000 people covering 2,700 delegates—was causing serious security problems.

After he ran my piece about the expected demonstrations, he had me do a retrospective on Chicago '68.

He was trying to trash the convention, he was so crazy, and nothing blitzed him more than Dixby's giving credentials to Vincent Akelroyd!

Akelroyd had not yet come crawling back to the paper, but we had heard through the grapevine that he had been spiritually down on his hands and knees when the call from Dixby came. A tryout at BBS for a role as a television columnist had not gone well. We heard he had performed for a woman producer who had told him to "try to make the viewer feel you like him," and Akelroyd had got into a long argument with her about why this was necessary, and the argument used up so much studio time that only three "takes" were

**225**

filmed. He was told BBS couldn't use him "just now." We heard that the man who had to tell him this then recommended that he join a men's rap group.

Akelroyd in his pain had spilled out the story to Flicka Poinsby, who was trying to get him to teach her to write. She, in turn, had reported it to Ron in hopes that such loyalty would be rewarded with a second-chance promotion, and Ron then gleefully had spread the story around the newsroom so as to teach everyone what happens to reporters who think they're too good for *The Newspaper*.

He had been anticipating that Akelroyd would beg to be taken back at his old salary, but Dixby hired him for the convention at twice that, not paying him through the National Desk budget but rather through the free-lance budget of the Sunday magazine. This meant Ron would have to double Akelroyd's salary, *if* Akelroyd was to come back. But now Akelroyd might not come back at all. That was the terrible thing Dixby had done with his power.

Ron was having conniptions. It got so bad, he wouldn't even go out to lunch. He made Freddie bring him sandwiches and started sending Willie into the front page story conferences in his place so he could stay at his desk every minute and keep us busy writing about the awful things that were going to happen in the city the next week.

I must say that Ron was not the only member of the Metro staff who resented Dixby's malevolent use of the convention credentials. It did not feel good to any of us to be excluded from a national convention in our hometown. And to be excluded when eight thousand others were going, a lot of them jerks from dinky radio stations and dinkier country weeklies—that really bugged us!

We were all in the dumps, those of us who weren't going. We developed a certain outcasts' camaraderie. Greg and I became reconciled to one another as soon as Dixby's list went up, and we started eating lunch together in the cafeteria upstairs to avoid seeing the obnoxious National Desk men eating on out-of-town expenses in our favorite dives.

Greg was getting like Ron about the convention, projecting onto it all his frustration about not being there. He hated the two front-runners. He despised the Democratic platform proposals. He'd say things like: "They've got a bunch of dykes writing that stuff! A woman's control over her body, shit! They're all lesbians!" Then he'd say, "The Democrats don't know who they are anymore. Abbie Hoffman could walk all over them now, and they wouldn't even say ouch!"

He claimed it wouldn't make any difference whether Udall or

Muskie won. "They're interchangeable now," he'd say. "Listen, the only two people who think there's a difference between them are Meyers and Vanderkamp, those assholes!" Iggy Meyers and William Vanderkamp were the two National Desk reporters who had been covering Udall and Muskie. Greg called them either assholes or "dumb turds."

For argument's sake, I would say that they seemed to be working pretty hard.

"Yeah, working hard to write a lot of bullshit!" Greg would respond. "Vanderkamp knew Muskie was finished in April when he walked out of that news conference where they asked him about the famous crying episode. You think he wrote that? He kept writing that Ed Muskie is holding strong. Holding strong! Udall gained on him from then until the first week in June. And he'd still be way ahead if he hadn't blown it with the 'Americans should relinquish the automobile' speech. Mo dropped twenty points the next day. What does Meyers write? He writes there's been a plateau in the campaign!"

Then I would usually say, "Well, one of them *is* going to win, Greg."

"Yeah," he'd say gloomily, "it's gonna be the most boring convention since Ike was renominated in 1956."

Then we'd go back downstairs to let Ron yell at us again. In the circumstances, that was almost cheering.

# XXXII

On Friday morning, Ron got quiet again, and everybody was depressed. Eddie looked worried. He had seven hundred dollars riding on Ron. He went around asking a few people if they'd go against him for Ron, let him bet on Dixby. He didn't get any takers. Vic Veblen said he'd put two hundred on Dixby to fifty from Eddie for Ron. Susan Braithwaite, who passed through on her way from a National Desk meeting, gave Eddie ten dollars for Dixby and said she'd pay ten to one if Ron won.

"I hate to lose," Eddie said to me, shaking his head mournfully. "I hate to *know* I'm gonna lose. I've called every election right since I got to this place, but I think I've got my money on the loser.

Matter of fact, I think Ron's conceded."

It certainly looked that way when Ron retreated into his private office at eleven-thirty and left Willie to make the day's assignments. When people saw that Willie was in charge, they headed into the bathrooms, but the loudspeaker worked in there too, so Willie got Eddie out, and I heard later that he had assigned Eddie to do the pointless profile of Lindsay. Lindsay was in Montauk. Eddie had to rent a car and drive out there with Marco Fellini. While this was happening, I was sitting on the ladies' room couch doing the crossword puzzle. I heard Willie call Greg's name. Then I must have dozed off, because Flicka Poinsby came into the bathroom and told me Willie had been calling my name for ten minutes.

"Tell him I'm not feeling well," I said.

"You'd better tell him that yourself," Flicka said.

I dragged myself out to Willie, beginning to think that I might actually be coming down with something.

"Where the hell have you been?" he snarled. "We've been looking all over for you!"

"I was in the ladies' room, Willie. If it's about a story, I don't think I can—"

"Ron wants you right away in his office," he said.

"Oh," I said. "What about?"

"He'll tell you," Willie said nastily.

So I expected another bawling out for not having predicted a return of Chicago '68.

But Ron greeted me with his enormous grin. Greg was in the office with him.

"Sit down, Sarah," Ron said. "Greg and I have a *great* assignment for you! The two of you are going to work as a *team*."

Greg gave me a lewd wink and puckered his lips at me.

"We want you to go to the delegate parties," Ron said, "as many delegate parties as you can get to. Greg will be doing the same thing. We want you to ask the delegates if they're really satisfied with the way things are going."

"You mean, like, get any complaints about hotel service and cabdrivers?" I asked.

"No, no, no!" Ron said. "I mean questions about the issues and the Love factor. I want you to find out how many of them want to drop their pledges to Udall and Muskie. I want—"

"But I don't have credentials, Ron."

"You don't need credentials to get into those parties, Sarah," Greg said. "The host committee is giving them."

"Mrs. Heller is giving one," Ron said. "I don't know why she would bother," he added in a hurt, quizzical tone. "They're all being given in people's apartments. You don't want to cover the smaller states. But the big ones, like Pennsylvania, New York, Alaska—"

"Alaska may be big, but it doesn't have many delegates, Ron," said Greg.

"Well, you two use your judgment," Ron said, flopping his hands impatiently. "Mrs. Heller has the list of them all. She's on the host committee. I really don't know how she gets herself into these things. Call her up. She'll give you the list."

"What am I supposed to be finding out, exactly?"

"I *told* you," Ron said. "You're to ask about the Love factor and what the delegates are going to do on the second ballot."

"Love factor?"

"Greg will explain it to you," Ron said. "Why don't you two have lunch together. I've got a meeting."

This time Greg suggested we go to Sardi's. The idea of doing a delegate piece must have boosted his morale. We got a little table deep in the downstairs dining room, and Greg ordered shrimp scampi.

"This is on me, kid," he said. "I'm putting you down as Mrs. Heller."

"But Ron knows—"

"Ron doesn't give a shit. What are you having?"

"I guess I'll get steak tartare, then, and a Bloody Mary."

"That's the spirit!" Greg said. "Well, well, well! Will you look who just walked in!"

I craned my neck to see Vincent Akelroyd jabbering rapidly in the ear of Willard Dixby.

"What has he done to his hair?" Greg asked me.

"It looks like he dyed it."

"More than that," said Greg. "It's been styled. Look at that! He practically pulled Dixby's chair out! Get down and kiss his ass, Vinnie!" Greg kissed the air.

Just then a lock of Akelroyd's fluffy new hair came down into his eyes, and he quickly flipped it back with his fingers. It promptly fell into his eyes again, and he blew upward, looking cross-eyed toward the heavens. Greg snorted loudly. Akelroyd recognized the sound. He spotted us and gave a condescending smile. Dixby did not bother to acknowledge us. As we watched, four other men joined them. Gil Foley was the only one I recognized.

"Well, I'll be damned!" said Greg. "I'm glad Ron didn't come with us. It would break his heart."

"I didn't know Gil ate lunch with reporters."

"He doesn't. Kleinfreude must have invited him."

"Kleinfreude? The publisher? Which one's he?"

"He's sitting next to Gil. Haven't you met him?"

"No. I've never even laid eyes on him. He looks very young. Also fat."

"That's Bill Vanderkamp, stupid! Kleinfreude's the one on the other side of Gil."

He was a slender, graying man who looked as though he was adept at keeping inconspicuous. I couldn't get a good look at his face because he was wearing tinted aviator glasses. They made him seem slightly sinister, like a genteel gangster's lawyer.

"Is that Gloria Steinem's influence, the aviator glasses?" I asked.

"What are you talking about?" Greg said.

"Ron told me Gloria Steinem made a big impression on Kleinfreude."

"Nobody makes a big impression on Kleinfreude. He's got terminal boredom."

"Who's the other one?" I asked. There was one more strange face in the group, a knockout with dark curly hair, dimples, and devastating black eyes.

"Which one?"

"The guy between Kleinfreude and Akelroyd."

"That's Iggy Meyers. He's the great kingmaker who's gonna put the country to sleep with Mo Udall."

I thought it best to find a topic of mutual interest.

"Gil doesn't look well," I said.

"He never looks well," Greg said. "Not since Curaçao."

"*The Newspaper*'s got a bureau in Curaçao?"

"Of course not, stupid! Gil was on vacation there two years ago. The guy's been all around the world. He's covered wars, famines, cholera epidemics, and he never gets a serious illness. Then he takes his wife to Curaçao and he gets hepatitis from the water in his luxury condo."

"Maybe he didn't drink the water in the old days."

"Yeah, Ron says he used to put it away."

"Still does sometimes."

"How do you know?"

"I got looped with him," I said proudly. "In his office. He gave me the strongest vodka tonic I've ever tasted."

"When was that? Right before Ron tried to fire you?"

"Ron didn't try to fire me, Greg! I wish people would get things straight around here."

"Okay, okay. Why'd Gil give you a drink?"

"I don't know if I should tell you. But I told Ron."

"You'd better tell me, if you know what's good for you. Gil's a strange guy, Sarah." ·

"He sure is! You know what he really wanted to talk about? How the *Eye* was planning to steal his garbage."

"What!"

"That's what he said. Because he read that they were going to go around snooping in garbage cans where famous editors lived."

"Who'd want to know what was in Gil's garbage?"

"He said another weird thing. He said his job made him feel lonelier than God."

"The guy's a complete loon!"

"But you can't tell anybody, Greg."

"If you told Ron, they know it in the Moscow bureau by now. Ron can't keep a secret."

"Now you tell *me* what's going on. What's this crazy business he's doing with us?"

"It's not crazy, Sarah," Greg said, lowering his voice. "I've been telling you the voters got sick of Udall and Muskie months ago. The primaries take too damn long."

"Well, they've got the delegates."

"Who says they have to keep them?"

"They're pledged."

"On the first ballot they're pledged. After that it's open season. Do you know who's leading the polls now? Do you know who's the number one candidate with John Q. Citizen?"

"Who? Teddy Kennedy?"

"Guess again."

"Gerry Ford?"

"I'm talking Democrats! Guess again."

"I can't. Tell me."

"George Foster Love."

"Greg, you're not telling me—"

"It's gonna be a hung convention, Sarah. Anything's possible."

"But Love has about three delegates."

"He might get New York. That's enough to put him in a swing position, and from there he could go anywhere. The voters love him."

"But I still don't understand what we're supposed to do."

"We're going to find out how many delegates would swing to Love if they thought he was going for it."

"That's what Ron meant by the Love factor! I couldn't figure it out—I thought he was talking about the left wing, you know, the new left! He really is out to trash— Greg, I should tell you that I got a tip about Love. He may be gay."

"Those rumors have been around for years!" Greg said, wrinkling his nose in disgust. "Listen, any politician who's very good-looking is going to get smeared like that when the going gets rough. When did you hear that? Probably when this last poll was released."

"I heard it about three weeks ago, and not from anybody in politics."

"They're getting scared! That means they're getting scared! They know he's creeping up on them!" Greg said.

"But I told you, it wasn't a political source. I mean, he's a member of the Village Independent Democrats, but—"

"There, you see! The VID is for Udall. They probably came to you, Sarah, because you're gullible now after that thing with the mayor. You always have to watch it after a scoop like that. People can make you believe anything for a while."

Greg signaled for the check, and then he said, "Cross your legs. Here comes Iggy. If he puts the make on you, ask him about his live-in girlfriend, Clare."

"Weren't going to say hello to me, were you, you horny bastard!" Iggy said as he reached us. "Can I help it that you don't have credentials? I put in a word for you, you know. Just now, in front of the publisher. I said you were the best political reporter in New York City."

"I don't need any help from you, Meyers," Greg sneered.

"But I lied," Iggy said, turning his heart-wrenching eyes on me. "I understand this is the lady who scooped you, the incomparable Ms. Sarah Makepeace. Your story was the talk of Washington. Did you know that? The *Washington Post* did a follow-up on escapist dreams of politicians. They got Henry Kissinger to say he sometimes sleeps with his eyes open. We're hoping it'll start a trend in absentee officeholding. Washington is a bore. Iggy Meyers, at your service," he said with mock gallantry, putting out a hand.

When I shook it, he clamped his hand around mine and would not let go.

"What are you doing with this has-been?" he said. "I hope you are aware that he is a happily married man, whereas I am happily separated."

"Greg tells me you live with a lady named Clare," I said. Greg patted my knee under the table.

"I'm sorry you won't be at the Garden, Greg," Iggy said, by way of a rejoinder. "It's going to be interesting. Too bad Ron let you down."

232

"Fuck off, Meyers!" Greg said.

"He's got no class," Iggy said to me. "What are you doing later? Would you like to go to the *Newsweek* party with me?"

"I don't know," I said. "I may have to—"

"You go right ahead, Sarah," Greg said. "You should find it instructive. You'll learn how the big boys look when they don't know which ass to kiss first."

# XXXIII

That was how badly Ron wanted to trash the convention! As if he thought he could rewrite history, throw Udall and Muskie out the window! Ron's genius must have cracked. This wasn't any little zoo funds trick. This was on the order of national subversion. Why should I say national? Global! The man had deluded himself into thinking that he could pick the next leader of the free world. I tell you, I was flabbergasted. Ron Millstein had finally flipped.

After lunch I looked around for Eddie, but by then he was two-thirds of the way to Montauk. I wanted to tell him to take his money off Ron *fast*. Meanwhile Greg told Ron that Iggy had invited me to the *Newsweek* party. Ron said I should definitely go, even though it would only be for the media. He and Greg told me the idea was to throw Iggy Meyers off the track while also finding out whether anyone in the press was going to make anything of Love's interesting lead in the popularity polls.

"How'm I going to find out whether they're going to make anything of it without making them think they should?" I asked Ron.

"Don't worry about that, Sarah," he said. "They won't think you know anything."

I was too worried about the whole harebrained scheme to be insulted by a remark like that. Greg didn't seem to be worried, but I figured he was only humoring Ron and probably glad to have an excuse to go strutting around among delegates. Greg was too smart to take Ron's idea seriously. He had to be in it for the ride. In which case, there might not be much point in worrying, I told myself. But I worried. Still, it was the next best thing to actually covering the convention. Why shouldn't I ride along too?

Flicka Poinsby told me half the famous people in America were supposed to be going to the *Newsweek* party. I didn't know if I could handle that. Then Freddie said somebody had said Dustin Hoffman and Robert Redford might go, because they'd become press groupies since *All the President's Men*. Or was it the other way around—Katharine Graham and Ben Bradlee had become Hoffman and Redford groupies? Freddie couldn't remember.

I left a note in Eddie's box as I took off for the party, and on the way over, I wondered who else might be invited. What if Joan Baez showed up? Nobody had said she would, but ever since Chicago '68 the Democratic party had been trying to make itself over in her image. Why shouldn't she be there? What if I had to talk to her? What would I say? Why did you leave Bob Dylan? Was I supposed to ask questions like that? Joanie, did it ever bother you that you didn't finish college? What do we do now that the war's over, Joanie? I wouldn't have the nerve. People might see my hand tremble if I lit a cigarette. I was so *nervous!* How could I hide it? If Carl Bernstein heard me in action, he'd psyche me out right away, and then he'd write that *The Newspaper* was trying to do what Tricky Dick tried to do, and Ron would hate me and fire me for good, and Iggy Meyers wouldn't fall in love with me.

*What is this sudden mention of Iggy Meyers?* said a voice inside me. *Stay away from him! You are in love with Kevin.*

"This," said a woman going up in the elevator, "is the first party that counts."

Polite men in white jackets checked our invitations at the door. (Ron, not wanting me to arrive with Iggy, had given me his own.) They ushered us toward Mrs. Graham, who smiled, nodded, shook our hands, and sort of stroked us past her into the room. She kept the traffic flowing at a good pace.

At first I was afraid to look at people. I went over to one of the big windows. The late afternoon sun was glinting off the Hudson. New Jersey shimmered in the distance. How many people were sitting in their undershirts on their stoops over there drinking beer? Kevin's cousin, the one who knew about Uncle Nick and the super's wife, lived in New Jersey. People did just what they wanted over there. Dumped poison chemicals off the highway. Left dead bodies in plastic bags. Bribed their state assemblymen. Families on East 118th Street that showed up every two weeks looking destitute really lived in New Jersey. Welfare commuters. A comfortable way to live, always doing what you wanted. I took a deep breath, lit a cigarette, and looked around.

I did not recognize a single face. What a relief! No Dustin Hoffman! No Joan Baez! Two hundred total strangers. Or maybe a hundred and fifty. Or maybe five hundred. Anyway, a lot of strangers. I could feel my limbs relaxing. I puffed on the cigarette, watching the people, enjoying the scene. It looked very cheery and New Yorky, with the big windows letting in wide bands of brilliant hard-edge sunlight.

I saw a man raise his arms and let out a yell, then charge for a far corner. There were other loud greetings, back slappings, yells of nicknames. People's eyes slid right past me. It was quite pleasant to be so anonymous. Maybe I should just watch. Ron wanted me to mingle, but how? What should I say? These were all old friends. Should I fake it? Say, Didn't we meet in Chicago? I couldn't pull out a notebook. Ron didn't want people to know what I was doing. Oh, Ron!

Ah, there was a familiar face. Mayor Simon. So there were some pols. Couldn't let Simon see me. Too awkward. I stepped out of his line of sight. Oh, no! There was Dixby, over near the bar. Best to step out of his line of sight too. I walked around a conveniently massive rubber plant.

"Sarah!" said Jenny Locke in alarm. "What are *you* doing here?"

"Ron didn't want to come," I said in a queer high voice. "He thought I might learn something."

"Ron sent *you* in his *place?* He must be feeling suicidal!"

"Well, I'm not representing him. He just gave me his invitation," I said lamely.

"So you're back in his good graces," Jenny said accusingly. "Must have been that story you did on the mayor. With Ron you're always as good as your last story. He'll be down on you again before you know it. Ron has the loyalty of a flea. You should join our suit. Then he couldn't fire you."

"I'm not sure I'd do your suit any good. Ron has given me a lot of breaks, too many—"

"I didn't say we needed you. I said you're going to need us. By the way, I hear you were never on the *Crimson*. Where did Ron get the idea you were a big star on the *Crimson?*"

I opened my mouth, but no sound came out.

"*There* you are!" said Iggy Meyers, clapping a hand down on my shoulder. "I've been looking all over for you. I thought they might have stopped you at the door. Oh, hi, Jenny!" he said, and he leaned forward to kiss her on the cheek.

Jenny kept her eyes on me. They seemed to be silently asking, "Well?"

Neither of us had spoken to Iggy.

"Hey!" he said. "Am I interrupting something? You two having a Feminist Faction meeting?"

"Oh, no!" said Jenny. "Sarah thinks she doesn't need us."

"Well, she needs a drink," Iggy said. "And I'm not letting this little lady out of my sight. She might scoop me!"

He, however, scooped me off with an arm around my waist.

"I figured you might want to get away from her," he said. "She was pretty upset when she heard you were in Sardi's with Greg. She's still carrying a torch for him, you know."

"I have heard that."

"What do women see in Greg? He wears elevator shoes. What do you want to drink? Is there anything that renders you senseless with desire?"

"I think I'd better just have a glass of white wine. I have to go to Alaska after this."

"You have to go to *Alaska?*"

"No, no! The Alaska party."

"Wine it is, then. Don't go away."

I thought I saw Walter Cronkite in the distance. Wasn't it time for the evening news? Maybe they had a stand-in for him to send to parties. And wasn't that what's-his-name talking to him? What was his name?

"Oh, Edwin Newman!" I said aloud.

"That's right," said a voice in my ear. "What are you doing, Makepeace? Counting them up?"

"Oh, it's you!" I said. It was Walrus Face.

"Forgot my name, eh? You're so important now, everybody remembers yours. What are you going to do for an encore? Tell us who's going to get the nomination?"

"I remember your face perfectly well. You helped me out at the Mishiyoko dinner. You're with UPI."

"That's not good enough. My name's Dick McCarthy. I only remember yours because you left an indelible impression, getting hauled away by the Secret Service."

"Of course, Dick! It's nice to see you. You saved my life that night. That was my first assignment."

"But you fucked me over like a typical woman."

"I did?"

"Yeah. You didn't tell me about the Forsythe Foundation. I'm supposed to be UPI's freak specialist. You made me look bad."

"I'm sorry!"

"What are you doing here? Did you come alone? Are you working?"

"Well, I'm just sort of picking up the vibes."

"Ahah, I get it. Gonna do a nasty piece about the press, right?"

"Oh, no! What are you doing? Are you covering the convention?"

"Would you believe that my boss forgot to put in for my credentials? You can put that in your piece. His name's Bart Sawbuck, and it's spelled the way it sounds. I'm so pissed off! I've been getting ready for this thing for a year! I'd quit, but I can't get another job."

"I'm sure you could get another job, Dick. You're very good."

"Wanta bet? Nobody's hiring. Not unless you're a black lesbian. And you can quote me. You don't have a drink. What do you want?"

"Iggy Meyers is getting me one."

"Iggy Meyers, eh? Isn't he married?"

"He's just getting me a drink."

"Who do you think's going to win? What's the word in your shop?"

"Oh, Willard Dixby. That's quite clear now."

"Come again? I was asking who you thought was going to get the nomination."

"Oh, that! Oh, I don't know." Then I said tentatively, "Some people are talking about Love, but I don't know."

"You mean Senator Love from New Mexico? He's got about ten delegates. And Governor Feely," McCarthy said. "Love's just in it for the visibility. The guy's only thirty-eight. He's got time."

"Yeah, I know," I said. "People like to bullshit, I guess, because they can't predict, really."

"You guys aren't doing a story on Love, are you? I mean, he's not *really* going for it?"

"Gosh, I'm the last person to ask," I said. "I just heard Greg Swenson talking about how Love's ahead in the polls."

"Swenson's been selling that idea?"

"What idea?" asked Iggy, handing me a huge plastic glass full of wine.

"That Love might have a shot at it because he's ahead in the polls," said McCarthy. "Are you guys going with that?" he asked Iggy.

"What's he talking about, Sarah? Who is this guy?"

"I'm sorry," I said. "This is Dick McCarthy, with UPI. Dick, this is Iggy Meyers."

"We met a long time ago, Iggy," Dick said. "At the Cambodia

**237**

May Day thing. You went off with the piecy chick from Wisconsin."

"I don't remember that," Iggy said, showing his dimples. "Where you staying, Dick?"

"Me? I live here. I'm in the New York bureau now."

"You're lucky," Iggy said. "New York's big news these days. UPI. Oh, yes! I'm sure I've seen your by-line. Richard McCarthy. How are you calling this thing?"

"What, this?" Dick said, looking around. "I'd say it's a draw between the competitive and the complacent. And you can quote me on that too, Makepeace. There's a high complacency factor in here."

"Quote him? Are you doing a piece on this party?" Iggy asked me.

"Ooops! Let the cat out of the bag!" McCarthy grinned.

"No," I said. "I'm just drinking the free wine."

"What do you think, Meyers?" Dick asked. "Who walks off with the prize?"

"Read my story tonight," Iggy said.

"This guy's a lot of fun," said Dick. "Where are you staying, Meyers? Maybe I can bribe a bellboy and go steal your notes. Come on, tell us who it's gonna be."

"I'm in the St. Regis," Iggy said, rocking back on his heels. "My story says I don't know who it's going to be. Nobody knows."

"Hey, there's Bosco!" said McCarthy. "I bet *he* knows! *Hey, Bosco!*" he shouted, waving a fist in the air as if in a revolutionary salute. "Bosco and I were at Columbia together," he told us.

"Sarah, let me show you—" Iggy started to say, but was interrupted by a wild-haired guy with bug eyes who had blocked his retreat.

"Hi, Meyers," he said, then he turned to McCarthy and went, "Heeey! How about that, Dick! We made it to the convention!"

"Not me," Dick said glumly. "I'm not going."

"Not going! What's the matter with UPI? We can't pick the candidate without you, Richard!"

"Sarah, let me—" Iggy tried again, but he was pinned in.

"Who's the lovely lady?" Bosco said. "Have I met you?"

"This is Sarah Makepeace," McCarthy said. "Watch out. She's doing a piece on the press."

"I am not, Dick!"

"You should have been on the bus with us," Bosco said.

"That's been done, Nat," Iggy said snootily. "Sarah is not doing a piece. She's my guest."

"Watch it with this guy, Sarah," Bosco said. "I've been riding around the country with him for—what is it? Eight months? I lost track. Iggy here left a lot of broken hearts in the canvassing offices."

"Nat works for the *Washington Post,*" Dick McCarthy said. "How are you calling it, Nat? Who's gonna win?"

"Beats me," he said. "Look at the numbers. Nobody's got it. What do you say, Meyers? You still talking to me?"

"Too close to call," said Iggy. "It's not secret."

"What do you say?" Bosco asked me.

"Before big boy here shut her up, Sarah was saying she heard some people at *The Newspaper* talking about George Love," McCarthy said. "You heard any rumblings about Love?"

"Pretty Boy Love? Shit, he's only got something like fourteen delegates, but what the hell, everybody's sick of Ed and Mo! You people know something we don't know?" Bosco asked Iggy and me. "Is Kennedy going for Love?"

"Where are you staying, Nat?" McCarthy asked.

"At the St. Regis."

"You're big stuff now, man!"

"It's too far from the Garden. I'm serious, can anybody find out what Kennedy's doing?"

"He's not going in," said Dick.

"Are you sure?" Nat asked.

"That's what he told us," Dick said, looking at Iggy.

"He keeps his word," Iggy said enigmatically.

"You mean like 'Hang in there, Mary Jo. I'm going for help'?" Bosco said.

"Oooh!" we all moaned in unison.

"What's the Bronx cheer for?" asked Willard Dixby, suddenly among us.

"That's not a Bronx cheer," Nat said. "A Bronx cheer is like this!" And he demonstrated so vigorously that a drop of spittle hit Dixby's nose.

"We-ell," said Dixby, after an awkward pause, "Ah didn't expect to see yew here, Sarah. Did Ron send yew up here to do a little snoopin'?"

"I invited her," said Iggy.

"Ah want to have a word with yew," Dixby said to Iggy, and he took him by the arm, the two of them going off through the crowd.

"Who was that?" McCarthy asked.

"Our national editor," I said.

"Willard Dixby?" Bosco asked.

"Yes," I said.

"He didn't seem too friendly toward you," Dick said.

"He hates the city editor," Nat said. "Everybody knows that."

**239**

"Listen, I think I'd better go while the going's good," I said.

"You can't leave us!" Nat said. "We want to hear more about this Love strategy."

"I don't know anything," I said. "I'm not covering the convention."

"She's a scoop artist," McCarthy said. "You won't get anything out of her."

"Honestly! I don't know anything!"

"Listen," Dick said. "Spell my name right. And put in that I'm single and only a sexist when it comes to sex."

"A scoop artist. Hey! She's the one who got that story about the mayor. Hey, Sarah! Come back here!" Bosco called as I retreated, waving at them over the crowd.

When I reached the men in white, I thought I heard Iggy calling, "Sarah, wait!" but I didn't look back.

# XXXIV

The Alaskans were eating and drinking as though they had not been fed since the last political convention. But that was plainly not the case, because they were enormous. Their large hands engulfed the lesser mitts of New Yorkers in the big living room of Mr. and Mrs. Richard Goldmark, where they had come to be welcomed but instead seemed to be the ones doing the welcoming, so friendly and ready were they to boom down in their huge voices, "Ha! Ah'm Harree from Fairbanks. Who're yew?" They all seemed to have Texas accents, which further dislocated the purported theme of the evening, a sort of "Whither Alaska?" symposium that Mrs. Goldmark had hoped to elicit from the king crab and some leaflets piled casually on the two drinks tables. The leaflets had been supplied by two young men from the Whole Earth Society, who stood talking to each other appropriately near a Sierra Club poster, anticipating that any minute Mrs. Goldmark would quiet her guests and introduce them. Her guests, however, were not the quiet-down kind. Some of them had not seen each other since they had left Houston, and there were whoops of recognition, great back-slappings and calls of "Son of a bitch!" going on all around. In decibels they were to the

240

*Newsweek* gathering what grand opera is to sixth grade glee club. Mrs. Goldmark approached one of the tallest delegates, a man who appeared to be a leader because of the number of hands he was shaking. She modestly asked whether he might like to open the "little panel on the environment." He said, "Paaardon?" And a man next to him said, "Shoot! We been talkin' about thayat all year. If Ah hee-er one more person say the word 'environmeyent,' Ah'munna peeuke!"—a threat not empty of promise, considering the amount of king crab, spare ribs, coleslaw, green olives, red wine, potato salad, and strawberry shortcake that particular speaker was consuming. The one who'd said "Paaardon?" shrugged, and Mrs. Goldmark threw an anguished glance at the two Whole Earth Society representatives, who looked bland and ecologically superior. The man who had said he might puke stuck out a gargantuan hand to them.

"Ha!" he said. "Ah'm Foster Jarvis from Nome. Who're yew?"

They each had to shake his crude hand.

"Why don't ch'all have a drenk," he said. "Miz Goldmark, these boys don't have a drenk!"

That was the end of the panel on the environment. Foster Jarvis, who turned out to be co-chairman of his delegation along with "Miz Lee Reynolds, our inteeellectual," got to talking investments with a small, balding Manhattan stockbroker, who looked like a midget next to him. I moved around the room, eavesdropping here and there, picking up fragments of conversation about the flight east, the lost luggage, the twenty-dollar taxi fares, and Harry from Fairbanks's enthusiasm for Linda Ronstadt.

"You thenk she'll come?" he asked me when he learned I was a reporter. "You thenk you could fahnd out where she's stayin'? Ah'd shore lahk to meet her. Ah'm in the Sheraton. Room 2150?"

"Who are you going to vote for?" I asked.

"Me? Ah'm pledged to Boothby, yew know, our favorite son."

"Yes, but that's just a holding operation, isn't it? Who are you really for?"

"It's too early to start askin' thayat, Miz Marcus; we got fahve days to go."

"Well, who do you like, of the other candidates?"

"That depeyends."

"Depends on what?"

"The ohwell pipeline stayance, what they've got to say about cap'tal gains. Yew're a reporter. Ah don't have to tell yew."

"What do you think of Senator Love?"

"Thayat faggot? Ah thenk he's a Commanist!"

241

"He's way ahead in the polls."

"He'd hafta to ease up oan offshore ohwell rahts 'fore Ah'd go for him."

"But you like him otherwise?"

"Oh, sweet Jesus, there's Billy Leeds!" he exclaimed, spotting someone behind me. "God damn it, Leeds!" he yelled, and a wild hoot rent my ears and something as big as a water buffalo hit me from behind and sent me sprawling over the back of a couch. Harry and Billy were practically humping each other standing up. I heard a glass crash to the floor. I saw the Whole Earth Society Brahmins beat a quick path to the door.

"Yew alraht, darlin'?" a big blond woman asked me.

"Yes, I think so," I said, hoisting myself to my feet.

"Mah name's Julie Ann Jarvis," she said warmly.

"I'm Sarah Makepeace," I said. "Is everybody here from Texas?"

"Weyell, we're from Nome. Where yew from?"

"Manhattan."

"Yew don't sound lahk a New Yorker."

"Where are you from originally, Mrs. Jarvis?"

"South Car'lahna."

"It's weird. I mean, everybody I meet here is from the South."

"Weyell, everybody in Alaska had to come from *sum*place else, honey. 'Cept the Eskimos. Our co-chairman's from New York City. Yew talked to her?"

"Who are you going to vote for, Mrs. Jarvis?"

"Oh, Ah'm not a delegate, darlin'. Ah'm jess here with mah husband."

"I think I met him. Foster Jarvis."

"That's raht."

"I suppose you think the way he does, that Senator Love is a Communist."

"Senator Luv? Ah luv Senator Luv! He's so ceeute! An' he's young, too young to have too many moneybags behahnd him. Ah'd vote for him if I wuz a delegate, that's for shooer!"

"Really?"

"He's so nahce to his po-wer wahfe. That's what Ah *truly* lahk about him."

"How long have you lived in Alaska?"

"Fahve long yeeyers! Yew ever been there?"

"No."

"Yer lucky, honey. It's so cold an' dark an' *ayem*-ty, Ah swear Ah doan' know whah anybody wants to save it. Ain' nothin' to save but ahce an' mosquitoes."

242

"Why do you live there, if it's so awful?"

"Honey, mah husband bult half the ohl pipeline! He's a petroleum engineeyer? He made more money last year than he made the whole first ten years we were married, Ah thenk."

"How do you know the Goldmarks?"

"Ah don't. But they're oan the board of Foster's comp'ny—that is, he dudn't own it. The Comp'ny he works for, Standard Development? An' they're frens of Lee Reynolds, our co-chairperson. Yew oughta talk to her. She's real smart. Lemme see. Oh, *there* she is! Over theyere, talking to Mr. Goldmark."

She pointed toward a handsome woman wearing a white pants suit and smoking intensely as she watched Richard Goldmark shape an idea with his hands.

"Excuse me," I said to Mrs. Jarvis, who in any case had been discovered by Mrs. Billy Leeds. I squeezed my way toward the far corner, hearing a man say, "Hell, Bob, if you and I go together, we won't get mugged," and farther on, a woman pleading, "But, Gerald, yew promised me yew wouldn't have mower than fower!"

"We can swing it if we get the conservatives," Richard Goldmark was saying as I drew near.

"Oh, hello, Sarah," he said, seeming to warn Lee Reynolds with his eyes. "Lee, this is Sarah Marcus from *The Newspaper*. Sarah, this is Lee Reynolds, co-chairperson of the delegation."

"Sarah Make—" I started to say, but Lee interrupted:

"I wish there were something better than 'chairperson'! It sounds so awkward! And 'co-chairperson' is even worse. Why does the word 'man' have to apply only to men?"

"I understand you're from New York, Lee," I said. "Why did you move to Alaska?"

"Oh, god! Is this an interview? Do you know how many interviews I've done? The *Fairbanks Journal* stringer just got through with me. Where do they *get* these people? He'd never heard of Bill Boothby. No more interviews, please!"

"Well, perhaps a few questions for *The Newspaper*, Lee," said Richard.

"Why didn't they send Iggy Meyers? I mean, honestly, Richard, *everybody* knows why I moved to Alaska. The girl doesn't read her own clips."

"I'm sorry, but I didn't have time to read the clips before I came on this assignment," I said. "I only—"

"Oh, heavens! I'll tell you about her," said Richard. "Lee represents our law firm in Fairbanks, that's Simpson Tweed Thatcher and Ross. She's thirty-eight years old. She was third in her class at Columbia Law School in 1965. She would have been first but she was editor of the *Law Review*. She's divorced. She served for three years on the Tri-Lateral Commission. She cooks fantastic French meals, and she will probably be on the Supreme Court. Lee and I have known each other for—how long has it been? Sixteen years," he said with the sort of quiet solemnity that betokens a significant memory.

"All I really want to know is how the delegation's going to vote," I said.

"I have no idea," Lee said. "We haven't caucused yet."

"I thought you were just talking about it, rallying the conservatives or something."

"Oh, that was business," she said, tapping out a new cigarette.

"Oh," I said.

"Yes, business," said Goldmark. "I thought you were pledged to Boothby."

"He's released us," Reynolds said. "Off the record, Sarah. Boothby hasn't told the press. I think that he's going to announce it tomorrow."

"Did he make a recommendation?" Goldmark asked. "Who is his man?"

"Between us, I think he's pushing for Love."

"Love? Love's a lightweight!" Goldmark said. "And he's way too young! What kind of a record does he have? He's only been in the Senate one term, and he spends half his time in the swimming pool, I hear. He ran such a corny campaign, Lee. 'Love Is All You Need'! I mean, talk about vapid hypes!"

"Calm down, Richard! I'm not supporting him," Lee said. "But he *is* popular, you know."

"His wife is popular—the champion skier, mother of four, tragic leg amputee."

"Don't knock it, Richard! Betty Ford's popularity went way up when she had the mastectomy."

"What is it? We're going for the bathos vote now. Bring back Senator Eagleton! The country can feel for a man who's had his brains fried!"

"She's taking notes, Richard."

"That was *off* the record, Sarah Marcus. I'm in my own house," Goldmark said huffily.

"Okay, okay," I said. "But I'd be interested, Lee, if you could say just what Senator Love's appeal is."

"I'd just be guessing," she said. "I mean, he's not my candidate. But—well, let's see. He's good-looking, he's got a populist image, raising funds in small contributions—and he's very clever with the media. I'd say it's a kind of Kennedy appeal—you know, all the outdoorsman stuff: Outward Bound, rock climbing, walking to Washington from Santa Fe, riding his bicycle to the Senate every day—"

"But what does he stand for? What does he really stand for?" Goldmark asked.

"He inspires people, Richard. They look at him and say, If he could do it, I can do it. When he gets up in front of a crowd and tells about his father losing the farm and the years he spent living in a pickup truck and singing songs to keep his brothers and sisters warm, he makes people feel good. His life has been a real shaggy dog story.

"And then his romance! Coming back from the Vietnam War so depressed, meeting that angel who made him want to live again! Think about it, Richard. People can look at him and say, There's a good guy who got what he deserved."

"But why does that qualify him to be President?" Richard asked her.

"I'm not saying he should be President. She asked me what his appeal was."

"I'd sooner take Jerry Brown," Richard said. "At least he's got the brains—"

"Wheyer's that little laydee from *The Newspaper?*" someone bellowed. "Theyer she is!" And Harry from Fairbanks came charging toward me.

"Hey!" he said. "Yew kin tell me. Is this really the building wheyer they filmed *Rosemary's Baby?*"

"Yes, it is," I said.

"Hot dog!" he said. "Ah was raht!" he yelled to his friends across the room. "This is eeyit! This is the Deekoter!" Turning to me again, he said, "This place is chock-full of cee-lebrities, ain't it?"

"A few," I said.

"Hot dog! Hey, y'all," he called to his friends. "Whadda yew say we go pay Mr. Caree Grayant a call!"

"Oooweee!" whooped a woman. "Ah adoh-wer Caree Grayant!"

"I don't think—"

"Yew know which apartment he lives in, little laydee?" Harry asked me.

"Oh, I don't think Cary Grant lives here," I said.

"Does, too! Does positively live heeyer. Yooohooo!" Harry yelled, galloping back across the room. "Come on, y'all!" he summoned. "Come *oan!*" And with that he went charging out the door, and a stampede of drunken people followed him.

Mrs. Goldmark scurried over to her husband.

"Richard, do you think we should go after them?" she asked.

"What do you think, Lee?" he asked her.

"It's a little too late," said Lee. "You should have watered down the wine."

"What do you think they'll do?" Mrs. Goldmark asked.

"It's hard to say," said Lee. "They may forget what they're about before they reach the elevator, and then Foster will suggest they go hang one on, and he'll take them to the nearest bar. I hope he doesn't kill anybody."

"Oh, Richard!" said Mrs. Goldmark.

"I wouldn't worry, Joanna," he said. "Lee's just teasing us."

I thought I should circulate among the delegates a little more. The party had lost its momentum, though. The New Yorkers were talking in little clusters by themselves. The remaining Alaskans had divided up along sex lines. The men were talking hunting and fishing. The women were talking New York department stores. Nobody would stick to politics. When I asked about Love, I got polite shrugs, and comments like: "I guess he's nice enough. Perty young, though," or, "My daughter likes him. I think he's a little too liberal." One Alaskan woman asked me for the address of the Women's Liberation Movement. The balding stockbroker said to me, "Boy! You sure took a dive in the second quarter!" got a perplexed frown in response, and went off to say goodbye to his hosts. Pretty soon everybody was drifting over to say goodbye to the Goldmarks. I was the last in line.

The stockbroker, who had lingered to discuss an investment with Richard, was just ahead of me.

"Joanna! Great party!" he said. "I learned a lot. They're not all dumb!"

"I'm so glad you could come, Paul," she said. "You met Sarah Marcus, didn't you? You can share the elevator with her."

A doorman appeared in the doorway.

"Gino," said Mrs. Goldmark. "Did someone forget a jacket?"

"You gotta do something, or we're gonna have cops all over the place!"

"Oh, Richard!"

"Your party's spreadin' all over the building, Mrs. Goldmark. Everybody's callin' me."

"They said they were going to knock on *doors*, Richard!"

"They're trying to knock *down* a few doors," said Gino.

"Where are they now?" Richard asked.

"There's some on the sixth floor, some on the fifth, and some on the second," said the doorman. "Take your pick. People have been calling the cops."

"That's not necessary," Richard said. "I'll go down, and Lee, you come with me."

The stockbroker and I followed them to the elevator. Gino came too.

"Who are your friends, Mr. Goldmark?" Gino asked.

"They are delegates to the Democratic convention," Lee said, "from the state of Alaska. They're very excited to be here."

She and Richard got off at the sixth floor. We could hear a ruckus, some pounding shouts of "Wake up, Mr. Grayant!" and then the elevator doors closed.

"New money," said the stockbroker.

"That's why I switched to Republican," said Gino.

When we reached the ground floor, we saw two cops talking with another doorman. He was telling them, "It's nothing, officers, just a little party," as we went by. I thought I should wait outside the courtyard entrance to see whether any arrests were made. But the cops left after about thirty seconds.

The stockbroker had insisted on waiting for me.

"Listen, you can get your purse snatched around here at this time of night," he said. "You going east?"

"No."

"Well, let me get you a cab."

As we stood on the corner of Central Park West, he said, "What did you say your name was?"

"Makepeace. Sarah Makepeace."

"That's what I thought, but when Joanna said Marcus . . . Makepeace. Of course! You're the one who got that story on the mayor. What's the real story? What's his problem?"

"He didn't tell me."

"He's finished now. What are you going to write about that bunch of rednecks? Aren't they awful!"

"They're just having a good time."

"I shouldn't complain. They're our biggest clients."

"Who? The Alaska delegation?"

"Standard Development. We do all their environmental impact work. Where are you going now? Would you like to get a bite to eat?"

"Oh, no! I've got to get back to the office. Thanks anyway."

"I can't believe you're the same person who wrote that story. I really can't."

"Why not?"

"I mean, I thought you'd be gray-haired and maybe have wing-tipped glasses. It's your writing style, I guess."

"Really?"

"You can't help it, of course. *The Newspaper* wants you to—What's your sign?"

"My sign? I think it's Leo, but why—"

"Leo! Fantastic! I'm an Aquarius—like Norman Mailer! We're an ideal match. Could I call you sometime? I could give you some good stories. Do you have a listed phone? Have you done any TM? Are you a women's libber? I'm all for it. Hey! Nobody owns your body but you."

"Oh, look, there's a cab now," I said, managing to free my elbow as I stepped forward to hail it.

He kept pace with me, but I could tell he didn't know whether to also raise his hand for the cab, as that might seem to contradict what he'd just said about being all for women's lib. He fidgeted. The cab stopped near us. The stockbroker gripped my shoulder.

"You want to know the real secret of this convention? It's right under everybody's nose, but they don't see it."

"What's that?" I asked.

"It doesn't matter who wins," he said. He released my shoulder. He watched me settle into the cab, then he stuck his head into the window to repeat: "It doesn't matter."

# XXXV

Try telling that to Ron Millstein. It doesn't matter who wins! Why do you think we call ourselves the human race? That's what he would say. If you don't want to win, you don't want to live.

When I arrived back at the office, I discovered Ron wasn't the only one who felt that way, that Greg, too, was hell-bent on winning and had convinced himself Ron's scheme might work. He and Ron were pacing back and forth in Ron's little office, like two expectant fathers. Greg had been to four delegate parties and found what he said was "total indifference" to the front-runners. I dreaded having to tell them how little I had learned. What was worse, I had stupidly mentioned Greg's name at the *Newsweek* party. I left that for the last, and only confessed it, haltingly, to Greg when Ron went out for a minute. To my astonishment, Greg looked delighted.

"You hear that, Ron!" he said as Ron came waddling through the door again. "Nat Bosco thinks we're onto something! I *knew* Sarah would do that! Oh, Sarah, baby, you're brilliant! And Dick McCarthy heard her too! Ron, we're going to have to move this thing up a day."

"What thing?" I said.

"Would you like a sandwich?" Ron said to me. "You've done great work, Sarah. Great work! Finding out that Boothby's going for Love. You're a scoop artist. Have a sandwich. You have to keep up your strength. We want you to do the Pennsylvania brunch tomorrow morning, and there are two or three other—oh, yes, the Florida breakfast. Do you have an alarm clock? That's at eight."

He handed me a soggy sandwich while Greg consulted the list of delegate breakfasts and brunches.

"She can catch Connecticut after Florida," Greg said. "It's on the East Side too. And then, Sarah, you'll have to go by California before you hit Pennsylvania. Give them each at least an hour."

"And get back here by two," Ron said, "because Greg will have an early deadline for the first edition."

"Greg's writing tomorrow?" I asked.

"Oh, yes!" Ron said. "He's right. It's got to be tomorrow. We can't let this wait, if Nat Bosco knows—"

"Because Strauss will be on *Meet the Press* Sunday," Greg said.

"What's he going to say?" I asked.

"Strauss hasn't committed himself," Greg said. "The national chairman can't—"

"No, I mean you. What are you going to write?"

Ron and Greg looked at each other as though I had just asked which way was up.

"Why, Sarah, he's going to—" Ron said.

"That depends on what you find out, Sarah," Greg said swiftly. "We won't know how extensive this swing to Love is until you tell us."

I was too tired to argue, and the next morning at the Florida breakfast, I did hear quite a few reporters asking each other about a swing to Love. I sat at one of the press tables when I probably should have been talking to delegates, but the speculation was interesting. Everybody at the table said the voters were bored with the front-runners. A man from the *Baltimore Sun* said the candidates could have saved themselves and the taxpayers "a shitload of money" if they'd pooled all their literature and speeches at that

**249**

point in the campaign when they had started to sound alike, the point when each man believed he could take the nomination.

"Yeah," said a woman from the *Texas Observer,* "what's the difference? Udall's saying, 'Strength with peace' and 'Heal the wounds,' and Muskie's slogans are 'Peace with strength' and 'Bind up the wounds.' What a drag!" The wounds were presumably the wounds of Vietnam and Watergate, but the *Baltimore Sun* man said, "Hell! The only place the country's bleeding from is its wallet, and nobody's saying anything about that since Mo blew it with the auto industry!"

"What's Love's slogan?" asked the woman from the *Texas Observer.*

"'Anything's possible,'" said a correspondent from the *Taos Weekly Times.*

"Don't I wish!" said the woman from the *Observer.* "But I think it's gonna be Muskie."

"That's Love's slogan, Sally," said the *Baltimore Sun* man. "'Anything's possible.' Speaking of Love, I hear Nat Bosco's doing a piece about his second-ballot strategy. Do you know anything about that?" he asked the *Taos Times* guy.

"I heard the networks were asking about it," he said. "Love's not saying anything."

A television crew came in and started filming interviews with delegates. Sally went over to listen to a couple of them. She came back to our table and said, "Yep. They're asking about some kind of a hidden Love vote. What's going on?"

The *Baltimore Sun* man got up and started interviewing delegates. My hour was running out, but I got a quote from a woman delegate from Orlando, who said, "Love's an attractive candidate. But we're tired of lost causes. We want to see what Strauss says about him on *Meet the Press* tomorrow."

I hurried over to the Connecticut breakfast. There were more reporters there. I heard one saying, "Listen, one-third of the voters don't even know who the candidates *are!* The party leaders are worried."

I asked a few delegates about Love. Every one of them said, "I just got through answering that question." I found a black delegate from Hartford, who described himself as "an Afro-American resource." He, too, had already been asked about Love.

"Yeah, I like Love," he said. "So what? I like Muhammad Ali, but nobody's askin' me about *his* chances here."

At the California brunch, all the press were crowded around Jerry Brown, and I couldn't get near him.

250

"What's he saying?" I asked a reporter who emerged from the crush.

"He's pissed off," said the reporter, and he walked away fast.

"What's he saying?" I asked a TV sound man, who frowned at me and put his finger to his lips.

I gave up and circulated among the delegates, asking them about Love, but being asked in turn if I knew what was going on.

A woman wearing a "Strength with Peace" button said, "Nobody tells me anything! What's Jerry saying?"

"I don't know," I said. "How do you feel about Love?"

"I like all kinds," she said, smiling at me. "What's your name, sweetie?"

"No, I mean Love the candidate."

"I figured you meant that. Oh, well, you're the tenth reporter who's asked me that this morning. I'm pledged to Udall. We all are."

"But people are saying that on the second ballot there might be a switch, Jane," a woman next to her piped up.

"I think it's a Kennedy move," said Jane. "It's got the smell of the Kennedys. Where else would this sudden Love thing be coming from?"

By the time I got to the Pennsylvania brunch, all the Bloody Marys were cleaned out, there were so many reporters there, and half the delegation hadn't yet arrived.

"Gee," I heard the chairman saying when I got within earshot. "All this sudden interest in Love is amazing! What's he done? Promised you all he'll move the White House to Taos?"

But the delegates were talking among themselves as though they believed Love was a serious contender. I heard one man saying, "People are starting to ask if we can go for him on the second ballot; then why not on the first ballot?"

"We can't, John. We're pledged," said another man.

"What if the rules were suspended?" asked the first. "It's just hypothetical."

"I don't know anything about George Love!" a woman complained. "Can anybody tell me about his record?"

At that point I had to leave.

I came charging through the third-floor lobby flipping through my notes, trying to see what I should say to Ron and Greg, and I ran right into Iggy Meyers.

"Sarah! What happened to you last night? You left without saying goodbye," he said in a hurt voice.

"I told you I had to go to Alaska."

"That's right. Why didn't you tell me the chairman of the Alaska delegation got arrested in the Dakota?"

"He did?"

"You want to have lunch? What are you doing here?"

"I can't."

"You're not working today, are you?"

"No, no. I mean, I don't feel well."

"What are you doing here? What's wrong? I'll take you home."

"No, I'll be all right. I just have to do, um, my expense accounts."

"You come in on Saturday to do your expense accounts? Come on, Sarah! What's Ron up to?"

"Gotta run," I said.

I made a dash for the ladies room. I had to come tiptoeing out like a thief and wend my way around the back passages to Ron's office. Greg was typing at Ron's desk while Ron watched over his shoulder.

"Sarah!" they both said. "How's it going?" Ron said. "Did you get to Pennsylvania?"

"I just ran into Iggy in the hall," I said. "I think he suspects something. He asked me to have lunch."

"Then go have lunch with him," Ron said.

"I told him I couldn't. I said I had to do my expense accounts."

"On a Saturday?" Ron said. "Sarah, that was a dumb thing to say."

"I know," I said.

"They won't catch up with us, Ron," Greg said. "Gil's protecting us. You *said* he was protecting us on this, right?"

"Of course he is, Greg!" Ron said. "This is *our* exclusive! When Gil makes a promise, he keeps it."

"Okay, Sarah," Greg said, "shoot. What's the story?"

"Well, I'm not sure," I said. "I mean, you were right that everybody's sick of Udall and Muskie, but only the reporters seemed interested in Love."

"What reporters?" Greg asked.

"All the reporters. They were all over the place. There were a couple of TV crews at the Florida breakfast and three press tables. There were *tons* of reporters at California and Pennsylvania, just *tons*. And they were all asking about Love, Greg. I don't think this is going to be an exclusive. I heard Nat Bosco is doing a piece about the hidden Love vote. Is there a hidden Love vote?"

"Bosco! It's working!" Ron said. "Come on, Sarah, type up your notes right away. Put in everything you heard, *everything*."

He made Greg get up so I could use the typewriter on his desk, and while I typed, Ron stood over me, coaching and taking peeks at my notes.

"Don't skip that! What's that? Wait, wait, you skipped a page here, where it says *Baltimore Sun*. Put that in. We want to see everything!" he said.

He started pacing the room as I typed, and when a page was finished, he took it from me and walked back and forth, reading. I heard him say, "That many reporters!" and then "Aaah!" and "Ummm!" and "Aha!" Greg took each page as Ron finished, and he uttered shouts of delight. "Oh, look at this!" he said. "We've got them running! Oh, boy!" And then Ron said, "Oh boy, oh boy, oh boy!" the way he had when he'd read the Missing Persons report on Mayor Simon, and then an exhalation came out of him, a sound not like a human breath but rather like what a great bear might produce when it wished to express perfect happiness, a long, sighing "Aaaaaaaaaah!"

"I tell you, it's working!" Greg said. "Lemme get in there, Sarah. I've gotta write this thing."

"What's working?" I asked, although I had a fair idea.

"The strategy," Greg said. "Love's strategy."

I vacated the desk, and Greg put in a fresh piece of paper and immediately started typing his lead. I came around behind him to read:

"On the eve of the Democratic convention, there is no sertain winner among the candedates the delegates must consider for their Presidential nommination, but a dark horse from the state of New Mexico is ganing momentum in a growing growndswell of xxxxxxxxxxxxx . . ."

"Um, Greg, you've got a couple of typos," I said.

"Don't bother me!" he said.

"Greg, are you sure there's a growing groundswell for Love? All we know is that the press—"

"Shut up, Sarah!" Greg said.

Ron came around to read the lead.

"I don't like 'growing groundswell,'" he said. "It's a cliché. Let's say something else."

"But we don't know if there's a growing whatever you call it for Love!" I said. "All we know is that the press is asking—"

"Ron, will you make her shut up," Greg said. "I can't concentrate."

"Yes, yes," Ron said. "Let's leave him alone, Sarah."

"You want to write my lead? Be my guest," Greg said to Ron.

Ron came around behind the desk again and leaned over Greg's shoulder. They both stayed quiet for a while. Then they both looked up and seemed surprised to see me watching them.

"Sarah, why don't you go out and get yourself a bite to eat," Ron said. "You've done a great job."

"What have I done?"

Ron looked at me as though he were measuring something in my character.

"I tell you what!" he said warmly. "Why don't we all have lunch together! Why don't you get us something, Sarah!"

So he got rid of me for a while. He ordered corned beef on pumpernickel with mustard and mayonnaise, cheesecake, a can of diet Pepsi, and a big cigar for celebrating when the story was done. Greg ordered tuna fish on rye with lots of mayonnaise, Tuborg beer, and a box of plastic-tipped cigarillos, plus the latest copy of the *Evening Star*. Ron insisted I go three blocks down Eighth Avenue to a sandwich place that had "the best corned beef in Times Square."

When I came back, they had composed this lead:

"On the eve of the 48th Democratic convention, Senator George F. Love, a favorite-son candidate from the state of New Mexico, is suddenly riding a hidden groundswell of support that may make him the strongest contender for the Presidential nomination by Wednesday night."

"I don't like to see 'may' in a lead," Ron was saying. "It's too tentative. And why call it a 'hidden groundswell,' Greg? What's hidden about it? For all you know, the Love story's going to be all over the networks tonight. We *know* that Love's going to be the nominee—"

"Ron, we can't go that far out on a limb," Greg said. "What if he decides this isn't the right time?"

"Could I ask a question?" I said. "How do we know Love's going to be the nominee?"

"All right, we'll save that for Monday!" Ron said impatiently. "But I'm warning you, Greg, if we're behind *any*body on this, if we're behind the *Chronicle* or the *Post*—"

"We won't be, Ron," Greg said. "They're too scared."

"You guys don't really think Love's going—"

"Will you do me a favor, Sarah?" Greg said. "Will you shut up or get out of here!"

So I shut up. An hour and a half later, Greg had his story well started. He had written (before Ron corrected the spelling):

On the eve of the forty-eighth Democratic convension, a sudden growndswell of support for Senator George F. Love, the favorate-son candidate from New Mexico, has throne a cloud of dout over the candadicies of the two front-runners, Senators Morris Udall of Arizona and Edmund Muskie of Main. Niether man has enough delagates pladged to him to capture the nomination on the first ballet, and each has been ardently courting Love for the "swing" vote of his 300 delagates.

Within the last two days, as delagates have conferred with one another here, a suprising number have said they would choose Senator Love as a comprimise candidate in a deadlock situation, and an informal poll conducted by *The Newspaper* showed Love would capture an immediate 61 percent of the delagate votes if the rules were suspended to free them from their pledges. . . .

"Love holds the cards in this one," said Party chairman Robert Strauss during a telephone inteview early yesterday afternoon. "Some people think he holds *all* the cards."

Senator Love's popularity with the voters has been the only constant in a campeign year when public opinion has shifted often and drasticly. But since he entered only one Presidential primary, that of his home state, he aproached the convention with no hope of winning the nomination. Since arriving in New York three days ago, however, the handsome Vietnam veteran's prospects have been raised so high that his campeign staff is now publicly declining to anser press questions about his intentions. In private, they point to the 287 independent delagate votes he has picked up here and smilingly say, "Anything's possible!"

The 38-year-old Senator, who is married to the former Olympic bronze medelist Betsy Bromley, has established himself as a leader among the new breed of activist legislaters in Washington. He has been compared to the Kennedys in his campeign style and bright good looks.

"He inspires people," said Lee Reynolds, a cochairman of the Alaska delagation. "They look at him and say, If he could do it, I can do it. When he gets up in front of a crowd and tells about his father loosing the farm and the years he spent living in a pickup truck and singing songs to keep his brothers and sisters warm, he makes people feel good. His life has been a real shaggy dog story. . . . Poeple can look at him and say, There's a good guy who got what he deserved." . . .

# XXXVI

"How can a groundswell throw a cloud, Greg?" I asked, putting my nose against a photo of Mrs. Muskie to smell the fresh ink of the first edition. Greg's story was two columns to the right of my nose, just barely above the fold on the front page. "Does it sort of splash up into the sky like spray from the sea?" I asked.

"You had your chance, Makepeace. I didn't hear you come up with anything better," said Greg. He was lolling back in his chair with his feet up on his desk, languidly smoking a cigarillo and keeping an eye on the National Desk. "You think it's easy to do that with three hundred pounds of boss breathing down your neck?"

It was six-thirty, and the first edition had been "up" for about ten minutes. There was no need for me to stick around. Ron and Greg had dismissed me hours before. But I wanted to see what the reaction would be when the others read Greg's story. And I had been trying to think of a way to get Greg to admit it was all a shuck.

"Where'd you get that sixty-one percent will vote for Love business?" I asked.

"That was a conservative estimate," Greg said. "It's probably more like eighty percent."

"Where'd you get it, Greg? Was there a poll?"

"Ron and I worked it out."

"You mean you made it up?"

"You talked to the delegates. You saw how many would go for Love."

"Greg, you don't really believe—you can't seriously believe—"

"Hey, Greg! That's some story!" Eddie Schwartz called out on his way to the men's room.

"I just don't understand how Gil let it get into the paper, Greg. I'm sorry, but I really don't," I said. "And without telling the National Desk."

"They missed Watergate," Greg said. "They kept telling Gil, 'Mitchell says it's not true.' That's why we all went to see a movie starring the *Washington Post!* Gil doesn't forget, Sarah. He doesn't trust National!"

"How come he let Dixby handle the convention credentials, then?" I asked.

"You ask a lot of dumb questions," Greg said.

"Here he comes," I said.

"I see him," Greg said.

"He looks mad," I said.

"You've got ink on your nose," Greg said.

That was the last thing Greg said to me for several hours. Dixby covered the ground between Foley's office and Greg's desk in nothing flat. We hadn't noticed him going into Foley's office, but he came out of there in a state of charge, and we figured, when the ambulance was stuck around the corner trying to get past the *Newspaper* trucks to come pick up Greg, that whatever had transpired between Foley and Dixby had been so downright infuriating, so insufferably debasing, so unconscionably and thoroughly insulting to the national editor's dignity—and he descended from a family with a long history of hurt pride going back to the battle of Vicksburg, where his great-grandfather sprained his ankle and was cruelly spared (this story Eddie told later over coffee at the hospital)—that Dixby could not answer back, and so he did the only thing left to him to do, came out and declared war on someone lower down the pecking order.

I wish I'd had enough nerve to look at him when he got to Greg's desk, but I was kind of afraid he might yell at me too, and say something about the *Crimson* (since Jenny knew and was working for him), and so at the last instant I opened my copy of *The Newspaper* and held it way up to make it look as though I was deeply absorbed. I could hear:

"You sneaky little cocksucker! Do you realize what you've done? You have subverted the election process of this country, Greg Swenson, and you have besmirched the integrity of this newspaper for all time! Get that goddamned smile off your face! This is no time to be smilin', boy! You are finished! You just wrote your own epitaph!"

I kept my head behind my paper, but out of the corner of my eye I saw Greg's legs swing to the ground.

"Don't tell *me* about the integrity of this newspaper!" Greg yelled. "Who told Gil Foley John Dean was a liar? Or have you forgotten! Who said Martha Mitchell was crazy?"

"We're not talkin' about no Watergate, Swenson. We're talkin' about twenty-six primaries that you are tryin' to goddamn throw out the window! Do you know what you have done?"

"Why don't you go yell at your pretty boy Iggy Meyers!" Greg shouted. "Go ask him what he's been doing. I'll tell you what he's been doing! Writing press releases! That's how much fucking integrity he's got! And the same goes for your prize boot-licker Vanderkamp. He's the worst. He gives advice to Muskie's speechwriters, for shit's sake. Ask them! They'll tell you! Vanderkamp orders his own handouts!"

"Handouts! Look who's talkin'! Goddamn son of a bitch! You took your piece straight from the asshole of Love's floor manager, Swenson! What'd you do? Follow him around with your notebook, trying to catch the turds?"

"You're pathetic, Dixby! You missed the story, and now you want to kick the guy who got it. You're a sore loser! You can't stand it that Strauss gave me an exclusive interview while your crew of boot-licking assholes were all sucking up to Kleinfreude and Katharine Graham!"

"Swenson, you know goddamn well you should have come to me with that interview. And you know why you didn't—'cause you know what I would have done with it, you sneaky cocksucker! You went to Ron because you knew he's too goddamn sore to care, didn't you? You knew Ron's so hot to get a story on this convention he'da taken it from a hooker who turns tricks for the hatcheck boys in the Garden. Don't you call me pathetic, you sneaky bastard! You're a coward, and you always have been. You and Ron are both cowards! That's why neither one a you would face me with this idea, this public relations pitch for that shiny-eyed ski bum. I oughta kill you!"

I heard a swishing sound, and I heard Greg say, "Jesus!" and then some grunts and a loud whop and then Greg's chair came careening over toward me, and I heard it coming and dropped my paper. Greg was on the floor.

"Get up, you yellow bastard!" Dixby was yelling. "Get up and fight, you sneaky bastard!" He kicked Greg in the chest a couple of times before Freddie got him into an armlock from behind and pulled him backward. Dixby struggled a moment longer, then suddenly relaxed and said to Freddie, "Okay," and Freddie let him go. He shook his arms and strode quickly back to the National Desk.

Ron game galumphing in with Willie, just as Dixby had reached his desk.

"What happened? What happened?" he asked Freddie, who was down on his knees slapping Greg's cheeks.

"Sarah, call the police. Tell them to send an ambulance," Freddie said.

258

"Sarah, what happened?" Ron asked me as I was waiting for 911 to answer.

"Just a minute, Ron," I said.

"Police emergency," said a female voice.

"Hello, we need an ambulance," I said.

"What is your problem, miss?"

"There's been a fight. There's a man unconscious."

"I see. What's the address?"

"The *Newspaper* building, West Forty-eighth Street."

"What's the address?"

"Ron, what's our— Oh, never mind! Listen, lady," I said, "it's the only building on the block. The entrance is right in the middle, between the two gates. They can't miss it. Tell them to look for our sign. It says 'The Newspaper of New York.'"

"Oh, *The Newspaper!* Why didn't you say so? Don't you people have cars?"

"Freddie, don't we have cars?"

"Nope," Freddie said. "Photo's got them all. Tell the fuzz he's bleeding. Tell them he was stabbed."

"Ma'am, could you please tell them to hurry up. He's bleeding pretty badly."

"Did you say there was a weapon?"

"Didn't I? He's bleeding *badly*. Hurry up!"

"Okay."

When I got off the phone, Ron was down on all fours, asking Greg's comatose form, "What happened? What happened?"

Greg was bleeding a little from his lip. But he was not waking up. We all took turns holding his head back. Freddie had read somewhere that you were supposed to do that with unconscious people. Eddie Schwartz came out of the men's room and said we were doing it all wrong. We shouldn't touch Greg. We should put a wet paper towel on his forehead and leave him be.

"What happened?" Eddie asked.

So I told them what I could remember, and Freddie told the rest.

"That bastard!" Ron said. "He should have come to me."

"You weren't here," I said.

"He couldn't have hit you, Ron," said Eddie. "He needed to hit somebody."

"I'll never forgive myself if Greg doesn't come out of this," Ron said.

Greg's phone started ringing. We ignored it. But then Ron said,

"That's Greg's phone. Get it, Sarah."

"Hello," I said. "Mr. Swenson's line."

"Is he there?" said a taut man's voice.

"He's here, but he's not all here."

"Look, could I talk to him, please?"

"I'm sorry, he's out cold."

"Tell him Flip Masterson's calling."

I cupped the phone and asked, "Who's Flip Masterson?"

"That's Udall's campaign manager!" Freddie said.

"Ask him what he wants," Ron said.

"What do you want, Mr. Masterson?"

"I want to talk to him about his story."

I cupped the phone again. "He wants to talk to Greg about his story."

"Ask him if he has a statement to give us," Ron said.

"Mr. Masterson, Greg's not available. Do you have a statement to give us?"

"Who is this?"

"Sarah Makepeace."

"You're not— Oh, switch me to the National Desk!"

While I was trying to do that, the second line on Greg's phone started ringing. I lost Flip Masterson.

The second call was from Lisa Pearl, Muskie's press secretary. She asked to talk to Greg. When I told her that Greg was out cold, she started shouting about bribes to newsstand dealers and somebody being on the payroll of the Republican National Committee. She wasn't making sense, so I said I had to take another call, and hung up on her. Ten seconds later the phone rang again.

"Whadda you bet it's Love," said Eddie.

The ambulance attendants came trotting in with their stretcher. As I picked up the receiver, they were pulling Greg's eyelids open, as though they were trying to see whether he was dead.

"Hello," I said.

"Is Greg Swenson there?" asked a cheery man's voice.

The other line started ringing again.

"No," I said. "Who's calling?"

"This is George Love. I understand you've got a story about—"

"Could you just hold on a minute. There's another call coming in."

"Sure," he said.

The medics got Greg onto the stretcher.

"Hello," I said. "Greg Swenson's line."

"You cut me off! I demand to speak to Greg Swenson!" Lisa Pearl shrieked.

"Just a minute," I said. "Does anybody want to talk to Lisa Pearl? Love's on the other line."

"Sure, I'll talk to her," Eddie said, and he took the call on my phone and had to hold the receiver a foot from his ear.

"Hello, Senator Love," I said, switching back to him. "Greg Swenson's not here." Greg's feet were disappearing out past Dayside. "Can I help you? I'm Sarah Makepeace."

"Well, Sarah, if you wouldn't mind, I was wondering if you could read me that story Greg wrote about me. We can't get any copies in the hotel, and I'm trapped in here. There are quite a few reporters out in the hall."

I read him the whole piece. He thanked me and hung up. Eddie was still getting an earful from Lisa Pearl.

# XXXVII

We watched Strauss's *Meet the Press* interview in Greg's hospital room the next day. Greg's wife, a compact little woman with beautiful, trusting blue eyes, was stretched out on the bed beside him. They were holding hands. Their four kids were stretched out on the floor playing the Monopoly game they had brought for their father. When the program started, the oldest boy, whom Greg called "Bean," tried to watch it. This annoyed his siblings, who kept saying, "Come on, Bean!" "Your turn, Bean!" "Step on it, Bean!" very loudly during Strauss's first comment. I didn't hear anything of it after Strauss said, "Thank you, sir."

"Shut up or take that goddamn game out of here!" Greg yelled.

Ron, Eddie, and I decided to move closer to the TV. We sat down on the floor, blocking Bean's view. Bean then moved up beside us. After that his siblings only whispered, "Your turn, Bean," and it was possible to hear what Strauss was saying.

"What we've got is a case of overexposure," he began in answer to a question I hadn't heard. "You know, gentlemen, our primary system is a little like an engagement that goes on too long, and there've been too many Sundays with the future in-laws in the living

**261**

room. You kind of want to get on with it or call the whole thing off, if you know what I mean. We have two fine fellows to offer to the American public, but the bride is having second thoughts. That's how I see it. I'd hate to have her locked into a bad marriage, you know, feel forced into it because the banns were posted up in the town square. I'd like to see her make the choice of her own free will, right up to the wedding day."

"Here goes! He's for it," Greg said.

"Shhh!" went Bean.

". . . for an open convention, Mr. Strauss?" we heard a reporter ask.

"Well, now, that's kind of a misnomer," Strauss said. "There's nothing closed about this convention."

"Would you be for a suspension of the rules?" a reporter asked.

"That's not up to me," Strauss said, smiling like the father of the nervous fiancée. "That's up to the delegates. Unless our two fine gentlemen wanted to release them, but I haven't heard either of them say they would."

"He's not for it," Eddie said.

"Yes, he is!" Greg said.

"Wait!" said Ron, but Strauss was being asked a question about the ERA.

Wait though we did through the whole half hour, Strauss said nothing more about the question of rules suspension.

"Greg, you've got to call him," Ron said, jumping up from the floor. "You've got to tell him he didn't make himself clear."

"Greg is not doing any work," his wife said quietly. "I'm sorry, but you'll have to find someone else to do it."

"But I just want him to make one phone call," Ron pleaded.

"Mr. Millstein, you've already exceeded your visiting time," she said.

"Greg!" Ron said torturedly. "Greg, tell her!" And then he actually clasped his hands and looked as though he might kneel down. "You don't understand," he cried. "There's so much at stake here. Greg's reputation! His story!"

"You don't understand, Mr. Millstein," the heartless woman said. "Greg has had a concussion. He is supposed to lie still and do nothing."

"Just a phone call," said Ron, still clasping his hands. "One phone call can't hurt. It's a matter of life and death!"

In answer, Greg's wife pressed a button to summon a nurse.

"Greg, please!" Ron tried once more.

The nurse came very fast.

"What's this? What's this?" she said. "We're not supposed to have any visitors, Mr. Swenson. How did these people get here? Come on, everybody but wifey's gotta go. Out! You want a shove?" she said to Ron.

"Yes, yes, everyone out," said Ron, waving us toward the door. He picked up a stray Monopoly piece and handed it to Bean. We all exited. Ron did not follow.

Greg's children went down the hall to a little waiting room. Eddie and I lingered in the hallway. We saw two uniformed guards go past.

In no time at all, Ron was striding toward us, shouting, "You'll regret this!" over his shoulder. Nevertheless, he kept moving fast. We went out with him.

"It's up to you two now," he said to Eddie and me on the street.

Eddie said, "Ron, you really want me to work overtime today? How much are we gonna get workin' the phones?"

"I don't have anybody else," Ron said. So Eddie shrugged, adjusted his hat, and said to me, "Come on, kid. Here goes nothin'."

We did work the phones, hard. All afternoon. Everybody was "in a caucus" and couldn't be reached.

At six o'clock I went back to Eddie's desk.

"This thing isn't going to go any farther, is it, Eddie?" I said.

"I dunno, kid. I just don't know."

"Did you take your money off?"

"Half," he said. "I still got three hundred ridin' on him."

We left before the first edition came up. But at ten o'clock, I went out to Sheridan Square to buy it. National had the lead story, but so did everybody else. It was:

### UDALL AND MUSKIE RELEASE THEIR DELEGATES
### IN UNPRECEDENTED CALL FOR OPEN CONVENTION
Strauss Said to Urge Step; Wants Delegates
To Choose from "Free Will"; Muskie Bitter;
Love Now Openly Seeks Nomination

I got kind of scared, looking at the headline, I remember. I thought: *Did we do this?* And then I said to myself: *No, we couldn't have. Could we?*

# XXXVIII

I heard sirens all night long and could not fall asleep. I was lonely for Kevin. Toward dawn I dropped off and dreamed that his wife came to confront me. When the telephone rang, I reached for it with sleepy foreboding.

"Is this Sarah Makepeace?" said a woman.

"Yes."

"Sarah, this is Lee Reynolds. We met the other night at the Goldmarks'?"

"Yes, I remember. How are you holding up?"

"I'm surviving. Listen, Sarah, I'm a little concerned. Greg Swenson quoted me in that story about George Love. I never talked to Greg Swenson."

"Yes, but you talked to me. I gave him my notes."

"That's not what I said."

"It *is* what you said, word for word. It's in my notes."

"But you didn't tell him what I said first, that I'm not a Love supporter."

"Well, he had my complete notes. I guess he didn't think it fit in with the thrust of his piece. But he had the full quote."

"I expected someone from *The Newspaper* . . . there are basic standards . . . your motto is 'The Truth . . .'"

"I know. It's a fiction."

"I don't think this is any laughing matter, Sarah. I would like a retraction."

"What?"

"Well, a correction. I'm asking you to print a correction."

"Gee, I don't know what the policy is on that."

"This has caused me a great deal of embarrassment! Don't you know I am head of Citizens for Udall in Fairbanks?"

"Uh, no, I don't think you mentioned that."

"I *do* expect you to know the minimum. Honestly, Sarah, it was in your clips! I may have to write a letter to your boss."

"Look, Lee, I wasn't the one who pared down your quote. Why don't you call Greg Swenson."

"But you are the one who knows what I actually said. I would like the record set straight. I'm being accused of leading a defection!"

"You are? Where's everybody defecting to?"

"As if you didn't know!"

"I really don't."

"I can't believe you don't know that Love has picked up all the Udall delegates."

"*All* of them?"

"I'm talking about Alaska. But I'm pretty sure it's the same story elsewhere. Richard says he may carry New York unanimously now. You can imagine how upsetting this is!"

"Well, I guess, but I don't know what I can do about it. I'm not sure the paper prints corrections for snipped quotes."

"No, I didn't think so. Would you mind doing me a favor? You owe me one, it seems to me. Would you mind calling Flip Masterson and telling him what happened to that quote?"

"No problem," I said.

"Good," she said. "I have to live with those people, you know."

"You don't think Love's going to win, do you?"

"I think it's up to Kennedy now."

"Why Kennedy?"

"Because you people all go to him and stick your goddamn microphones under his nose."

"Oh."

"I hate to think that the fate of the nation is between his two temples."

"The fate of the nation?"

"Yes!"

"Lee, who are you going to vote for?"

"Off the record?"

"If you like."

"Off the record, I don't know. On the record, I'm still for Mo."

I had just fallen back asleep when the phone rang again. This time it was Ron.

"Sarah, listen. I want you to go up to the Statler," he said. "I want you to go see Ted Kennedy. You can do it! He likes young women. Wear something sexy. Have you got anything sexy? And comb your hair. Put on lipstick. You should fix yourself up more often, Sarah. You could be glamorous. There's no rule in the Women's Movement that says you have to look like a slob, is there? How soon can you get up to the Statler?"

"Ron, you have to have credentials to get in there."

"Don't worry, you'll get in. You got that story about the mayor, didn't you? Call me as soon as you get there. But don't let any other reporters hear you. Find a phone out of the way. I don't want anybody to know we're trying to reach Kennedy. 'Bye."

The day had a close, sticky feel to it, uncomfortable on the skin. As I walked down Seventh Avenue from the subway exit, I saw a couple of derelicts scratching themselves across from the Garden. I saw another one asleep on the sidewalk between Thirty-fourth and Thirty-third, and then three more seated on a little stoop on Thirty-third Street, sharing something in a brown paper bag. Farther down the avenue, I passed a shopping bag lady who was pulling her cart of papers and rags and talking to herself as she scratched away at her rib cage. My skin felt itchy all over, and then I had an odd sensation, almost like ESP, that there was a weirdness center somewhere in the vicinity, a concentration of molecules like a polarity of the smell of cheap wine or old pennies in the gutters, something with hidden magnetic powers to attract the lowlifes from all parts of town.

I figured I'd walk up to the side entrance of the hotel, get turned away by the cops, and then go back into the subway and straight to the office, where I'd tell Ron I couldn't get in. Seeing me in the flesh, he might dream up another assignment.

I was carrying my press card in plain sight, but I knew this wasn't enough. All the National Desk boys had been wearing their special red-white-and-blue convention IDs around their necks for three days. These had their pictures on them and were the real credential. The press card was yellow.

There were barricades on the sidewalk in front of the door. They were carelessly zigzagged. I easily slipped between them. The four cops at the door watched me. I smiled at them and showed my card. They smiled back. I walked on into the hotel. Simple as that.

The lobby was absolutely jammed. I managed to shove my way in the direction of the telephones. But there were reporters everywhere. I could pick them out by the IDs. There was a depressed-looking TV crew drooping by the telephones, and half the people in the lobby seemed to be interviewing the other half. I saw Iggy Meyers talking up a pretty hotel clerk. I tried to keep my face turned away from him. This meant walking with my head turned sideways, and I banged into several people, who didn't like it. Finally I got close to the phones. There were about thirty people waiting in line to use them, and every single one was occupied by a reporter.

As I stood pondering the situation, I heard a bustle around the corner. The droopy TV crew sprang up. Flashbulbs flashed. All the reporters in the lobby tried to move toward the flashbulbs. I heard a few "Ow!"s and there was one big scream. I tried to move too. Something caught me around the waist. I saw Teddy Kennedy's face in the center of a thicket of microphones. Then I fell down, and someone kicked me in the shins and yelled, "Let go! Let go! Let go!" Only from sheer terror, rolling away from the man's feet, did I manage to extricate myself from the electrical cord. I had somehow got tangled in the droopy TV crew's mike wiring.

By the time I stood up again, the bustle was moving toward one of the hotel exits, flashbulbs and Teddy Kennedy at the center.

"What happened?" I asked a reporter near me.

"Nothing," he answered. "All he said was, 'It looks like rain.'"

I decided to give up on the phones in the lobby. Maybe there were pay phones upstairs. I got into an elevator. Several women got in with me.

"Did you see him? He was right next to me!" said one.

"I know, Doris. Those photographers nearly killed us!" said another.

"I wish he was running," said Doris.

"Maybe he is," said a third.

"I thought you hated the Kennedys, Doris," said the first.

"I hated Bobby, because he ruined Gene's campaign. And he was too chicken to go in first."

"Gene ruined his own campaign."

"Gene was too intelligent for politics. It broke his heart to be losing to a guy who had nothing but charisma."

"How can you like Teddy, then? You *know* he never swam across that bay."

"He's been punished. I think he's suffered. I like a man who knows he's fallible—"

The door had opened. The women got off, and Robert Strauss got on, pressing the lobby button. I quickly pressed the twentieth-floor button. The doors closed.

"I think this is going up," I said.

"Going up? Oh, hell!" he said. He pressed buttons all over the board.

"Is it going to be Love on the first ballot, Mr. Strauss? Is Kennedy going to endorse Love? What if Kennedy decides to run himself?"

"Kennedy won't— You wouldn't be from the press, now, would you, sweetheart?" he said, crinkling his eyes at me.

"Actually—"

The door opened onto the tenth floor.

"Ta ta!" he said. I followed him out, heard a buzz of voices and then someone calling, "There's Strauss now! Come on!" and a pack of reporters came thundering down the hall.

"Oh, hell!" Strauss said again, punching the down button.

But the pack reached him before the elevator came. TV lights were turned on, mikes thrust in his face, and I was crushed behind him against the wall.

"Mr. Strauss, what's the situation?" asked a man with a mike. "What is the count for Love?"

"Gentlemen, I have no idea. I just finished breakfast." Strauss smiled.

"We've heard a report that Teddy Kennedy has thrown his support to Love. Is that true, Mr. Strauss? Have you talked to Kennedy?"

"Senator Kennedy and I have had many discussions," Strauss said, crinkling his eyes. "He's a good Democrat. As you know, he did a great deal of work on our platform. We're grateful to him."

An elevator opened to the left. Strauss lunged for it, and I was shoved into an ashtray.

"Mr. Strauss! Mr. Strauss!" the pack called.

"See you later," Strauss said, waving as the door closed.

"Who's she?" someone asked.

"Are you with him?"

The lights were beamed at my face.

"Are you with the Democratic National Committee?"

"Is Love going to get it on the first ballot?"

"Has Mr. Strauss met with Senator Love?"

"I wouldn't have the faintest idea," I said. "I'm a reporter."

"Why didn't you say so!" the foremost mike bearer yelled. "Cut it, Jack!" he said, and the lights went off. The pack dissolved. A few members were heard asking, "Who's she?" as they walked away.

An elevator opened behind me.

"Hello, Sarah!" It was the voice of Iggy Meyers. I felt his hand on my shoulder. "Interesting expense account you put together the other day. What's going on?"

"You tell me. How's your boss's hand?"

"How's Greg?"

"Recovering."

"Little bit of excitement on the job. Sorry I missed it. I would like to have seen Greg get decked. He deserved it. Look what he's done to this convention! Do you really want a flitty nature boy from the Land of Enchantment to be President of the United States? He hasn't even had one full term in the Senate."

"Why do you say flitty?"

"Well, wimpy, then. Full of moral beatitude. How can you vote for a guy who won't drive a car? He won't use shaving cream out of a can, either. Did you know that? What if he gets in the White House and outlaws cigarettes?"

"He won't get in. Do you think?"

"He might, child, he might."

"Gee."

"But don't you go quoting me in a story as a seasoned pundit, you sly creature. I'm not helping him. There's something about the guy, I dunno—he's too wholesome. He thinks he's part Sierra Club poster."

I chortled disloyally.

"I can't figure out why Ron would go for a guy like that. He's not Ron's type, not at all. Ron will find out. Love doesn't play along."

"Do you know what Teddy Kennedy's doing?"

"Save yourself the trouble. He's not saying a word until tomorrow. Hey, are we working for the same paper?"

"What are you doing?"

"Nothing that can't be improved by a drink with you."

"Not now."

"This afternoon. You want to get to know me better?"

"I've got to find a phone."

"There's one at the end of the hall."

"What's going on down there?" I pointed to a cluster of reporters.

"California caucus. But we've got it covered. Art Loosh is on the spot."

Art Loosh worked for the National Desk.

"This is pointless," I said.

"It's brought us together," said Iggy.

We had reached the end of the hall. It ran into another passageway, going off in two directions.

"This way," said Iggy, steering me to the left with fingers on the back of my neck. His touch communicated a certain sensitive knowledge.

He showed his dimples while I dialed.

"Ron!" I said, not bothering to close the phone booth door. "Listen, Teddy Kennedy's left the hotel. He's not going to say anything till tomorrow afternoon."

"Where's he gone? Did you find out where he's gone?"

"No, Ron, but there were about five hundred other reporters trying to—"

"Find out where he's gone, Sarah. I want you to *talk* to him. I want you to get this ahead of the others! Did you dress up? Did you wear something sexy?"

"Ron, I'm sure he's not going to say anything—"

*"Tell him Teddy doesn't want to swing the delegates before they've had a chance to caucus,"* Iggy whispered.

"Is there someone with you, Sarah? Who's with you?"

"Um, yes, but it's just a guy from the Democratic National Committee," I said. "He's telling me Teddy doesn't want to swing the delegates till they've had a chance to caucus."

"That's ridiculous! The *Committee* doesn't want him to swing them! Get rid of that guy!"

"Okay, Ron," I said. I cupped the phone and waited a few moments.

"Ron, I can't scoop eight thousand people," I said.

"What do you mean? You and Greg did that on Saturday!"

"Greg did. I didn't. Everybody's on this story now."

"I don't like to hear you talk this way, Sarah. I've just removed you from probation. I don't want you to disappoint me."

"Okay, Ron. I'll stick around."

"That's more like it. You let Kennedy get a look at you. Tell him you want to talk to him *alone*, Sarah."

Teddy Kennedy did get a look at me, about two hours later, when he walked back through the lobby. I said, "I'd like to talk to you alone, Senator." He looked once quickly, frowned, and then walked right past me.

True to Iggy's prediction, Kennedy announced his endorsement of Love on Tuesday afternoon in the Statler lobby, with five hundred reporters crammed inside trying to hear his every word and about three thousand more having a riot outside, trying to get in. (The cops stood firm, citing the fire laws.) That night Walter Cronkite said Love's name was "sweeping the caucuses like a brushfire in a California canyon."

"This is your candidate!" Iggy Meyers said to me when he came charging into *The Newspaper* late that afternoon. "I hope you like him!"

By then, of course, Love was no longer the City Desk's candidate. He belonged to Dixby and the nation. And by six-thirty we could see that Ron was in an awful grump. Freddie claims to have heard him say, "I'm quitting!" but no one corroborates this. Perhaps

Ron said he was quitting for the night.

With Greg in the hospital, and with Akelroyd and Jenny working for Dixby, there was nothing else Ron could do on the Love story. It had got way too big for Eddie and me. The other political reporters from city side who were without convention credentials were all trying to stay out of sight to avoid the humiliation of being seen in the office without a red-white-and-blue convention tag.

Foley must have known that Ron would be suffering the tortures of the damned by now, with his ace reporter out of commission. He sent Ron a set of credentials for Wednesday night, nomination night, with tickets for the publisher's private box. Ron and his wife were both invited. It was a nice gesture. The publisher's box was miles away from the press section, over which Dixby, I was told, strutted like a bantam cock.

## XXXIX

I was feeling low on nomination night. I'm not sure why exactly, because I didn't believe Greg and Ron and I had wrecked the primary system all by ourselves. Eight thousand other reporters had been in on the act, and we couldn't help it if the delegates didn't know what they wanted. I refused to believe that Ron had planned the thing precisely down to the minutest blunders I would make at the *Newsweek* party. Still, I had made the right blunders, precisely the right blunders to set off the chain reaction Ron had wanted, and maybe I sort of knew at the time or sort of willed myself not to know because of wanting to be in on things, and so maybe I was guilty too, and we had wrecked the primary system, and eight thousand innocents had gone along with us scared to death of missing a scoop. The worst part was I had enjoyed every minute of it, and now I wanted to be with Ron at the convention, watching his crazy plan play itself out to the end from a front row seat.

There was another thing bothering me. Kevin hadn't shown up on the last Saturday night. The previous week I had given him a copy of Marcuse's *Eros and Civilization* to encourage him to leave his wife. When he called to say he couldn't make it the following Saturday, I asked him what he thought of the book.

"It sounds like it was written by a professor who likes to fuck his

**271**

students," he said. "I couldn't finish it."

Now I didn't know when I would see him again, and the uncertainty was making me think about marrying him.

I settled in for one of my lonely evenings, missing both Ron and Kevin and trying to console myself by switching channels a lot while I waited for the convention to begin. The networks all had a shot of Robert Strauss getting a pie in the face in front of the Garden. I tried to see if I could recognize the young man who threw it, but the shots were all blurred. The sight of pie made me hungry. I went out to Smiler's for my usual paper bag supper, and I was sitting at my table eating it and watching a woman with trembling nostrils sing the national anthem when Kevin called.

"Hi, Flash," he said. "Want some company?"

"Kevin! What a nice surprise! You can watch the convention with me," I said. "Where are you?"

"Criminal courts. I had a collar. I was working the four to twelve at the Garden, but the sarge said to get lost after court."

"Who'd you arrest? Anybody I know?"

"Could be. He threw a pie at Robert Strauss."

"That was just on the news! You'll be famous."

"I know. I had to fight off a fuckin' mob to get to the guy. Almost lost him."

"Oh, hurry up! I want to hear all about it!"

He brought a Chinese take-out meal from Suzie's on Bleecker Street and a six-pack of beer. We sat opposite one another at my little table, belching like man and wife.

"The Secret Service was so pissed off!" he said. "They've got fifty guys staked out in front of the garden and all of 'em looking for known assassins and famous egg throwers, you know, 'cause they've memorized a bunch of photos Rinkel's office gave 'em, and this guy doesn't look like any of 'em, he looks like somebody you've forgotten about who used to live next door, and he comes up to me and asks me what time it is. He's holdin' a cake box. He's dressed like a deliveryman. I tell him it's twenty past four. I'm guessing, 'cause I just came on duty.

"Next thing I know, Strauss comes walkin' across the street, and the TV guys make a rush, and we have to go in and bust some heads, give him some air, and while we're holdin' back the cameras, this guy walks right up to Strauss and pops the pie in his face. Strauss said, 'Aw, shit!' Was that on the news?"

"No," I said. "I didn't see you, either."

Kevin said he arrested the pie thrower at four forty one and testified at his arraignment at nine-ten, which was a miraculously swift turning of the wheels of justice for any day of the year, most especially during the Democratic convention, when night court was jammed with prostitutes, all bitterly aggrieved and loudly demanding to be moved up on the docket.

"They charged him with assault in the first degree, which is a felony," he said, "and then they let him off with a summons. His old man's on the Financial Control Board. That's why. He's one of your Crazies for Hire, you know," he said, and then he tried to drink from his rice container and got rice down the open V of his shirt. He had to untuck the shirt and flap it to shake all the rice to the floor, then he leaned down, scooped it up, and brushed the soggy grains into an ashtray.

"You want a fork?" I said. "How's your cousin?"

"Which one? I got about three hundred cousins."

He dug his hand into the paper bag from Suzie's and unearthed a plastic spoon.

"The one who told you about Uncle Nick and the super's wife."

"Oh, Tommy. He's okay. Theresa's pregnant again. Poor Tommy."

"Too many kids?"

"Naah, the girlfriend."

"It's not his wife who's pregnant?"

"She is, and Tommy's gotta drop the girlfriend."

"Why? I should think—"

"He's got a rule. He never screws around when Theresa's pregnant."

"Do you have a rule like that?"

"I don't know. We've never had a kid."

A ponderous silence. Then I said, "Well, it's only nine months. The girlfriend will probably take him back."

"In nine months most girls will find somebody else," Kevin said.

"Yes, but not permanently. I mean, he doesn't expect her to be celibate, does he? Women are—promiscuity should be more natural for them than for men."

"You think so?" Kevin said with a thoughtful frown.

"Oh, yes! Women's sexual needs are enormous. Have you read Masters and Johnson?"

"Yeah."

"You *have?*"

"I was looking at it last week. I think the people they had for, like, subjects weren't normal. Who'd be a volunteer for something like that?"

"Kevin, you haven't started sleeping with Helen again, have

you? I mean, I don't think it would be wrong or anything, but I'd just like to know is all."

He didn't answer immediately. He spooned up sweet and pungent pork, took a sip of beer, spooned up some beans, drank some more again, ate some more, drank some more, and then set the beer can down with a bonk of finality. He held onto it with his whole hand and appeared to be fascinated by the label. A long, deep, well-fed burp came from his chest.

"Damn, I was hungry!" he said.

"Yes, you were," I said. "That's the first time you've brought food."

"Got any cigarettes?"

I tossed him a pack. He lit one, and I lit one.

"I think Helen's going out with somebody," he said.

"Oh, brother!" I said. "I *thought* there was something wrong."

"No, it's okay," he said. "Listen, we've both got to find out what we want! This is good. It's going to show her, you know, how she feels about . . . about . . . And it's going to show me, too. Shit, she might figure out she's the one who doesn't want to be married. Dr. Festniss says it could be just the thing to provide a resolution."

"What makes you think she's seeing somebody?"

"She goes out on her nights off. She doesn't tell me where she goes. She's getting her hair fixed a new way. She bought a couple of new dresses. She's acting real sweet. All the signs are there. She even left a copy of the *National Enquirer* around, like she's dropping an unconscious hint. It's got 'Ten Ways to Tell if Your Husband Is Cheating' right on the cover. She checks out in all ten ways."

"But she's not a husband!" I said, though already I shared his suspicions.

"The *Enquirer* said a lot of the signs are the same for wives."

"Do you ask her where she goes?"

"I can't. I don't want her to ask me where I've been."

"And Dr. Festniss thinks this is *good?* This is a disaster! Since when is he so free with his opinion, anyway? I'd like to tape his mouth back up."

"You're the reason. I finally decided you were right, that it's a lot of money to pay a guy who sits there and doesn't say anything. I told him I was gonna quit if he didn't talk. He said, 'Fine,' and he started talking. Now I can shoot the breeze with him, throw things back and forth. I'm getting feedback. I feel good."

Kevin looked at me with a new glow in his eyes. He dragged on his cigarette and blew out. For some reason, the gesture annoyed me.

274

"I'm sorry, Kevin," I said, "but I don't think you're getting somewhere. Or rather I think you're getting to the wrong place. The man is a creep! He has no feelings. He's talking about resolution as if you're some kind of math problem. What if it breaks your heart to have your wife go out with somebody else? How about that for a resolution? And what about me? Where do I fit into the resolution?"

"He said you would react this way if I told you about Helen."

"That's another thing I hate about him! He thinks he can analyze me, and I'm not even paying him!"

"He said you're afraid of having the whole thing resolved, just like me. He thinks you don't know what you want, either, and you know I've got a big jealousy thing, so now you're afraid I'll go back to Helen."

"Afraid! I *know* you will!" I said. I started to cry.

Kevin came over to me and stroked my head.

"Come on," he said. "Don't do that. If I got blown away tomorrow, you'd be in bed with somebody else next week."

"Oh, Kevin, don't say that!" I moaned, and then I really let go, and he pulled me up against him and hugged me. The crying fit didn't last too long. At the height of it, I felt a familiar ecstatic twinge, and some part of my brain said calmly: Better not waste too much time.

"Okay, Kevin," I said, "but if you start sleeping with Helen, I want to know, because it's only fair that I should be able to—"

"Is there somebody else?" Kevin said, holding me at arms' length. "Is there?"

"Not now, but—"

"But what?"

"I think the woman should be able to do whatever the man does."

"Take your clothes off!"

But he didn't wait for me to do it. He opened my shirt and bit my shoulder. Delicious shivers went down my arms. What Felix Lebwohl could learn from him! Kevin pulled my shirt off and inspected me for bruises. His rough fingers made goose pimples rise all over me. He pulled me into the bedroom and threw me onto the bed. Then he undressed himself. The sound of the zipper made my heart go faster. I didn't hear the gun go clunking to the floor, but probably it fell into his jeans. He smelled so good! Sweaty and soapy, like boys after a hot night of baseball. Oh, the feel of him! I can still remember the curve of his shoulders. They made me think of horses ridden bareback, muscles rippling under their flanks. Was it only the animal in us? I thought it was love, the thing we recognized in each other in Seymour's Deli. Or maybe when he asked me to roll a joint. It isn't so easy to tell love from lust these days. What would Juliet have done with Masters and Johnson? What would happen if Kevin and I got married? What if he didn't like *Masterpiece Theater?* Should I ask him?

"What's wrong?" he said.

"Nothing," I said. "Don't worry about me."

What was wrong? I still loved him, didn't I? Oh, yes, I still loved him! Did this ever happen to Helen? A mistake to think of Helen.

"Are you sure there's nothing wrong?" he asked.

"I'm sure," I said. "The only thing I can think of is I just ate dinner."

"Do you want to stop?"

"No, no! I told you, don't worry about me."

Finally he came. He sighed and kissed me on the forehead. Then he rolled over onto his back.

"I'm sorry," he said. "But you said go ahead."

"It's okay," I said. "I feel fine."

He nuzzled against me and fell asleep. After about ten minutes, I got up as quietly as I could and fumbled around for the cigarette pack. I found it, lit up, and took a deep drag.

"I shouldn't have told you about Helen," he said.

"I'm sorry I woke you, Kevin."

"I wasn't really asleep. Maybe I was. I think I had a dream about that guy throwing the pie."

"Where's your gun?" I said.

"I left it in the car. Why?"

"I was just wondering. I thought you didn't bring it with you."

"You want to shoot me now?"

"Oh, Kevin!" I couldn't help smiling. "I just thought you'd be worried. You're usually so careful with it."

"I hate to take it with me everyplace. You don't know what it's like to have a gun on you all the time. You'll never know."

"It must be awful! Why do they make you keep them when you're off duty? It scares me. It makes you scary. Just knowing you have it on."

"They say it turns women on."

"I suppose, in a sick way."

"Hey, you don't think that's why."

"Oh, me? Of course not! I was too full. I had two beers. That's all."

"You've had more to drink than that before."

276

"Hey, Kevin, come on out here! They've already started the countdown for the nomination!"

## XL

There are some things about ourselves we're better off not knowing, if you ask me. I guess that's what I have against psychoanalysis, that it eliminates the screen between you and yourself. By the time you're finished with it, you can't take credit or blame for anything you've done because you've found out your kindness is really aggression in disguise, your hostility is really terror behind a mask, and your feelings of love are not the ultimate flowering of adult humanity but actually transmogrified infantile cravings to be back in the womb and sucking your mother's breast at the same time. According to psychoanalysis, we don't grow up, we just grow more confused. Imagine what sort of a picture of human beings the Martians would form if they got their only descriptions from psychiatrists and psychoanalysts. My god, they'd think we were all these giant babies in giant baby clothes drooling through the toy corridors of our toy office buildings between weekends back inside Mommy's womb. What would they think Mommy looked like? Christ!

Well, you can guess how I felt. It was as though Dr. Festniss had pointed his finger at my naked body and said, "There! You see! It was his gun all along!" Not that I hadn't suspected some link between the gun and that ecstatic power Kevin had over me. But I had never guessed Kevin might suspect the same. If there's anything worse than knowing things you shouldn't know about yourself, it's worrying that your lover knows them. What was Kevin supposed to think? He couldn't have been very flattered, fearing that his magic was all in his gun. I felt awful! Even I hadn't thought the gun could make *that* much of a difference. Maybe there was something wrong with me. We'd been so busy always wondering what was wrong with him. Was I a pervert? A gun fetishist? Why hadn't I always had trouble with unarmed men, then? Would I from now on? Was that what happened with a sexual perversion: once you knew you had it you could never forget it?

When Kevin stood up to go to the bathroom, I thought he

**277**

wanted to get away from me. When he propped himself against a pillow on the couch and put his legs over mine, I thought he was trying to be subtle about getting away from me. When he later said, "Stretch out next to me. It's more comfortable," I thought he was temporarily repressing his desire to get away from me so he could exhibit the condescending tenderness people show you when they're about to break up with you and get away from you for good. After I moved back to lean against the couch arm beside him, I discovered he hadn't left me enough room, and I knew this was a subconscious gesture of contempt. But I didn't dare say anything. I was so humiliated! I even wondered whether Dr. Festniss had *instructed* Kevin to leave his gun in the car.

What would Doris Munster think of me now? Naturally, she had to pop into my mind at the worst moment of self-discovery. Jesus, would she go to town on me! Not only smitten with a cop but unable to function without seeing his gun. How much more unliberated could you get? Didn't matter how many orgasms I'd had; I would never make the grade now. How many had I had? I wondered just for the record. How many Saturday nights? But then, he had come by during the week sometimes, and there had been that one other time when it hadn't worked. Zowie! He had brought his gun that time! So maybe I wasn't a pervert. Maybe I was just a normally malfunctioning female. Except, now that I *knew* about the gun, knew I had subconsciously missed it, I couldn't be normal.

So I couldn't beat Doris. None of those orgasms could count. It would be like cheating to count orgasms caused by a gun. The racetrack wouldn't let drugged horses take the prize, after all. Why should women be impressed by my ability to turn into a quivering mass of sensuality in the face of centuries-old sexist symbolism? Even their mothers could do that. The challenge of our era, our real secret contest, ought to be in learning how to swoon over a man who had no recognizably masculine traits whatsoever. Not a fag. Fags were too sexy in their own way. No, the new object of adoration ought to be one of those wimpy guys who never got to first base with us in college because they took us at our word when we said, "Get your hand out of there!" and then wanted to reason with us in a tone of understood mutual respect about the need for sexual release in every normal adolescent's life. He should be no taller than ourselves and no brighter or stronger or braver or any less apt to cry under pressure. He should look bland of gender, be neither handsome nor pretty, act not the least bit ambitious in his work, and frequently express misgivings about the uses of the penis. He should offer to cook for our friends when we were busy and ask whether on hot days he might borrow our skirts. He should be uninhibitedly experimental in bed and ought to try at least once a week to perform erotically without an erection. He should say, whenever we asked him what he thought of anything, "What do you think?"

Women who swooned over the old heroes, over men who had deep voices and obnoxiously forceful opinions and who kissed them and felt them up before asking permission, must be penalized heavily, if not disqualified altogether from the liberated women's sexual sweepstakes. And women who let themselves rely on *any* if not all of the centuries-old sexist symbols must certainly be given demerits for each. It could be like handicapping in the America's Cup race. Thus the judges would have to mark them negatively in each case where the man made the first phone call, where they urged him to order the wine, where they allowed him to assume the driver's seat, where they maneuvered him into divulging first how he voted in the last primary—and most negatively when they told him they preferred to lie on the bottom facing up. What about a fucking gun!

"What's going on here?" Kevin asked, causing me to flinch.

"I think it *was* your—"

"I thought the *Times* and your paper said Love had it in the bag," he interrupted. "How could they be so wrong? Look at this. They're all going out to caucus."

I hadn't noticed. At least half the delegates were gone from the floor, and more were in the process of leaving it. All Love had had in the bag, apparently, was the gullibility of the press. The delegates were still walking around vacillating at will.

The situation should have created a thrilling suspense, I realize now, but it did not. It was terribly boring. I didn't realize quite how terribly boring at the time, as I had my own private suspense mechanism going with Kevin and the question of how deeply he understood me. Only the surface of my mind was watching the business on the tube, but now I can remember that Kevin complained aloud a great deal, saying, "Oh, come on already!" "Will you people get a move on?" "Is this going to take all night?" "Why don't they shit or get off the pot?" "Why don't they draw names out of a hat?" and suchlike.

The networks weren't prepared to have to fill in time, so they made the process even more boring by showing long shots of delegates lost in all the classic symptoms of indecision, sitting with their mouths hanging open, falling asleep, watching themselves on TV. The coverage was like a cinema vérité film about a bunch of people waiting up all night at the airport after a missed connection.

At some point when I was nearly asleep on Kevin's shoulder, my

**279**

father called up. That's how boring it was. The alert sentinel of democracy thought he could take a breather from watching.

"What are you doing with the Democratic National Committee?" he asked me. "You go from the frying pan into the fire. I hope you don't think they're any better than *The Newspaper!*"

"What are you talking about, Dad?"

"I saw you on television with Robert Strauss."

"Oh, that was just because I got squashed in behind him when a camera crew came along. I'm still with *The Newspaper,* Dad. Same old enemy."

"I saw your story about the mayor. What was the point of it?"

"The point. Well, it was—"

"I'm not sure I approve of that kind of story. I think a man, even a mayor, is entitled to his solitude."

"Nobody knew where he was, Dad. There was no one to give the orders."

"The city's probably a better place then."

"They have to have somebody around to sign bills. They just have to know where the mayor is, Dad. New York is too big. He shouldn't have run for office if he minded people knowing where he was all the time."

"I still maintain he is entitled to his solitude. Privacy is a citizen's right."

"If he's a private citizen."

"You're adopting the ethics of Fleet Street, Sarah. I don't like what the newspaper business is doing to you."

"Let me say hello to Mom."

"I'm pleased with this party revolt. Love seems a shade more ethical than his elders. But why was *The Newspaper* so keen on him? Do you think he's assured the Kleinfreudes that he doesn't mean what he says?"

"Please let me talk to Mom."

"Hello, dear," said Mom. "Isn't it exciting! Are you watching the convention?"

"It's kind of slow going, I think."

"Well, you know, watching your father is—"

"I know. Listen, Mom—I just got accepted on permanent staff at *The Newspaper.*"

"That's wonderful, dear!"

"Well, I don't know if it is or it isn't, but I'm going to stay there for a while because I have to. I'm in debt, kind of."

"Sarah!"

"I mean, I could very well be in debt. See, a couple of kids from

East Harlem got in trouble, and I posted their bail. Well, what it is is a surety bond. If they show up in court, I won't have to pay anything. They're the ones I worked with, you know. Their mother says they were framed."

"Of course you had to help them, Sarah. The police do such terrible things! Adam will be proud of you."

"Yeah, well, tell him to stop threatening to get me kicked out of my job until this case is over, okay? Because I could be in hock for twenty thousand—"

"Oh, yes, I keep telling him to stop that. Twenty thousand, Sarah!"

"Well, maybe the boys won't run away. Oh—California's coming back in. I'll let you go, Mom. Maybe this is it."

"All right, dear. Are you coming to see us soon? Ann Walker was here last week. She asked about you. They've all seen your name in the paper." Then she whispered, *"I think Adam likes that."*

"Gotta go, Mom."

"Bye-bye, dear. Will you have a story in the paper tomorrow?"

"No. 'Bye, Mom."

The California delegation had indeed begun to amble back into the Garden. But once on the floor, they seemed to lose track of the reason they had returned. The chairman of the delegation went off into a huddle with a small knot of delegates, leaving the rest of them to sit in their chairs with their jaws dangling.

"Fuck this!" said Kevin. "They're gonna take all night."

He reached for the pack of cigarettes.

"You didn't tell me you've been posting bond for crooks," he said. He said "crooks" with the cigarette between his teeth, like a tough cop. My heart ached.

"I was sort of embarrassed about it," I said. "I didn't think it was the smartest thing I ever did. It was a sentimental gesture."

"Who's the bail bondsman?"

"Sy Shimmer. You ever heard of him?"

"*Shimmer?* Shit, Sarah, you don't pay up with him, he'll send the guys with the baseball bats! Shimmer's a fuckin' crook himself. How'd you get hooked up with him?"

"The Legal Aid lawyer brought me to him."

"Sure! What does he care? He gets paid every week no matter how many clients skip."

The BBS reporters were trying to trace down a rumor that Love had offered Muskie the vice-presidency. The camera focused on Willard Dixby for a moment. He was standing in front of the press section with his hands resting in the small of his back, his elbows protruding like little wings. He looked utterly rapt, as happy as only a man watching his enemy's plot come undone could be.

BBS couldn't get confirmation of the Muskie rumor. The reporters' voices took on a resentful edge. The network ran old news footage of the campaign. The same footage had been shown five times previously that evening. Each time it was shown, we saw Betsy Love drop her crutch on important occasions: the day she was filmed at home in Taos after Governor Feely endorsed her husband, the afternoon Kennedy endorsed her husband, and approximately seven hours before this deadlock, when she had been filmed saying, "Oh, I hope he doesn't get it! I would hate to spend more time away from the mountains!"

BBS still could not get confirmation of the Muskie rumor. The two anchormen, Bobo Jenkins and Mike Mossbacker, said it was "an unprecedented cliffhanger." They had said that quite a few times already.

"They can pick the dodo without me," said Kevin.

He went into the shower, and I could hear him singing in there. It sounded like a very accepting-of-status-quo sort of tune. When he came out, he kissed me on the nose, said, "See you around the campus, kid," and went out the door still humming. So maybe it was all right with him.

Now it appeared that the California delegation had at last counted itself. The chairman moved toward a microphone, clutching a little sheet of paper. "California has a vote count," he said. Scurrying forms were visible behind him. A hand tapped his shoulder. He went into a huddle with the knot of delegates again, leaving Mike Mossbacker at a loss for words. Bobo Jenkins said, "This is a cliffhanger inside a cliffhanger."

Presently the delegation chairman moved to the mike again. He announced that the last holdouts for Muskie and Udall had just capitulated. "California, the fastest-growing state in the nation, casts all of its delegate votes for the junior senator from New Mexico, the next President of the United States, George Foster Love!"

There seemed to be a ten-second lag while the delegates were waking up, but eventually a big cheer was heard, and then the dominoes started falling. One by one, delegations fell in line: Missouri for Love, Pennsylvania for Love, Arkansas for Love, Florida, Mississippi, Colorado for Love, all of them unanimous, Rhode Island for Love with two Muskie votes, Massachusetts for Love with three abstentions, Alabama for Love unanimously, Texas, Nevada, Nebraska, North and South Dakota unanimously for Love. The roll call went zigzagging among the states that had made up their minds.

New York State held out until it could announce in time to put Love over the top. The count went on after that, but nobody heard it. The whole convention hall fell to singing the Beatles song "All You Need Is Love," and Love came out onto the dais, supporting his wife with an arm around her waist and holding up his other hand in a V for victory. The four children, ages three to nine, clung to their mother any way they could, appearing to drag her down as hard as their father was pulling her up. She did not have a crutch with her.

Love kissed her on the lips, then turned back to the crowd with eyes brimming. *"Love is all you need, Love is all you need, Love is all you need,"* the crowd sang over and over and over, egged on by the loud blaring band. Love's youngest child, a little boy dressed in overalls, put his hands over his ears and made a face. The BBS anchormen audibly cooed with delight.

The singing was so tumultuous that at first I did not hear my phone. When I picked it up, I could barely hear someone saying, "Hello, Sarah. Is that you?" I turned down the volume on the TV and asked, "Who's calling?"

"Roger Einstein," he said.

"Roger! I thought you and Ellie were on the Vineyard."

"Ellie is. I had to come back in to see a patient. Sarah, have you been watching? This man Love—I never thought he'd get the nomination! He's not—I mean, he's—I must talk to you. Not over the phone! There's someone I want you to meet, someone who knows . . . Are you free tomorrow night?"

# *XLI*

The next morning *The Newspaper* carried an Iggy Meyers profile of Love that made him sound like the nicest guy in the world, the very one who ought to marry your daughter. Wholesome but also deep, optimistic but also concerned, troubled by his memories of the Vietnam War, yet still willing to say America was a good country and there was no place better.

It didn't take the brains of a Sherlock Holmes to figure out that Roger wanted to introduce me to the homosexual who claimed to have been Love's lover. I had told Roger I would meet his "someone who knows," but what was I supposed to do once I met him?

Take down the details in my notebook? Did Roger actually expect me to write a story about the Democratic presidential nominee's old boyfriend? Me? The one person out of all seventy Metro Desk reporters whose City Short alluding to the density of homosexuals in Greenwich Village had been called to the attention of the top editor! Why me, for god's sake? Was this my punishment for having allowed my roommate to marry her psychiatrist? What on earth would I do with the information? Tell Ron? Tell *Ron!* Ron was now in a state of beatific happiness of the sort that comes only to those for whom the end has justified the means. He had walked into the paper that morning with a face resembling that of an ecstatic water mammal, a smiling manatee, perhaps, swimming in an element of pure pleasure. He had kissed me good morning. He had kissed Jenny Locke good morning! He had sent Greg Swenson a case of Château Lafite-Rothschild, sent it to his hospital room along with a complimentary corkscrew and a note saying, "All you need is Love!"

Why should I want to destroy Ron's happiness? And anyway, who didn't have a crazy sexual history nowadays? Ellie had told me she once did it with a couple, back when her friends were all saying, "Smash monogamy!" ("Hated him, loved her," she had said. "But it was kind of pornographic. I didn't want to do it again.") Had she ever told Roger about that? She had done it only that one time. Whereas apparently, from what Felix had hinted, this thing between Love and his friend had been fairly continuous for a while. But so what? Why should the world know about it? Because he was running for President? Why should that make it any less private? It would be different if he was a guy like Nixon, a right-wing sleaze with a creepy five o'clock shadow and all sorts of nasty finger-pointing in his background. Nixon looked like he sold dirty books for a living. And finger-pointers were fair game. But Love was a nice guy. Maybe a little too much Ron's creation for my taste, but I didn't want to sink him. Why should I be the one to publicize his past? To protect him from KGB blackmailers? That's what they always said about homosexuals in government, wasn't it, that they'd be vulnerable to KGB blackmail? But how could Love be blackmailed if the press refused to print anything about it? What kind of a person wants to ruin his former lover's career?

Not someone you'd very much want to meet.

That was my thought at thirty seconds to eight, thirty seconds before Roger was due to arrive. My next thought was that I should scram fast. Later I could say I had forgotten our appointment.

I was searching for my keys when the buzzer sounded. Roger was fifteen seconds early. Ought I to ignore the buzzer? Pretend I got held up at the paper? Roger would call there. He was like that. He buzzed again. I pressed the release button.

"You . . . should . . . be . . . more . . . careful," he said breathlessly as he came through my apartment doorway. "Don't . . . you . . . have . . . an intercom? . . . What if . . . someone else . . . had buzzed you?"

"They didn't," I said.

Roger sat down in Kevin's chair, still puffing. Apparently he was not used to climbing two flights of stairs fast. So much for my theory about Megan and him.

"Look, Roger," I said, "I think I know why you're here. I mean, I think I know what you're going to tell me. Is it about the guy who claims to be Love's former lover? Were you planning to introduce me to him?"

"How did you know?" he cried, jumping to his feet and darting his eyes around the room.

"I—a source—a source told me," I said.

"Sarah, if you've been talking to the Secret Service— A man's life is at stake!"

"Calm down, Roger," I said. "I didn't get it from the Secret Service. Sit down. Would you like a beer? We're not meeting this guy tonight, are we?"

"That depends," Roger said, "on where you heard about him. I need to know that immediately, Sarah, or the deal's off. I'm not staying."

He stood with his arms folded and his beard pointing at me accusingly. He looked like a Russian prosecutor. (Roger in the KGB?)

"I'm not even sure I want to meet the guy," I said. "But I guess I can tell you, Felix Lebwohl was the one who told me."

"No one else?"

"No one else."

"Felix shouldn't have done that," Roger said, but he was obviously relieved. He let his arms drop and he took a seat again.

"Would you like a beer?" I repeated.

"The attending therapist should never make a disclosure like that. I'll have to speak to Felix," he said, frowning and stroking his beard. "Oh, coffee, please, if you have it. You can make it instant."

"Sure," I said. I filled the kettle and fetched myself a beer. "Felix didn't tell me very much," I said, leaning against the sink at approximately the point where Felix had trapped me. "He was quite concerned about the man's privacy. I think it just sort of slipped out. I wish you wouldn't speak to him. Then he'd know I told you."

"Well . . ."

"Roger, I'm not sure I want to go calling on this person."

"You don't have to," he said a little too readily.

"I've been thinking about it all day. I mean, I did have a pretty good idea from what you said on the phone. And, Roger, if this man opens up to me, I'm not sure *The Newspaper* will want to print his story. They don't usually print things like that, you know. I'd hate to disappoint this man. It must be hard for him to tell people. Maybe he shouldn't have to go through that if it's not certain that *The Newspaper* will print. Maybe I shouldn't go to meet him."

"You don't have to," Roger said again. "He's coming here."

"What?" I said. It was my turn to freak out.

"I said he's coming here."

"To my *house?* You gave him my *address?*"

"He lives right around the corner from you, on Gay Street."

"Oh, god!"

"You'll like him, Sarah. He's quite appealingly childlike."

"But around the corner from me, Roger! Don't you see? Now he'll be bothering me all the time. Shit! I wish you'd ask me before inviting one of my *neighbors* to my house!"

"Damn it, Sarah, his place may be *bugged!* Now, *do* you want this story or *don't* you? Because if you don't, I'm going right to the *Washington Post!* They've got an office in New York, you know. I checked that out. I almost called them first. Maybe I should have. But I thought I'd do you a favor because you're an *old friend.* I thought you should be the *first* reporter to know that a presidential candidate has been threatening the life of his former lover! If you don't think *The Newspaper* wants that story, you'd better tell me *right now!*"

"Roger, don't get so upset! I've never *seen* you so jumpy. What do you mean, Love's been threatening his life? Do you have any proof?"

"I don't be*lieve* this! She asks me do I have proof! What do you think I am, Sarah? Do you think I'm an idiot? Of course there's proof. Renato has the proof!"

"What kind of proof?"

"What are you going to do, Sarah?"

"I have to ask you these questions, Roger. My editors will ask me the same questions."

"Renato recorded a phone call that was made to him. It wasn't the first, but he didn't have a recording device for the first couple of calls. I told him to bring the tape. And the letter."

"What letter?"

286

"His last letter from Love. That's why he got the phone call. He'll tell you all about it. Now," Roger said, looking at his watch, "do you want the story or don't you?"

"Yes, of course I want it."

Fifteen minutes later, my buzzer sounded again. I heard light footsteps on the stairs.

Roger opened the door and stood waiting for Renato, who arrived also out of breath. He was dressed in black leather pants, a black sleeveless undershirt, and black leather shoes. A hefty gold chain hung around his neck.

"Oh, god!" he said. "These pants are so . . . hot! You must be . . . Sarah. Hi. I'm Renato. Dr. Einstein *said* . . . you had a small . . . place. But it's bigger . . . than mine! God, it's so *hot!* Do you think I could have . . . a glass of water? . . . How are you, Dr. Einstein? . . . I don't usually dress . . . like this, but I'm trying to look like somebody . . . from the Mafia. The guy followed me here, Dr. Einstein."

He fanned himself as he spoke, the way Blanche DuBois fanned herself in *Streetcar*. No way in the world was anyone going to mistake him for a member of the Mafia. He looked like—

"Here," I said, handing him a glass of water. "Do you go to the Leroy Street pool?"

"Not anymore!" he said. He took a seat on the couch. "I'm so glad you called me, Dr. Einstein!" he said. "If you hadn't called me, I would have called you. I don't know about Dr. Lebwohl. He's kind of a controlling person. He had the nerve to ask me why I wanted to be a dancer! I don't think he likes dancers, Dr. Einstein. I know that sounds paranoid, but I can't be paranoid about *every*thing. There've got to be some people who don't like me for real. But I don't think it's personal with Dr. Lebwohl. I just think he really doesn't like dancers."

"What makes you think that?" Roger asked, putting a hand to his chin.

"I can just tell."

"But think about it. How can you tell?" Roger's fingers curled around his beard.

"The way his eyes get when I start talking about the dance world. He squeezes them very tight and then opens them very wide, like he's angry. What else can I talk about? I mean, dance is my life."

"Have you noticed this reaction in other people when you talk about the dance world?"

"What? That thing in the eyes? No. He's the only— I mean, people get nasty. They ask me what I've been in and how much money I make, you know, because they get uptight in New York if you're not earning money. I get all sorts of hassles about that! Listen, I think it's worse to be a *dancer* than it is to be *gay!* People have more respect for hustlers than they do for dancers. I said that to Dr. Lebwohl. That's when his eyes went like *that*." Renato tried to demonstrate.

"Unless he's trying to keep from falling asleep. Do you think it's that?" Renato asked. "I just thought of that."

"It could mean he's intensely interested in what you're saying," Roger said. "You must try not to read too much into these little details. You are still quite paranoid, don't forget. Fear can do that."

"Are you two going to have a therapy session?" I said. "Maybe I should leave you alone."

"Oh, I don't mind!" Renato said. "I've got nothing to hide. You wouldn't have a cigarette, would you, sweetheart?"

"Of course, this is all off the record," Roger said.

I handed Renato a pack of cigarettes.

"Thanks, doll," he said, and then to Roger he said, "Why? As far as I'm concerned, my life is an open book."

"The name of your therapist. That wouldn't be ethical," Roger said.

"Well, if you think *he* doesn't want people to know he's treating *me*," Renato said woundedly.

"Oh, heavens, no!" said Roger. "It's merely for appearances, the professional ethics. It wouldn't look right, letting you talk about how your therapy is going."

"I won't tell Dr. Lebwohl I told you," said Renato.

"Well, shall we change the subject?" I said. "You want to go on the record?"

"Why don't you tell me what you want to know," Renato said to me. "Are you going to record this?"

"I don't have a machine."

"Oh, well, I guess you can take notes."

"Yes," I said. "That's what I was planning to do."

I fetched a notebook and a pen.

"All right," I said. "Why don't you tell me about yourself."

Renato took a deep drag and blew the smoke languorously to one side, raising his shoulders as he blew, like a female vamp.

"Maybe I should have a glass of wine," he said. "Do you have any wine?"

"I've got beer."

"Oh, I'll take that!" he said.

"Are you sure you should?" said Roger. Renato nodded. Roger said to me, "You have to understand, Sarah, that Renato wouldn't be here if it hadn't been for the threats on his life."

"The killer," said Renato. "He's always outside my house."

"Killer?" I said.

"Oh, I call him the killer because that's what he looks like. He's got this big neck, bigger than your waist. He came to see me about three weeks ago. He was real nice at first. He said he brought a message from George, that George would have come himself, only he was too busy. Then he started asking me what I wanted with George, and he sounded kind of funny, the way he was asking, like he was implying things, you know, hinting? It was in his voice. His voice scared me. I said I didn't want anything with George, except it would be nice to see him when he came to New York. That's when the killer started cracking his knuckles. You thought they only did that in the movies, right? He cracked his knuckles real loud and looked at me with his eyes all squinty—not like the way Dr. Lebwohl squints; you know, meaner, like a killer. I got so scared, I almost screamed!

"He was looking at me like that and telling me George never wanted to hear from me again, that I should *never* try to contact him, because if I did . . . and then he, like, paused and looked at me like he was trying to tell me he didn't have to say what he would do.

"I said, 'Did George tell you to say that?'

"And he goes, 'Who else do you think?' And he's still cracking his knuckles. God, I was scared! He was blocking the door.

"And then he asked me if I had saved any letters from George, and I said yes right away, so *stupid!* I *had* saved them all. George was my first real love.

"'He wants 'em back,' the big goon said.

"I asked why after all this time. See, I had no *idea* that he was going to get the nomination. I just knew he was coming to the convention, because I had read it in the paper. Anyway, I ended up giving that guy the letters, all but one. I kept one. And now I wish I hadn't! That man has called me *fifty times!* He calls at three o'clock in the morning, at four, at five. Oh, it's so *creepy!* He says, 'Renato, do you know who this is? Do you know why I'm calling?' And then he starts asking me if I understand the situation, how grave it is. He says 'grave' a few times to make sure I get it. Then he says he's going to break both my legs. God, he's so awful!"

"Why don't you just hang up on him?" I asked.

"I did that once. He called me right back, and he sounded terribly angry. He said, 'You won't hang up this time if you know what's good for you.' So I didn't hang up.

"Oh, I'm so *nervous!*" Renato cooed. "You wouldn't have another cigarette, would you, doll?"

"Sure," I said. "Help yourself. The pack's right on the table."

"Renato's tape will show you what sort of person he's been dealing with," said Roger. "A real psychopath."

"I told him I was recording him," Renato said. "Then *he* hung up."

"Could I ask a simple question?" I said.

"Be my guest," said Renato, exhaling like Marlene Dietrich.

"Why haven't you called the police?"

"Oh, I wouldn't want to get George in trouble with the police!" said Renato, rolling his eyes in a way that combined self-incrimination with coyness.

"And yet you're willing to tell *Newspaper* readers that you had an affair with him and that now he's harassing you to keep it quiet," I said.

"The man shouldn't be President," Roger said. "The public has a right to know what he's been doing."

"*I'm* not ashamed of our affair," said Renato.

"But if you publicize what's been going on with this goon person, you *will* get Love in trouble with the police," I said.

"Not if I refuse to testify," said Renato.

"What if you were subpoenaed?"

"I'd just go to jail." He made his face thin and soulful.

"I don't trust the police on a thing like this, frankly," said Roger. "I think publicity is Renato's best protection. You see, as long as he exists, he's a threat to George Love."

"I have another simple question to ask you, Renato," I said.

"Shoot," he said.

"Why did you call him up?"

"Call up who?"

"You said the goon told you never to call again."

"Oh, you mean when I called *George!*"

"Yes. Why did you do that?"

"I read about him in the paper, you know, that he was going to be the favorite son candidate from New Mexico, and I realized that meant he would be coming to New York. So I thought wouldn't it be

290

fabulous if we could get together! I even thought I could introduce him to some of my friends in the Gay Activist Alliance—because they've got people on the Democratic National Committee, you know."

"Did you *say* that to him?"

"I never got to talk to George. They put me on with some person from the Senate office. He sounded like a very *junior* person."

"Did you tell that person you had contacts in the Gay Activist Alliance?"

"Of course not! I said I wanted to leave a message for George, from his old army buddy. I said they should tell him to call me when he got to New York because I was living there, and we could get together. That's *all* I said."

"But you left your name and address. Did you get the junior person's name?"

"I left my phone number. No, I don't know what his name was. It didn't seem important at the time."

"They must have been afraid you were going to make trouble for him," I said.

"But I didn't say *any*thing to make them think *that*. They didn't know about George and me!"

Roger and I exchanged a look that said: As soon as they heard that voice they knew.

"But still," Roger said, "he should have called Renato to find out what he wanted."

"All I wanted was to *see* him," said Renato. "I haven't *seen* him for ten, eleven years."

"Maybe we should begin at the beginning," I said. "Renato, when and where were you born?"

"I was born in Pittsburgh on Groundhog Day in 1944, and my real name is Art—well, Arthur—Arthur Weinstein, but I chose Renato for aesthetic reasons."

"So now you're Renato Weinstein."

"Oh, sweetheart, no! What kind of a dancer would call himself Renato Weinstein? I'm just Renato. Period. A lot of dancers only use one name. Nijinsky. Nureyev. Baryshnikov."

"Are you a ballet dancer?" I asked.

"Oh, don't I *wish*! I started too late for that. I took some barre, but *everybody* does that. I do modern. I almost got into the Graham company last spring. Maybe you should leave that out. It doesn't sound too impressive to say he almost got into the Graham company. Is this going into the Sunday paper? I would like it to go into

**291**

the Sunday paper. Maybe I should make that a condition."

"Fine," I said. "I'll tell my editor you're making that a condition. And of course, you want it on the front page, right?"

"Oh, right!" he said breathily.

"Now, you were saying, Pittsburgh, on Groundhog Day, 1944. . . ."

# *XLII*

Renato talked for two hours, one hour and ten minutes longer than his ex-lover took to read the acceptance speech centered on the themes "Bind up the wounds," "Peace with strength," and "Anything's possible." (One cruelly sarcastic columnist was to commend Love for the "exemplary intellectual conservation" he had displayed in "recycling his opponents' discarded acceptance speeches into his own.")

I forgot to turn on the TV at nine. Renato, I later calculated, started his own rap approximately four minutes before Love said, "Brothers and sisters, fathers and mothers, children, grandparents, aunts, uncles, cousins, nephews, nieces, sweethearts, buddies, friends and fellow Americans, I come before you tonight to thank you. . . ." At about that point, Renato was saying, "I'm not sure I can remember my toilet training. I mean, my mother says that there was no problem about it, but if I've *completely blocked* it . . ."

But of course, as I say, at the instant of Renato's unfolding, we were not aware of the counterpoint. Renato held our full attention. Whatever Roger had heard before did not seem to have dulled his interest in the story. In fact, Roger was such a responsive listener that I suspect he made Renato even more long-winded than he ordinarily tended to be. For Roger's benefit, Renato kept interjecting psychoanalytic material. Every once in a while, Roger would say, "Fascinating!" or, "Very significant!" which did not help to keep Renato on the track. His narration went like this:

"I'm not sure I can remember my toilet training. I mean, my mother says that there was no problem about it, but if I've *completely blocked* it, doesn't that mean I hated it? Ma says I learned in a week and everybody told her that meant I was a genius."

292

"Fascinating!"

"I had a *lot* of trouble with that genius thing! You can imagine, a Jewish kid in Pittsburgh. My parents were too poor to send me to private school."

"Very significant!"

"I went to school with the Hunkies, you know, kids from steel-worker families? We didn't live in a good neighborhood. Ma was always talking about that, and I think she was afraid I'd get killed walking to school because I was small and delicate, and so she walked me to school every day and picked me up every day."

"Very significant!"

"I mean, Jewish mothers are supposed to be normally over-protective, but she was *ab*normally Jewish—I mean— Why did I say that? I meant to say *ab*normally overprotective."

"Fascinating!"

"I hate thinking my mother can remember things about me that I can't remember. She's so possessive anyway, and it's like she owns more of me than I own, if you know what I mean. Do you know she walked me to school when I was a sophomore in high school?"

"*Very* significant!"

"Do you know what she said when I told her I was gay? *That's* a whole other story! She said I was going to kill my father—"

"Fascinating! *And* very significant!"

"—but that's not the first thing she said. The first thing she said was, 'I *knew* I shouldn't have let you walk to school by yourself.' She was talking about when I was sixteen years old! She finally let me go to school by myself when I was a junior!"

"Ah!" said Roger at that point, and I felt that we had got to the crux of Renato.

But new cruxes kept being reached. The story, as I indicated, took a long time.

Renato said that during family fights he had heard how his father was a "charity case" in his uncle's dry cleaning shop, and his father sat around reading books about the British royal family when he was meant to be sewing.

"Why the British royal family?" I asked, but Renato did not answer the question. He never had been very close to his father. Apparently the mother had made sure of that. He wasn't even too sure about how his mother and father had got together. The father's decline, he somehow divined, had started when the army rejected him for having flat feet.

Renato's mother had pinned all her hopes on her son, and they eventually weighed so heavily that he ran away to the army, obviously the symbolic and actual liberator of Weinstein manhood. Renato was blessed with sound arches, and he volunteered for duty in Vietnam. George Love, who concurrently had been suffering the twin burdens of sibling worship and sexual guilt (for activities he never explained to Renato because "gentlemen don't tell"), had volunteered for Vietnam duty. He was also then fulfilling an obligation to ROTC, which had put him through the University of New Mexico. He headed a small search and destroy unit that Renato (who was still Art Weinstein) joined shortly after arriving in Vietnam. They were assigned to the Mekong Delta, which was controlled by Americans, South Vietnamese, or Vietcong, depending on the time of day or night.

"We fell in love. What more can I say?" Renato said with touching brevity.

"Well," said Roger, in a rare moment of expansiveness, "you were both fleeing from women at that point."

"We were together from June '64 to April '65," said Renato. "I was his first man. He was my first *anything*."

Roger did not call this significant.

"Why did you split up?" I asked.

"Those things just *hap*pen," he said. He sighed theatrically and reached for another cigarette. I noticed Roger glancing at his watch, which said twenty to eleven.

"Who knows why?" said Renato. "Maybe it was meant to be. Our signs didn't match. I'm a Cancer and he's a Leo. That's a very bad mix, you know, like, astral dissonance? My best match is Aquarius, so of course I end up in Greenwich Village. I don't know if I believe in that stuff, but René sent away for my horoscope once from this real professional astrologer, and it predicted, you know, that someone very close to me would become king. Of course, we don't *have* a king, but the President is kind of like our king. René thought it meant him, that he was going to make it very big. I haven't told you about René yet, have I? If you want to know about craziness, Dr. Einstein, René is it. I think he's had every mental illness there is—"

"You were going to tell us about your breakup with Love," I said.

"There I go blocking again!" said Renato. "I must be still in love with him!"

"How did you break up?" I asked.

"It just happened," he said. "George got wounded. He was sent to the hospital in Saigon. I couldn't stand being in the Delta without him. So I *pretended* to have a mental breakdown. That's when I first thought seriously about acting, you know, because a lot of guys pretended to go psycho and couldn't fool the doctors. But I could. I did such a good job, they sent me back to the States and put me in this *horrible* veterans hospital in the Bronx, where I really did go a little bit bonkers. There were men, you know, who thought they were General Douglas MacArthur—most of them were World War II vets—and this crazy *spade* character who went around calling himself Elijah. About once a month Elijah would see the devil in somebody and try to kill them. *He* was really crazy! Even the guards were afraid of him. One day they helped him escape. They took him outside the grounds and told him he should be doing his work out in the world because the devil was all over the place out there. I don't know what happened to him. Where was I?"

"You were in the hospital," I said.

"Oh, yes. Well, I was still in Bronx Veterans when George was shipped home. He came to see me. He said, 'What are you doing here? You'll go crazy in here.' I left the hospital that week.

"George stayed around for another week, and we went down to Greenwich Village and stayed in some fleabag hotel down there and talked and talked. George didn't like it in the Village. He said he never wanted to live in a homosexual ghetto. That's what he called it. He wasn't cut out for the Village anyway, you know, because he hated what he called bohemian thinking. He was a square. I don't know why I cared so much about him. We couldn't have been more different!

"Anyway, we had a lot of talks that week. We talked about what we were going to do. I had decided I wanted to become an actor, and I *loved* New York! So it was definitely going to be New York for me. But George still didn't know what he wanted to do, only that it had to pay well and keep him away from bohemians. I was the one who said if he felt that way, he should become a lawyer or a businessman. Of course, I was kidding! But right away George liked that idea. I don't know why he'd never thought of it on his own.

"He decided to go back to Albuquerque. He had all those brothers and sisters back there. He was sort of the head of the family, you know, because his old man turned into a drunk after they lost the farm. Sometimes I think I wanted George to be my father, you know, and that I had a kind of reverse Oedipus complex about him, but I couldn't let on to him, you know, how much I wanted him to stay, because he always used to tell me the one thing he liked about me was that I wasn't clingy. I wasn't like women.

"So anyway, he went back to Albuquerque, and I got a job as a waiter at the Village Gate, and I started taking acting classes, and of course, I was young and *gorgeous*, so people kept falling in love with me. You know what the scene is like down here! You don't stay lonely long.

"But I still got upset when the letter came. It sounded so final, like we'd never *ever* see each other again. I was very low for a couple of weeks. I even went into this group therapy group because I was feeling so unattractive. That's where I met René, and he turned my life around. René got me into dance. He was my first dance teacher. He taught Limón technique. He was a wonderful teacher. Well, he still is, I guess. I don't take from him anymore. He got mad at me when I performed with the Aesthetic Realists. When René gets mad at you, you don't want to *know* him! He throws things. He screams. He has tantrums, I mean *real tantrums*. His problem is he's got a prima donna complex, only he's never been a prima donna. Well, I guess you can be a prima donna—I mean, he's never been a star. You know what his biggest part was? It was understudy for a member of the chorus in *West Side Story*. But the person he was understudy for never missed a performance. René never went on stage the *whole* time! How long did *West Side Story* run? Three years? I can't remember. Of course, I was a *child* and still being walked to school. But anyway, that scarred René for life. He turned into a bitch. His students even *call* him Bitch! You would think he had been a member of the Royal Ballet or something, he's so fussy!"

"Renato, what about the letter?" said Roger, now pointedly looking at his watch. "Did you bring the letter?"

"I'm getting to that," said Renato.

"It's getting late," said Roger. "I think Sarah has enough of the story now. Why don't you give her the letter and the tape, and then if she has any questions she can call you."

"I don't want her calling me! What if my phone's tapped!"

"Well, then you can call her—from a pay phone. Show her the letter, Renato."

Roger's voice had an edge to it. Renato frowned mincingly.

"I think the letter might be worth a lot of money," he said. "If George gets elected it could be worth a lot of money. Look how much they pay for notes from Jackie."

"But, Renato!" Roger said. "I thought we agreed that George Love must *not* be elected. Because he has been threatening your life. We can't have a man like that in the White House, now, can we?"

"Oh, I *want* him to get elected!" Renato exclaimed. "I just don't want him to kill me!"

296

Roger groaned.

"I think your best protection is in turning the letter and the tape over to *The Newspaper*," I said. "Then the next time the man calls you, you can tell him *The Newspaper* is onto him."

"I can't believe this is happening to me!" Renato whined. "These last few weeks have been like a nightmare!"

"If you want to keep the letter, just let me make notes from it. Or let me make a Xerox," I said. "But I can't pay you for it. *The Newspaper* doesn't pay for stories."

"I can't believe George would do this to me!" Renato said. He leaned down as if to weep, no, to scratch his ankle. He pulled a folded envelope from his shoe.

"Here! Take it! Take it! I don't want it!" he said dramatically. "You're right! The next time the killer calls, I'm going to tell him *The Newspaper* has it!"

"Gee," I said, unfolding the envelope. "Maybe if he calls tonight, you shouldn't tell him *which* newspaper has it. I wouldn't want him to try and grab it from me when I was on my way in to work. Try to stall him if he calls tonight, Renato, okay?"

Renato sighed.

"I wish I'd never called George!" he said. "All I wanted to do was *talk* to him!"

The envelope was postmarked Santa Fe, June 18, 1967. It smelled mildewy, I noticed. This is what it said:

Dear Art,

I don't know how to tell you this, I guess there's no easy way to say it, so here goes. I've fallen in love with someone else. It happened a couple of months ago, actually, and I put off telling you because you were so nervous about the *Oh! Calcutta!* audition. (I hope you made it, even though it sounds like a lousy show.) I'm sorry about us, Art. I'm very sorry. You've meant a whole lot to me. I guess I don't have to tell you. I'm sure I wouldn't be in law school if it wasn't for you. I probably wouldn't be alive, either, because you're the only thing that kept me from cracking up in the Delta, old buddy, and I'll always love you for it.

You're not going to believe this, but the person I'm in love with is female. Her name is Betsy Bromley. Maybe you heard of her. She was in the Olympics three years ago and lost her leg in that awful fall. At first I just wanted to be nice to her because I felt sorry for her, and I guess I thought we kind of had something in common, you know, because of my wound and everything. I guess I was afraid of quote unquote normal women. But Betsy is really special, Art. You would love her. You really would. And I know she would love you. I've told her a lot about you, although I haven't worked up my nerve to tell her how it was between us. Someday I will. But I have to wait and pick the right time. So please hold off coming out here until I tell you everything's cool. I'm afraid she'd guess about us right away if she met you. She makes lots of jokes about fag jocks, but I don't think she really minds them. She's been through too much herself to [here a phrase was crossed out thoroughly, though I thought I could make out the word "misfits," and then the sentence continued] be nasty to people with hangups.

Did you go to that big demo with the kids wearing flowers? I've been to a couple of protests here. Some of the Vietnam Vets are starting an antiwar group here, and they want me to join and bring my Purple Heart. I'm not sure if I will. One asshole from their group carried a Vietcong flag in the last protest. Betsy says I don't understand how things are now, that the kids are saying a lot of things they don't mean. She says I'm a fifties person. But she is too. She was a Curved Bar Girl Scout—that's like Eagle. Now she's got me going to church again. She has taken over my life. She says she's going to make me President of the United States.

Art, old buddy, I hate to sign off. It's like signing off on a part of my life. But I think Betsy's right about me being a fifties person, and I think you are a sixties person, one of the few I really like. Sooner or later, we would have gone our separate ways. But let's not make this goodbye forever. Just until I give you the All Clear. Meanwhile, take care of yourself, and I'll be looking for your name in lights.

Love always,

George

"Renato, is this the last you heard from him?" I asked. I noticed that the name Love was written on the envelope in the same handwriting.

"Until that creep came to my house."

"Were you in *Oh! Calcutta!?*"

"Oh, god, no! You think I'd still be working at the Gate if I had been in *Oh! Calcutta!?* I should have been in *Oh! Calcutta!* I was fabulous in the audition. Everybody said so. But they pick their friends. Listen, it's *all* connections! Everything in New York is like that. *You* know. You must have had connections to get on *The Newspaper.*"

# XLIII

The next morning I made a mad dash for the subway. I thought everyone in my car was eyeing my purse with keen interest. I still hadn't decided what to do with Renato's story. He had given me the tape before he left my place, and all night long I had imagined noises on the roof and on the stairs. Of course, I couldn't listen to the tape until I had a machine. Freddie was in charge of the scarce supply at the City Desk, and I had heard Eddie complaining that National had taken all the working ones. He said Lindsay had been very annoyed when he showed up without a tape recorder and asked him to talk slowly. Why tape recorders should have been scarce at America's most accurate newspaper was a question nobody asked there except when they needed one fast.

That morning Freddie told me he had no machine at all. I made a mental note that I should tell Gil about this during our next talk and perhaps then offer him a chance to philosophize about men and machines and then gently steer the conversation to the subject of polygraphs. No one knew what conclusions management had drawn from the lie detector tests, and now, with Ron's candidate victorious but Dixby's desk on top of the story, no one could tell how things stood in their contest. Eddie's challengers were demanding payment. Eddie was standing firm, saying Ron wasn't beaten.

Ron did look unbeaten. He was basking in congratulatory phone calls, accepting compliments from his staff, and going about his work in a genial, easy way. He assigned me to do an obituary on the deputy water commissioner, which he said would be a "piece of cake," and then he went off for a three-hour celebratory lunch with his idiots. We heard later that he had spent the entire lunch discussing who should be appointed to the Love cabinet.

He surely wouldn't like a scandal about Love, not unless it was big enough to create a sensation of Pulitzer Prize–winning magnitude. And it would only do that if Love really had been threatening to have Renato killed. So everything depended on what was on that tape.

But not until late in the day was I able to listen to the thing. Mark Lindenbaum's death turned out to be rather complicated.

That is, not the death itself—he had died, aged forty-three, of a massive heart attack at the Brooklyn Bridge Tennis and Squash Club at seven o'clock in the morning—but the life he had been leading. The deputy water commissioner had breathed his last in the arms of his "fiancée," twenty-three-year-old Kimberly Jones, a very physically fit Pan Am stewardess who had been runner-up for Miss Utah. Ms. Jones became so distraught that she asked the police to call her beloved's sister out in Queens, a woman she had never met but instinctively knew to be not crazy about stewardesses. The sister turned out to be the wife of the deceased and the mother of his five children. She, poor woman, was beside herself with fury when I reached her. She felt her husband had died to elude her wrath. But she soon came to her senses, said she didn't know why it was any of my business, and hung up on me. Thereafter her telephone line gave off a busy signal.

This made it difficult to find out the endearing details necessary for obituary writing—the deceased's favorite authors, his hobbies, men he had most admired, and what he had said in his high school valedictory address. Kimberly Jones was also incommunicado. No one at Lindenbaum's office seemed to know much about him other than the fact that he had been a fitness fanatic. (He died in the pink of health.) "And of course, everybody's told you about the fountain," his secretary said, going on to describe the waterwork that the late deputy commissioner had had installed on his Executive Sweep desk. The only clue to his passionate nature, it continually pumped rose-colored water out of a jug held by a naked figure of Aphrodite. Jess Flicker and I racked our brains trying to decide whether we should call it imitation Rococo or imitation Renaissance. We also puzzled lengthily over what to term Kimberly Jones. We finally decided upon "fellow fitness enthusiast."

The obit ran only to three-quarters of a column, but it was a bitch of a thing to write altogether. Reading it over, Jess shook his head sadly and said, "The wages of sin are unequally distributed in this world. Has Figland read this?"

Finally, at seven o'clock, Freddie found me a tape recorder. I took it into an empty office in Culture, where the walls were decked nicely with dance posters. This is what, watching Nureyev's cloying eyebrows, I heard:

"Hello?" Renato's voice, sleepy and peevish.

"Hello, Art. Have you found that letter yet?" A calm, clipped male voice, which, coming from a cockpit, would build passenger confidence.

**300**

"God, it's *you* again! What time is it?"

"I thought I'd have you all to myself at this hour, Art. Are you alone?"

"You're not coming up here! I won't let you in! I'll call the police!"

"I thought we agreed, Art, that I'd have to smash your face in if you call the police."

"What do you want?"

"I want that letter, Art, the one you kept out of the packet. Why did you keep it, Art? You weren't thinking of showing it to anybody, were you? I'd hate to have to fit you with a pair of cement shoes."

"Don't be stupid! You think you can scare me with that dumb gangster talk? How do you know I haven't given the letter to somebody for safekeeping? How do you know I didn't tell them to open it if anything was to happen to me?"

"They wouldn't be able to prove anything, Art. You don't know who I am."

"Yes, but if someone was to recognize George's handwriting—"

"So you admit now that you did keep that letter!"

"I don't admit anything!"

"Art, let's stop playing games. What do you want for that letter?"

"This is ridiculous! I'm going to sleep!"

"Don't hang up, Art. I asked you a question."

"I told you, there *isn't* any letter."

"You wouldn't be planning to sell it anyplace else now, would you? Because if you are, Art, that would be going back on your word. I don't like a man who goes back on his word, Art. I think a man who goes back on his word is scum. Do you know what I would do with you if you sold that letter, Art? I wouldn't kill you right away. That would be too easy on you, Art. Do you know what I would do?"

"I think you told me already. You'd smash my face in. You might hurt your big, ugly hand, you know."

"Don't be funny, Art. We're not kidding around. Have you ever had one of your fingernails removed? You get your fingernails manicured, don't you, Art? My friend says those are easier to pull out. He's had a lot of practice with manicured fingernails. The Italians use him."

"This is so *stu*pid! I have to get some sleep!"

"Yes, you need your beauty sleep tonight because you're going to that audition at the Graham school tomorrow. At eleven o'clock, isn't it, Art? And then you're going to the gym, and at five you're

**301**

going to work at the Gate. Do the people at the Gate know you were once diagnosed as psychotic?"

"They wouldn't care."

"Do they know you were never discharged from Bronx Veterans? I bet you haven't told them, Art. The hospital has you listed as escaped."

"Go ahead and tell them. That was *years* ago!"

"The Secret Service would like to know too, Art. They like to know everything about people who threaten presidential candidates."

"I haven't been threatening him! All I did was call him!"

"Oh, no, Art, you don't remember. We have witnesses. You were overheard threatening the candidate."

"Yeah? Well, I wonder what the Secret Service will think when they hear *my* side of the story. I wonder what they would think if I had a letter to show them."

"I think I will have no choice but to tell the Graham school that you lied about your age."

"Don't do that! You can't do that!"

"Of course I can do that, Art. I've obtained a copy of your birth certificate from the Pittsburgh city clerk's office. Unusual first name your father had, Theobald—"

"Please! You can't! I'll look for the letter again! Maybe I'll find it!"

"Sounds German. Theobald. How can you have said you were twenty-two, Art? I was glad to see you did use your real name on the résumé. But twenty-two? Twenty-eight, maybe. You could pass for that. But not twenty-two, Art. I think the school already suspects you lied."

"You can't tell them! Please! It's not fair! I haven't done anything wrong! I haven't hurt George! You can't *do* this to me! I told you, I'll look for that letter again!"

"But I thought you *had* been looking for it, pal. How is it you haven't turned the thing up by now?"

"I've moved around a lot. Maybe I left it behind somewhere."

"That would be very careless, very careless."

"Well, how was I to know George would want his letters back? I haven't spoken to him in ten years. He didn't care what happened to *me*. He could have asked for the letters a long time ago."

"You wanted to remind him, is that it, Art? You didn't want him to forget about you. That's dangerous, Art."

"We were friends! Why shouldn't I call him?"

"If it was up to me, Art, I'd take care of you right now. You're lucky it's not up to me."

"Please give me time. I need to think where the letter might be."

"You're not going to talk to anyone about this, are you, Art? You're not going to tell your psychiatrist?"

"Of course I wouldn't tell anybody! I *loved* George!"

"Because if this leaks out, it's curtains for you, Art—or should I call you Renato?"

"God, you're so tired!"

"Tired? I'm wide awake. You're the one who's wrecked. Your degenerate life is burning you out. I'd be doing you a favor if I put you away."

"I think I'm going to record you."

"You wouldn't dare, would you, Art. You know what I would do. I've got your birth certificate."

"How do you know I'm not recording you right now?"

"You wouldn't dare, Art. You're too chicken. I'm glad you're chicken. You might stay alive, if you listen to me. Think of me as your keeper, Art. I'm your keeper for the rest of this campaign. The minute you step out of line, I'm mailing your birth certificate to Martha Graham by registered mail."

"Please don't!"

"And then I'm going to take care of you for good. Do you know what I mean when I say for good?"

"Oh, God!"

"It doesn't necessarily mean I'll put you out of your misery. It could mean I'll just make sure you never dance again. You could wake up one morning in the gutter with pulverized kneecaps."

"Come on! I've got you on tape!"

"Think of it, Art. Pulverized kneecaps."

"Do you get off on this stuff?" Renato asked, but the goon had hung up.

I heard a dial tone, Renato's voice saying, "What a creep!" a click, and then the *scritch-scritch-scritch* of the tape spool turning. I lost control and went running out into the newsroom, waving the tape recorder in the air and yelling at the top of my voice, "Ron! Ron! Ron! Ron! Ron!" When I reached his desk, I shouted, "Ron, get off the phone! I've got something bigger than Watergate!"

"Quiet!" he shouted, but I could not stop. I yelled:

"Ron! It's all true! Love *did* have a homosexual affair! When he was in Vietnam! And his ex-lover lives here! He's a dancer! I interviewed him! He gave me his last letter from Love! And he gave me a tape! Love's people have been threatening his life! See, he tried to call Love before the convention, and Love sent this goon to get all the love letters back, and Renato—that's the ex-lover's name—Renato gave all the letters back except one, and I've got it, Ron! *I've got it!* This goon has been calling Renato, trying to get the letter back! *I've got him on tape, Ron! It's incredible!* He actually says, 'It's curtains for you' on the tape, Ron—"

"How *could* you?" Ron finally erupted. "How could you *do* that to me?"

"It's the truth, Ron. I can't suppress the truth!"

"How could you interrupt me when I'm talking to *Bill Kleinfreude!*"

"You were talking to Bill Kleinfreude?"

"Why did you *interrupt* me?"

"Because—because I thought you'd want to hear—"

"You thought I'd want to hear *dreck*, a piece of dreck that's not even fit for the *National Enquirer?*"

"But, Ron, the man is running for President, and he's got a gangster threatening his former lover's life! A man's life—"

"*I don't want to hear any more!*" he shouted.

"But, Ron!"

"*Not one word more!*" His face was purple.

"Okay, Ron," I said, and I backed away.

## XLIV

I suppose I could have walked straight over to Dixby's desk with the tape recorder, but it didn't occur to me then, and as soon as I realized how stupidly I had shocked Ron with the news, I decided to hold off. I figured that Ron would come around after a couple of days. My story would give him the edge on Dixby again, and I honestly believed that the juiciness of it would overcome his reluctance to ruin a candidacy of his own making—if he could also foil Dixby.

I decided to wait out the weekend. That proved more agonizing than I could have guessed. The nights were awful. I kept hearing people crawling over the roof to come murder me. Along about four in the morning, I would start wondering whether it was possible to send poison gas via the telephone. To make matters worse, Kevin failed to show up on Saturday night. I suffered a long-drawn-out heartbreak and at about midnight resigned myself to life as a sexual cripple. Rather than lie awake listening for murderers, I watched TV until the networks closed down, but it was little comfort. The late movies were cop stories, and I kept bursting into tears whenever a man went home to his wife.

The telephone woke me late Sunday morning. Renato wanted to know why the story wasn't in the paper.

"It's kind of embarrassing," he said. "I told all my friends it would be on the front page today."

"How many friends do you have?"

"Oh, that guy called again—the goon?" he said. "I told him you had the letter and the tape, and I told him I was going to tape everything he said to me from now on. He dropped the phone like it was radioactive!"

"Do you think he'll carry out his threats?"

"You mean send my birth certificate to Martha? I failed the audition anyway."

"I mean, do you think he might beat you up or something?"

"My friends are protecting me. But that's the problem. They can't keep it up forever. We thought the story would be in today."

"It will be in the paper very soon, Renato," I said firmly. "My boss is mulling it over."

"Tell him I can't go anywhere! My friends are sleeping on the floor in my apartment. It's very uncomfortable for them. What is your boss waiting for?"

"Renato, how many people have you told about this thing?"

"Only the people in my classes. I figure the more people who know, the better it is for me."

"How many people are in your classes?"

"About thirty, maybe a couple more. No, wait! I forgot to count stretch class. So maybe it's um, about fifty in all."

"Well, shit, Renato! If you told *that* many people, it could break somewhere else! I thought you wanted to give this to *The Newspaper* as an exclusive. Do you know what the *Chronicle* would do with a story like this?"

"Nobody can print the story without the letter and the tape. I asked a lawyer friend of mine."

"So that's fifty-one people you've told, not counting the two headshrinkers."

"If you're so worried about somebody else getting the story, then why haven't you printed it already?"

I couldn't answer that one. I urged Renato to be patient and signed off.

On Monday morning, I marched hollow-eyed to Ron's desk. He was foraging through the press releases and pointedly not looking at me.

"Ron, we're going to lose that story if we don't run it right away!" I said. "My source is not being very discreet."

I felt a clammy hand on my arm. I spun around, to see Willie Crespi hunching at me.

"Sarah," he said patronizingly, "you're going to have to stop barging in on Ron whenever you feel like it. If everybody did that, he would never get any work done."

"When *can* I talk to him?" I asked.

"I'll let you know as soon as he's free," Willie said, adding, when I didn't move, "Trust me."

Ron was not free to see me all day, however, and the following morning I found a memo "From the desk of Ron Millstein" in my mailbox. It said:

"Report immediately to Akelroyd in eighth-floor test kitchen. RM."

# XLV

I was to spend the rest of my life in the eighth-floor test kitchen helping Vincent Akelroyd fathom the meaning of such phrases as "creamy and springy," "done to taste," "whip until stiff," "lightly browned," "to the soft ball stage," and "cook until done." Neither Akelroyd nor I was happy with this arrangement, needless to say, but our happiness was not uppermost in the bosses' minds. Akelroyd had, through a series of back-stabbings, budget cuts, and his own inability to comprehend how Muskie had lost the nomination, been dropped from the National Desk team at the end of the convention. At the same time, the Sunday magazine editors had informed him that they did not want a profile of Muskie after all, and they had offered him a kill fee that was not even a third of the sum he had been promised. Dixby and the Sunday magazine editors got into a very ugly exchange of memoranda about who was responsible for Akelroyd's phone bill, and several things which should never have been put down on paper were put down on paper. The argument started in low-key, professional fashion, one desk asking another who had authorized a separate phone line for Vincent Akelroyd at Madison Square Garden, why it had been installed in his name and not in the name of *The Newspaper,* and incidentally, which desk had asked him to call Rangoon? But side issues were soon brought in. Dixby's early preparation for the Baptist ministry was mentioned along with his alma mater, Heavenly High. We heard that a retaliatory suggestion then came from Dixby concerning the source of the wardrobes of the Sunday magazine editors' wives. From there the memos had descended into gutter journalism, and the magazine editors, under the pretext of substantiating their charge that the National Desk played fast and loose with money, cited in the most insinuating fashion a certain Upper East Side apartment rented by (but not the home of) the national editor. For his part, Dixby stooped to making a most pointed reference, while impugning the news judgment of the entire magazine staff, a reference to a certain exhausted-looking couch in the foyer of the Sunday magazine's editorial suite.

Akelroyd was left without a job and without any free-lance assignments. Flicka Poinsby turned him down for lunch on the Monday after the convention, and that afternoon he had called Ron to beg for his old job back. Ron tortured him, made him wait by Dayside for everyone to see, and then took him into his private office to torture him in some way Vinnie has never disclosed. Whatever Ron did to him, Vinnie emerged with downcast eyes and hurried out of the newsroom. We soon learned he had agreed to come back to the paper as second-string food critic. Ron had given Vinnie's column to Greg.

In the history of *The Newspaper,* the second-string food critic had never been given an assistant, but the new position was created about three hours after Vinnie had been on the job, although I didn't find out about it until the next day. Vinnie had apparently gone berserk after suffering an accident with his first assignment, Mrs. Heller's recipe for Soufflé Shirley Temple (the one containing the phrase "creamy and springy"), and if it had not been for the intervention of *The Newspaper's* day nurse, Vinnie might have blown himself up. She worked next to the kitchen. She had heard him throwing things around and had smelled gas. She called building security, who came with a straitjacket and a fire extinguisher. Someone, probably the nurse, called Ron to tell him what was going on, and Ron told Vinnie to forget about the soufflé and go home for the night. Ron allegedly spent the next hour or so feeling real remorse, until Willie asked him what assignment I should get for the following day.

It wasn't until I had worked with him for several days that Vinnie began to talk about anything to do with *The Newspaper* in front of me, but I had figured out something was up because of phone calls he kept getting from a man in accounting, who sounded not unlike Renato's goon. Vinnie usually took the phone into the supply closet, so I couldn't hear him talk to the guy. But one day the man phoned him in the middle of a very tricky flambéed Hawaiian shish kebab preparation, and he shouted heedlessly into the phone, "I have never called Rangoon in my goddamn life!"

My old buddies in the newsroom soon told me that Vinnie had been seen handing the phone to a very voluptuous BBS messenger in Madison Square Garden on the night in question, and although no one so far had snitched to the editors, it was that bit of glad-handedness with National Desk facilities which the office pundits cited in arguments that Vinnie had all along been Ron's mole and had helped to persuade Dixby that Greg Swenson was *not* doing a story on the hidden Love vote.

Eventually Vinnie confided in me because he was racked by fears. He had got it into his head that *The Newspaper* was going to give him a lie detector test to find out what, if anything, he knew about the Rangoon phone call, and he was certain he would fail the test. This would lead to broader inquiries, and he thought he might ultimately be indicted for pilfering company money.

He made me ask him questions and simultaneously feel his pulse, and even though he fed me the questions himself, he'd break out in a sweat every time we went through the routine, asking me anxiously, "Can you feel it? My heart stopped that time. Did you feel it? When I told you I didn't see the caste mark on her forehead. I lied. Could you feel?"

"No, Vinnie. I can scarcely feel your pulse, let alone any variations."

"Look at this. I'm sweating like a pig!" he'd say. "Do they measure sweat? I'm sure they measure sweat! How could I have been so weak? Anyone who calls herself Karima!"

It wasn't the money for the call that bothered him. The Rangoon call came to about four hundred dollars. It was what management would do when it dawned on them they should look into his expense accounts. He told me with trembling lips that there were times, there had been times—very rarely, but certainly more than once or twice a year—when he had not actually eaten lunch with the governor although he had put the governor down on his expense form.

"I can't have that on my record," he said. "It would ruin my credibility."

"Oh, Vinnie! Everybody does that! Anyway, they won't find out. The governor won't tell."

"If they asked him, if they gave him specific dates, he'd *have* to tell them!" he said. His face was ashen. "He can't protect me on this. A governor is too vulnerable."

"I told you, Vinnie, everybody does it."

"That's why! That's why! You see, even *you* know about it! And the desk is always looking for this sort of thing. They *know* everybody does it. But you see, when they're out to get you—"

"What more can they do to you, Vinnie?" I asked.

But he was not listening to reason. He was really becoming a bit unhinged. Another sign of it was his fussiness around the kitchen.

His job was to test three or four recipes a day. These were given to him by the first-string food critic (who covered restaurants) or by various editors or by editors' friends. Vinnie took the whole process terribly seriously. He would measure a teaspoon of something and then throw it away and measure again, just to get it right. And when he was writing up the recipes, he'd bother me for ages, making me taste things over and over again and tell him whether he was right in calling them "effervescent" or "tremulous" or "robust."

He wrote about the recipes in an ornate, faintly pompous style which was not unpopular with the readers of the recipe page, and I suppose he was becoming quite a good cook. But he went about it like a nervous bride and yelled at me and pushed me around and made my life miserable.

One day he got a letter from Mrs. Heller, which praised his work and asked why he had not tried her "scrumptious" recipe for soufflé. Vinnie decided to try it again. He was too nervous, however, to put his own hand to the task. He had me do it, and he hovered around me like a great Mexican jumping bean, banging into things and bumping me at the wrong times and hooting with excitement every time he got a glimpse into the bowl. Between the hooting and the jumping and the banging, I was not able to concentrate very well, and I do think I got something wrong in the proportions of eggs to flour. Anyway, the batter wasn't the right consistency. It was neither creamy nor springy, and as soon as Vinnie got a really good look at it, he banged and jumped and hooted more frantically. This unnerved me. I added more eggs when I probably should have added more flour. The batter became watery. Vinnie saw this and let out a terrible howl, and then he brought his hands up to his head, presumably to begin tearing his hair, only on the way up one

**309**

of his hands banged my elbow really hard. I said, "Ow!" The bowl slipped. The Soufflé Shirley Temple went all over the kitchen floor, and Vinnie let out a god-awful sound, a really inhuman howl, and then he came for me with both hands poised in the strangler's curled reach. To save my life, I had to step right into the middle of the soufflé, and as I ran down the hall toward the elevators, I heard both the sticky sounds of my shoes pulling away from the floor and, in the distance, a hopeless, grieving coyote howl that grew fainter and fainter as its sadness increased.

"Enough is enough, Willie," I said to him as soon as I reached the City Desk. Ron was nowhere in sight. "I know you guys don't care what you do to me, but do you really want to destroy Vinnie's mind completely? How long are you planning to keep up the punishment?"

"I just got through talking with Vinnie," said Willie. "He sounds fine."

"You're lying! Vinnie is in no state to talk!"

"He asked for another assistant, if you really want to know."

"Good! At least I won't have to watch him deteriorate."

"Go right back upstairs, Sarah. You haven't been trying up there."

"I need to talk to Ron."

"Ron's tied up."

"I want to know what Ron is going to do with my exclusive."

"If you know what's good for you, Sarah, you'll never mention that story again."

"Ron told you about it?"

"And you'll get back upstairs!" Willie said. "If you know what's good for you. Any minute now, he'll be coming out of Gil's office, and if he sees you here—"

"I'm not going back upstairs!"

"Sarah, I'm ordering you!"

"Fine. Then I'll quit!" I said, but Willie said simultaneously, "Here comes Ron!" and Freddie said, "Sarah, you've got a phone call. It's your bail bondsman."

Sy Shimmer told me Jesus and Fredo had jumped bail. I was to be in his office at ten the next morning with a banker's check for five thousand dollars. The other fifteen thousand I was to pay him over the next five years. The papers I had signed in his office gave him eighteen percent interest.

The *Newspaper* credit union loaned me the five thousand at eight percent interest, making me sign my name in blood under a promise that I would not quit the paper until the loan was paid off.

Nobody had heard me say I was quitting. After I signed for the loan, I had no choice. I went back up to the test kitchen.

There I came upon a wondrous sight. Vincent Akelroyd was getting atop a stool in the glistening-clean test kitchen, watching a woman in a big white apron stir something in our large stainless-steel bowl. He looked utterly rapt. The woman's back was to me when I entered the room, so for a second I feared Willie had heard me say I was quitting. But then the woman raised her head to see who had come into the room and I saw the happy, flushed face of Mrs. Reginald Heller.

# *XLVI*

From that day forward, Vinnie was a changed man. He acted like a man in love. Perhaps he was in love. He constantly quoted Mrs. Heller to me. He repeated her little jokes. He told me when her dog was sick. And whenever she dropped by the test kitchen, Vinnie went into that rapt, admiring trance and couldn't stop smiling.

Mrs. Heller must have been about twenty years older than Vinnie, so his feeling for her was sublimely platonic, the real agape of the human soul. It left me free to laze around by myself, to read in the corner or spend hours on the phone with Renato, telling him lies about why the story was taking so long to come out.

I really shouldn't have been doing that. I had lost all hope that the story would run. But Renato was terrified, and I sort of felt it was my fault and that if I told him the story would never run, it would crush him. Besides, he still could go to another paper—even without the tape or the letter—and I knew Ron well enough to be wary about anyone else getting a story he had turned down.

Renato had spotted the goon darting in and out of doorways everywhere. This had scared him so much that he took a leave of absence from his waiter's job and holed up in a friend's place on West Seventy-second Street. He started to talk about going to the police. I was afraid if he did that the story would leak out. I kept advising him to lie low and telling him my boss was still mulling.

I would have consulted Kevin, but for a long time I didn't hear from him, and then he called me from his home to tell me he had shot his toe off with a regular service revolver while he was trying to get it out of the holster. He got mad when I asked how it happened, and he hung up on me before I could tell him about Renato. Of course, I couldn't call him back. I didn't have his number.

Ron was certainly giving no sign of change in his attitude. He was still basking in the glory of Greg's scoop. He was also acting quite friendly toward Dixby. The reporters didn't know what to make of that. Eddie wasn't happy about it. "It's like he's selling out," he said. "Like he knows Dixby's gonna be his next boss."

Then one day, Eddie overheard Ron and Greg talking about some interview Greg was trying to get with Love, and Eddie had a brainstorm.

"Fuck it!" he said to me when I came down for my mail. "How could I have been so dense? Ron's not giving up. You know what he and Greg are trying to do? Get the first exclusive interview with the candidate!"

"Which candidate?" I asked.

"Love, of course!"

"But Love gives interviews to everybody."

"Yeah, yeah, but they want the first real in-depth thing."

I couldn't see how that would have a bearing on Ron's behavior toward Dixby, but Eddie explained that Love would never slight one *Newspaper* desk over another. He said everybody outside *The Newspaper* knew about the rivalry between Ron and Dixby, and any political candidate worth his salt would go out of his way to keep both of them happy. The desk that got slighted might otherwise do an investigation of the candidate's finances or find out he had cheated in college. And of course, with Love running for national office, his relationship with the National Desk had to come first. If Greg and Ron were going to get anywhere with him, they had to make it look as though they had become bosom buddies with Willard Dixby, have it get all around town that they were cooperating with him, be seen eating lunch with him, seen piling into a cab with him.

"They're gonna steal that story right out from under his nose," Eddie said.

About a week later, Ron called me on the test-kitchen phone.

"Could you come down to my office right away, Sarah?" he said. "I'm just having a little meeting with Willard, and we'd like to talk to you."

He sounded conciliatory, so I allowed myself to think Eddie was wrong. The cooperation *could* be sincere. And maybe *both* Ron *and* Dixby now wanted to run my story. Maybe they had heard it was getting around town.

Dixby was seated on one of the couches in Ron's office, smoking a cigar. His cheeks had two pink spots on them. Ron's nose was red. They must have just had a long lunch together.

"Now, Sarah," Ron said, "I know you're probably a little upset about the way I reacted to your story about Love the other day--"

"It's been weeks, Ron," I said.

"Well, well, I hope you're not *still* upset! Willard and I have been talking about it. I think I told you we don't usually print stories like that, didn't I?"

"Well, not in so many words, but I assumed—"

"Yes, we don't print stories about the private lives of public figures unless . . . unless . . ."

"Unless the story is rey-levant to the man's public duties," Dixby helped him out. "When Wilbur Mills gets stopped for drunk driving in Washington, we print it, but when somebody calls us to say Teddy Kennedy is having lunch with a woman, we don't print it."

"Sarah," Ron said, "the Love people have somehow become aware of the fact that you have those materials, um, which could damage Love severely, and it wouldn't be fair—"

"They want to know if you're planning to use them," Dixby said.

"What did you tell them?" I asked.

"How did they find out what you had, Sarah?" Ron asked. "You didn't *call* them about this thing, did you?"

"No, I didn't. I didn't want to tip them off unless the story was going to run," I said. "I guess Renato must have—yes, he told me he told the goon."

"Renato? The goon? What's she talking about, Ron?" Dixby asked in a tone that implied he considered me peculiar.

"Renato is Love's former lover, and the goon is the man who was threatening him at the behest of Love's campaign," I said.

"That's crazy!" said Dixby.

"Sarah, could you bring us the letter and the tape?" Ron said. "Oh, and bring your notes too."

"If you want," I said. "Are you going to run the story?"

"Sarah, honey, if we are going to decide what to do with that story, we will have to see the ev-i-dence," said Dixby, with oily sweetness.

"That's right," said Ron, "and bring any copies."

"I didn't make copies," I said. "Do you want me to make copies?"

"Oh, no! That's all right!" Ron said. "Where have you been keeping them?"

"In my purse," I said.

He and Dixby looked at each other in a what-did-I-tell-you sort of way, and afterwards I wondered whether they had had somebody go through my desk to look for them.

When I came back from the test kitchen with my purse, I said, "I suppose you'll want to talk to Renato. Do you want me to call him?"

"Call him?" Ron said absentmindedly. "Oh, I think we'll have to talk to Gil about this first."

"He's pretty nervous. He's been talking about going to the cops."

"Oh, tell him not to do that!" said Ron.

"Yes, that might be a mistake," said Dixby.

"Well, what can I tell him about the story? He calls me every day. Will it be running soon?"

"Oh, tell him that we'll at least have a judgment on it in the next day or so," Ron said.

They took the letter and the tape and thanked me. A little too profusely, I thought, as I went back upstairs.

Half an hour later, Renato called me on the test-kitchen extension.

"Sarah! Sarah! You've got to do something!" he said. "He's found me!"

"I've got good news, Renato," I said. "The editors are taking it to the top man. We'll hear—"

"Sarah, he's coming here! He called me! He said I got him *fired!* And he said he's going to *kill* me! I'm so *scared!* I have to call the police, Sarah! I have to! Even if it means George has to go to *jail!*"

"Renato, don't do it!" I said. "Don't do it! Come down here. Get in a cab, and come down here. He can't kill you in the *Newspaper* building. There's a guard downstairs."

"But what if he's on the street? What if he's got a gun?"

"If he's got a gun, he can shoot his way into your apartment. Hurry, Renato! Come down here!"

"What was that about?" Vinnie asked me.

"What have I done?" I said, and I rushed down to the third floor. I barged in on Ron in his private office. He was on the phone. He looked at me for one second with such a panicked expression that I was afraid he might already have heard that Renato had been killed. But then he said, "What *is* it, Sarah?"

"Ron! Ron!" I said. "He's coming down here! Renato's coming here! The goon just called him. He said Renato had gotten him fired, and he was on his way to Renato's house to kill him. Only

314

Renato isn't staying at his own house. God, it's creepy! Ron, we've got to protect him! Call the police!"

"I'll call you back," he said into the phone, and quickly put down the receiver.

"What are you saying, Sarah? That you told that nut to come here? What are we going to do with him? Sarah—"

"Ron, we have a responsibility to him. He gave us his story, and it's because of that that the man who was hired to shut him up has been fired. I'm *sure* it is, Ron! That man is a killer!"

"Calm down, Sarah!" Ron said, wringing his hands nervously. "Now, we have to think. What are we going to tell him?"

"That's not important! We have to get the police!"

"No, no, no! We don't want the police coming in here because some nut has told us there's a killer after him!"

"Some nut! Ron, you have the letter! You've got the tape! Did you listen to it?"

"Not yet."

"Where's Dixby? Don't you want to tell him Renato's coming? Maybe he'd like to talk to him."

"No, no! He's busy, Sarah. We can't bother him right now. Would you go out and get Greg? Send him in here. And you'd better stay by your phone. You know, in case Renato shows up. The guards will call you."

The guards never did call me, but in the ensuing confusion, Renato was to manage to slip upstairs by himself.

He had rushed out to a cab, just as I had urged ("I thought of Jack Ruby, you know, and I decided I'd be safer down here than with the police"), but the goon, who had taken his own cab to Seventy-second Street, arrived in time to see Renato stepping into a loose-limbed Checker and promptly did a screeching reversal. Renato's cab pulled up in front of the building in a bad state of repair. The goon's cab, a sleek little Peugeot diesel that was part of a demonstration project commemorated in one of those City Hall ceremonies that perhaps caused Mayor Simon to disappear, had had no trouble catching up with the battered Checker. Renato made a dash through the revolving doors just as the Peugeot stopped at the curb. Renato shouted, "There's a madman after me! Ask Sarah Makepeace!" and he attempted a grand jeté in the direction of the elevators. But the trusty guards grabbed him before he could get off the ground, and three of them pinned him against the reception counter with their truncheons, saying, "You're not going anywhere, buster!" and "Oldest trick in the world. Thought you could fool us, eh?" At which point, the goon, who may have been delayed by a fare dispute, emerged from his cab with his gun blazing. The bullet ricocheted off one of the revolving doors, causing a starry cracking of the glass and then bouncing back to graze the forehead of the gunman. This did not stop him. He went plunging into the lobby, bursting out of the revolving door in a terrifying shower of broken glass, and he waved his gun at a bunch of frightened sixth graders who had just completed the midday tour of the great metropolitan daily. They shrieked and dropped their "The Truth Is Our Business" bags. The guards ducked behind the reception counter. Renato dove in among them, and for a brief eternity, the goon held possession of the institution which modestly called itself America's most accurate newspaper. However, as luck would have it, Eddie Schwartz was just then returning from a quick jaunt to the OTB parlor, where he had placed three two-dollar bets on horses named Sweetheart, Passion Flower, and Courtship, losers all, chosen only out of the gambler's sentimental belief that three things on a common theme bring good fortune. He came through the revolving door rather slowly because he was trying to remember the last time the motif of love had brought him good luck, hence the door did not make its usual whooshing sound when he came through, and the goon did not hear his approaching footsteps—Eddie wore orthopedic shoes in case Willie was doing assignments—so surprise gave Eddie the advantage. He knocked the gun right out of the goon's hand. It fell to the floor and discharged a tremendous boom. The schoolchildren screamed. Renato shrieked. The goon turned to dash toward the doors. Eddie picked up the gun and said, "Freeze, mister, or I'll put a hole through your shiny leather jacket." That was language the goon understood.

The brave guards then came out from behind the reception counter and seized their quarry, and it was at this point that Renato slipped away upstairs. When the cops came to arrest the goon (Josh Spitzer, a failed middleweight amateur and retired cop), they took statements from everyone in the lobby. But no one remembered to mention Renato.

He found me in the newsroom, and I took him straight to Ron's office, where Ron and Greg were waiting. Ron told me to go upstairs to the cafeteria to fetch coffees for everybody. When I came back, Greg and Renato were gone, and Ron was on the phone again.

"You can leave the coffee right here," he said. "Thanks, Sarah."

"Where did they go, Ron?"

"I don't have time to explain now," he said, waving me away.

316

Out in the newsroom there was a buzz of excitement. People had by then heard about the shooting downstairs, and everybody was asking about Eddie. Someone said the man with the gun was a hit man for the Mob. Someone else said he was a lunatic homosexual. Another person—Steve Figland, I think it was—said the guy was Eddie's loan shark. When Eddie came upstairs, everybody cheered.

"Who was the guy?" Steve asked him.

"Beats me," said Eddie.

Ron soon came out and took over the supervision of the story. He said Eddie shouldn't write it because he had been so centrally involved. He said he was going to let Flicka Poinsby do it, to give her a boost. He had her type it in his office, and he was in there with her for quite a while.

I couldn't find out what had happened to Renato. He disappeared that night with Greg, and there was no mention of him in Flicka's story. There was no mention of the Love campaign in the story, either. All the piece said was that a demented fifty-four-year-old man had come into the *Newspaper* lobby waving a gun and talking incoherently, and that a sixty-two-year-old police reporter had surprised him from behind and disarmed him. The story said the gunman was subsequently arrested, charged with attempted homicide and assault with a deadly weapon and taken to Bellevue for psychiatric observation.

Greg started avoiding me. Ron sent me back up to the test kitchen and pulled his too-busy-to-talk-to-you act again.

I buried myself in a copy of *How to Make a Million Dollars Before You're Too Old to Enjoy It*, the newest literary sensation.

One week later, *The Newspaper* carried a front-page, top-of-the-fold story based on the first in-depth exclusive interview with the Democratic presidential nominee. It was written by Iggy Meyers.

# XLVII

I was not astonished when Ron called me at home the next morning.

"Sarah," he said, "I had a talk with Gil yesterday. He was very disturbed about that shooting, you know, very disturbed."

"Where's Renato, Ron?" I asked. "What did you do with him?"

"Renato is fine," he said. "Greg has been looking after him. Now listen. I think Gil is leaning toward running our story, but it's going to be tricky. Dixby is still against it."

"And you are for it now? What changed your mind, Ron?"

"I've always been for it, Sarah! I've been working on Gil. Do you think I've just been sitting on my hands? These things take time! Gil has never run a story like this. He thinks it could ruin Love."

"He's worried about whether he should ruin a man who tried to have his ex-lover killed?"

"Well, the Love camp has been saying that wasn't authorized. Sarah, there's going to be a meeting in Gil's office at eleven. I want you to be there. But I don't want you to say anything unless Gil asks you a question, is that clear?"

"Okay, Ron, but—"

"Because this is going to be very tricky, Sarah. It involves a serious departure from policy, and I don't want Gil to be upset by anything about you. Otherwise he might say we should give the story to Greg."

"It's *my* story! *I* got it!"

"I know, I know, Sarah, and I want you to write it. But you have to make a good impression in there with Gil. Wear something sensible. Have you got a nice summer suit?"

"No."

"Well, wear that yellow dress. It's not bad. And *don't* wear your sandals. Why don't you get rid of those sandals, Sarah?"

"I don't have any other summer shoes, unless you want me to wear sneakers."

"So buy some shoes! I want you to look reliable, Sarah. This whole thing is riding on you!"

"On my shoes?"

"I know what I'm talking about, Sarah. Now, remember what I said. Only answer questions from Gil. And be on time. The meeting starts at eleven."

"Okay, Ron."

I shouldn't be telling you this, but I did buy a pair of shoes to wear to that meeting. Ron said they were "just right," but he seemed awfully nervous. He had just found out that Gil had invited Willie Crespi to take part in the meeting, and he hadn't invited Willie himself. Greg whispered to me as we went in, "Watch out for Mike Weathervane." I didn't know who Mike Weathervane was, but I recognized a face from National's copy desk when we were seated, and I figured that must be Mike. Greg had called him "a tight-ass, but smart."

It was sort of like a court. Gil was sitting down at the end of a long table, and on one side were Dixby, Iggy Meyers, and Mike Weathervane. On our side were Ron, Greg and me, and then Willie. But Willie sat up close to Gil, as if he was trying to provide a reassuring presence for him, not for Ron.

Dixby took a chair diagonally opposite Ron and immediately facing me. He was in a mood to glare—at me, steadily and obviously. Iggy winked at me. I winked back and then worried that Gil might have seen me.

Gil cleared his throat, closed his eyes, and put his hands together under his chin.

"Gentlemen," he said, "and, ah, Sarah, we have a solemn and awesome responsibility here, deciding whether to—which we have never done in the past—because there were many times when we could have. J. Edgar Hoover, Kennedy's peccadilloes—we knew about those when he was in the White House. And of course, Johnson's whole off-camera character, and then the Martin Luther King episode, although that—well, in retrospect, I am glad we didn't, but it still gives me pause to think that he was a spiritual leader. Still, it wouldn't have been proper for us to print that sort of thing, especially when it came from a wiretap of dubious legality. And we never have, actually, gone into the sexual history of a man running for the highest office before an election, so we must decide that—or rather whether—we must decide whether this is a different case, and if so, in what way. Now, the facts as I understand them are this: George Love had a homosexual affair when he was a young man in Vietnam—"

"Not so young," said Ron. "He was twenty-five."

"Well, I think that's young. Twenty-five," said Gil. "Am I wrong?"

"Absolutely not, Gil!" said Willie. "Absolutely not!"

"I know at that age I was guilty of hotheadedness on many occasions," Gil went on. "All right. We've established that he was young when he had the affair. He was probably also in a disturbed state of mind. A young officer in charge of a search and destroy unit. We can all remember how dangerous the search and destroy work was. Yes, and when men are frightened—or women—they will turn to anyone for comfort. How many of us can say what we might have done, or indeed, how many of us have, in moments of extreme danger, turned to the nearest at hand? I'm not asking for a show of hands, gentlemen, but I do want us all to search our souls. Those who cast— Well, George Love turned to one of the young soldiers in his unit. They had an affair. The affair terminated at the end of their

**319**

tours of duty, approximately. The two men saw each other in New York for two weeks, and that was it. George Love went back to New Mexico. The other man stayed in New York.

"The two men wrote to each other, however. . . ."

I could feel Ron tapping his foot impatiently under the table. Gil went on and on and on. My mind strayed. I wondered where Renato was. I felt a kick from my right side. My eyes met Greg's, and then he looked down, signaling me to do the same. He had a copy of *The Evil Eye* casually open to its Bits and Pieces column on the table in front of him. While turning his gaze attentively toward Gil, he very faintly tapped an item with his index finger. I read it.

"Is *The Newspaper*'s Gil Foley going off his rocker?" it began. "A little bird on 48th Street says the usually uncommunicative editor recently invited Sarah Makepeace into his office for a little chat, during which he downed three stiff drinks and confided to Ms. Makepeace that he sometimes feels 'lonelier than God.'"

". . . and I would like to hear from Sarah on this," Gil was saying, "but my understanding is that she was introduced to Renato, also known as Arthur Weinstein, by her psychiatrist, and—"

"Not mine; his," I said.

Ron kicked my left leg.

"Excuse me?" Gil said.

"It's not important," I said.

"You're not feeling very *communicative* today, are you, Sarah?" Mike said pointedly.

"I was just trying to explain that the man who introduced me to Renato was not my psychiatrist. He was *his* psychiatrist. That is, Renato had gone to see him once," I said, feeling myself grow red.

"And, ah, why did this psychiatrist arrange for, ah, Renato to meet you?" Gil asked me. "Does he support Ford?"

"I don't think so," I said. "He belongs to the VID."

"The VID?" said Gil.

"The Village Independent Democrats," said Dixby. "Didn't they endorse Muskie?"

"I think we're all familiar with the facts, Gil," Ron said.

"I'm not sure," said Dixby. "I'd like to hear more about the fellow who made the introduction to Sarah, the one she says isn't *her* psychiatrist."

"I don't think he would want his name used," I said. "But I've known him for years. He married my college roommate."

"Ah," said Gil. "So it was the close connection."

"But I still don't understand why he arranged for this patient of

**320**

his to meet Sarah. It is against the canons of ethics for a doctor to do that to a patient, introduce him to a newspaper reporter," said Dixby, keeping his eyes fixed on me.

"He had Renato's consent," I said. "If you mean you want to know his personal motive, I guess it was just like what anyone's would be. He said he didn't think a man like Love should be President, because of what—"

"So he *was* a Ford supporter!" said Dixby.

"Oh, for god's sake, Dixby, you heard her tell you he was a reform Democrat!" Greg said sharply. "What are you trying to imply? That Sarah's been duped in some kind of dirty tricks scheme? You think Gerry Ford hired somebody to come shoot up our lobby?"

"If we are gonna ruin George Love's chances for the presidency, Greg, if we are gonna ruin his lahfe, Ah thenk the least we can do is consider every angle of this storee before we print it!" Dixby said. His accent seemed to grow more thickly regional as his blood rose. "And Ah certainly thenk we ought to consider the motivation of every source. And yes, Ah thenk it's possible Sarah has been duped. You thenk running for the pres'dency is nahce and straightforward? How long you been coverin' politics, boy?"

"As long as you've been kissing ass with the right people, Willard, and that's a long time!" said Greg.

"Gentlemen! Gentlemen! We must try to keep personality disputes out of this," said Gil. "This matter is too important for petty rivalries, and I *must* ask you to rise above them today. Now, you have both raised important questions about experience, judgment, motives, and it *is* important for us to ask whether we have indeed all been duped. But the issue we must decide, the central issue we must deal with and upon which *I* must decide this, is whether a presidential candidate's sexual history is a proper subject for this newspaper. Now, I would say no if there were not any special, ah, extenuating factors, so to speak. But this case is not a simple one, since we do not have a simple cover-up of the past. We have, in addition, a case of—well, I don't know what to call it. Reverse blackmail? Extortion? Does this added element make the story doable?"

"Well, we're not clear about the added element, Gil," said Dixby. "Love's people are denying—"

"You told the world about Betty Ford's mastectomy," said Greg.

"That's right!" said Ron. "I don't see how a breast is any less private—"

"Or any more tasteful," said Greg.

"Honestly!" Iggy burst forth. "There's no relation whatsoever between a mastectomy and a homosexual affair. What's shameful about a mastectomy?"

"I'm glad you asked that question, Iggy," said Gil, "because I'd like to ask what's shameful about a homosexual affair. Haven't the gay rights people, the re*spon*sible gay rights people, been trying to tell us—"

"Well, of course, Gil, we can all agree on that!" said Ron. There's absolutely nothing shameful about a homosexual affair! On the contrary. It's something to be proud of. I mean, if you're a homosexual—"

"Oh, cut the sheeit, Ron!" said Dixby. "A week ago you were arguing that if this leaked out, it would ruin Love's careeuh! And Betty Ford's mastectomy is a horse of a completely different coluh. She told us about that herseyelf! An' if you remember, we *did* thenk a mastectomy was shameful and in bayad taste. If you recollect, you were one of the ones who argued that we should play it down. You said it was a tacky play for the public's sympathy. Hell, Ron, you cain't juss sit there an' tell me any candidate in his right mind gets hit with a homosexshul history theng is gonna stand up an' say he's *praowd* of it!"

"Why not? One of Lindsay's health commissioners did that," said Ron.

"You know goddamn well if Love gets hit with this theng he's gonna go rahght down the *tube!*" said Dixby, pounding his fist on the table.

"Gay rights is very strong in the party," said Greg. "And they backed Love. Besides, we really don't know how many voters are secretly gay."

"Since when is being gay an issue?" said Iggy. "People don't vote for you *if* you're gay or straight. They vote on the issues now. But we're way off the point. The point is—"

"That's a good point," said Mike Weathervane. "Does anybody know how Love stands on gay rights?"

"He made strong statements in favor of gay rights in San Francisco and New York," Greg said. "He made strong statements *against* in Florida, Alabama, and Utah."

"That's right," said Iggy. "He's been all over the map on the issue."

"Well," said Gil. "I don't think anyone disputes what Willard said, that this story would ruin George Love's political career."

"Yes, but our obligation is to the voters, isn't it?" said Greg.

"I'm just wondering how good this will be for New York," Willie said. All eyes turned to him. "I mean, New York already has an image as a homosexuals' town."

"But the affair didn't take place in New York, Willie," I said. "It broke up here. You might as well worry what the story will do to the image of the Vietnam War."

Ron kicked me again.

"I'm sorry, Willie. I don't see your point," said Gil.

"I was thinking of the federal loan negotiations," Willie said. "Every time Simon has to go to Congress, all the New York haters in the country write to their congressmen calling New York a haven for homosexuals and welfare cheats."

"Who told you that?" Greg asked him.

"Well, it doesn't matter!" Ron said hastily. "I certainly don't think parochial considerations ought to come into this."

"Huh!" uttered Dixby.

"We have to ask ourselves what's best for the country," said Ron.

"Indeed, what is best for the free world," said Gil. "It is not inconceivable that the Communists could exploit this secret—if we keep it secret."

"Exactly!" said Ron. "There's no telling what Love will do to keep this story quiet! Look at what he's done already!"

"You weren't so awful fired up about what Love has supposedly done—and Ah'm not sure he's done anything—but you weren't so fired up abeyout this last week, Ron," said Dixby. "Or don'choo remember that one week ago you said it would be yellow journalism to put Love's name into that shootin' piece, since the guy had already been fired by the campaign? You said he was a free-lance operator, Ron. Or don'choo remember?"

"We've all had time to think about it," Ron said.

"Is this true?" Gil asked Ron. "The gunman had been fired *before* he came here?"

"Well, that's only what the Love people say," said Ron.

"He said it to Renato," I said, "right before Renato came down here. But that doesn't make any difference, does it? The tape—"

Greg and Ron both kicked me.

"Renato was here? In the building? At the time of the shooting?" Gil asked. "Why wasn't I told?"

"Apparently he was here," Ron said, "if Sarah says she saw him—"

"Sarah, what happened?" Gil asked me. "Why wasn't he mentioned in the story?"

"Well, Gil, that's just the thing," Ron said, as his face took on the most appealingly boyish look of honest embarrassment. "If we had put Renato into the story, we would have had to explain the background. We would have had to go into the whole thing, and I believe you were not at the front page meeting that day, and Willard and I decided together, didn't we, Willard, that in your absence we couldn't see making the break with tradition, because there was very much the chance that this man Josh What's-his-name was a free-lancer, or that he had been fired because of his violent nature. We just couldn't blame Love for his conduct at that point. And we couldn't open the whole can of worms, the homosexual history. And I must admit, I do like Love. I have biases. I think we all like Love, and we like him better than Ford. But if it's between a man I don't like so much and a man who could be vulnerable to KGB blackmail, then I'm afraid—because I've had time to think about this—I'm afraid we'll have to print this story. I've seen Renato. I've been in touch with him since last week. You asked me what changed my mind, Willard. Well, Renato did. He has been through hell!"

Ron's tone was so sincere, we could see it having a very palpable effect on Gil.

"Oh, that KGB blackmail stuff is sheer fantasy," said Mike. "They don't play that way."

"How do you know?" I asked.

"Mike used to cover the CIA," said Iggy.

"Blackmail is a thing of the past," said Mike. "Electronic eavesdropping is too easy now. I'm sure they already know about this story, and I'm sure the CIA knows too. That could well have been an agent putting the heat on Renato."

"Whose?" I asked.

"Why, ours, of course!" Mike said. "The agency would want to know what he would do under pressure. Then they would know how to protect Love if he got elected."

"Who's indulging in fantasy now?" Greg asked. "Come on, Mike! Love's people hired Josh Spitzer!"

"Yes, but they maintain he wasn't meant to do what he was *doin'*," said Dixby.

"They have to say that," said Greg. "Look what Nixon said about the Plumbers."

"Ron believed 'em last week," said Dixby. "An' I don't thenk it was Renato who changed his mahnd. Ah thenk it was Iggy's storee. Fact, Ah know it was Iggy's storee. 'Cause Ron promised the Love people he'd suppress Renato's storee if they gave Greg Swenson here the first exclusive! That's the whole reason we're in here, Gil!"

"I would *never* make such a promise!" Ron declared haughtily.

"You take that back, Willard! I demand you take it back! I would *never* trade with the pages of this newspaper!"

"Aw, come on, Ron!" said Dixby.

"Then what did change your mind, Ron?" asked Mike.

"I *told* you! Renato did! He has been terrorized for weeks! Love's people were trying to get the letter back. They knew what they were doing! They can't pretend they didn't! They would have killed him to get that letter back!"

"Perhaps we all ought to talk to Renato," said Gil. "Do you think you could get him in here?"

"Right now?" Ron asked.

"Why not?" said Gil. "You said he was staying at the Pierre, didn't you? Could you give him a call and tell him to take a cab over?"

"Not right now," Ron said.

"He's not there?" Gil asked. "Isn't it dangerous for him to go out?"

"He wasn't our prisoner," said Greg. "We couldn't force him to stay in."

"What do you mean, he wasn't?" said Gil. "You mean he's left the Pierre?"

"Yes," said Greg.

"And where has he gone?" asked Gil.

"We don't know," said Greg.

"Oh, I'm sure he'll be in touch with us today," said Ron. "He's been in touch with us nearly every day."

"How long has he been gone?" asked Gil.

"Since yesterday," said Greg.

"Ron," said Gil.

"It doesn't matter, Gil," Ron said. "We have the tape and the letter and Sarah's notes."

"Anybody can write a letter. Anybody can make a tape," said Dixby.

"A man who doesn't want to be identified," said Gil. "I don't like it, Ron. What if he should retract?"

"Well, there's always the gunman," said Greg. "If we can get hold of him."

"You mean you haven't talked to him yet?" Gil asked.

"He's disappeared too," said Greg. "He slipped out of Bellevue last week."

"This is beginning to sound quite doubtful," said Gil.

"But we have the letter and the tape!" Ron said.

"I cannot see going to press with a story of this importance when our main source has disappeared," said Gil. "I cannot see us doing that, breaking every precedent, going against the wishes of the Kleinfreude family, ruining an otherwise fine young politician's career with a story that is not properly sourced."

"You've talked to the publisher about this?" Ron said. "I thought you weren't going to do that, Gil, until we had discussed it here."

"Bill told me they were planning to endorse Love on Sunday."

"On Sunday!" said Ron. "Well, that makes— I'm glad you told us that, Gil. And when you mentioned this story to Bill, what did he say?"

"Well, he said of course it was up to us, Ron, but he wants us to be very, very certain. I don't think he would like it to run. But you know how he is. He won't interfere," Gil said.

"Oh, well, then!" said Ron.

"Mr. Foley," I said, "I believe Renato."

Ron kicked me very hard.

"My dear," said Gil, "you have had very little experience. Even I find it difficult after all these years to detect the truth. Now, the question is, gentlemen, do we believe, are we convinced—because the publisher will ultimately hold us accountable for this—are we convinced that Gerald Ford is presidential material?"

"But he's already President!" I said.

"Sarah, be quiet!" Ron said.

"Well, Ah, for one, will not support goin' against the publisher's man with a story which to mah mahnd has been questionable from the very beginning," Dixby said. "It becomes even more questionable with the disappearance of the major source. And there is another very serious reason to hold back on this story. Ah doubt the credibility of our reporter, and if Ah doubt it, you can bet that Love's people would tear it to ribbons."

"What are you trying to do, Willard, say that because she is new, Sarah isn't credible?" Greg asked. "Don't you like having your Georgetown glamour boys scooped by a girl from *The Evil Eye?*"

"Ah was not going to go into this," Dixby said. "But it looks as though Ah'll have to. Sarah's credibility would be zilch just as soon as that story hit the newsstands, because she gave false credentials to this newspaper. She never was on the Harvard *Crimson*. She never was on the university restructuring committee. She never was on the mayor's task force on crime. How can we run a story like this under the by-line of a reporter who has lied to us?"

"That's enough, Willard," said Gil, and then, blinking his eyes very fast, he said to me, "Is it true you never worked on the *Crimson*, Sarah?"

326

Everyone looked at me.

"Well?" said Gil.

"It's true. I wasn't, but I never—"

"Sarah!" said Ron. "I'm shocked!"

"But, Ron, you know I—" I started to say. Ron grabbed my knee under the table and at the same time interrupted.

"Shocked, I tell you, absolutely shocked. Well, this puts a whole new light on it. Yes, it certainly changes the picture. Sarah, I will have to deal with you. Let's go."

"Yes," said Gil, white-faced. "You two will have to have a serious talk. Well, that settles it for me, gentlemen. Unless anyone has anything to add."

No one did.


# XLVIII


In spite of everything I knew about Ron, I had not expected him to betray me like that in front of his archenemy. To make me look bad was really to make himself look bad too, since I was his protégée, his hand-picked representative of—what did I represent? The world below Fourteenth Street? Permissiveness? Hidden (deeply) talent? Youth's capacity for being co-opted by money and promises of power and fame? Or the boss's right to hire anyone he pleased for reasons known only to him? Whatever I stood for, when its currency went down, so did Ron's credit for being a good judge of it. Or so I had thought until the moment he said, "Sarah! I'm shocked!" He shocked *me* so much, I couldn't act fast enough. And the moment was over before I had fully taken in what had happened. I was still taking it in as the meeting broke up, and I thought surely Ron must have a plan, a cunning but ultimately right strategy which would explain his abominable behavior. Probably he had been working a feint to throw Dixby off the track and make him think the Love-Renato story was not going to run. Yes, that was it! Ron *did* know where Renato was! He just didn't want Dixby to know.

I followed him into his little office expecting that as soon as the door closed he would tell me what was going on and how I could help the scheme along. What a surprise I got then! Instead of his explaining anything to me, he demanded that I explain to him why I had *misled* him into believing that I had worked on the *Crimson*. I couldn't believe my ears. For a split second I thought maybe he feared his office was bugged. "But, Ron, surely you remember—" was as far as I got before he cut me off. "But, Ron—" I tried again. He cut me off again. He looked livid. He told me that I was a "disgrace to the profession," that I had "some nerve walking in here," that he couldn't work with someone "who doesn't play it straight," and then he showed me the door, and he kept yelling at my retreating back so that at least half the people in the newsroom heard him repeat his "misled me" line.

I thought I had been fired. I walked out and went straight to the Poor Mouth, where I accepted several drinks from a sympathetic trio of unemployed poets. Then I went home to telephone my parents. I have a dim memory of the conversation, but I must have told them the whole story, for they demonstrated a familiarity with the details on later occasions. I think my father told me he would take out a mortgage on the house to help me pay Sy Shimmer and the credit union.

But it turned out there was a problem with firing a *Newspaper* employee who owed the credit union more than a thousand dollars. Freddie informed me of this the following morning. His phone call awakened me into the worst hangover of my young life. My eyes hurt when I moved them in any direction. I felt simultaneously hungry and nauseous. I had intimations that I was on the brink of a profound discovery, as if I might be about to settle the question of the existence or nonexistence of God. Freddie said I was to return to the test kitchen.

I did not know it that morning, but I was entering into one of the more pleasant periods of my life, an extended hiatus of the sort that befell me between the date of my college acceptance and the date of high school graduation, a honeyed time when a weekly contingent of feckless hedonists, I among them, had wildly elected to take the bus into New York instead of going to school. We had scarcely had time on those criminal ventures to do more than browse the pornography shops before we were compelled to rush for the homebound bus, and we had less money than time, but the traveling so far in a forbidden direction was pleasure enough for us, that and being immune to punishment.

How tame those trips seem to me now! We didn't even take liquor or pot with us. But wickedness, like beauty, is in the eye of the beholder. If your experience of it is narrow, so is your taste for it. Still, I realized before reaching college that my experience with deviance was way below the norm. And my freshman year at Radcliffe was strewn with painful moments when my deficiency was revealed to me in front of others. And if the truth be told, even in my hometown I had been regarded as a dullish grind of an adolescent, hence the importance of the trips to New York, status-wise. But I started with ground zero status in college, pitted as I was against the sophisticates of Hunter College and the Dalton School, who had grown up in the pornography capital of America. They came to Radcliffe with diaphragms supplied to them by the family physician, and they had the telephone number of a Cuban doctor in Miami who was the diaphragm's backup. They labeled me both a grind and a hick. One night during the winter exam period of freshman year, Ellie, who was (relative to me then) among the most terrifying of Hunter High graduates, had managed to pry me from the *Norton Anthology of English Literature* by showing a warm interest in my love life. A girlish heart-to-heart chat began, but it soon became a monologue punctuated by exclamations from the listener such as, "Don't worry about him, Sarah!" "Oh, you poor thing!" "I know the feeling!" and "No one does the first time." The more I talked, the more I exposed myself, but Ellie seemed so sympathetic and I so badly needed a confidante that I could not stop. The talking seemed to carry its own momentum. Even I did not know what I would say next, and suddenly I was telling a story I should never have told anyone. Ellie's face began to look oddly strained. She put her hand to her mouth. She snorted through her nose. Just as I reached the terrible ending of this tale, she went "Ha ha!" instead of "You poor thing!" and I realized my error. Too late. Ellie let out a tremendous guffaw and, to my eternal chagrin, yelled down the dormitory hallway, "Oh, my god, Sarah Makepeace, you didn't really think that meant you were actually supposed to blow on it!"

With considerable hindsight, it is easy to conclude that there was a cause-and-effect relationship between my fear ever after that I would be taken for a bumpkin and my eventual fascination for characters like Jesus and Fredo and Ron and Kevin, all of whom had considerable sophistication derived from their courage to do wrong. How far into doing wrong I wanted to go myself I wasn't certain, but I sure as hell wanted the sophistication. It was I who came to the city culturally deprived. I think I subliminally knew this and was all along searching for urban cads who could teach me how to survive better than my honest, forthright, morally uncompromising father ever could. Maybe I disapproved of the cads, maybe not. But I yearned for their gifts for getting what they wanted out of life, which seemed ineluctably linked to their ability to defy what was left of morality, their ability, especially, to lie.

This was what I came to recognize when the dust settled in my head after a few days, and I was able to admit to myself that I had not challenged Ron's lie at the moment of his betrayal because I had not wanted to expose him. To expose him when he lied *against* me in front of Gil would risk ruining his credibility when he lied *for* me. The likelihood that he ever would lie for me again was very slim, but it was there. And it seemed to me that I had nothing to gain from trying to set the record straight. I couldn't be fired, so why ruin Ron just to get myself restored to the Metropolitan staff? How would I fare, after all, working for an honest boss?

I did not delve very deeply into this question.

It was not, strictly speaking, true that *The Newspaper* couldn't fire me. *The Newspaper* could fire anyone it chose to, but before the employee could be got rid of forever, he was allowed to demand a hearing. In the case of an employee heavily in debt to the credit union, extensive hearings were called for. I would have been given a chance to cross-examine the bosses at length, should the procedure have been set in motion. Freddie said it had never yet been set in motion.

Vinnie told me that managers on a higher level than Ron were wary of the hearing process because the final ruling, to be made by an ostensibly impartial arbitration panel, would be binding on the company as a general policy. Vinnie said the real reason *The Newspaper* would not fire me, then, was the possibility that the outcome of a dismissal hearing might further restrict its ability to fire people like me.

I could relax. I didn't have to do anything. I probably could have stayed home every day except payday, but I wasn't sure about that, so I still came to the test kitchen every morning. Once there, however, I lost all sense of responsibility. I settled into an old easy chair and commenced to read. Being stuck on the career ladder where I couldn't move up or down (there was no lower rung) had done wonders for my appetite for reading. Vinnie could not get me to answer him. I did not hear him. Sometimes I looked up to see him watching me, but I ignored this and looked back down at the page.

One day I made the mistake of bringing in a funny book, though, and my chortling annoyed Vinnie. The book was *Pnin*, by Vladimir Nabokov, the story of the odd Russian émigré who kept making mistakes with words and social customs. After about the fourteenth chortle, Vinnie said:

"What's so goddamned funny?"

330

"You wouldn't appreciate the joke, Vinnie, unless you knew what came before it in the story."

"Then read me the book," he said.

"You mean begin at the beginning?"

"Where else, pray tell?"

And thus it became our system that he should do all the cooking while I should read to him, and we were both very happy.

I don't mean that we always read funny books all day long. I mean we forgot ourselves like children. I brought in many serious books. Vinnie liked them because they were longer than the comic ones, and he couldn't bear to have a story end. Dickens was eminently suitable, but we did eventually tire of him. Then Vinnie said he had a taste for Flaubert (like Sy Shimmer, who, incidentally, had recently been asked to peruse a grand jury subpoena). Neither one of us had read *A Sentimental Education*, and we were not prepared for the power that Flaubert would have, after Dickens, to make us believe in the reality of his world. Vinnie got so caught up in the story that when he had to interrupt it for a trip to the New Orleans Shrimp Specialists Convention, he pined for it, and he called me each evening from his motel room and insisted I read him a couple of chapters over the phone. So prolonged was the reading that the story of Frédéric's unrequited love for the beautiful, virtuous Madame Arnoux worked itself very thoroughly into our emotions. By the next to last chapter, where Frédéric and Madame Arnoux finally declare their love for one another, we had become quivering Jell-O in Mr. Flaubert's hands. The moment when the exquisite black-haired woman, the object of Frédérick's lifelong unfulfilled passion, about to give herself to him at last, took off her hat to reveal her gorgeous tresses gone all white, Vinnie and I gasped together, and then the tears began to flow. I had to keep wiping mine away to be able to read on. Vinnie let his drop freely.

"'Sometimes your words come back to me like a distant echo, like the sound of a bell carried by the wind; and when I read about love in a book, I feel that you are there beside me,'" I read in a scarcely audible voice. My eyes filled up and overflowed before I could read Frédéric's reply.

"Hello!" came a sudden hearty greeting in our doorway. "Now this, boys and girls, is our test kitchen, where the famous food writer Vincent Akelroyd tests out his recipes. Have you seen that by-line? *A,k,e,l,r,o,y,d*. And that's Mr. Akelroyd himself right there. Hello, Mr. Akelroyd! This is the fifth grade class from P.S.41."

"Hello, Mr. Akelroyd!" said one of the fifth graders, looking at

**331**

him from the hallway. The beefy *Newspaper* tour guide seemed to be hesitating, holding the class in check. Vinnie had not responded. Vinnie was blinded by tears. He stood absolutely still except for a slight tremor in his shoulders, his features contorted with sorrow for all mortality.

"He's crying!" said one of the children, and several pressed through the door and leaned their heads around each other to see Vinnie.

"Oh, no, no! Don't be silly!" said the guide, trying to shoo them back outside. "Come along," he said. "These people are busy."

"Crying!" "Crying!" said one child after another. The guide scrambled around, trying to collect them. They kept popping out of his grasp like baby chickens popping out from under a hen's wing. "Crying!" they said. "Look! Why's he crying?"

"Don't be silly!" the guide scolded. "Come along now. We're going to look at the *presses!*"

He finally swept them all out the door. I heard one of the children asking again, "Why's he crying?" from the direction of the elevators, and the guide's voice came back dimly: "Onions, of course!"

That incident occurred about three days after George Foster Love was inaugurated. By the end of January, everyone in the newsroom had heard that Vinnie was seen crying into his mixing bowl and that I had been seen sniffling in sympathy. Vinnie became popular for the first time. His former colleagues started asking him to lunch.

I was very pleased, because I had been swamped with requests to have lunch with our former colleagues ever since the day after the meeting in Gil's office. I did not like to leave Vinnie in the lurch. His new popularity made everything perfect.

My popularity derived in part from the same source as his: I was down on that bottom rung and made everyone at *The Newspaper* feel superior. But I had one added attraction. I knew about the Democratic nominee's (then President-elect's, then President's) homosexual past.

Everybody who took me to lunch wanted to know about it. Every single one. I had some pretty classy luncheon companions. Newbold Hardscrabble of the Moscow bureau, a really distinguished foreign correspondent who had won the Pulitzer three times, took me to Lutèce to ask me about it. Gunther Effing, the Paris bureau chief, chose La Côte Basque, sent back three bottles of wine and pronounced the restaurant "shabby" before very confidentially trying to get me to tell him the tale (*"Entre nous,* of course"). I prolonged the process with him for my own reasons. But with the three men from the London Bureau who took me out to lunch together, I was quite brisk and to the point. They had chosen the Poor Mouth for its Fleet Street informality. ("The girls you pick up here are after your body," said Sylvester Ponsonby-ffrench, the risibly dandyish swing man of the bureau.) A. J. Buttonweiser, the correspondent who had covered South America for twenty years before he was sent to Tokyo, took me to Sardi's, where he anxiously looked over his shoulder for editors throughout the lunch. He apologized, saying all those years in police states had made him leery of being seen with anyone who had the goods on the President.

The entire Washington bureau looked me up one by one, and I became familiar with their blood feuds, compared to which the contest between Ron and Dixby sounded like child's play. I was approached, too, by a goodly number of people on the City staff. Even copy editors wanted to dine with me, and tactfully refrained from mentioning any of our past differences. I met reporters I had never seen before, though we had worked in the same newsroom.

Reporters from other papers called me too. I put all but the single young men off, and in the end, I did not tell any outsiders except Miltie Clendenon and Dick McCarthy that the rumor they had heard was true. Miltie and Dick both swore they were going to get the story out, but neither one did.

Love, meanwhile, began enjoying his honeymoon with the public. The entire nation saw him trying out his new cross-country skis on the White House lawn after the inaugural parade. His wife was with him, skiing on one ski. The Love children had sung the national anthem after the swearing in, and then John Denver had led the grandstand in a rousing chorus of "All You Need Is Love."

The new administration started off with high hopes. The Congress seemed to be in a mood to tackle the energy problem, and Love kept saying that the "new American revolution" would begin momentarily. But when reporters gently asked him what he had in mind to replace oil, he accused them of "pointless negativism."

The press turned a little against him. The Congress didn't come up with anything startling on the energy front. Love didn't, either.

I was not following his career closely, though, because I had got bored with reading newspapers. I only became aware that Love's support was eroding when my father started calling me again. Dad said Love had "sold out to the oil companies" and had some plan to eliminate all taxes on American oil. I didn't listen alertly. I heard Dad say something about how it was like "feeding a wolf more sheep so he can have the energy to go look for more sheep to eat."

**333**

Dad also told me about Love's plan for developing compact nuclear weapons. That wasn't going down so well with his old friends "the Greenies." Dad said the President had had the nerve to push these things with Jerry Brown's slogan "Small Is Better."

Then Love announced he would be cutting out "government waste." I heard that one night on the television news. He said he would start with the elimination of wasteful welfare payments, which he proposed to do with a new "Disability IQ test." The idea was that there were enough service jobs available to give employment to anyone with half a brain, and a simple IQ test would establish who had half a brain. Anyone with less would be eligible for welfare.

Dad later told me this plan got snagged in Congress because the nation's leaders quarreled irreconcilably over what ought to be the proper level for a "disability IQ."

Love was going down in the popularity polls three months after he took office. By this time his liberal supporters were bitterly critical of him, and they had already begun to talk of a "Dump Love" campaign. My father was in this group, and he wanted me to find Renato for them.

The next time Kevin called me, I told him the Renato story. He said maybe I should report Renato as a Missing Person. So I did—without telling Ron, of course. But it came to nothing. A detective from the Sixth Precinct called me about two weeks after I had filled out the form. He said he had talked to Renato's friends and was satisfied that he had moved out of town.

"They think he's gone to San Francisco," he said. He told me he was closing the file.

As for Kevin and myself, that had turned into a cordial estrangement. It was his doing. He stayed away from work for ages with his foot wound and then, after the Department gave him a desk job, he told me he was trying to make a go of it with Helen again. Yet he kept calling me every three or four weeks, as though he needed to know I was still there. But he did not confide in me anymore. And he didn't ask about other men.

I don't think I would have told him the truth. I had gone through a startling number of men since he had last seen me. I had so many to choose from with all the luncheon dates. Once I tried and rejected three in one week. Gunther Effing I tested out after our lunch at La Côte Basque. He was an exquisite blond with aristocratic features. He had survived a German concentration camp because of his Nordic beauty, and the story of his adoption by a GI

334

unit (*Mein Buddies*) had been sold in paperback to over one million readers. It was a story that made him irresistible to women, he told me. I was flattered when he said he'd never forget me, because he hinted that he had made love to hundreds of women. I said I would never forget him, either, and I meant it. He had unwittingly proved to me that I was not a slave to the gun.

I thought it unwise to take up with *Newspaper* reporters who lived in the city, so after Gunther, the men I chose came from the Poor Mouth or from a small pool of admirers I had ignored during the affair with Kevin. None of them could do what Kevin could do, not even Gunther, but one orgasm will suffice in most instances. And actually, I was glad to find that no one could replace Kevin. It made me feel faithful to him.

I took up other pleasures that winter and spring. I had my hair done. I joined a health club. I practiced dwelling on my strengths (as recommended in a book called *Zen Techniques of Self-Expansion*) whenever I was alone. I learned about wines so that I could always order the best ones when being taken out to lunch. I went to the racetrack with Eddie Schwartz. I went to the opera with Vinnie. I wandered through SoHo on Saturday afternoons with Ellie, flirting with strangers and occasionally popping into art galleries. I bought a cheap camera and took pictures of people in the Poor Mouth, who then usually bought me drinks.

It was a very happy time, and when spring came, I felt even happier. Spring came very suddenly, boom, after a harsh winter. One day the air was bitter cold. The next day it was balmy and soft and full of expectation, and everyone was walking around smiling.

I felt so good that day that I decided to leave a note in Jenny's box offering my support and signature for the Feminist Faction lawsuit. A couple of days later, she left this note for me:

> Sarah, that's great news! Come to our next meeting, May 1, in the back of the conference room, 1:30 P.M. Let's have lunch sometime soon to celebrate your conversion.
>
> On the lawsuit, I spoke to our lawyers. They think you probably aren't needed for the case. Management's getting nasty, and the arrest for corrupting the morals of minors could hurt us if they put you on the stand. But it was great of you to offer. That took guts. Yours in the struggle, Jenny.

I was a little hurt at first, but then I told myself she was being very kind, considering how long I had ignored her cause. I *would* make a bad witness for the lawsuit. There was no denying it.

**335**

I decided to call Jenny and propose that lunch date before she could call me. I got her at her desk right away, and she was very apologetic about the lawyers rejecting me.

"You know lawyers," she said.

We made a date for the following Tuesday, and as I hung up the phone and looked over at Vinnie, happily kneading Anadama bread on the test kitchen pastry board, I had a fine sensation of completion, and an inner voice said, "There now," as though I had finished a psychic assignment, paid my last outstanding dues, and nothing more could go wrong.

# XLIX

No sooner had I embraced that foolish filament of faith than our little paradise was invaded by—well, let me tell you how it happened.

I had been reading from *One Hundred Years of Solitude,* our latest accomplice in the conspiracy against boredom. That morning I had started with the chapter beginning: "Colonel Gerineldo Márquez was the first to perceive the emptiness of the war," and I had been reading at a great pace, for the strange vertiginous book had a hypnotic effect on me, and I did not seem to grow tired reading it. Vinnie loved it too, but he had been waiting for a good place to interrupt me to ask if I'd seen the garlic press, and he was growing a little impatient, as I never paused and never seemed to come to the end of a paragraph, so finally, as I was in the middle of the passage about Aureliano Segundo's supernatural good luck, reading, "The more he opened the champagne to soak his friends, the more wildly his animals gave birth and the more he was convinced that his lucky star—"

"Sarah!" Vinnie said. "Stop a minute. Where's the garlic press?"

"How should I know, Vinnie? I haven't touched it."

"Well, can you remember seeing me with it?"

"No, Vinnie! You interrupted in the middle of a sentence!"

"Okay. Start again."

It was because of this interruption that I did not pay attention when Vinnie cleared his throat or when he fidgeted and banged against a cupboard door. The noises made me read louder and with angry force, and I do not know how much the figure in the doorway heard (while holding a finger to his lips to stop Vinnie from speaking). I had my back to the door. I read:

"'The more he opened champagne to soak his friends, the more wildly his animals gave birth and the more he was convinced that his lucky star was not a matter of his conduct but an influence of Petra Cotes, his concubine, whose love had the virtue of exasperating nature. So convinced was he that this was the origin of his fortune that he never kept Petra Cotes far away from his breeding grounds and even when he married and had children he continued living with her with the consent of Fernanda. Solid, monumental like his grandfathers, but with a joie de vivre and an irresistible good humor that they did not have, Aureliano Segundo scarcely had time to look after his animals. All he had to do was to take Petra Cotes to his breeding grounds and have her ride across his land in order to have every animal marked with his brand succumb to the irremediable plague of proliferation.

"'Like all good things that occurred in his long life, that tremendous fortune had its origins in—'"

*Whaaaaangawhaangawangawangawopwopwopwangawop*, went the huge pasta pan that Vinnie in desperate chivalry had nudged off the counter.

"What the fuck made you do that?" I said before he could stop me.

"I did," said someone, stepping through the doorway. "He was trying to warn you, I'm sure. I'm Bill Kleinfreude."

"Oh, Mr. Kleinfreude!" I said, jumping out of the chair. "Oh, hello!"

"Cozy little setup you've got here," he said, smiling inscrutably.

"Here, Vinnie, let me help you now," I said, stepping around behind the counter and bending over to hide my flushed face.

"Have a seat, why don't you, Mr. Kleinfreude," said Vinnie. "Would you like to watch us at work? We're going to make a simple pesto sauce this morning. It's one of your mother's favorites. Why don't you take it home to her!"

"It is?" said the publisher. "Well, you probably know more about her culinary tastes than I do by now. I hope she doesn't bother you too much. She's apt to bother cooks. But thanks for the kind offer. Actually, I came here to borrow your assistant for a little while. Where's she gone?"

"Sarah, what are you doing?" Vinnie asked me.

**337**

"I'm looking for the garlic press," I said.

"Down there?" said Vinnie. "I already found it, Sarah! Get up. Mr. Kleinfreude wants to talk to you."

"Please call me Bill," said Kleinfreude. "Everyone does."

"You want to talk to me?" I said, trying to look unterrified.

"Yes. What was the name of that strange book you were reading?"

"Oh, Sarah was just giving me a sample—" said Vinnie.

"*One Hundred Years of Solitude,*" I said, feeling the dreadful prophecy of the phrase.

"Strange book, very strange book. Well, then, Vincent, can you spare this young woman for a half hour?"

I looked at Vinnie with naked fear in my eyes. He sent me a feeling, sorrowful glance.

"Well, only for a half hour," Vinnie said earnestly.

"She's that indispensable, is she?" said Kleinfreude. "Very well. I'll have her back in half an hour."

He led me around several corners and into a small private elevator, which opened, three floors up, onto a comfortable sitting room. There he poured me a cup of coffee from a pot warming over a hot plate on a sideboard. I asked timidly whether he might have any cigarettes, as I'd neglected to bring my own. He clucked his tongue at me and dug a pack of Gitanes out of a sideboard drawer.

My fingers trembled alarmingly as he lit my cigarette, and to my horror, I asked him the first thing that popped into my mind:

"Don't you have a secretary?"

Luckily the question seemed to amuse him. He smiled broadly, sat back in his chair, tapped his fingers, and looked at me as though he now had my measure.

"You can relax," he said. "I never make passes at my employees."

"Why—did you think—because I asked— Oh, god, nothing could have been further from my mind! That was the last thing in the world— I just meant because you make your own coffee!"

"I don't make it. I do have a secretary, and she made the coffee. But she doesn't pour every cup for me. That would be excessively chauvinistic, don't you think?"

"I guess," I said. He waited for me to say something more. I looked down at my feet. Of course, I was wearing the sandals!

"In my father's day," he said finally, "*The Newspaper* had only male secretaries."

"I've heard that," I said quaveringly. "Why was that?"

**338**

"Oh, I think it was true everywhere, except maybe it lasted a little longer at *The Newspaper*. This place is very slow to change. Twenty years ago, we had three women reporters. Journalism used to be considered too vulgar for women! They couldn't have women covering murders. And the language in the newsroom . . . Well, *that's* all changed. Are you in that Feminist Faction?"

"No," I said, "not yet."

He tilted his head to one side and cocked an eyebrow—he was not wearing the aviator glasses. Then he said:

"I promise you, I am not going to make a pass," and his lips curled with amusement again.

"Mr. Kleinfreude, I told you, that was the last thing I expected you to do!"

"It's true that I have something of a reputation," he said. "You must have heard gossip. And you are quite an attractive young woman."

"Thank you," I said, starting to wonder whether this was a pass. The thought gave me courage. "But why did you want to see me?" I asked.

"Why do you think?" he asked, drawing in his legs and sitting up. He was seated on a plush chair. I was bunched together in a corner of a couch.

"That's not fair," I said.

"Why not?"

"It's a trap question. You'll get me to list my shortcomings."

"Do you have any?"

"What do you think?"

"That's better! Now you're starting to relax. You thought I brought you up here to fire you, didn't you?"

"Yes, I did."

"Sarah, tell me honestly: What do you think of Ron?"

"What do I think—of Ron?" My voice had gone all funny and strangled-sounding.

"Yes. I want to know what you think of him, really."

"Gee, Mr. Kleinfreude, in what sense do you mean?"

"Please call me Bill. Everyone does. I mean in every sense, Sarah. I want to know what you think of him in every sense."

"Wow! I hardly know *what* I think of him, to be perfectly honest with you. You see, Ron changes a lot. I mean, he changes his mind a lot. But I like him. I mean, you can't help liking him. Ron is so full of—well, angles. And he's really a very good city editor. He's got tons of ideas. He's enthusiastic. Ron has foresight too, you know. He was really ahead of the ball with that Love story during the Democratic convention, and—"

"Is that why he killed your story about Love's boyfriend? Because Love was his candidate?"

"Where did you hear that? Ron didn't kill that story. Gil killed it. Ron wanted to run it. Maybe he's changed his mind now," I added quickly. "It wasn't an easy thing to decide. I was all for it at the time, of course, because it was my story. Now I'm not so sure."

"But you're positive Ron wanted to run it?"

"Oh, yes! Ron and Greg and I argued for running it, and Dixby and his crew argued against it."

"Then your father has his villains mixed up."

"My father? Have you been talking to my father? He doesn't—"

"Not talking to him. He sent me a letter."

"Oh, god!" I said with all my heart.

I promptly lit a new cigarette from the old one.

"Would you like to see it?" Kleinfreude asked.

"Oh, god!" I repeated.

He took this to mean yes. He reached into an inner pocket and pulled out the long-dreaded missive. It was several pages thick. He unfolded it and handed it to me.

"'Dear Mr. Shield,'" I read.

"But this isn't to you!" I protested. "It's to Lars Shield at *The Evil Eye!*"

"Your father sent me the copy, though," said Kleinfreude. "If you look at the end, you'll see he typed, 'cc William Kleinfreude III.'"

And so he had.

My father had recounted the entire story of Love and Renato. He had also recounted the entire story of my efforts to get it into *The Newspaper*, not forgetting to include mention of *The Evil Eye*'s Bits and Pieces item in which Gil's lonelier-than-God quote was reported. And he explained that the Harvard *Crimson* lie had been Ron's lie all along. He had everything right.

His final paragraph said:

"It is your urgent duty, Mr. Shield, to print the facts as I have presented them to you. I am certain that my daughter will confirm everything in this letter. In closing, I can only say that an institution which so badly cheats the American people of their right to know the truth about their President does not deserve the name newspaper. I have known this for many years, as have all readers alert to the increasing problems of pollution, the most insidious of which is winter road salting. *The Newspaper* has not once reported on the dangers of road salting, and it is currently overlooking the even greater danger in the White House. We must not allow *The Newspaper* to strangle the truth."

He signed it, "Sincerely yours, Adam Makepeace," I was glad to see, not "Power to the people! Adam X. Makepeace," as had been his custom of yore.

I think I cried out. I was dazed and unaware of my own movements.

"Is it true?" Kleinfreude asked me.

This time I heard myself sigh. As if by its own volition, my head began to move slowly up and down.

"Maybe you'd like another cigarette," said Kleinfreude.

He seemed to sense that I couldn't move my arms. He shook a cigarette out of the pack for me and held it up to my mouth. My lips opened and took it. Kleinfreude gave me a light. I inhaled and was finally able to lift my hand to take hold of the cigarette.

"Now," said Kleinfreude, "what are you going to do?"

"Do?" I said forlornly.

"Sarah, I know this must be hard for you, but you've got to think now. What are you going to do?"

"There's nothing I can do. What can I do?"

"You could confirm it. Have they called you to confirm it?"

"No. When did they get it?"

"Well, I got my copy this morning. It's dated only three days ago. I would guess that Shield got his this morning also."

"Why did he *do* it?" I asked the gods. "Why, why, *why?*"

"I was hoping you could tell me that."

"Mr. Kleinfreude—"

"Bill."

"Well, B-Bill, my father is kind of a professional iconoclast. He's been writing letters to *The Newspaper* for thirty years. They've never printed a single one. He's got a real thing about *The Newspaper*. Oh, god! He *knew* how much I needed the job! How could he do this!"

"Calm down, Sarah. No one has said anything about your job. I want to know what you plan to do, though. Are you going to confirm it?"

"Of course not! Why should the *Eye* get our story!"

"It's more than that," he said. "This could be quite embarrassing."

"What do you think I should do?"

"Could you talk to Lars Shield? You used to work for him, didn't you? Could you persuade him that your father violated a confidence,

341

that it was an off-the-record conversation?"

"Lars doesn't talk to me. He thinks I sold out to the enemy when I came here."

"Well, then, what about your father? Could you talk to him, get him to withdraw the letter? Maybe if we promised to print one of his other letters—"

"I don't think you understand, Bill. My father also thinks I sold out to the enemy when I came here."

"But he's your father! Surely he—"

"He's a man of principle. He won't budge."

It was the publisher's turn to sigh.

"Give me one of those cigarettes," he said. "We've got to think of something."

# L

We got through three-quarters of the pack, arriving at the brilliant notion that I should call Lars Shield after all, although not with that feeble argument about my father's letter being a violation of confidence. We both thought it would be stronger to lie, to say my father was crazy and had made it all up.

I dialed from Kleinfreude's desk. I had little hope that Lars would speak to me, but I had even less hope that he would believe me if he did take my call.

I heard the *Eye*'s double ring. Kleinfreude held up crossed fingers.

"It takes them forever to pick up the phone," I said. "Where are the cigarettes?"

A buzzer sounded. Kleinfreude pressed a button on a little squawk box.

"Yes, Vanessa?" he said.

"Your mother's here," said the secretary. "Should I send her in?"

"No!" Kleinfreude ejaculated. To me he said, "My god! I don't want Mother to hear about this!"

"She wants you to take her out to lunch," said the secretary.

"Tell her I'll be right out," he said. "Can you manage?" he asked me.

342

"The cigarettes!" I said.

"*Evil Eye*," said the switchboard lady.

"Hello, is Lars Shield in?" I said.

Kleinfreude frantically dug the cigarettes out of the couch.

"Who's calling, please?" asked the switchboard lady.

"Sarah Makepeace," I said. "Tell him it's important."

"Everybody says that, dear," said the switchboard lady.

"I'll be back as soon as I can," Kleinfreude whispered, dropping the cigarettes on the desk.

"Matches! Ashtray!" I said.

The publisher dashed back to fetch them from the coffee table. He set the precious objects down in front of me just as a white-haired woman appeared in the doorway and Lars said to me:

"God damn it, Sarah, your old man already called me! What do you want?"

"Mother, this is Sarah Makepeace, one of our new reporters," said Kleinfreude. "She's been telling me about how we can attract young readers."

"Just one moment, Lars," I said. I cupped the phone in my hand. "Hello, Mrs. Kleinfreude," I said.

"Hello," she said flatly. "Maureen's told me about you."

"Mother, we mustn't disturb her," Kleinfreude said, and he led her out the door, closing it behind him.

"Lars, I'm sorry about that," I said.

"Look, Sarah, if it's about that letter your father wrote, I am not going to listen to another word. I've made up my mind!"

"Made up your mind?"

"Yes. Did he tell you to call me?"

"I haven't talked to him today, Lars. I—"

"Look, I don't have time for this. We're not going to run it, and that's final!"

"You're *not going to run it?*"

"Sarah, now that you're a *daily* journalist, you may think it's no holds barred, everything for a scoop. But we don't operate that way. If a gay has not come out of the closet, we do not expose him. I'm *not printing* that thing!"

"You're not? None of it?"

"No! And don't call me about this again. And tell your old man not to call me, either. He is off the wall. Your old man is certifiable! Look, I've wasted too much time on this already. Goodbye!"

"Bye, Lars."

"Sarah?"

"What, Lars?"

"I mean it. Don't call me on this again. Do you know how many people have tried to tell me the President is gay?"

"Don't worry, Lars, I won't."

I went back to the test kitchen all atremble with relief. Vinnie, of course, wanted to know what had happened upstairs, and I really yearned to tell him, but I had just been taught the cataclysmic consequences of indiscretion.

"Well, at least I'm not being fired," I said, rubbing my arms and shivering.

"What happened, Sarah?" Vinnie asked worriedly. "You look awful. What did he want?"

"I think I'm having a delayed reaction," I said.

"To what? What did he *do* to you?"

"He didn't *do* anything, Vinnie. It was a false alarm. He just wanted to have a little chat. He said he meets all the new reporters, and somehow he was a bit late getting to me."

"But, Sarah, you're trembling! If that man took advantage—"

"Vinnie, I'm just trembling with relief. I thought he was going to fire me. He asked me what I thought of Ron. God! I didn't know what to say!"

"What did you say?"

"Oh, I said he was enthusiastic, full of ideas, and very changeable."

"I'm going to fix you some camomile tea. You look just awful," said Vinnie, and the interrogation ended.

We settled into the magical century of Macondo again. A peaceful hour passed. Vinnie served up the pasta with pesto sauce. He insisted I stop reading to eat, although I wasn't hungry. In the middle of our little meal, the test kitchen phone rang. Vinnie answered it.

"It's Kleinfreude again," he said. "Be careful, Sarah."

I took the phone into the supply closet.

"Hello, Sarah. What happened? God, I'm sorry! I completely forgot Mother was coming for lunch. What happened? Did he buy your story?"

"He's not going to run the letter. He said—"

"Not going to run it! *None* of it? Are you sure?"

"That's what he said. He was pretty annoyed. My father—"

"Oh, you little *genius!* You're wonderful! How did you do it?"

"I didn't—"

"Damn! There's my buzzer. Look, I've got a meeting. I want to hear all about this. Oh, you're great! But then, you're a 'Cliffie.

Listen, do you want to have dinner later on this week? How about Friday?"

"Gee, I—"

"There's a little place called the Chaumière on West Fourth Street. You live down in the Village, don't you? I looked at your personnel file."

"Yes," I said.

"Okay. Meet me at La Chaumière at eight o'clock Friday. I'd pick you up, but people recognize me sometimes. So I'll see you at the restaurant, right?"

"Okay," I said.

"What was that about?" Vinnie asked as I emerged from the closet.

"Oh, another false alarm," I said.

Vinnie appeared to be on the verge of asking me another question, when Mrs. Heller came in and he forgot I existed.

# *LI*

He wasn't old enough to want me to marry his son, so his calling me a 'Cliffie had interesting implications. And if I had been attracted to him, I might have felt less guilty about accepting his dinner invitation. But he didn't turn me on. It wasn't merely that he had no gun. He looked too smooth, too tailored, too coifed and polished. Too rich. He seemed to be the kind of guy for whom life is like an endless supply of expensive wine, something he took for granted and hardly noticed going down.

My motives for having dinner with him were pretty bad. He *was* the publisher. I *was* in a nothing job. For the first time in my life, I wanted to take advantage of somebody else, *really* take advantage, get all I could get out of him. All week I tried to think what Ron would do if he were twenty-seven and female and had caught the eye of the married publisher. Of course, I couldn't tell Ron that Kleinfreude had asked me out to dinner. Ron would go bananas. He'd either try to get the date canceled or try to make me wear a hidden tape recorder and give me all sorts of outlandish advice that wouldn't help at all. He might even ask to come along as a chaperon! I couldn't tell *him*.

Still, I kept trying to think what Ron would do in my place, and naturally, I was sure he would lie like crazy, but the question was, what lies would he tell? First of all, he'd have a fantastic one ready to explain why he (in my shape) had told his father all those things he shouldn't have told him. His father listened in on a phone conversation? A conversation with whom? His best friend, a person as discreet as a well. But where did Dad overhear me making this phone conversation? In my apartment? When he came to visit? When was that?

I had to think, you see, of every detail. I had to be ready for any question. I had to be *better* than Ron. Ron's lies contradicted each other. That's why people were onto him.

I never did get it solved, how I would explain why my father knew everything that he had put in that letter to Lars. I got distracted by the problem of the conversation with Lars, which I knew Kleinfreude would ask about right away. I tried to imagine Lars resisting me while I pleaded with him to have pity on a poor crazy man's daughter. "Think how Cordelia felt, Lars, when the world was mocking her nutty old man!" That's the way I was planning to start the dialogue for Kleinfreude. I was going to tell him I knew Lars was very literary and we could sometimes get him to cry when we quoted poetry. I had it worked out into a long spiel. Lars was going to have got sidetracked correcting my quotations, and it would be a very drawn-out thing, with Kleinfreude hanging on my every word. I wouldn't give him a chance to ask how my father knew what he knew, or maybe on the way to the restaurant it would come to me, what to say about that.

I told Vinnie I had to leave early on Friday afternoon to go home and wash my hair. He wanted to know who my date was, so I said, "Oh, just a guy I met last week."

Then I went home and soaked in the bath with this scented bath salt stuff that had a woman kissing her shoulder on the package. I washed my hair with Blonde Tone shampoo and pinned it back with little forget-me-not barrettes that Jim the Shorter had pronounced "*real* cute!" I wore a new silk camisole top without a bra and a filmy cotton skirt. And my new shoes.

When I got to the restaurant, a small, dark place below street level, Kleinfreude was already sitting at a table, sipping from a glass of very mellow Pommard. The maître d' knew him and had given us a table in a little room by ourselves. Kleinfreude held up his glass to me as I sat down, and he said:

"To the lady with the cinder on her nose!"

"Oh, have I got a cinder on my nose?" I sat down at the place to his right and tried to rub it off.

"Here, I'll do that," he said. He dipped his napkin into the wine and rubbed my nose with it.

I must have looked worried, because he said, "Don't worry. I am *not* going to make a pass at you!" He poured me a glass of wine, handed it to me, and said, "Now tell me, how did you really come to work for *The Newspaper?*"

I told him. I told him the true story.

"Ha!" he said, slapping his hand on his knee. "That's a gas! Ron's really something, isn't he!"

"Yes," I said. "He is."

Kleinfreude poured me another glass of wine.

"Are we going to order?" I said.

"Oh, we've got all night. Drink up. Now I want to hear all about your father."

"What do you want to know?" I said.

"Everything! Tell me all about him. Tell me the story of his life."

By the time I had finished that, we had finished a bottle of wine. Kleinfreude called a waiter, and we ordered the spécialité de la maison, which had no price next to it.

I was feeling good, and he seemed to be having a fine time too. Every once in a while, he would look at me flirtatiously and say, "What if somebody saw us here? They'd get the wrong idea, wouldn't they!" Then he'd ask me something else about my life or my dad's life, and I'd babble on kind of gushily, trying to think when I might drop in something about Dad listening to my phone calls. He made it so easy for me to talk. He was clearly attracted to me. He thought everything I said was interesting. I began to think maybe he wasn't such a creepy smoothie after all. And I began to think we were going to get through the whole evening without talking about Lars. The wine was making me go off on tangents a little bit. I sort of thought something might go wrong in the Lars story if I was that drunk. Anyway, it really looked as though he wasn't going to ask about it.

We finished dinner at ten-thirty or eleven. He ordered a cigar and poured the last of the second bottle of wine into our glasses.

"Now," he said, "I've been saving the best for the last. Tell me what you said to Lars Shield."

"Well, I—I told you Lars was very angry when I called. He almost didn't want to talk to me. He—"

"No, wait! Let me guess! I've been trying to guess all week. Let me try this out on you. You told him he'd be picketed by the Gay Rights Movement. That must be a third of his subscribers right there."

"No," I said. "Lars is used to being picketed."

"They picketed us, you know. They wanted us to stop using the term 'sexual deviance.' Between us, I thought they had a point. But we told them we don't let outsiders edit the paper."

"That's what Lars always says. He says all activists are natural censors."

"What did you do to turn him around? No, wait, I want to guess again. I bet you told him it wasn't right to expose a gay who hadn't come out of the closet."

"How did you know?" I heard myself saying.

"Is that what you said?"

"Yes. That's exactly what I said."

"I knew it! I knew it! You're so smart! Boy, Ron knew what he was doing when he hired you! Did it take you a long time? Did he argue with you?"

"No. Actually, I think he had his own misgivings anyway. That's why he was angry when I called. I could tell he was worried underneath."

"He must have asked you why you had changed your mind, why you didn't want the story to run anymore."

"Well, I said I'd had a long time to think about it and that when I read my father's letter, I got a gut feeling it would be wrong to print the story."

"And what did he say to that?"

"He said he had the same gut feeling, and he guessed he might as well go by his gut."

"Go by his gut! Of course, Sarah, you are a sly one! Using his language! Go by his gut! Let's have a brandy and drink to Lars Shield's gut!"

I had run out of cigarettes by then. Kleinfreude bought me a cigar. We sat over the brandies puffing our cigars like two tycoons. He kept smacking his lips and shaking his head with satisfaction, and I think I was glowing.

"Now you can tell me what you really think of Ron, Sarah," he said.

"Ron? Ron is the most brilliant man I have ever met," I said. "Also the most unscrupulous."

"You think so? You really think he's unscrupulous?"

"He'll do anything to get a story."

"He's supposed to. That's his job."

"He sucks up to people in power."

"He's a realist," said Kleinfreude, grinning at me around the cigar like Miltie Clendenon. Gosh, but I was getting to like him.

"I can't tell you anything. You've got your mind made up," I said.

"Go on."

"Well, he's a liar. He lies all the time."

"Ron? He's a terrible liar! Everybody sees through him. He's a terrible liar. I can read him like a book. Not like you. You could make me believe anything with that wide-open face of yours."

"Me?"

"Tell me something. Did you think I might try to seduce you tonight?"

"I can't say I didn't consider it at all."

"And what would you have done if I had?"

"What would I have done?" I took a puff of the cigar. "Honestly? What would I have done?"

He nodded.

"I don't know."

"That's what I like about you. You're so honest. Ron knew what he was doing when he hired you. Ron is a brilliant editor. You're right about that. Gil thinks so too. He thinks I've made the right choice."

"Choice for what?"

"This is just between us right now, Sarah, but I told Ron and Willard this afternoon. Ron is going to be the next editor of *The Newspaper*. Let's drink a toast to him. To Ron Millstein!"

"To Ron Millstein!"

# LII

We were both so drunk that he decided to take me home in the limousine that had been waiting for him on Jane Street the whole time we were in the restaurant. He walked me to my door. I started to open it. He put his hand on my arm.

"Thank you so much, Bill!" I said. "That was really fun! Let me go in. Someone will see you."

"Let them," he said. "I'm not doing anything wrong. I would

like to see you again, Sarah. I like bouncing things off you. Are you free next Friday?"

"Gee, I don't know—"

"Think it over," he said, giving my arm a little squeeze, and he dashed back to the limo and was gone.

On Monday morning, I stopped by the newsroom around eleven, when the reporters were coming in. The place was hopping. People were crowding around Ron's desk, trying to edge in there and shake his hand. Eddie saw me and reached into his back pocket to pull out a wad of money.

"Here, kid," he said. "You get a piece of this."

"I didn't bet, Eddie."

"Yeah, but you helped Greg on that story. Go on. Buy yourself a new dress."

"Eddie, I won't take it!"

He was trying to hand me a hundred-dollar bill, but I ran away from him. I went over to the crowd around Ron. I sort of wanted to congratulate him. There was too thick a crowd, though, so I turned away and started walking back to the elevators.

"There's Sarah!" I heard Willie calling out. "Sarah, wait!"

So I turned around and the crowd parted and Ron stood up to let me shake his hand.

"Isn't it great!" he said. "We just found out this morning."

"It's wonderful, Ron! You deserve it," I said.

"Sarah, I'm going to do something about you," he said. "You come see me this afternoon."

"Okay," I said.

I came whistling into the test kitchen, and Vinnie said to me sharply:

"What are you so happy about?"

"Ron's going to be the next editor, Vinnie! They just announced it! He won! Isn't it great!"

"You can't tell me that's why you're looking so—Jesus, Sarah, can't you be more discreet?"

"But everybody knows! They're all down there congratulating him. You should go down, Vinnie. Ron's in a fantastic mood."

"I'm not going to congratulate him. But that's not what I meant, Sarah. I wasn't talking about Ron."

"Who were you talking about?"

"You and Kleinfreude. You are in the *Chronicle*. And Figland saw you on the street together. He's been telling everybody."

"Oh, no!"

The telephone rang. Vinnie answered it.

"It's for you," he said.

"Who is it?" I asked.

"Guess," he said.

It was Kleinfreude. I took the phone into the closet again.

"Well, Sarah, I'm afraid I'm going to have to cancel our date," he said.

"I just heard there was something in the paper," I said. "How did they find out?"

"You didn't tell anybody, did you?"

"No. But Vinnie says one of the reporters saw us."

"Have you seen the *Chronicle?*"

"No."

"I'll read it to you. It's in the Wining and Dining column. It says: 'Is Bill Kleinfreude's marriage on the rocks? It's been ages since we've seen him in public with his lovely wife Susan, and a little birdie told us he was seen dropping off one of his reporters at her doorstep late Friday night. She's the one who broke that story about the mayor, pretty Sarah Makepeace. Our birdie said she stepped out of the *Newspaper* publisher's limo with him, and he walked her to the door and stood having a little heart-to-heart with her before letting her go, alone, inside.'"

"Oh, brother!"

"Are you sure you didn't tell anyone?"

"Absolutely not. But I just heard Steve Figland saw us."

"Figland? He's on our paper, isn't he?"

"Yes, but maybe—"

"This couldn't have come at a worse time. Susan is in London. I can't even find her. She's going to hear about this before I talk to her!"

"Oh, I'm sorry!"

"It's not your fault. I should have realized. Well, that's the way it goes."

"I'm sure your wife knows that gossip columnists don't tell the truth."

"At this point, she may be having me followed."

"Really? Is there anything I can do? Do you want me to call up the *Chronicle* and deny it?"

"Oh, no! That would only make it worse! It just means we can't see each other again."

"Yes, I can see—"

"I'm sorry, Sarah. I really enjoyed your company. I wanted to get to know you better. But we'll have to take a rain check on that."

"Well, good luck," I said.

"I didn't make a pass at you, did I?"

"No."

"I can't drink anymore. Ciao, Sarah. Keep your chin up."

"'Bye."

When I came out of the closet, Vinnie said, "You'd better watch your step, Sarah. You're playing with fire."

"Oh, Vinnie! The whole thing was completely innocent!"

"Figland says he saw you kissing him. Right out on the *street*, Sarah!"

"He did *not* kiss me!"

"What's going on, Sarah? Are you going to have an affair with him?"

"Of course not! Kleinfreude doesn't mess with the staff."

"You don't know about Flicka Poinsby, apparently."

"What about Flicka?"

The telephone rang again before he could answer. I picked it up.

"Hello, this is the test kitchen," I said, thinking it might be a gossip columnist.

"Hello, Sarah! This is Wendy. You remember me, don't you? Mr. Millstein's secretary?"

"Oh, yes, Wendy. Hello!"

"Sarah, Mr. Millstein would like to make an appointment with you. Would three-thirty suit you?"

"I already told him I'll be down this afternoon."

"Well, come at three-thirty, all right?"

"Fine," I said.

"That's funny," I said to Vinnie. "Ron just asked me to stop by and see him this afternoon, and then his secretary calls to make it an appointment. Weird. Vinnie, you don't think they'll fire me because of this thing?"

"*Au contraire,* my dear. If Ron thinks you're going to be the publisher's next mistress, he'll put on the white gloves. Don't you know Ron by now?"

When three-thirty rolled around, I reported to Ron, feeling intensely aware of the openness of the newsroom, the heads leaning together down the aisles.

"Sarah!" Ron said, though he was on the phone. "Here, Willie, you take this," he said, and he handed it to Willie. "You look marvelous, Sarah! Did you do something with your hair? You look wonderful! You're just glowing!"

"I pinned it back, if that's what you mean."

"We miss you down here, Sarah. You don't come down to see us often enough," he said.

"I don't work on this floor."

"You mean, as soon as your assignment changes, you forget your old friends? We didn't forget *you*, did we, Willie?"

"What, Ron?" said Willie, covering the receiver.

"I was telling Sarah we haven't forgotten about her."

"Oh, right, Ron!" said Willie.

"Everybody's been asking about you," Ron said.

"That's right," said Willie.

"Yeah," said Freddie, wriggling his eyebrows at me.

"Come into my office for a minute," said Ron. "Have you got a minute?"

"Well, yes. Wendy said I—"

"Good! I want to have a little chat with you."

We took our usual positions opposite each other on the couches.

"I think you're ready for a change, Sarah," he said. "You must be tired of the test kitchen."

"Oh, no, Ron! I like it up there," I said forcefully.

"You don't have to pretend, Sarah. I know you're a good sport. We've had our little differences, and we've been angry at each other, but that's all in the past, isn't it, Sarah? You're not angry at me anymore, are you?"

"No, Ron, but—"

"That's what I like about you, Sarah. You don't hold a grudge. You and I can argue and we can get over it. I like my reporters to argue with me. I like them to care about their stories. I was saying that to the publisher this morning, you know, when he told me I was going to be made editor."

"You must be very pleased."

"Thank you, Sarah. I'm a little awed, actually, at the prospect of— Well, I suddenly know what Gil means, you know, when he says it's lonely, because it does feel that way—the responsibility, the awesome responsibility. And you know the publisher feels that way too. He told me that. He and I agreed that what this paper needs is more young, energetic talent like you, Sarah—yes, like you. I don't know whether I've told you this, Sarah, but you've got what it takes to be a great reporter. People remember your stories. You're famous now, do you know that? I went to a cocktail party on Saturday night, and two people asked me why they hadn't seen your by-line lately. They remember your story about the Mayor."

**353**

"That was just luck," I said.

"Don't say that, Sarah! It wasn't just luck! It was talent and persistence. We make our own luck, Sarah. That's what a smart person does. You see, that's what Jenny doesn't understand—"

"Jenny!" (I had just remembered the lunch date I had made with Jenny. It had been for the previous Tuesday, the day Kleinfreude showed me Dad's letter.)

"Yes, Sarah, Jenny does *not* understand that we cannot have a system bent backward trying to make up for centuries of discrimination against women. Discrimination is not something we can suddenly make up for. You see, *that's* why we couldn't print that story about the President, Sarah, because it wouldn't make up for what's happened to homosexuals, and the country wasn't ready for it. You *do* understand that now, don't you?"

"I—I think so."

"And I know you won't tell anyone about it, Sarah. It has to be our secret, our responsibility. Maybe someday, when he is no longer President . . . But, Sarah, I want you to expand and spread your wings on this paper right now. I want you to be a *star!* Well, you already are a star, but a *bigger* star. How would you like to take over the Urban Diary?"

"Not the column! Greg—"

"It doesn't belong to Greg. It was Vinnie's column before it was Greg's. And it was Steve's before it was Vinnie's. It belongs to everyone, to all of us, because it belongs to *The Newspaper!*"

"Ron! I don't know how—"

"I'll give you a week to get started. I've already told Greg. He'll break you in this week, and next week you'll start writing. You'll have to do some columns right away, though. We always keep a few advance columns in case you get stuck one night. But Greg will tell you about it."

"I bet he will."

"Sarah, he won't mind. He likes you. He thinks you're going to go far."

But what will happen to Greg? And what about Vinnie? What do I tell him?"

"Don't worry about them, Sarah."

"You should put Vinnie back on the column. He's the best."

"Vinnie doesn't want it back. He's got a hundred-thousand-dollar advance to do a cookbook."

# LIII

Thank heavens Mrs. Heller intervened before any of my columns appeared in print! The public was spared such phrases as: "When spring comes, throwing up flowers," "My mind reels backward, boggling at the Manhattan skyline," and "It behooves the urban individualist whose heart beats to a different piano." Jess Flicker let it be known around the office that he had never seen such awful writing, not even in his Queens College Journalism 1 class, and all those Jess hadn't told, Greg told. Greg had, after all, his own columnistic pride to preserve. There had been quite a number of letters from readers asking what had become of "that graceful writer Vincent Akelroyd." People who read the Urban Diary apparently did not read the food page.

In any case, before my week of preparation was over, another gossip item appeared in the *Morning Chronicle,* this time in its People column, to wit:

"Keep an eye out for the by-line 'Sarah Makepeace,' *Newspaper* readers. We hear she's going to be writing the Urban Diary column soon. Her star is certainly rising! She is the publisher's favorite reporter. You heard it first in Wining and Dining last Monday. We have now learned *Bill Kleinfreude* was seen dining très intime with his favorite reporter in the private room of a Greenwich Village bistro last Friday night."

This time Mrs. Heller called me. She asked me to have lunch at "21" again. We took the same upstairs table.

"Now, dear, you can tell me," she said as soon as the Bloody Marys were served, "what's going on between you and Bill?"

"You mean Bill Kleinfreude?"

"Of course! It's in the *Chronicle* again this morning. Didn't you see it?"

"No. What else could they say? I think I'm going to call them. It's all so stupid!"

"Don't you *dare* call them! Sarah, tell me. How serious is it?"

"It's nothing at all! We had dinner once, and that was it. We had to talk about a problem at the paper."

"What problem?"

"I don't think he would want me to—"

"He's the one who asked me to have lunch with you, dear."

"Then why are you asking me what's going on? Ask him. Why'd he ask you to have lunch with me?"

"This business has been bad for his marriage. Frankly, I think he *is* fond of you. He can't very well be seen with you himself. Susan is an extremely jealous woman. You must stop telling people you had dinner with him."

"But I haven't told anyone! A reporter saw us."

"How did you become a columnist? Bill can't understand. It really doesn't look right."

"Believe me, Mrs. Heller, I don't want to *be* a columnist. Not yet anyway. It's too hard."

"But you must have asked for it."

"No, I didn't. Ron called me in on Monday and told me I would start next week. He wouldn't let me say no."

"On Monday. I see. That's the day the first item appeared. Oh, Ron!"

"You think he did it only because of that? Ron's so crude!"

"He's subtler than you think. I begin to see the workings of a plot here. Ron has been seeing a lot of Bill's mother, you know, and she hates Susan."

"I thought you were a friend of hers."

"Oh, yes! But I don't like to see her interfering in her son's marriage. She won't listen to me. I'm *too* good a friend. She's always made trouble for Susan. You *mustn't* repeat this, Sarah."

"Of course not! But you mean you think Ron wants to make it *look* as though Bill gave me the column?"

"I'm afraid so. How's your writing?"

"People whose judgment I trust say it's awful. I don't want to *do* it, Mrs. Heller!"

"Maureen. Please, dear. You make me feel so old when you call me Mrs. Heller!"

We concentrated on our food for a while. She had ordered ratatouille. My stomach had been bothering me since I'd been trying to write columns. I ordered vichyssoise.

"Is that all you're having, Sarah?" she asked me.

"I don't feel very well these days."

"You don't think you're pregnant, do you?"

"Honestly! Don't you *believe* me? I told you there's *nothing going on* between Bill and me!"

"You call him Bill."

"He asked me to. Look, I spent a whole evening with him, and I have no idea why he's making Ron the editor—I mean, over Dixby. Could you tell me that?"

"I do know Mr. Dixby's being a Baptist didn't help him. *The Newspaper's never* been run by a Baptist."

"Oh."

"You don't look well, dear. We have to do something about you. We can't have you writing that column. It simply doesn't look right. Actually, I think we can't have you in the city. You know the saying 'Where there's smoke there's fire.' Bill is a weak man, and Susan can usually sense when he's headed for a fall. If she stays away for the summer again, and you're here, he'll try to see you again. I know him well, Sarah. He would never leave her for you. He loves Susan very much. But he doesn't like to be alone. Most men don't. He would hurt you. He would never leave her for you."

"But I don't want him! I'm not attracted to him. He's perfectly nice, but I don't want him. He's too spoiled."

"It would be better for you if we sent you out of town."

"Mrs. Heller—Maureen, how many times do I have to tell you, I am not interested in having an affair with William Kleinfreude!"

"But where to send you—"

"Why don't you send me to Paris, ha ha! I've never been there."

"Paris," she said, watching me take a drag on my cigarette. "Why, yes! What a splendid idea!"


## LIV


They shipped me off two weeks later. Mrs. Heller was determined to get me away fast. I hardly had time to pack and see my parents and say goodbye to all my friends. Kevin actually came around to see me, he was so stunned to hear I would be moving away. He warned me over the phone that he and Helen had really got back together, so I figured he meant he didn't want to go to bed with me. But when he appeared, he grabbed me and ripped my clothes off and ravaged me to an ecstatic pulp. Afterwards he said, "Well, it couldn't have been just my gun."

I said, "Of course it wasn't, you fool!" and kissed the little pool of sweat below his throat. "You mean you're not carrying a gun anymore? How can you be a cop?"

"I quit," he said. "I'm doing management training. It's boring, but Helen's happy. I think I miss the street."

"You're just saying that to make me feel better."

"If it doesn't work out with her, will you marry me?" he said.

"Kevin! Listen to what you just said!"

"I just said if it doesn't work out with Helen and me, will you marry me? Well? Will you?"

"Oh, Kevin! What am I going to do in Paris without you?"

"I don't want to think about that. What's your answer?"

"It will work out with Helen. I just know it."

"And if it doesn't?"

"What does Dr. Festniss say?"

"Fuck Dr. Festniss, lady! I want to know what you say!"

"I say it will work out."

"But what if it doesn't?"

"Okay, I'll marry you. What kind of a ridiculous proposal is that?"

But he kissed me so that my mind boggled and reeled backward.

I spent the last weekend with my parents. Noah called me from the depths of his lab, and my father did not once complain about *The Newspaper* or about road salting. He never said anything about the letter he'd sent to *The Evil Eye*, either, and I naturally didn't mention it. But on Sunday, when he and Mother were driving me to the bus stop, he asked me:

"What is a homophobe?"

And after I explained, he said:

"Do you think I'm a homophobe?"

"Oh, don't be silly, dear!" said Mother with her usual good sense.

I have to admit I was stumped.

Some of my peers took my going to Paris as a personal affront. Jenny Locke let it be known through the grapevine that I was disinvited to join the Feminist Faction for good. My buddies down in the Poor Mouth all insisted I should buy them farewell drinks, which I did, and then they ungratefully spread the word around that the Paris bureau was no longer a prestige assignment.

Ellic, who had recently obtained a job in a center for dog psychology, found it deeply painful that her former roommate was going to be a foreign correspondent in Paris. She disloyally told her women's group that I couldn't speak a word of French.

Even my dear friend Miltie Clendenon got a little testy with me when I told him the news. He said:

"I guess that crap we've been printing about you isn't so crappy."

On my last day in the office, Ron's new appointment was officially announced, and everyone from the Metro staff came up to congratulate him again. Willie Crespi produced a case of champagne, which we all thought very sporting, as the official announcement also said that Greg Swenson would become the next city editor.

Ron got tipsy and told us he couldn't have done it without us. Greg proposed a toast to "the best editor in the world." We all seconded him. Eddie Schwartz whispered, "Wherever he may be!"

As I was walking to the elevators, Ron came hurrying over to say one last goodbye. He put an arm around me and gave me a pillowy squeeze.

"Didn't I tell you I'd send you to Paris?" he said. "I keep my promises!"

# LV

Everything happened so fast, I couldn't believe I was on my way to Paris, even when I was halfway there. I slept fitfully on the plane and tried to read *Le Monde*. Eventually I gave up and read *Time* magazine. It said *Kojak* was the most popular television program in the world, a piece of news which put me to sleep again. When I awakened next, *Time* had fallen open to another page, and I looked down to see Renato! Oh, my god! Renato Weinstein was alive and well and working in the White House! He was there, all right, unmistakably smiling from behind the President's right shoulder in a photograph captioned: "President Love conferring with White House aides over the problem of Japanese auto competition." What did Renato know about Japanese auto competition?

I fell asleep again, and when I woke up we were in France. As I came into Paris the sun was just coming up over the Tuileries, and the birds were singing away like mad. The taxi driver gave me a little tour before he took me to the Place Vendôme, where our office is, so I saw the beautiful bridges over the Seine and Notre Dame and the Tour Eiffel in the distance and the imposing Place de la

Concorde. The *Tabac* signs looked familiar because I had pictured them so many times from Simenon novels. Gunther met me at the door and carried my bags to the little room in our office suite where I'll be staying until I find an apartment. There's a poster on the wall of the room which says, *"La Vérité, c'est nôtre affaire."*

It will be touch and go with Gunther. He has forgotten me completely, so he thinks I would be a fresh conquest. I am not keen on taking up with a German in a city full of Frenchmen.

I have been here for three weeks now, and already I smoke only Gauloises. I also have a source of my own. He is an agent for Interpol, but you never would know it. He looks like a taxi driver who fell on hard times. His name is Gérard de Gaulle. He says he is a distant relation. I find him very boring, but he tells me who is sleeping with whom all over Paris. He says Interpol does not have to worry about laws against wiretapping.

To induce Gérard to share information with me, I told him the story of Love and Renato. He said he was glad to hear that Americans have learned "to keep some things out of the newspapers." Afterwards he took me on a walk through Montmartre, and I saw how Parisian bums sleep stretched out right across the sidewalk, forcing pedestrians to step over them or step down into the gutter. I told him our bums in New York would never do that, for fear of being trod upon. Then I remembered the bum in the park last May, all covered with newspapers, and I told him the headline I saw: THOUSANDS WAIT IN LINE TO SEE FACE OF JESUS ON TORTILLA.

He said something like: "How wonderfully innocent you Americans are!"

When we got back to the Place Vendôme, there were two letters waiting for me. The first was from Sy Shimmer, bearing a return address on Riker's Island. It said:

Dear Ms. Makepeace:

An unfortunate misunderstanding has landed me temporarily in jail. I am entrusting all my business affairs to an able young attorney, Mark Blossom. I believe you know him. You will continue your payments to me in care of Mr. Blossom, 2150 Park Avenue, New York, N.Y.

Perhaps you have heard that your two friends Mr. Cintron and Mr. Vasquez were arrested in Queens on bribery charges. This does not cancel their old bail debt.

I trust you are pleased with your transfer to Paris. I would give my eye teeth to be in your place, if I had them to give.

Sincerely yours,
Seymour Shimmer

The second letter was from Eddie, and said in part:

There's a story going around that you were carrying on with both the publisher and Ron and that when the situation got too hot, the publisher's mother intervened and had you sent to Paris. I don't believe a word of it. But how did you get there, kid? These things don't just fall from the sky.

Hizzoner, you'll be happy to know, is not going to run again. He says he's "a fulfilled man." Rest of us think Jenny Locke finished him off. Greg took Jenny off the dirty restaurants list and sent her down to City Hall, where she emptied the press room. Greg, by the way, is getting to be a worse pain in the ass than his predecessor. He demands receipts with all expense accounts and has instituted a new system by which the source must sign a little slip saying he had lunch with you.

You should see Ron. He walks through the newsroom talking to nobody, practicing that glassy-eyed look Gil used to have. If you wanta say hello to him, you gotta make an appointment. But he still gets attacks of gung ho. Last week he talked to London and we had sixteen stories on England in two days. Watch out. He'll discover Paris one of these days.

We miss you around here, kid. You always looked so confused, you made everybody else feed good.

Love,
Eddie

P.S. Word is, the reason Dixby didn't make it to the top spot is that *he* cancelled those hotel reservations himself to make Ron look bad. Supposedly that proves he doesn't have the integrity to run this newspaper. And did you know that toward the end Gil was using *Newspaper* security men to guard his garbage?

P.P.S. Ron just told Figland, who told me, that the reasons you were sent to Paris are: you speak French like a native, and your great-great-grandfather was a member of the Paris Commune. What *is* the story about you and the *Crimson*?

**361**